CONTACT

REALMS' ANCHOR I

CONTACT

REALMS' ANCHOR I

SECOND EDITION

WILLIAM H. NUGENT

Contact: Realms' Anchor I
First Edition Copyright © 2018 William H. Nugent
Second Edition Copyright © 2022 William H. Nugent

Publisher Name: Wiesbaden Press
Legal Names: Tom Kuhar and William H. Nugent
Location: Forest, Virginia USA

This novel is a work of fiction. All the characters, names, incidents, organizations, and dialogue are either products of the author's imagination or are used fictitiously. The expressed explicit and implicit views are story-telling devices and do not necessarily reflect the opinions or beliefs of the publisher or author.

ISBN: 978-1-7327950-7-5 (hc)
ISBN: 978-1-7327950-4-4(sc)
ISBN: 978-1-7327950-6-8(e)

Library of Congress Control Number: 2022915471

Because of the dynamic nature of the Internet, any web addresses or links contained in this book may have changed since publication and may no longer be valid.

CONTENTS

Capabilities are potential; men are kinetic.

FOREWORD FROM THE AUTHOR

Welcome to the Second Edition! I wanted to call it the "Get Some Edition" but realized that'd be better served down the line when the content delivery tech is more advanced. In that world, you still get the physical, cover-bound book, but within is steel instead of wood pulp. A blade for your hand wired with microchips, speakers, and brain lojackers to deliver narrative straight to your adrenal implants. You hold the knife; the words flow. You grip it tighter; the cinematics start. You raise it in the air, and the thunder comes down. Suddenly you're on the field charging in with Gunny Brines and Captain Saunders. Black Robes melting your face. You don't even care about the story, just your rib muscles pounding harder on your lungs so you can out-scream your own screams. RARRRRAAAR-RWWW!!!

But that's still a few years out. So, yeah: Second Edition.

Realms' Anchor: Contact was and still is my debut novel. I got hooked on the idea of modern warfighters in an epic fantasy setting during college a million (20ish) years ago. Wrote the early drafts of the first three books (plug for book III below) and then spent the intervening time relearning how to write and tell a story. For those interested in writing, it's a process. Hence the Second Edition.

But really, the 30th edition.

After about four years of total dedication to books II and III, returning to the world of Contact is nice. Feedback from readers has helped identify snags and points of confusion in the story. Also, with so much more of the universe canonized, I've had more fun with my foreshadowing. It's crazy how far the characters have come while trying to stay true to their various missions.

Zooming out to the grander designs of this whole thing, Realms' Anchor is epic fantasy cauterized onto the Earth you know from the late 20-teens. It's a clash of tech and the supernatural, informatics and prophecies, a military honed by ten thousand years of human warfare and one birthed by cosmic chaos. An easy comparison is those superhero movies in which the armed forces are overwhelmed by advanced technology and magical powers. Except here, no one is coming to save them. Training, discipline, and the frothing desire to win are the only ingredients in the mix.

And humor.

I've got six (6)—you like that legalese?—books planned for the series. There are, of course, more stories to tell and fun within the Realms' Anchor universe, but that's the current projection. For those savvy folks who made it this far into some random author's forward, this is also a great spot to embed the title reveal for book III. The Begotten Some: Realms' Anchor III will dip you into Ajid's Winter and the outset of all-out war. If that means nothing to you, then you've got some reading to do.

But if it does mean something, then . . . right? Yeah, cool as fuck.

Should be out a few months after Contact's Second Edition. In the meantime, enjoy.

PROLOGUE

Nothing happened.

No change in the passage of time, bright light, harrowing sound, or searing touch upon his cloaked skin. It was an emptiness between two places so brief he wondered if anything had happened.

It had.

Crumbled rock and dry dirt instead of soft grass now crunched beneath his riding boots. Each breath brought a refreshing parch to the tongue, and all was silent. Truly silent. Lifeless.

The two others stood by his side, but he sensed nothing of their arrival. They just . . . existed. Their surprise mirrored his own as they kicked the dry ground and scoured the darkness in disbelief.

He calmed his desires to scry this new land until it baked beneath his feet. It was not needed. The others sensed it too. It was less a matter of reason or confirmation of signs from an ancient text than a warmth in the heart. A secret knowledge contained unknownst by all men. *Our search is ended.*

He was First, so he would speak.

"Strange."

"But familiar," said Second.

"Familiar to the eyes and ears, perhaps. But . . ." First said, searching for the like.

"As an apparition to what was life," finished Third.

"Yes, yes," cried Second. "But there is more."

"It is safe," said Third.

"It *is* safe," agreed Second. "Our task will not be difficult."

"We cannot perceive the dangers," First said. "No home of the *Corsan Carre* could be safe."

"None of the writings describe them or their home as dangerous. Only the danger they bring," said Third.

First was no longer listening. His eyes settled upon a flash on the horizon. It came again. Again. Now it was constant and growing. The light of a star brought near.

"Curious," said Second, now seeing the light. "I *sense* nothing."

"It is constructed," First decided. "As a lantern might be."

The other two chuckled but could offer no alternative.

"The noise . . ." began Second.

"The lights have split," said Third.

First forced himself away from the spectacle to their surroundings. He brushed his thumb along the Renderweave of his robe and asked the dark brighter to his eyes. And night became day for him alone.

The land was a waste for all he could see, but a clear path of packed dirt lay only steps away. Worn by many pairs of wheels, it stretched toward the rumbling lights.

"It is a wagon," he said.

"Horseless and capable of such noise?" cried Second.

"Should we fear?" asked the Third.

First watched the wagon slow and make the sound of a blade across rust as it came to a stop. The impossible brilliance and motion of the metal contraption commanded attention. To mere men, it was likely formidable and impervious.

"We fear nothing," he whispered.

CHAPTER 1

HUDUD

Dr. Pat's last memory of the new normal was the two assholes fornicating in the neighboring tent. Not unusual in what the military called a *forward position,* but with the green display on her watch flashing 3:15 a.m., they'd been at it almost five hours now.

Five.

She rolled over in place—a careful maneuver to prevent the narrow cot from tipping onto its side—and wished she hadn't misplaced her earplugs. Sleep was at a premium, and unlike the grunts next door, her medical skills required a degree of focus and concentration.

At least, that's what she told herself.

It was a better argument than admitting an infantile jealousy of the younger girl's pleasure cruise with one of those vibrant, hard-bodied twenty-somethings at the helm. Dr. Pat's mind drifted to her slightly wilder college and early postgraduate days. There were a few occasions when the hours in the sack totaled somewhere near five, perhaps six.

But never continuous.

People inevitably needed to eat or take a phone call. Hell, that was before people had phones to "check" all the time.

The girl screamed again.

Maybe that's the key, Dr. Pat thought. No cell reception out this far; nothing to do but fuck.

Shouting now.

Anger? At first, it didn't make sense. Then Dr. Pat deflated as she came to a new understanding. If they could screw for five hours straight, how long would a fight last?

Before she could fully sink into the despair of another sleepless night, everything went dead quiet. *Finally.* Instead of relief, the hairs on the back of her neck rose. It felt wrong, too abrupt like someone hit mute on real life.

Dr. Pat lifted her head and strained her ears. There was somethi—

The world exploded.

. . .

Blank. Chaos.

A hail of white noise focusing to a gray blur.

Dr. Pat gulped at an inhospitable, soundless vacuum, finally gagging on a lungful of sulfur and smoke. Her hands and face scraped against rough canvas as she tried to push herself up.

The atmosphere sucked another breath.

Instincts took over. She dropped back down, burying her face in her arms. A second later, her skull rang like a bell struck from within. Then her back burned as it was sandblasted by the unseen hell above.

No question she was about to die.

Somehow, the winds died down, and she was still a thinking, feeling human being. She fought the urge to turtle and tried to open her stinging eyes.

No luck.

A nervous tremor rattled her body as she coughed on the air. *Did they drop something on the camp?* All the hype about the Taliban having chemical and biological weapons roared to the forefront as she tried to wrangle a list of symptoms. Unrevealing considering anything short of her skin melting off was indistinguishable from the acute shock of being bombed.

She groped for the toxic release personal protective (MOPP) gear the United States Marine Corps security force had issued. Nothing. Not even her cot was in reach.

Forcing through the pain, she opened her bleary eyes. The tent and all her meager possessions were gone. She was laid bare to the night's sky amid flickers of gunfire coming from all directions.

Cocooned in the muffled world of acoustic trauma from the initial blast, she relied on the slightly clearer vision in her left eye to assess the situation. This was no sporadic rocket attack. A fierce battle was underway, with flashes and waves of baking heat detonating throughout the camp and Marine fighting positions. There was nowhere to run, but she had to move. A quick pat down confirmed her nighttime scrubs were still functional clothing.

She kept low, rummaging through the tattered remains of her tent's floor until she felt the light, plastic crunch of a half-empty water bottle. Rolling onto her back to wash out her eyes, a high-pitched ringing began to cut through the silence.

Tinnitus.

A promising sign—in this case—that her auditory nerves were rebooting.

She was breathing better, too. Thoughts of a chemical attack took a backseat to planning her next steps and . . .

Another explosion smothered her in hot atmosphere.

Gagging on acrid smoke and the sour taste of metal, she recovered faster than before. Blinking the last crud from her eyes, she dared to raise her head . . .

. . . and took in the horror that remained of the multiorganizational relief mission attached to the Pashtun village of Hudud in Kandahar Province, Afghanistan.

The security lighting was out, but the monochromatic glow of a full moon left nothing to the imagination. The village proper resembled a forest of ashen trees as smoke columns rose straight into the night sky. Scattered explosions continued to tear through the few remaining structures. *Not structures,* she thought, *homes.*

This wasn't a battle; it was a slaughter.

She closed her eyes to fight back the rising wave of panic and refocus on her job. When she opened them, two partially nude forms—foggy gas masks and all—crawled out from a tattered canvas and made a beeline for the Marine combat outpost.

Down, but not out.

Camp Dud, as the Marines called it, was a collection of tents and antenna towers walled with sand-filled dumpsters. It spent most of its life as a glorified bullet and bombproof clubhouse. But now, it was a bright beacon of defiance holding firm against the storm of bombs. Fighting back with long streams of gunfire and zipping rockets.

It was little comfort, though, in the context of the damage already done. For all the Marines' talk of advanced warning networks, claims of owning the skies, and assurances of Hudud's low threat levels, they were clearly caught by surprise.

And incapable of helping anyone but themselves.

Sharp crackling noises joined the ringing in her ears as more auditory nerves recovered from the shock. It was far from a clean bill of health but sufficient situational awareness for what she needed to do.

Dr. Pat waited for the concussive score of weaponry to fully focus on Camp Dud and then sprinted hard and fast into the chaos. From quick glimpses, it was evident that the attack had focused on the tent clusters within the extended Camp Dud fencing. Then they'd gone after the village.

Kill the weak first.

Completely inhumane, but it opened the possibility they hadn't hit the field hospital. She put everything she had into her pavement-pounding jogger's legs and headed in that general direction. Her lungs were about to catch up to the energy burn when another flash lit up the hospital's former location.

Pulverized.

Uncertain of how to proceed and not keen on heading toward the Camp Dud firestorm, she entered the smoldering debris field to search for supplies. It wasn't long before she stumbled on an unarmed Marine with a length of rebar threaded through both sets of quadriceps.

"Hey," he said as if they'd just met for drinks.

The wound looked ghastly but was self-controlled with minimal hemorrhaging. Hard to know if that rod missed the femoral arteries or just pinched them off, but he was stable for the moment. Her most critical intervention involved slapping away his attempts to pull it out. As she tried to calm and focus him, she became acutely aware of the many cries of "corpsman!" and "help!" around her.

She could hear again, for what that was worth.

"Pat! Dr. Pat!" called a familiar voice above the roar.

Dr. Pat let out a slow sigh. In this austere world of mind-numbing destruction, that voice triggered an untapped reserve of pure anxiety.

Micky Toms was a spike in the cocktail of professionals and altruists here at high personal cost to do good. She would be a good fit in a sorority or as a drinking buddy, but in a conflict zone, she was lost. From the low-cut shirts to obtuse advances at everything with two legs, she could almost be forgiven for treating it all as some sort of joke. But it wasn't. It was a handicap. Worse, she was one of those super clingy energy vampires who preyed on introverts.

So it was no wonder that, in defiance of the mathematical probabilities, Dr. Pat caught sight of Micky's ballasted form stumbling through the field hospital debris. If killing the weak first was a thing, this girl was in extreme danger.

"Get back!" Dr. Pat shouted, voice coming out like she'd been at a pack a day since college.

Micky did not oblige. Instead, she managed to trip herself up and crash shoulder-first into the impaled Marine. The man sucked a breath, paled, and promptly passed out from the pain.

"Christ, Micky, watch yourself!" Dr. Pat checked the rebar. Thankfully, it was still plugging the bleeds.

"No time. You're safe; I'm safe. Let's go!"

"Calm down," Dr. Pat said to herself as much to her number-one fan. Micky wasn't just clingy; she was like a stray that thought she'd found her mother.

"No, no, no. Time to be amped up. Let's go!"

"I'm needed here."

"Here? Bad. Far away? Good! Let's go."

Dr. Pat shook her head at the infantile phrasing and tried to keep her voice even. "I'm not one of your kindergarteners. I'll be fine. Go to Camp Dud." She crawled to the next moaning body and cleared away a sheet of charred canvas so she could get to work. Everything else was a distraction.

"Pat, that's the worst place in the world right now," Micky insisted, following.

"Then go down to the village," Dr. Pat said, pushing her away. "It looks like the Marines are taking the brunt of the battle now."

"I'm not leaving without you."

"Go!"

Micky huffed, threw her hands up, and ran off toward the village haze.

Finally. Dr. Pat refocused on her patient. She applied pressure to the wounded trooper's upper leg, staunching the spread of soppy darkness across his beige trousers. After a minute, he was responsive to questions, easing her concerns about how much blood he'd lost. She replaced her hands with his and showed him how much pressure to apply. When she was confident he could hold it together, the firefight was already fading in the distance.

Good, MEDEVAC won't be far behind.

She sprinted to the next writhing form, the severed torso of an Afghani worker for whom she had no hemostats, gauze, or painkillers. He was a lost cause, a low priority in a triage scenario. But she stayed anyway. She never learned the language but listened as he listed several seemingly proper names in a final parting. It wasn't long before she found herself at another cry for help, tearing at her own sleeves for bandages.

"Hey, Doc," said Micky, reappearing and dropping down next to her. "I scored some goodies."

Dr. Pat shook her head without looking up. "Micky, you need to find shelter." Elbows deep in the blood and guts of another useless battle in a pointless war, there was no time for the chipper little girl who wanted to go for a ride along through hell.

"There is no shelter, Pat," Micky muttered, pushing a yellow case forward.

Confused, Dr. Pat stole a look back at Camp Dud. Expecting to see the last dying embers of their only hope fading into the darkness, she was surprised to see the place lit up and buzzing with activity. They'd gotten power back and were directing searchlights over the wire at several large fires.

Micky is crazy.

Ignoring the emotional roller coaster beside her, Dr. Pat put a reassuring hand on her patient's shoulder. "Looks like they're getting things under control." He gave a weak smile in response. Satisfied by the pulse in his neck and wrists, she scanned the wreckage for the next one.

"Spotted someone on my way back," said Micky hoisting the conspicuous yellow case off the ground. "I'll show you."

Dr. Pat hesitated but then noticed the cross patch on the case. It wasn't yellow, either, but desert beige. Micky had stumbled on a fully intact triage package, probably from the remains of the field hospital.

Micky, who could barely tell the difference between a dinner plate and a chuck pad.

Too desperate and frazzled to be ungrateful, Dr. Pat nodded and followed. They found a female security contractor dragging herself with a slow and painful crawl toward a rifle a few feet away.

"Calm down; it's over," Dr. Pat soothed. It was a struggle to roll the woman over and inspect the extent of her injuries. Her anterior side revealed widespread surface area burns everywhere not covered by her vest.

Micky opened the triage kit and began passing over various dressings. Her dismal attitude lifted as the two fell into a tenuous rhythm. She even found time to don a tattered lab coat to look fashionable for her part as "Dr. Pat's nurse." After a time, Dr. Pat found herself marginally grateful for the help.

"Welp, I'm not leaving without you," was all Micky had to say.

The heavy fighting ended, and the Marines shifted to damage control. Other survivors emerged to help with the wounded. They passed word along that reinforcements from nearby Kandahar Airfield were expected anytime. So, it was no surprise when the thudding of heavy lift choppers filled the air.

Relieved, Dr. Pat looked at her temporary nurse and said, "We need to switch gears and focus on prioritizing the injured for evacuation. There should be some colored tags in the kit. Red, yellow, green. This many, this far out ... we only need the green and yellows." She paused to convey the emotional weight of what she was about to say. "Not everyone can be saved."

Micky stared past her into the night sky. Silent.

"Micky?"

Moments later, Camp Dud opened fire in the direction of the incoming choppers.

A second wave!

As Dr. Pat's hopes for MEDEVAC fell, a new fear rose. This attack was coming in slow and confident like her brothers when they had a deer cornered.

Camp Dud continued to pound away with everything they had. Still, that dreadful thudding grew louder and closer until it drowned out the normally deafening noise of guns and missiles. *Maybe Micky's negative attitude was justified after all.*

Then, the unimaginable happened.

A column of blue light shot down from the heavens and engulfed Camp Dud. The color was brilliant, cohesive, and totally not of this world. Mesmerized, Dr. Pat watched as the Marine combat outpost scintillated brighter and brighter. As if every atom were a little star expending a billion years' worth of light in a single, amazing strobe. And then, just like that, the sky was slapped by a giant flash bulb.

Camp Dud was gone.

The blue column lingered for several seconds, then slowly—impossibly—collapsed from the top, leaving nothing but dry earth at its base.

All thoughts of rescue left Dr. Pat's mind as it raced to rationalize the possibility of this new weapon in the context of her worldly understanding. She barely registered it when Micky gave a half-hearted tug at her arm. But soon, she too was mesmerized by the empty real estate that used to be Camp Dud.

What remained of the village and Marine garrison offered no resistance as the ugly gray helicopters with bright searchlights landed. Neither Dr. Pat nor Micky moved a muscle as shouting soldiers with rifles swept through the wreckage. They remained still until those shouts were inches from their ears, and overheated men pushed them face down onto the ground.

Dr. Pat managed a weak protest claiming they were MSF—a neutral entity in this conflict. Sharp zip-ties cut into her wrists, binding them. Her words were lost in a series of shots as the soldiers began executing the wounded—all the people she'd tried to save.

Those strong enough to walk were herded onto giant helicopters covered in foreign markings. As the doors closed, Dr. Pat's mild sense of claustrophobia snapped her out of the daze. It was a packed cattle car with too many breathers. She gulped for air.

I'm trapped!

In her panic, she charged at the line of well-armed guards along the rear wall.

She never made it.

Strong arms pulled her back into the mass of people. A calm voice urged her not to fight. Not to give them a reason. She looked up and saw half a friendly face. The other half was covered in second and possibly third-degree burns. But his jaw was set and his eyes intense.

Defeated, disarmed, but still defiant. One of the Marines.

"Right now, it's our job to stay alive, ma'am. To wait." Now his eyes were on the guards who looked ready to spray their rifles into the huddled mass of survivors.

The Marine's voice dropped to a whisper. "'Cause they done stirred up the hornet's nest."

CHAPTER 2

C-MONSTER

Dawn bubbled up over an unremarkable expanse of the Arabian Sea. Golden rays slipped along gentle waves, leaving a bright, blue day in their wake. The process continued unimpeded, far from the troubles of land as it had for millennia.

Until something new was there.

A smattering of silhouettes emerged from the shimmering waters into an armada of gray, metallic hulls whose sharp, angled bows and hard planes cut an undeterrable course.

Foreign ships were sailing in foreign waters.

And they were angry.

At the heart of the double-stacked fleet was the USS *Harry S. Truman* (CVN-75). The aircraft carrier loomed large against its concentrically arrayed escort and support vessels. A pair of cruisers and two destroyer squadrons stalked the surface, while a nuclear attack submarine lurked below in case a capable enemy appeared.

But the chances of that were slim.

Any naval force capable of challenging the fleet—especially this fleet—had no reason to risk a war with the United States. Rogue surface threats could be identified, engaged, and dispatched before they entered the same time zone. The same went for enemy aircraft as the Nimitz-class carrier maintained tight, round-the-clock combat air patrols supported by anti-air assets distributed among the ships. The most significant threat to the fleet came from land-launched anti-ship missiles. Quick, unmanned skimmers with microscopic profiles that were difficult to detect and engage.

Cue the age-old promise of retaliation.

A compliment of Ticonderoga Class AEGIS guided missile destroyers ensured that static and dynamic launch sites did not get a second shot.

Combined with their enhanced anti-ship missile interception technology, which used advanced RADAR, identification, and integrated electronics to target and stop high-speed incoming threats, the Tomahawk cruise missile systems ensured no high-value target within 1600 miles was beyond reach.

By overlapping these air, sea, and strike capabilities, the armada sailed with a full-spectrum defense shield. But the threat of America's supercarriers was a known quantity in the geopolitical landscape. What made this fleet unique was what that shield protected.

The second largest ship within the naval womb was a landing helicopter dockship—a flattop like the *Truman*. The USS *Storm* (LHD-9) was a Wasp-class amphibious assault vessel named after the famous operation to liberate Kuwait from the 1991 Iraqi invasion. Configured with nine helicopter bays and a well deck, her sea and air-based delivery systems were a threat to every shore and inland installation within hundreds of miles.

The USS *Storm* and her two sizable sister dockships carried the United States' response to the attack on its outpost at Hudud. The reason for turbulence in the global markets and whole armies drilling for war. It carried a statement. Commitment.

The Marines.

————

Wet, hot, and over-salted.

That was the early-bird special waiting for Gunnery Sergeant Michael T. Brines, senior NCO of Charlie Company First Battalion Second Marines assigned to the special operations capable 25th Marine Expeditionary Unit.

His cotton skivvies were damp from sweat within seconds of stepping onto the USS *Storm's* flight deck. Panning the dark-gray turf to get his bearings, a gust of headwind hit him like someone had opened an oven. It was almost enough to consider the possibility of entertaining the thought of heading straight back into the ship's climate-controlled interior.

Maybe a lesser man . . .

No, the heat was just the melted sludge at the bottom of the shit sandwich. A shit sandwich that everyone knew would taste worse than it looked, yet no one could wait to take a bite.

He spat, and the gob of saliva hit the deck with a spattering sizzle.

Another hot day in hell.

A flurry of activity astern distracted him from his science experiment. A small chopper, a Huey, lifted off landing pad eight. It hovered for a minute, dangling a tether of gray crates, and flew toward the *Truman* like the pilot just needed his air hours and had nothing better to do. Other than that, it was dead on deck.

Brines noticed the idle deck crews chatting in groups of three or four as he began working the blood into his thick leg muscles. If he gave a damn about naval operations, he would think this was a prank designed to mess with his sense of vigilance. The way things seemed, they'd be hurting to launch within the hour if the order came through.

The fact was that he didn't give a damn. He let go of his control issues a long time ago. At least when it came to making sense of the military's thousand moving parts.

He bent forward and grabbed the tips of his sneakers, producing a satisfying pull in his lower back and hamstrings. He knew his job and his people, and that shit was locked-down tight. But, from the situation reports and trickle-down intel, executing the job—this job—properly was banking on a lot of assumptions. It would've kept a younger Brines awake at night.

The old Brines.

The new Brines figured that even if this battle plan survived abortion, hatched into the world an abomination, crawled on its belly across a burning desert of good ideas, and begged his Marines to save it with its last breath—and that's exactly what would happen—he had zero fucks to give. He wasn't going to say shit or give it a second thought until someone handed him the mic.

That's when he'd start caring.

That's when Charlie Company would rear that disaster into a miracle. The rest was out of his control. And he didn't mind that.

Anymore.

For now, he would enjoy the fruits of a clear flight deck. He sucked in a deep breath, stretching his green Marines PT t-shirt tight over his barreled chest, and allowed himself half a moment to soak up the orange glow on the horizon. The nice thing about the sea was the view and no one staring back. Satisfied, he jogged toward the cluster of Marines near the ship's bow.

Enroute, he tried to focus on the men, the training, but the lack of top-side activity was a ball burr. The largest carrier-supported battle group to sail these waters in recent history didn't just shut the fuck up for no reason. Something was different today, and it wasn't concerns over jet-fuel conservation.

He thought back to the recent press releases and continuing coverage of the "Crisis in Pakistan" but came up empty. Sure, the shit-talking liberal media was questioning capabilities, screaming World War III, and looping that haunting footage of the failed rescue operation in Iran over thirty fucking years ago. But they weren't reporting anything new. And he'd hear about a draw-down from the news long before it was announced ship-wide.

Quit thinkin' about it.

Brines tightened his fists and shifted focus to other parts of his shit list. Trying to sell mom's house during a deployment came with endless headaches. Painting. Staging. Pictures. Fake signing computer forms with a click instead of a ballpoint.

And the middlemen.

The civilian chain of command was the exact opposite of the military's. Instead of going up, it went down into the dirt where all the deciders were buried. Then there were twenty guys standing around with golden shovels offering to dig 'em up for a cut. No face-to-face discussions, just invisible assholes hell-bent on raking each other over the coals.

Can't sell anything unless you let 'em feel like they raked you.

Brines blamed coupons. People couldn't stand to buy anything unless they had that $0.10 discount shit-ticket in hand. It didn't matter that the store was just purging old or otherwise nasty, unsellable inventory. Ten cents off had them lining up for it.

Those were the people in the voting booths and pushing their opinions into the social media. They were an army of idle, undisciplined children looking for ways to incite mobs and tear down everything decent in the world.

He took another look around the barren deck and ground his teeth. He didn't give two shits about the uprising in Pakistan or the political infighting it caused back home. Let the historians argue whether Hudud was an act of war or an act during war. It was all political bullshit at this point.

If men were fighting, it was a war. No question about it.

As bad a response plan as the one the brass had dreamed up—not that he gave it a second of analytical thought—its one high point was that it would use Marines as God intended.

Ground combat.

It was a tantalizing, once-a-career-mission. The focus and objectives were clear, and the stakes were actionable. American lives. No oil, no regime changes, no knocking on doors. Just plain doin' the right damned thing.

Redemption.

He banished the last thought immediately. That line of thinking led to a dark place. Instead, he sucked another breath of the baking, humid air and let it clear his mind. *This ain't no draw-down,* he decided. If anything, it was a ruse. Maybe he was lying to himself, just like when he thought that first offer on mom's house was too low. Still, he could feel it just as he could feel his nuts pulling away from his already overheated body. A change—any change—in the fleet meant they were days, if not hours, out from something decisive.

Action.

He locked the realization away in the dungeon deep within his mind, a cellmate for his control issues. He had no business worrying about where he was going or doing until it was live fire.

Gunny Brines—the sure-footed, commanding force of discipline and war—approached the dozen or so Marines loitering near landing pad four. The tall, fit form of his commanding officer Captain Ronald E. Saunders, stood out among them but not apart from them. Somehow the captain's dark-haired high and tight had trimmed up since they'd last seen each other at 0030 hours for midrats—the midnight rations millennials liked to call "fourth meal."

He squeezed in a haircut? Fucker never sleeps.

A casual glance at the lean-cut group similarly dressed in their skivvies might make one think they were getting ready for volleyball practice. Or since they were already soaked in sweat and had just finished.

Brines would've known the truth of this group even if they weren't standing on the deck of a two-billion-dollar dockship. Their casual arrangement in an otherwise safe environment was anything but accidental. No single man bothered scanning the horizon; instead, they watched each other's backs and faces. It was a silent partnership that spoke volumes to the warrior-forge that produced them. Individually, these men were dangerous; together, they were indomitable.

And Brines was their alpha.

Captain Saunders tossed him a nod. "Morning, Gunny. We were just discussing the impact of heat on human performance." It was a polite way of suggesting there was some bitching about physical training this AM.

"Sir," Brines started to say, but it came out as a drier than usual rasp. He cleared his throat. *Just gotta warm up the pipes.* The pause gave him a chance to pan the other Marines in attendance. Only two officers—First Lieutenant Lyons and Second Lieutenant Weber—had managed the early wake-up. All four of his staff sergeants were accounted for. The remainder included junior non-commissioned officers (NCOs) and enlisted like Sergeant Gilbert and Lance Corporal Light. Brines didn't expect to see a huge turnout given their rigorous schedule. Still, one notable absence was the newly minted Sergeant Jason Smith.

Dammit, Smith, don't piss and moan about the "boys club" when you ain't showin' up for meetings.

His Marines eyed him with that hopeful glint he'd seen a thousand times. It wasn't longing. They'd never expect him to cancel physical training because of the weather. That was like asking dad something when mom already said no.

Ain't gonna happen.

Some might call it admiration, but he refused to acknowledge that. He was the same damned guy staring back at them, just older and, in some cases, less educated. The career, the sacrifices, the bedtime stories they told each other at night were bullshit. Only thing that mattered was here and now.

No, they were looking for that *'rah.* The guy who'd drag them into the suck and breathe it double-hard.

As the ranking grunt, he was all too happy to oblige. "Expectin' it hotter later, sir."

Captain Saunders smiled. Wind sprints it was.

Sergeant Jason 'Bone' Smith drooled over the pile of food on his tray. He was a big dude with an appetite to match, but since the deployment got extended, it was straight feast mode. No matter how much he packed in for breakfast, his stomach would be chewing his ribs by 1000 hours.

It's because you're not sleeping.

His mom's words. And her being a doc, there was a whole lecture behind it. But she was also mothering her baby, who chose the Marines instead of college. She couldn't see it like his body was compensating for the lack of shuteye with calories.

Energy.

Smith liked that thought. Shrugging off the need for six hours of weakness in favor of recharging like Superman sucking energy from the sun.

"Don't forget to chew," came a quiet voice from behind.

"'Bout time you showed up, Pete," Smith said. "Saved you a seat."

The long-faced Italian shook his head, drawing the eye to the unkempt mess of black hair that edged on regulation. It gave him a wild look, which ensured that no one would mistake him for run-of-the-mill combat arms. Most people stopped guessing at *scout sniper*. It wasn't wrong, but that didn't give him the credit he was due.

Francisco—Pete to those who took a minute to dig deeper—was a man who called the wet and soggy places of the world home. He was slug-eating, nature-loving, and handsy with all the nasty shit Smith wouldn't touch through a plastic sheet. And the guy didn't get that love from a book, either.

"Come on," Smith urged.

Francisco kept walking, pretending he was going to find some Marines who would be comfortable eating next to his cold ass. Then he came right back and took his seat. He dropped a paper bag—same quart-sized throwaway Smith carried every day to that prestigious elementary school his parents paid for—and pulled a banana. Smith waited for him to break the peel before tearing into his pile of scrambled eggs.

"You didn't have to wait for me, you know," said Francisco.

Smith wasn't listening. Three forkfuls in, and his mind caught up with the fact that he was eating. He slowed down, taking a moment to savor a single bite instead of swallowing several. He was hungry, sure; right now, the box it came in was enough to get him salivating. Still, there was something else. A freshness that he'd not experienced since . . .

"You find a fingernail in that mess?" asked Francisco.

"Naw. Man, we into some fine dining today," Smith mumbled, trying to keep a straight face. The sailors and Marines at the other tables were already studying him. They were sensing his feel and looking forward to another round of laughs. His appreciation for what they called *superstition* and *omens* was often premium material for ridicule. He lowered his voice further. "Somethin's up, dawg."

Francisco removed a plastic food bag of unknown origins from the larger brown bag. "Negative, full moon tonight."

"Maybe we go in the day. We trained for both."

"Four-hundred-mile insertion. Everyone knows we're coming. Broad daylight? The captain wouldn't send Nickels on that run."

"It ain't up to him, Pete."

Francisco sighed. "You've been wrong every day this week."

"Today, I got proof. I know you on some fucked up diet but taste this shit." He nudged his tray across the blue plastic covering the metal cafeteria-style table. "Tossin' the choice cuts to the hounds 'fore an op."

Francisco rolled his eyes and grabbed one of the biscuits. He knocked it on the table, trying to show it was three days stale, but all he got was pastry flakes falling off. One bite and those rolling eyes stopped to tell a story about moist deliciousness.

"See?"

"Tastes alright."

"Yeah? And why you think that is?"

"Health inspection."

Smith batted the thought away. "Bullshit. This a sendoff." Still, the possibility was hard to ignore. "Why would any of them inspectors be up our asses way out here anyway?"

"Regulations." Francisco took an unheard-of *second* bite of the mess-deck biscuit.

"My God, y'all," came a shout from the meal service exit. "I have survived long enough in war to witness the unthinkable."

Francisco snorted at the comment and took a *third* bite of the biscuit.

"The end days are nigh!" cried the voice. "Francisco hath ate the processed fruit!"

"Another omen, brotha," said Smith waving Lance Corporal Ted 'Fish' Fischer over. The rest of the enlisted mess was already wearing smiles.

The pasty, southern doughboy with a short crop of reddish hair waded through the rows of bolted chairs and tables. Deftly evading some grab-ass by fellow Charlie Company Marines, he stopped by Francisco and said,

"G'morning, boss." Then he paused like he had to polish something first before adding, "Sergeant."

"You ain't gotta be like that. Fish, sit the fuck down."

A wicked smile sprouted on that freckled face. "Francisco reckoned I should mind my elders."

"Appreciate you respectin' the respectable," Smith said, sitting up taller in his chair. Everyone had been joking about his recent promotion. At least Fish had some class. Two Marines from Second Platoon, who still refused to own up, had filled his locker with "sergeant sex" condoms and doggie treats—a jab at his hard-earned nickname *Bone.* Thankfully the condoms were unused.

"So, what's y'all's deal?" said Fischer pointing to the biscuit. The thick way his southern accent came out, it was a wonder he hadn't spotted the difference in quality from across the ship.

"Bored Marines on a boat," replied Francisco going back to his brown bag. "Idle speculation."

"About a biscuit? Or ... is this one of them metaphors?" Fischer searched their faces for answers. After a moment, he stuffed one into his mouth. The effect was immediate. "Damn, like momma used to make."

"I thought you said your mother couldn't cook," said Francisco.

"She couldn't. But she could add water to that buttermilk boxed shit real good."

Smith let a smirk pop but said nothing. Staff Sergeant Carneal had been on him about churning the rumor mill. But that didn't mean he was responsible if others connected the dots themselves.

"So y'all're thinkin' this is a last meal of sorts?"

Smith nodded.

"S'posed to be a scorcher today ..."

"Our loadout is for a night op," dismissed Francisco.

Fischer sat back and folded his arms across his chest. "So, what, we get three squares solid before feet dry? I could live with that."

Smith shrugged.

"Full moon tonight," Francisco reminded them. "Not happening."

LCpl Fischer dropped his eyes and chewed on his lower lip. After a moment and a slight chuckle, he said, "I wasn't gonna say nothing. But talk of the town says they're makin' a final decision."

"Course they makin' a decision ..." began Smith.

"Today."

Hard stop; rumor mill be damned. Smith leaned in, eager, while Francisco cocked his head.

"Where'd you hear that?" they both asked.

"Nickels."

———

"Chuh . . . gag . . . ing?"

"Chugagin', baby. Totally chugagin' on it. Like I was in her fuckin' stomach or somethin'. Fighting to take more down while trying to chuck it back up. Back and forth. Gulp, gag, gulp, gag. Her whole body rockin' the love boat. Chugagin.'"

Lance Corporal Timothy 'Stone' Gladstone gave a slow nod as he digested the Charlie Company Corporal's story. In a strange sense, the locker room talk was mildly refreshing. A call back to boot camp and the camaraderie that arose just before lights-out when leaden limbs mixed with the thrill of getting some rack-time. Everything was light. Everything was funny as hell.

Still, as the corporal's eyes darted between his and another Marine's—a Private First Class Licht—Gladstone wasn't getting a warm and friendly vibe. He'd known this dude all of two sips of coffee and had to check too-much-time-in-the-tanning-bed's right breast pocket to recall his name.

Nickels.

Come to think of it, the forgivable crassness during boot came from a platoon of guys shitting, showering, shaving, scrubbing, sweating, chowing, and shitting together for weeks on end. Not a five-minute welcome-to-the-company during chow.

"You ever blow a dude, Private?" Cpl Nickels asked randomly.

Gladstone lowered his eyes, suddenly embarrassed for the corporal. In another life, this guy was a used car salesman. One of those short, fast talkers who spent too much time pumping up his chest in the gym and not enough time filtering his thoughts. And judging from what was coming out of his mouth, he probably spent most of his time looking for work between firings.

PFC Licht looked over and, for an instant, appeared to be readying a wicked comeback. Not the ideal approach to dealing with an entrenched superior when you were a PFC who somehow shot out of boot straight into a coveted Marine Expeditionary Unit. Mercifully, Licht became intent on his scrambled eggs after a moment. *Smart.* Before Gladstone could relax, though, the corporal's mouth opened to nudge the situation over the edge.

"Jersey!" boomed a deep voice, saving the PFC from a world of trouble.

Cpl Nickels' head snapped up, and Gladstone relaxed as one of Charlie Company's bigger black dudes sporting sergeant's chevrons marched over.

"What up, Sergeant Smith?" asked Cpl Nickels.

"You know what's up, dawg."

"Yeah? Okay, Sergeant *Dawg.* Guess rank ain't enough to drop that asshole jive and embrace the fact that you grew up on the white side of the tracks."

"So, it's like that, huh? Extra stripe means I'm privileged?"

Cpl Nickels shrugged. "Even this dick-sucking PFC knows you don't fit the bill, Bone."

Sgt Smith folded his arms and raised a trim eyebrow. "You know you ain't supposed to say that racist, discriminatory shit after we got the sensitivity training."

"The fuck?" Cpl Nickels was now panning the table for support. "How is that discriminatory?" Gladstone avoided eye contact hoping someone would back down so they could get back to breakfast. "Maybe it's 'cause I didn't say *Sergeant* Bone. My bad, bro."

"Makin' the assumption the PFC likes cock, dawg," Sgt Smith clarified.

Cpl Nickels turned away and muttered, "That ain't discriminatory, neither. He's white."

"What's that?" Sgt Smith demanded, his volume rising. "Like you can't hunt your own or something? You tryin' to self-identify as some cracker motherfucker now? Look in the mirror sometime, pig skin."

"Pig skin? Bro, you know it's just your race they're worried about. Right?"

A hush fell over the entire lower enlisted mess as Sgt Smith stepped forward and puffed out his chest. Gladstone didn't move. For whatever reason, things had just gone from zero to sixty, and he was about to be pegged as a witness in a murder, or at least a court martial.

"Least I got a race, son," growled the towering sergeant balling up his fists, "'nstead of some species of mushroom that grew outta the boardwalk."

The two stared in a pistol-less duel. It wasn't until a quiet chuckle rippled through the compartment that Gladstone remembered to blink. Finally, Cpl Nickels raised his hands in defeat.

Sgt Smith's thick lips thinned out, and he playfully slapped Nickels on his tan, nearly shaven head. "You lucky you're my boy, Jersey." Then he turned his attention to Gladstone and the still wide-eyed PFC Licht. "Don't pay this guy any mind. He just razzin' you."

The bladder of tension in Gladstone's shoulders released like it had five dicks. He couldn't say he was looking forward to future interactions with a superior like Cpl Nickels, but at least he appeared to be the exception.

Gladstone stuffed his nerves into that box for feelings he wasn't allowed to have as a Marine and waved the incident away. "It's that rifle company love I keep hearing about."

"Yeah, bro. We all pretty tight here in the C-monster," said Sgt Smith. "I know I seen you around lately. We just been too damned busy to shake hands and shit."

"I'm with the combat demolitions squad on loan from Bravo."

Sgt Smith raised an eyebrow. "Like explosive ordnance disposal?"

Gladstone shrugged. "Our sergeant is an EOD. The rest of us are a mix of close-in fuse lighters and combat engineers."

"Huh, ain't never rolled with nothin' like that."

"Yeah, we've been trying to figure it out ourselves for the past few weeks. I guess this whole thing got thrown together so fast that they have to mix and match all over the place."

"Sounds right. We all tip here, no shaft. You dig?" Sgt Smith laughed, so Gladstone laughed.

Charlie Company—*C-monster* as Sgt Smith called it—was composed of one heavy weapon and three rifle platoons. Usually, they'd clear ground for follow-on support platoons containing the combat engineers, EOD specialists, and anything else needed to get the job done. But this time, the ride in was tight on seats and even tighter on time. Everyone was training to double up on assignments.

"The D?" asked Cpl Nickels, suddenly taking a renewed interest in the conversation and displaying a severe case of selective hearing. "You two are getting real tight real fast, Bone."

"Everybody knows I'm a friendly guy," said Smith.

"Everyone knows you're looking for a new body pillow," quipped Cpl Nickels.

"Nothin' wrong with my old one," Smith said, reaching down to massage the corporal's comparatively smaller shoulders.

"Rape!"

"Can't rape the willing, baby," said Smith with a deep laugh. Then, turning to Gladstone, he added, "I'll treat you right, man. Take you out to breakfast and shit."

Gladstone chuckled. "Appreciate it." He liked Smith. The dude was a bull, brimming with testosterone, yet approachable with an easy-going charisma that made you feel like he had your back. Cpl Nickels, on the other hand, seemed totally ingenuine. As if the only way he could participate in a serious conversation was to drive it sexual. Gladstone had met plenty of these types through online gaming. Sure, a couple witty zingers were funny. But the constant reminders that the squeaky voice coming through his headphones possessed an organ of substantial size, girth, and prowess got old fast.

Cpl Nickels shrugged off Smith's hands and focused on the all-too-quiet PFC Licht pushing his food around the tray. "So, seriously, what's your deal?"

"My deal?"

"Yeah, dude," said Nickels. "Who'd you blow to get into Charlie? Ain't often we get reinforced *before* a mission. Combat demo-boy here makes sense. But a PFC? C'mon."

Gladstone could've sworn he saw the faintest hint of playfulness come over the PFC's face, but it was gone in a flash. Seemed like trading insults was a pastime for Licht, but then he remembered his place in the pecking order.

"They need a field radio operator trained on the new SINCGARS upgrade. That's me."

The two Charlie Company vets looked at each other, confused, like it was uncharted territory. Equipment upgrades happened all the time, but they were weeks, if not days, from going to war. Seemed a risky time to trial new gear.

"What's wrong with the old one?" asked Smith.

"You sayin' my boy Buontempo can't figure out your new-age shit?" said Cpl Nickels, probably referring to the radioman in his squad.

PFC Licht shrugged and sat up a little straighter. He was totally feeding off the fact that he possessed some secret, a bit of knowledge that gave him a microscopic edge over his superiors.

Gladstone had to admit, he was hooked too. His first real taste of combat was shaping up to be one for the history books. A rescue mission that was going to roll out like a full-blown, blitzkrieg-style invasion. At least, if those crazy joint task force training exercises last week were any indication,

The whole world was watching, too. Waging a war of words over the internet with insane predictions ranging from new terrorist caliphates to nuclear exchanges to the Second Coming. Digital hyperbole at its finest, but there was also the matter of scale. They were talking big because this was big.

And that made the little things super interesting.

Licht kept calm but made it clear he had nothing else to say on the subject. Understandable considering Cpl Nickels' hazing ritual or whatever just happened. Gladstone figured he could find the PFC later and get the details on those radios. A couple grainy YouTube videos of drunken assholes jumping off backyard sheds between the two of them, and they'd be best buds in no time.

"Yeah, well, this ain't the first tight-lipped playa around," said Smith setting a firm hand on Cpl Nickels' shoulder. "Makes me wish I'd gone for some tech schoolin' after boot 'nstead of carrying the duty."

"You mean carrying da business, bro," said Cpl Nickels, pretending to shoulder fire an obnoxiously oversized rifle.

"Hells yeah," laughed Smith. "Speakin' of, that summbitch needs some love 'fore I meet up with Staff Sergeant Carneal. Good meetin' you guys. We'll be seein' each other."

"Likewise," said Gladstone. Licht nodded.

Cpl Nickels stood up and piled his utensils onto his tray. "Good chat, boys."

Gladstone smiled and waited for the corporal to leave so he could talk to PFC Licht alone. But Sergeant Smith grabbed Nickel's arm and spun him around. "Got a minute? I heard you know some shit . . ."

Cpl Nickels smiled. "Well, well, well. Sergeant Bone comes seeking knowledge from the lowly corporal."

"Come on, man. You ain't really about that."

"Tell you what. I got a call to make, and then I'll come fill you up. Er, I mean in."

"Yeah, okay, but don't leave me hangin'."

Gladstone watched the two head out separate exits and turned to PFC Licht.

Gone.

The guy must have bolted the second Cpl Nickels turned his back. Meanwhile, Gladstone was left wondering if he should send that weekly check-in email to his mom sooner rather than later.

Elsewhere . . .

The shrieks became fierce thudding, which soon slowed and dulled. Finally, only the grunting and gasps of laboring men remained as their latest victim was dragged from a nearby cell.

Stupid, thought Dr. Pat retreating from her rusted door to the worn sleeping bag that served as her only piece of furniture. They'd all been shown the price of resisting. The brutal logic of her analytical mind boiled it down to a simple choice: compliance or irreparable brain damage. The guards were going to get their way regardless.

She glanced at her petrified cell mate and wondered if there was a difference. Marie had gone quietly, and, true to their word, they didn't lay a finger on her. But the same quick-moving nurse who coped with captivity by telling stories of her countless nieces, nephews, and cousins came back nervous, fidgety, and flinching at things unseen.

She also hadn't spoken a word since.

Dr. Pat's heart fluttered as her brain visualized the abject horrors used to induce such a state. What was the point of torturing medical and humanitarian personnel? Of course, not everyone was the same as Marie. A few she had passed in the hallways during bathroom breaks glided like they were drugged. Others seemed empty, like lobotomized but without the cranial incisions.

Then there were a few who were allowed to walk around free. The guards stayed away from them. Dr. Pat recognized one as the Marine with the burns who'd comforted her when they were first captured. Except now, those defiant eyes were dark and devoid of recognition.

When the guards finally came for Dr. Pat, she offered no resistance. They were rough as they dragged her through the dusty, cell-lined hallways, but no more so than a hurried owner yanking his whimpering mutt through the busy streets.

A whimpering mutt. And this isn't even the bottom.

Despite her rising terror and the constant pushing and shoving of the rifle-toting men, she finally got to see outside the prison.

And lose all hope of rescue.

The prison was well-fortified with walls, wire, guards, and big guns aimed skyward. After they exited the front gate, it was evident the complex was part of a sprawling military compound. Soldiers, weapons, and heavy equipment were everywhere. Nothing like the quiet, town-like naval bases she'd visited back in the states. This place was a division headquarters or something, and it was ready for war.

They brought her to a sand-bagged, concrete bunker near a pair of large runways lined with military aircraft. Jets.

Fighter jets.

At least two took off before she passed through the bunker's substantial blast door. Any thought that this was some terrorist group was gone. These people were professional military with money, supplies, and an agenda.

Inside was a bright complex of meeting rooms, armories, computer equipment, and well-dressed military officers. It looked like something out of a James Bond movie, complete with a super creepy guy in a hooded, black robe. Somehow wherever they took her, he was always there when she turned her head. But she never saw him move a muscle.

At the end of a long hall was a more extensive, open room where she was bathed in pale fluorescent lighting and the nasal tingle of caustic ammonia.

The infirmary.

One of the guards brought her to a passable attempt at an isolated operating area and pointed to a bloody mess on the stainless-steel table. He then asked in perfect English, "Can you help her?"

It was Micky.

CHAPTER 3

JUST KÔZ

Captain Ronald Saunders kept his eyes forward and step regular as he traversed the tight corridors of what the naval brass called Officer's Country.

It wasn't easy.

Every fiber in his being wanted to double-time it and get this over with. Rip off the band-aid instead of processing the myriad of reasons behind the sudden order to report to the fleet admiral.

He didn't want to go negative, but no way was this a social call or some sort of career-maker. Someone must have identified him as a malfunction in the MCPP operations plan. One significant enough to get the strike group's commanding officer involved. That meant looking forward to a chew-out session with his adrenals squeezing hard enough to crush walnuts.

We just need more time.

Truth be told, the current state of the mission was awful. The 25th Marine Expeditionary Unit (MEU) was commissioned over a year ago in response to instability in the Pakistani government. But the predicted enemy consisted of insurgent forces operating out of scattered safe-havens. Not half the Pakistani Armed Forces dragging the country into a full-blown civil war.

And no one had expected them to hit Hudud.

Bold. Insane. The media had almost gagged itself talking through the rationale. End of the day, it was a provocative move by someone—the purported leader was a PAF general named Khel—who thought he was a global player. A maniac who thought he was invincible because there were a few question marks in accounting for Pakistan's nuclear arsenal.

And for a while, he was. No one in the Pentagon wanted to touch it.

Almost no one.

This General Khel didn't just grab American hostages; he grabbed US Marines. And while Washington bricked up over talks of appropriating, negotiating, and flagellating, the Navy quietly tasked a full amphibious ready group to the rescue mission. Two-thousand five-hundred Marines with enough firepower to win in the air, on the sea, and anywhere they might land.

When COMMARFORCOM (Commander: Marine Corps Forces Command) grabbed the podium and described the mission with the words "Ground Combat Element," the rest of the joint services got hard. Men on the ground was steak, sex, and rock&roll. It was wins. It was medals. It was the Department of Defense's highest mission.

Suddenly, everyone wanted in.

And, for some reason, once those floodgates opened, they stayed open. The result ballooned a straightforward rescue *in extremis* into a full-blown wartime operation.

Saunders figured the only explanation was something like the military equivalent of political pork—everyone adding on their pet capabilities to ensure future funding. Either that or intervening in Pakistan's civil war was suddenly the safest way to make American safe.

It deserved at least an eye roll.

It wasn't all bad. Saunders' command, Charlie Company, was pegged to run point for the landing force. An in-country demonstration of what this new battalion-strength special operations capable force could do.

Career-maker.

Also, it came with a ton of cross-services support and firepower. Fighting with an overwhelming advantage never hurt, especially considering recent reports of General Khel making surprising gains against superior forces.

Despite all that, today's itinerary was scrapped, with all meetings canceled or placed on pending status. And here Saunders was, meeting with someone outside his chain of command. It was a wonder his brain didn't cook itself.

Charlie's getting canned.

The thought ripped through him like a stray bullet. He tried to dismiss, rationalize around, and even shelf it. The problem was it made so much goddamned sense, and now that it surfaced, it had the podium. He started to sigh but sucked that low motivation shit back in and clenched his fists.

Not upset. Pissed.

Pissed about all the spent time and effort. All his time. From here until

Christmas he'd be a worthless fuck because he'd mortgaged months of his yet-to-be-lived life to this. Sacrificed big on a personal level to operate at the top tiers of military planning and administration. *And don't forget that side-hustle of commanding a rifle company.*

All that. Then HUA, sidelined.

Maybe he did his job too well, and suddenly, the Corps didn't want to risk him on the ground. Or, more likely, they wanted someone with less personal attachments.

Sarah. Tommy.

He cocked his head to the side as if that would help suppress stray personal thoughts. Time for that later. The tangent was enough to get his mind to jump tracks, though. Instead of snaring on something useful to analyze, it dared to tease him with an alternative scenario. One where the entire mission was greenlit. Not just greenlit, but trigger pulled, powder spent, fire and forget we're going to war. *Yeah, right.*

This meeting meant one thing: canned, scrapped, whatever.

Saunders ducked through a hatch faster than intended and nearly collided with Colonel Jacob Ridge, Commander of the 25th Marine Expeditionary Unit. Before Saunders' mind could cut through the startle response to find the correct greeting or acknowledgment, Jake flicked him the briefest of nods and stormed right on by. That was all the confirmation he really needed. Charlie Company was thirty pounds of tomatoes in a 16.5-ounce container.

Canned.

The Marine guard—Cpl Benson from Bravo Company—posted at ship Captain Strom's port quarters snapped to attention at Saunders' approach. He opened the door and said, "Go right in, sir. Admiral Bowman is expecting you."

Saunders nodded mechanically and stepped through the hatch with his cover tucked beneath his arm. Moving into the modestly appointed cabin with the guard on his six, his mind kept the hits coming. *Wouldn't that be shit if the Army was getting the duty?* He could see the headline now: "Army Rangers Avenge Hudud; Fuckin' Marines Deemed Not-Special-Forces-Enough."

The admiral looked up from behind a large, cherry-wood desk and dismissed the guard.

"Sir, Captain Saunders reports as directed," Saunders said, clicking his heels and snapping a crisp salute like he'd just been slapped in the ass by a drill instructor. He regretted it immediately. The last thing he wanted was to come across as an overeager junior officer, even if it was true.

"At ease, at ease," urged Admiral Bowman, returning his gaze to the desk. Instead of some ultra-important mission briefs or stack of *SSDD* docs awaiting signatures, he studied the photographs of Captain Strom's children, maybe grandchildren, and other non-nuclear family members. A possible conversation starter since Saunders had a family, but as time passed, it just seemed weird. Even weirder was Bowman's thousand-yard stare. Whatever he was seeing wasn't in those photographs but far away from here.

Saunders maintained clasped hands behind his back and a projection of outward calm and control. Finally, the admiral hefted himself to a standing position and paid him attention.

"I pulled your service record." A pause. "It's dense."

Was that a compliment or a push toward retirement? Saunders had no idea and accordingly gave no reaction.

Don't make me read the whole letter; just get to the point.

"I've met men twice your age with a thousand times your responsibility who can't say they've seen half the shit you have," the admiral continued. His tone and focus now carried the weight and authority expected of a career flag officer.

There was a definite dichotomy to the man.

"A battle plan is a relatively simple construct in our modern age. We've got more resources behind every operation, from concept to action to reset, than any military force in human history. But we're still subject to the same critical limitation as the earliest humans engaged in melee. The men, not the materials, make the difference." He tapped a stack of readiness reports on the desk. "The current executable—Operation *Sea Monster*—is bloated, ballsy, and downright certifiable. Shoddy, slapped together, and disrespectful of almost twenty years of global counter-terrorism operations are some other choice words I've heard." He let his gaze wander back to the photos while that sunk in.

Captain Saunders' abdominal muscles hoisted themselves into his rib cage, trying to crush his organs against his spinal cord as he braced himself for the hammer.

"But we're out of time, and it's the best we've got." He shot Saunders a look. "My question to you, son, is whether you're the best we've got to give?"

Saunders prided himself on reading people; right now, there was genuine curiosity, even eagerness behind those case-hardened eyes.

This can't be happening.

Was the United States really about to launch a full-on invasion of a recognized nuclear power? The hostages were a drop in the bucket compared to what he'd seen from the proposed combined-arms hyperwar. Was he the man for a microscopic ground force running defense for the Navy's premier special forces operatives—the SEALs—while all hell broke loose on the far side of the world?

"Oorah, sir."

The admiral snapped a nod, but it was more of an affirmation of some internal thought than a response. Perhaps the hostages had a lot more political value than Saunders realized. Or maybe Brines was right. This was a "just" mission, and only a cold-hearted monster would think the military was using it as an excuse to extinguish the biggest threat to Middle East stability since ISIS.

"*Sea Monster* is a go."

The knot of twisted muscle and compressible organs in Saunders' chest released. *Not canned!*

"Tonight."

And immediately cinched back up. *Fuck!*

The admiral offered a knowing smirk. "Apparently, some fresh intel grew someone in Washington some balls, and the plan's been fast-tracked."

Saunders swallowed hard. The greenlight meant everything from here on out (minus delays or an abort) was a well-orchestrated series of events. The military machine would move with exacting synchrony until Saunders and his men found themselves face-down or home alive.

So, what was Jake pissed about?

"On that note, I've spoken with Colonel Ridge, and we feel you are well-suited to complete a high-priority assignment."

"Sir?"

"One of the hostages is a VIP."

Saunders nodded slowly as he felt the last piece of a giant puzzle fall into place.

Admiral Bowman gestured to a red binder on the desk marked TOP SECRET//FOUO//ORCON//NORFORN//MR. "It's all caveated well above your pay grade, of course, but this is an especially sensitive situation." Saunders stared forward, confident he shouldn't even be reading the cover of something with that many restrictions. This was a single-source original data file, exempt from the Freedom of Information Act. No one was supposed to go near this without the explicit consent of the originator.

Full admiral must just be his day job . . .

Saunders shifted his weight, uncertain of what was being asked of him. At least it explained the off-the-record encounter with a high-ranking naval officer just hours before an op. Chain of custody trumped chain of command.

"You're cleared."

Verbal authorization? wondered Saunders picking up the folder. *More like an order,* he realized, scanning over the VIP profile. Other than a face and physical description, details were sparse. There was no information describing nationality, job, or even a name. It was literally a mug shot. If the VIP was among the hostages and needed this much anonymity, why inform him in the first place?

He waited for the admiral to look up from those insanely interesting pictures and selected his words carefully. "Shouldn't this be eyes only for SEAL, sir? Marine contact with the hostages will be minimal."

SEAL was 100% responsible for infiltrating, securing, and exfiltrating the enemy detention center. The only piece of that Saunders or his men might see would be over a hundred dirty and similarly dressed prisoners in a mad dash for the landing zone. Getting a positive ID on one of them was daunting at best.

Admiral Bowman nodded. "Initially, the plan was to maintain the VIP's cover and allow for extraction along with the rest of the hostages, but . . ." his voice trailed off.

"Compromised?"

Admiral Bowman stroked his cleanshaven chin as if struggling with some internal conflict. Like the contents of his meeting—now briefing— affected him personally. It did not instill confidence. "Unclear, but intel suggests the VIP has been separated from the main bulk of the hostages. Relocated to a C4I bunker."

C4I. That'd be the primary command, control, communications, computers, and intelligence facility. The TOC—tactical operations center—was as high a priority target as they got. Everything within one hundred meters would be ash and rubble before the enemy knew they were under attack.

Admiral Bowman pressed his fists into the desk and cut to the chase. "Your objective is to recover that VIP."

Saunders said nothing. He'd suspected there was more at stake than just the lives of 126 American relief workers, but he'd hoped that it was born from the need for a stable and legitimate Pakistan. Had this one *asset* pushed the greenlight? It wouldn't surprise him.

"I'll leave the details of extraction up to you." Admiral Bowman snatched a satellite image off the desk. It contained a birds-eye view of the concrete C4I with which Saunders had become intimately familiar. Its topside profile was small since it was dug into the ground but followed the basic layout. Four wings came off a central rectangle that functioned like a common area. The walls were thick and angled to deflect blast, and the doors steel. That new demolitions team they'd brought over from Bravo suddenly made much more sense. "But I need a positive ID, dead or alive, before you pull out."

Saunders' teeth clenched, and he hoped the emotional response wasn't as noticeable as it felt. "What's the probability of VIP presence?"

Admiral Bowman dropped his eyes. "As far as you're concerned, it's 100%."

"Sir, keeping that C4I intact is high risk to the ground element." Actually, it was insane.

Admiral Bowman shrugged, "The battle plan has sufficient redundancies to disrupt command and control without destroying the C4I. We're expecting ground resistance to fold on contact, but if they entrench and you can't advance, we'll reinforce with Alpha Company. You have my word."

Saunders wondered if he should call in a witness to this "word." Maybe Cpl Benson. The admiral could likely make a ship-wide announcement over the 1MC, and it wouldn't hold water.

"Understood?"

"Yes, sir," replied Saunders wearing his most dutiful face. *Sure, why not. Can't wait to tell Brines. He'll love it. Hey Mike, we're going to need some volunteers who don't have control issues and certainly don't like sticking to the plan . . .*

Admiral Bowman resumed his unfocused, thousand-yard stare and muttered, "We were considering removing this C4I from the target list anyway. Single-source and circular reports indicate they're using the eastern part of the structure as an infirmary. For all we know, there may be more hostages being held with the VIP." He shook his head, and his eyes sharpened. "Human shields. Be careful in there and remember you're clearing for . . . for friendlies." *Friendlies* hung in the air a moment, and it seemed like he had something further to add, but nothing came of it.

Saunders' pulse quickened as his analytical mind began poking holes in the new plan. The entire mission was predicated on rapid insertion and seizure to keep the enemy from making good on their promise to slaughter the hostages if attacked. *Now, there's plenty of time?* He dared to take a step as words began tumbling out of his mouth. "Sir, there's a chance they'll issue a kill order on any of our people in the bunker, same as within the detention center. We'll need to drastically alter the insertion pla—"

"No, Captain," the admiral held up a hand. "There's no kill order on the infirmary."

"Yes, sir." Saunders was a radio now, receive-mode only.

"Additionally, as with all classified information, you are not to disclose the nature of the VIP to anyone. Clear?"

"Clear."

"You are the only one who knows this face. That's how you'll make the ID. No names, no discussion with your men."

Hands dirty, balls deep, and tight-lipped. "Yes, sir."

Glancing down at those fucking photos again, the admiral chewed his lip. Before Saunders could step out of line again and ask if there was something else, Bowman regained his composure. "Update your operations plan accordingly, dismissed."

Saunders saluted and left without another word. Out in the corridor, he sucked ship's air as he raced to integrate this new directive. Tasking his men to do the job of the Navy SEAL hostage rescue team was NOT part of the plan. No wonder Jake was pissed.

Yes, true, we're special operation capable: trained and certified for shit like this.

But the SEALs! They were *actual* special forces operating under SOCOM authority. Experts at incursion and precision, this was the shit they lived for.

There wasn't time to make sense of it. Whatever the admiral's unspoken motives or needs, he wanted Marines to do a job. And they would. For now, and more importantly . . .

Holy shit, Sea Monster *is a go!*

———

Epic.

That was the word around town. Well, at least the ass-ridden stacks of racks lining the berthing area. Barracks for thousands crammed into an economy class, no-seat-selection steerage. With an airport overhead.

But it's all good, thought Corporal Nickels.

As of 1500 hours, it was all fucking good. The boredom, the stale air, and the below decks for days—unless you wanted to do pushups with double-gung-ho, triple-motarded Gunny Brines—were all worth it.

Get rested, get fed, get angry. Operation Sea Monster *is a go.*

Captain Saunders' words. A fucking greenlight for the kinda shit they'd write history books about. Not some patrol through a desert village knocking on doors and sweeping for IEDs.

Real action.

The sort where the entire three-dimensional battlefield was lit up and booming. Fire orders so danger-close that people were huffing air, hoping it still had oxygen. This was gonna be a brutal, violent incursion into the enemy's heart. The star attraction.

WE are the star attraction.

No supporting ops, but on-fucking-point. Three balls deeper than Alpha Company.

Nickels felt like hot shit as he ran the off-duty gauntlet to meet up with his fireteam. The captain gave them a few hours to deal with select personal affairs before the fleet went dark. But minus a call he still hadn't gotten to, his only responsibility was getting some dude action. Not dude on-dude action, but some serious bullshitting. Bone was being a bitch and pissing his time in the gym. And everyone else had their . . . rituals.

But the team was his. That meant they were paid by the US Government to participate in the motherfuckery.

A knock on Williamson's door had his sleepy, bottom-rack roomie mutter something about them going to the crew lounge.

A visit to the crew lounge found, unsurprisingly, sailors—*crew*—in an Xbox tournament. Loud and wild over stupid video game football. Fuckers were like Bone: big talkers, but mommy never signed the waiver. Nickels asked if they'd seen any of the green machine and got a real fucking whopper of an answer.

The library.

Had to be a wild goose chase. Sailors screwing with Marines shit.

But fuck if Nickels did not find his four-man team huddled around a little fold-out table in the motherfucking one-room library. Hours before the biggest operation the world had seen since Iraq, they were playing a board game.

LCpls Garcia and Buontempo looked up first because they still had an ounce of self-respect. But LCpls Light and Williamson were fucking gone. Enthralled by a medieval Monopoly board covered in stacks of cards instead of high-end real estate and a di with more sides than a fuck-yo-mommahedron.

"Corporal," said Buontempo. He was the new guy, a weird fifth wheel to their four-man fireteam. But like Bone was saying, something was up with the coms this time out, and radiomen were getting packed in every-where. Nickels wasn't about extra subordinates or work, but Buontempo was a cool dude who'd seen some shit out in Cali.

Williamson popped his little, red head up and opened his mouth to probably cast some sort of spell. Nickels shut him down. "The fuck is this?"

Light was the only one who straightened his back to show the proper respect before an ass chewing. The rest just smirked.

"Dry Mines of the Stone King," said Williamson matter-of-factly. "Part four of the Dark Bringer Campaign."

"Oh," said Nickels holding up his hands as if Lance Corporal Nerd had just dropped some ground-shaking knowledge.

"It's okay," said Light. The guy was great at missing social cues, especially sarcasm.

But Nickels had him covered. "Dry Vag of the Stone King definitely trumps SAVING THE FUCKING WORLD." Nickels slammed the table, knocking down all their little figurines. "Which is Part Ten Inches of the Global War on Motherfucking Terror, in case you forgot."

"So, 'personal time' was just a wink wink, nudge nudge suggestion to be circle jerkin' with our rifles?" asked Buontempo.

"He wants us hangin' out with Gunny, yo," said Garcia. "Playin' 'The Star-Spangled Banner' and sharpening our knives."

Williamson laughed. "Corporal just don't wanna make his call home. Nickels, let's roll you in as a level two. An hour of game time is like two in the sack. You know?"

Comparing Nickels to Gashface Gunny was a low blow. Even after a million years with a million drill instructors and officers beating the Marine Corps' history, hymn, and hymen into his skull, he would never turn out like Brines. That fucking guy grew up with the Eagle, Globe, and Anchor tattooed over his botched self-circumcision. A one-dimensional, tunnel-vision, zero-fuck giver about anything but getting the job done. Yeah, Gunny had some wins; the stories people told were crazy. But even crazier was what they always left out: the people who didn't make it back.

Worse than that was Nickels' team trying to drag him into their fantasy world fetish. Reading their beloved corporal like he was ballerina material instead of the cool, princess-fucking stallion he was. *Nerds. All of them.*

"Do I look like I get off playing pretend?" Nickels asked.

"You don't have to be a mage," said Light. "The fighter has a sword and—"

"This Marine has a machine gun, son. One spread, and your whole fucked fake world is gone. All those limp-wristed swingers got nothing on this. And that's where I need you to be: 21st-century badness ready to blow up on old news Pakistan."

"Just make that phone call, Corporal," said Williamson tossing that stupid di with too many sides. It landed on eight, and Williamson said something about the D doing damage. Whatever it all meant, Light folded like a kicked squirrel.

"Can you bring me back?" he asked.

"I might have a scroll," said Williamson.

"I need to sleep first," said Garcia.

It was too much. "You need to suck my dick first!" Nickels shouted. "You better shake this shit off and be Marines at zero dark."

"Wilco," said Buontempo with a laugh. Not laughing at, but he knew the whole nerdfest was fucking funny.

Nickels gave up and found himself back in the corridor, aimless and not in the mood for games or movies. His last resort for a distraction was taking pot shots at Francisco. The over-hyped marksman was probably napping topside right in that red box where the high-powered RADAR would zap a dude's nuts to croutons.

Nah, time to batten down and get in line for that call.

Unlike the rest of the world, this brand new dockship had bandwidth issues. It was probably just an excuse for APTS (Afloat Personal Telecommunications Service) to jack up calling card costs. Still, the official story said there was a device that connected the satellite network to the cell towers back home. It made the call legit—just dial the number—but that fucking machine only had 24 connectors or ports. Whatever. That meant on a ship of 3,200 before a major operation, there was a queue.

Except today there was also a C-monster fast pass.

The fo'c'sle in the bow wasn't an ideal location because it had a lot of space and only two phones. But fuck if it wasn't a Charlie Company exclusive lounge when Nickels entered. All the cool dudes, too: Baker, D'Arco, Staff Sergeant Riccardi … Not a hint of those axe-grinding psychos like Brines who did not have personal lives. Half of them were pumped for the fight, the other half jackin' at the thought of getting off the boat for a few hours. Didn't matter, though, because it was the high-moto Nickels craved.

The line moved fast too. Baker helped it along by showing off a dividend from his sext cache. The dude was a magnet, no joke. If he called tech support and got a chick, she'd send him a courtesy pic of her rack before they even got to rebooting the computer. If he got a dude, they'd transfer him to a chick just to watch the magic happen.

Nickels was finally having such a good time that he even waved over the PFC and that one demolitions dude—Gladstone—he'd fucked with at breakfast. They came, but like virgin lambs to the gangbang. Then when Baker gave them a taste of the spank bank, they reacted like … like it was a thing.

Like a bad thing.

Like they were the unbonable feminist chick who didn't want other chicks to get laid either.

But that just made it funnier. *Go find your soulmate, fuckers, and see how far into her pants the timid road takes you.*

When Nickels finally got the phone in his ear, he was bursting with stories. Operation *Sea Monster*, which was totally named after the C-monster—the Ground fucking Combat Element—was off limits to maintain operational security. And *they* were listening in on every call, ready to make good on the threat to shut it all down for one fuckup. But the ship wasn't in *river city*—reduced coms—mode yet, so he could plant some tiny seeds.

'Cause, this shit will be all over CNN this time tomorrow.

He wished he had time to call Uncle Harry too. *Plant so many seeds in that dismissive fuck that tomorrow he blows up like a dick-tree Chia Pet.*

She didn't answer her cell, so he tried the landline. It was usually a better connection anyway since she'd be on her earbuds and fill the call with feedback. One ring and it picked up. Classic.

"Hello?"

"Hey, it's me. Is—"

"She's gone."

Flat, straight to the point. Complete and final. In any other place, time, circumstance, or person, he would've asked the obvious follow-up question. Clarified the definition of gone. Asked when . . . when she'd be back.

But as the phone dropped from his hand, only one thing was left to ask. *Why?*

CHAPTER 4

PREPARATIONS

Pale rays from the high moon rained down on the black waters of the Arabian Sea. Its shimmering surface swelled and ebbed lazily, unbothered by the rising friction and tension of global affairs. Indeed, cast a man from his lighted and busy ships out into the friendless dark with only the daunt of hopeless infinity for companionship, he too might discover the insignificance of his worries. It was here within the sea's murky depths that creatures could still be called monsters, and man held no enduring power.

Tonight, however, was an exception.

Tonight, the undocumented, phantasmal denizens of the abyss would remain deep and still and keep whatever they used for assholes slammed shut as the three massive hulls of the Marine Amphibious Ready Group (ARG) loomed overhead.

Presently, the USS *Storm* was a cat waiting to pounce. Her portion of the Aviation Combat Element—callsign: Vulture—was now topside along with a compliment of red-shirt crew members running fuel lines and munitions carts to make it lethal. Three Super Stallion transport helicopters towered over the forest of smaller attack choppers. Waiting.

The ARG Commander (COMPHIBRON), Captain Simon L. Strom, stood on the bridge overlooking the flight deck. He listened to the battery of battle readiness reports from every department across all three assault ships of PHIBRON-12, the formal designation of his ARG. Everyone was bitching about everyone bitching about the timeline, which meant everything was on schedule. The administrator in him was satisfied, but the naval officer struggled with the reality that this mission was happening. *Sea Monster,* he thought as he stared out over the darkened waters.

More like 'Monstrosity.'

———

Beneath the USS *Storm's* flight deck, the empty hangar deck had transformed into a Marine assembly area. A growing mass of busy beige forms was checking and stowing gear into their modular war packs. Others were below decks catching midrats in the mess (though none dared to think of it as a last meal) or catching the last of some shuteye in their berths. As the officers wrapped up their final confirmation briefing with Operation *Sea Monster* green and go across the board, one Marine in particular was getting some alone time.

Deep within the bowels of the ship, far removed from the delicate electronics and clean glass screens inhabited by the command elements, laid the machine shop. It was a nightmare of twisted metal, presses, vices, sharps, heat, and grease, where the crew used good, old-fashioned sweat and muscle to forge their will upon raw alloys to build and maintain their weapons of war.

Typically pulsing with flesh and steel, it sat unused as the late hour of *Sea Monster* approached. But all was not still in the cramped compartment. Although the equipment slumbered, a steady scraping of steel against stone could be heard above the rumble of the ship's idle engines.

Gunny Brines sat alone in the shadows, surrounded by the primal components of man's killing machines, breathing an atmosphere thick with heavy metals and axle grease. With each passing of the blade over rock, he perceived the sparks that, for him, symbolized the smoldering furry of his lengthy career in the Marine Corps.

He said nothing, moved nothing save for each push of the metal from his thick arm over the stone. The work was repetitive, entrancing. The sparks took a brief flight into the air, only to cool and fade as they dropped toward the deck. They were his own history of intentions and actions. Some brighter and longer lived than others but always darkening at the end.

The Marine Corps would remember him for his accomplishments. Young Marines would whisper his name late at night between the quiet footfalls of the Fire Watch, but here in the dark with the blade, he could see past the bullshit. Right through the marketing and promotional topcoats to the substrate.

He never made a real difference.

Triggerman, mentor, warrior, and leader, he shouldered many roles. Men lived and died. Fatherless punks straightened their backs to his barking orders and called him sir. He'd supported and actuated multiple missions in the Global War on Terror, but at the end of the day, it would have gone on just fine without him.

He huffed.

The approach to the whole "war" was like one of those damned doctors who'd solved high blood pressure with some pills to slow the heart down. Sure, it worked. So did bailing out a sinking ship with some serious pumps.

But that ain't fixin' the problem, just making you dependent on the machine.

The same shit was happening here in the east. The threat was real and determined, but without clear battle lines, objectives, and an enemy with something to lose, the mission was counter to US military doctrine. Reactive. Withering. Another money-making machine for someone Brines didn't know or care about.

An enemy with something to lose.

A true enemy respected loss. They weren't out to notch a belt or steal bread; they wanted to win. That meant stakes, rules, and resolution. Iraq and Afghanistan started like that, at least in the mind of a younger Brines. Toxic regimes, people to save. It made sense. But once the coalition cleaned house, it became another lesson in what happens when good fighting men were used to buffer a foreign population against itself.

Wrong damned tool for the wrong job.

He wicked his fingers along the knife's warm, almost slippery edge. *Getting there.* He pulled out his strop for the last few passes.

The only time he'd made a difference was when his self-interests were threatened. He winced at the memory and felt the tug of the thin scar running the length of his left cheek as a final kick in the pants. It didn't hurt anymore, but it felt weird as fuck. As if all the nerves got scrambled while it was trying to heal.

He forced it back into his mind's brig and thought about the sparks again. Not their brilliance, but how quickly they grew dark and cold. That had been his reward for chasing the carrot. Bitter, cynical, and a heavy fucking drinking problem.

Well, not a problem, but a symptom of something invisible. A white-hot shard working its way through his brain, destroying him from within.

Alcohol had helped, but it was just coolant. Like a mouthful of ice water after eating a spicy habanero pepper. Relief, but only while there was more water. Eventually, the pain would go away on its own. *But sometimes you just keep drinkin'* . . .

He paused and slammed his fist into the steel decking at his feet as more pitiful memories surfaced.

Not now.

He willed his eyes to his knife and held it in focus. Not his knife, but Gramps'.

Always Gramps'.

He curled his meaty fingers around the ivory handle and recalled the first time he held it. The pink flesh of his tiny hand had struggled to cover a quarter of weird bone. Now, that oversized mitt was pocketed by dozens of little scars and callouses amid the lazy branches of bluish veins. There was a lot of history there, even before he attached the blade. The knife was a reminder, a partner, a silent witness. And soon, it would be again. Not from the comfort of its sheath but as an active participant.

He often wondered if Gramps would approve. Wherever Gramps found this bone, that took a diamond bit to even scratch, adding the blade was always more talk than action. Sure, he wanted to finish it but could never find the time or perhaps the will to get it done. When Gramps died, he'd left Brines with a bar of M390 steel and the handle.

There was a note too.

The steel is cold; the bone is not.

That was Gramps trusting him with the project. So, Brines apprenticed with an Amish blacksmith. The summer before he shipped out for boot camp at Paris Island, he grew enough confidence to forge the blade. Kept it with him ever since. Well, at least after he'd completed boot.

Maybe Gramps would've preferred the knife remain a mantel piece, but it also occurred to Brines that soon he would grasp the bone handle with the same wrinkled, marked-up hands as Gramps. So, fuck it. *It's mine.* Besides, the damned thing still looked new despite years of abuse.

The work with the strop resumed. Brines took a free breath as the blade reached perfection and moved beyond the dark thoughts into clear waters.

He turned the freshly whetted knife in his hand, examining the mirror-polished surface and taking comfort in the sharp hunk of peerless steel. Operation *Sea Monster* was different. A defined enemy had emerged from the sick soup of mixed ideologies and tribal bickering. Even the talking heads on the television he rarely bothered to watch agreed.

Real. Fucking. Bad guys.

His grip tightened on the blade's hilt. The rebels were led by a General Khel—a nobody who was kicking unbelievable ass against the legitimate government of Pakistan. It was all under the name of some new religion called Kôz. But devotion and a quarter of Pakistan's professional military assets weren't enough to do the damage this guy was causing.

Nah, there was another factor involved.

Whether it was foreign aid rigging up some kind of proxy war or a shit-ton of lies, that was for the people who cared. All Brines saw was a well-defined objective, the sort that embodied the Marine Corps mission. A standup fight against someone who wanted to win. With stakes.

Innocent human lives.

He drew a raspy breath, which reminded him of another time when everything made sense—his tour as Senior Drill Instructor at Marine Corps Recruit Training. He'd nearly shredded his voice box forging those people into Marines because they were the future. Make enough Marines, and you had your answer to war. Because: *Semper Fi.*

The next breath was deeper and clearer. The cynicism was gone now, and his mission, mind, and purpose were focused.

The session left both the warrior and the edge razor sharp. Not a moment later, as if on cue, the 1MC came to life:

"Now hear this, now here this. Marine rifle companies Charlie and Alpha are to report to the hangar deck with mission-specific gear. Repeat: all ground combat personnel involved in Operation *Sea Monster* are to report to the hangar deck. That is all."

Silence returned to the darkness. Gunnery Sergeant Michael T. Brines, resolute in his mission, slapped his keen blade into its chest-mounted vertical sheath and headed for the hatch.

———

"Ya heard 'em," bellowed Sgt Smith, marching down the corridor bulked up in so much gear his shoulders barely cleared the bulkheads. "Ground combat personnel report in!"

Ground combat personnel.

Not infantry. Not street patrol. Not fireteam XYZ. Ground combat personnel. Those three words sent a shiver down Smith's spine as they left his lips. The flyboys had their roles. The coms officers, the networking specialists, mission control, the dudes cleaning up the mess deck, the planners, the missile launchers, the president, the Army, and countless others had theirs.

Support roles.

For the Ground Element.

It was a narrow band in a Marine's career where he had the capability, let alone the opportunity, to take part in the purest mission of the Corps. Tip of the spear. The razor edge of contact. "That's us, ladies," he finished.

Smith was no stranger to combat. He'd witnessed its destructive fury both on and off the battlefield. The first time he thought he'd shot a man—never confirmed—was a shock. It left him hollow and dark. He'd seen Gunny Brines struggle with demons from a disaster he rarely talked about over the years. The physical scars from which he still bore. The men going in today would lose their pound of flesh, whether or not they made it out unscratched.

Smith had nothing to prove. But despite the risks and guaranteed cost, he was pumped. This mission felt right. Knowing that doing his job well was gonna pay off big for people who didn't have a goddamned hope in the world spurred him. Enthused him. He felt like he was saving the universe.

Like a superhero.

He might not be Superman, but the combined might of the C-monster was. And just to be part of that was worth the risk. *So long as I don't get shot in the dick.* He resisted the urge for a comfort tap on the XL steel cup beneath his vest's Kevlar overhang.

Smith nodded to the last two Marines from his squad as they hurried out of their triple-bunked cabins. *That's everyone, time to go topside.*

Damn, it's gettin' real.

His thoughts started to race, nearly tripping over themselves, visualizing how the mission would go once they touched down. They had run the plan into the ground during onshore, live-action mock-ups and virtual reality simulators that familiarized everyone with the layout of the objective. Overall, it was straightforward: touch down, establish a perimeter around the landing zone, and coordinate with Air to defend and destroy. Then pull out once SEAL had rescued the hostages. But shit never went right, and this time, he would have an entire squad looking to him for answers.

"... my favorite..."

Smith stopped at the hushed voice coming from where Nickels usually berthed. "Bro?" He called, peeking his head through the doorway.

Nickels was on the lower bunk with his back to the door, huddled over something. His head popped up, and there was a quick shuffle of hands ostensibly to grab the plate carrier on the deck beside him. But Smith also thought he saw him shove something into the side pocket of his trousers.

"Sup?" asked Jersey like it was nothing weird.

"You, uhm ... talkin' to yourself?"

"Talkin' to my balls, man," he said, coming out and slapping Smith on the arm. "Talkin' them down, I mean. Gotta restrain myself, so the rest of you can earn your keep. You know?"

"Appreciate it, bro. Let's get topside," said Smith shrugging it off.

Everyone had their superstitions and rituals. Well, except for Nickels. He was never one to take anything that seriously.

———

A faint electronic whirl echoed in the satellite phone's headset as it connected to the global communications network. The time difference between the east coast of the United States and PHIBRON-12's current position was nine hours. Late for him, but not for her.

Captain Saunders checked the black Timex that had stubbornly remained affixed to his wrist through multiple combat tours. Math came out to 1502 hours eastern.

Almost a half hour until her afternoon departmental meeting.

The phone rang on the other end, and he drew a calming breath. He'd let it go too long. Ten days since his last call, down from almost daily communication. And it didn't help that this was an extended deployment. Extra innings for a game no one wanted to see in the first place.

Hi honey. Remember me?

The timing of *Sea Monster* was bitter, in a personal sense, because their relationship had finally hit a smooth patch. Hell, there was even cuddling the last few times they slept together instead of back-to-back tortoises protecting little treasures.

His pulse quickened as the fifth ring came through the line. Would she even answer?

Ten days.

Suddenly, she picked up. "Ron!"

"Hey, babe."

"Oh, thank God," she breathed. A pause and then a quiet, "Are you alright?"

Saunders knew that tone and braced for the coming storm. "I love you, and yes, I'm fine."

"Fine?" An accusation.

"Babe . . ." said Saunders edging the earpiece away.

"Babe? Are you NUTS? I've been out of my fucking mind. You haven't spoken to me in two goddamned weeks. With all that shit going on over there, I thought you were dead. I thought you were fucking dead!" Her voice managed to fill the compartment, and Saunders wondered if she was sitting in as public a place as he was.

"It's like thi—"

"No, don't speak. You haven't said shit to me for two weeks. So, you can keep going if that's how you want it. You know, I held off. I didn't want to be the hormonal bitch hounding the Navy about why her husband isn't talking to her. I waited to hear something. Anything. But no, nothing. Just me waiting to see if the next guy knocking at my door is carrying a stack of papers or the fucking flag. You could have at least"—a sob broke in—"at least fucking told me you'd be out of contact. But you didn't say shit. You don't fucking care at all, do you?"

"Sarah, calm down," he said, trying his hardest not to make it sound like an order.

"Fuck you."

Sigh. When did it go from the two of them drunkenly flicking off the entire world together, in love, to "fuck you?" He knew the answer. Like anything else, things broke down when they weren't maintained. "Look," he began.

"No, you look!"

"Look at what? Huh?" The last thing he wanted to do was go on the offensive here, but he was on borrowed, begged for, and straight stolen time right now. "The picture of you I keep in my cover? The pictures you email of my life and my family that I can't be a part of right now?"

Silence.

"We're both hurting, babe. Turning on each other is NOT an option."

"If we need each other, then why aren't we talking to each other?" she asked in as quiet a voice as it got for Sarah.

It was blunt, painful, and spoke volumes about the underlying issues but also rational. Saunders could work with rational. "We *are* talking to each other. This extension is shit timing and a separate issue."

"You've been busy before and still had time to call."

"Not like this, babe," he said, wishing he could say more. "Net access has been totally firewalled for the past two weeks. Phone time is privileged and censored."

"Why?"

"Because . . . the fucking military."

He immediately regretted saying that aloud. All calls were being monitored.

Too late now.

She paused, then asked, "Is it a good day?"

He should've expected this, but the pace and stress were clearly affecting him. The question was coded to ask him if he was about to go into harm's way. He'd answered yes truthfully in the past, but in those situations, his biggest risk was sitting in a vehicle far back from the door-kickers.

"No," he lied.

He waited for a response—nothing. The pit of his stomach contracted into something small and heavy that tugged on his insides. That silence sliced through him better than any knife man could craft. Even Brines. Tightening his free hand into a fist and fighting off the urge to ram it into the steel bulkhead, he whispered, "I love you."

An eternity. Then, "I love you too, Ron. It's just . . . you're not on some business trip here. You're part of a war. Wars kill people."

"Babe, we're not at war . . ." *Semantics.*

"Whatever. Look, I'm not trying to sound like some powder-puff bitch here. I just need to hear from you. I"—she sniffled—"I like talking to you."

He bit his lip. She handled the dangers of his job better than most military spouses, and he had no one to blame but himself for pushing it too far this time. "I like talking to you too," he said. It was a simple thing to admit, but there was power in their sincerity. "I'm sorry."

"Ugh," she said with a deep breath. The tears were coming under control. "I know. Part of this is me being a girl, overreacting. Doesn't help that this week's been hell top to bottom. New director and the floors are in chaos trying to meet these damned government regulations. No one is happy." If Saunders' absence wasn't enough, her role as a hospital administrator was like napalm on a sunburn. She was on-call 168 hours a week to manage a structure devoted to human misery and suffering. And managing high-paid, hyper-educated doctors wasn't the same as keeping Cpl Nickels and Gunny Brines apart during rifle inspection.

Silence filled the line, and he could imagine her face contorted as she battled to separate job and relationship frustrations. Eventually, something clicked, and she continued. "I mean, I did get the flowers. So, I know you were thinking about me, even if you couldn't call."

Flowers?

"You said you got the flowers?" He was glad she couldn't see his face right now.

"Yup. Garden World did a pretty good job with them, but I'll give you a little credit for the note. It was nice."

Saunders licked his lips. It wasn't the first time someone had sent her flowers on his behalf. He would either have to buy that someone a cigar or some bandages. "Well, great. I hope they look good. And again, I'm sorry I haven't called."

"We're talking now; that's what counts," she said, calmer. "With all the shit on the news about the hostages and this manic wanting to start World War III, I was worried they might be sending you in."

Once again, Saunders was glad she couldn't see his face or the thirty-five pounds of combat gear he was wearing. "We're deterrence, Babe. I know that's no guarantee but have a little faith in my ability to avoid trouble. I mean, how many times have I gone and died on you?" He added a chuckle to keep it light.

"Only once," she muttered.

"That's right, and I was only dead for a few weeks," Saunders said. He and several of his men had been erroneously listed as killed in action during operations in Iraq. Over the ensuing years, he had dissipated her resultant trauma with jest and careful concealment of the events that took place while he was presumed dead. The fact that he could casually bring it up now was a testament to his success.

"Yeah well, I don't want to go through that again. I need to know where you are. Whatever happens."

"I can give you a ballpark—"

"Promise me that I'll always know where you are," she insisted suddenly.

It was an impossible request. She knew that. He knew that. But fuck it. "I promise," he lied, again.

"Okay," she whispered. He couldn't tell if she believed him, but she seemed to accept the fantasy. "And please stay safe."

"Doin' my best, babe. I'm just as pissed as everyone about this extension. You know I'd give anything to be with you and the boy right now."

"We miss you too. I'm sorry I'm messing up this call. I just want you home."

"I'm the one with shit to be sorry about. But I'll make it up to you. After this cruise, I'll have plenty of leave." He always made a point to plan on coming back and to never *if* the future.

"I've got a few ideas," she said.

"Oh yeah?" It was either a ten-page backlog of house projects or . . .

"Nothing too fancy, just a little getaway. I mean, if you don't want to, it's okay. I just feel like we need something to celebrate. Y'know," her voice lowered, "maybe we can get to work on a little sister for Tommy." It was music to his ears. Plus, she was in planning mode now. Planning mode was good. He let out a freeing breath. The discussion had gone from *fuck you* to *fuck me*. It was the sort of progress that made life worth living.

"A little bro for li'l T? Hell yeah. But you'd better start training now 'cause I could be home sooner than you think."

"No! It's not going to be like last time. I want flowers and kisses and the sound of the ocean to bring our little girl into the world. Not . . ." she trailed off, allowing his memories to fill the void.

"Ah babe, don't tease me like that when you know I'm not getting any out here." The conception of their son Tommy coincided with Saunders' return from being listed as KIA in Iraq. He jokingly referred to it as resurrection sex, and it was one hell of a week.

"Consider it your punishment." Her voice was playful now, and he finally smiled.

With the tension lifted, the conversation moved onto other pressing matters of state. Sarah vented the latest and greatest mishaps at the hospital. He shared a few nonsense stories from the Charlie Company archives. Precious minutes ticked away, but he didn't care.

The back and forth heated up when they got to vacation planning. She dismissed his suggestion of going to Hawaii and climbing the volcano outright, mainly because it didn't sound romantic to her. He disagreed. A volcano was the quintessential embodiment of romance.

More importantly, it was something to climb.

They mulled over a trip to upstate New York. She had relatives up there, and it had mountains—smaller things to climb compared to what he grew up with in the Colorado Rockies. But Upstate was always better in late fall and winter. Plus, Tommy was gearing up for first grade in a few weeks. "Babe, you need the beach and some quiet time. Like I said, start training now 'cause daddy's coming home soon."

"How soon?"

His mind worked on adding up the time for debriefing, possibilities of operational delays, expansion of the conflict, and the transit back to Camp Lejeune. "One week." It was a ballpark but reasonable.

"Bullshit," she said. "But I'm going to hold you to it, Ron."

"Babe, take li'l T out to the cottage and chill. You've been through a lot. I've been through a lot, and nothing will get me home faster than the thought of you two waiting for me. And the pitcher. Don't forget the pitcher." The pitcher was a mission priority when taking advantage of their beach cottage in Hatteras, North Carolina. Having the Atlantic as the backyard was relaxing, but beer and margaritas by the pitcher were downright medicinal.

"I'll see if I can arrange things with work, I guess." She paused and, for a moment, lost the levity they'd been sharing. "That reminds me, *your* son was sent to Mr. Benson today for fighting."

Benson. *That'd be the camp admin.* Saunders flashed back to some of his more memorable childhood brawls. "He start the fight?"

"He threw the first punch, yes. He says the other kid knocked his lunch off the table, but in the eyes of Camp Pony Oaks, it's all about who threw first."

"He win the fight?"

"Ugh, yes, he bloodied the kid's nose good. I had to deal with a call from the boy's father."

Saunders checked his watch and felt the sting of urgency. The only time he was ever guilty of losing track of time was when he was with her. "Okay, I'm running short here, but tell Tommy I'm disappointed in him for breaching the rules of engagement. You always let them throw the first punch. Give him a little *oorah* for kicking the shit out of that loser, though. And if that kid's dad gives you any more trouble, tell him I'll be happy to discuss it with him after I get out of the slammer."

"Yeah, I probably won't do any of that."

Saunders laughed. "All right, well tell T I love him. I've gotta go."

"Okay," she replied, used to his quick departures, "I love you; stay safe!"

"Love ya too, babe; I'll see you soon."

"Remember your promise."

A shiver rippled up his spine. Why did that bother him so much? She knew the military restricted communication and information on location and situation. He would try his best to stay in touch, but unrealistic expectations were unrealistic. *She knows that, dammit. So why do I feel like shit?*

"I love you, goodbye," was all he said.

He returned the phone to its hook and closed his eyes to give her a mental kiss. It started rough, but he felt better now. She'd forget about that location-finding bullshit. It was just her way of saying she wanted to keep working on the marriage. *Us working together.* Operation *Sea Monster* was nothing compared to the thought of losing her.

Approaching footsteps bade him stand.

"How's the wife?" asked Col Ridge, who'd made this late-stage personal call possible. The fleet had gone to operation-essential communications a few hours ago. As the 25th MEU's commander, Jake Ridge could pull a few strings for dickheads like Saunders.

"Ah, sir, she was a little pissy 'cause I haven't dropped her a line in a while." Jake also appreciated candor. There were limits, no junior officer was chummy with a full bird colonel, but a level of comfort was encouraged. "But otherwise, she sounds good."

"I hope the flowers helped."

Saunders smiled as a singular knot of the braided tension in his back loosened. "Ah, so they came from you guys. They certainly did. Thank you, sir."

The colonel waved it away. "You can thank me by staying safe out there."

Saunders tucked his lingering thoughts of family away for safekeeping and put on his game face. "Yes, sir."

"You pumped?"

"No distractions, Jake. I feel good about this."

"I miss it, Ron, but fuck if I'd be able to look me in the eye right now and say I'm not scared shitless."

"Sir. You never went into combat with the C-monster."

―――――

The two guards with batons and pistols strapped to their olive-green trousers were never far away. They loitered motionless on the periphery of Dr. Pat's visual field, casting the illusion of capable nurses ready to jump in at her beck and call.

No, not nurses. More like shadowing first-year medical students. Interested in what was happening, but otherwise, dead weight in the room. The guards wouldn't respond to her cries for forceps or compression. They wouldn't even change the radio station if asked. Yet they periodically questioned her actions with a disturbingly accent-free and firm command of the English language. Especially when she worked on one of their compatriots.

"Why not give him more of the fluid bag?"

"Because then his blood pressure will spike and risk rebleed."

"The leg will heal; do not cut it."

"No, it won't. Do you want a two-legged corpse or a one-legged survivor?"

"You must attend Omar; his pain is great."

"He's a heroin addict."

"He is a patriot. You favor your fellow prisoner too much."

Dr. Pat tried to avoid bias with her patients, but these were soldiers fighting a war. They knew the risks. Her people, as she'd come to view them, were victims of unwarranted, illegal abuse. Safeguards like the Geneva Convention were illusions, evidently, as there had been zero contact with any aspect of the international community. No church groups, do-gooding celebrities, or anyone from any non-governmental organization. So, the buck stopped here.

You're damned right I'm biased.

"With this one, you have spent enough time," urged the taller guard with that degree of finality in his voice. Another surprise was his ability to convey subtle inflections in his nearly perfect American English. But his sentence structure remained strange. It felt like talking to a translator. "Yes, of course," she replied unwilling to push the limits further.

Brutality also bred compliance.

She took stock of the bunker's cramped infirmary. It smelled of sick and rot and chemicals; the result of futile attempts to bring twenty-first-century sterile fields into a barnyard chop shop. She made eye contact with one of the actual nurses—female helpers covered from head to toe in dirty-white garb. "Please monitor blood pressure, pulse rate, and listen to the lungs on him," she gestured to the flaccid, pale man who—just a few hours ago—was a vibrant, hot-blooded Marine. Another reminder of non-compliance.

At least this stuff I can heal, not like . . . the psych-job they did on Marie and that other Marine.

Arriving at Omar, the next "priority" patient, Dr. Pat sighed. Another self-inflicted, superficial injury. *More drug seeking.* If there was one thing this Pakistani rebellion had, it was opium. And although it was mostly in questionable lyophilized—white powder—form, they knew exactly how to administer it for maximal pain relief. Read: maintenance.

"Give it to him," urged the shorter guard, on the other side of the bed.

The effects were immediate. Solubilized and injected intravenously, the opioid drained the tension from Omar's face. His eyes, so frantically searching, grew vapid, no longer interested in their surroundings.

It was reminiscent of how some of her people had returned to the prison. Altered. But they had stayed like that for days, whereas this Omar would be searching for another score in hours.

What was happening to some of her people didn't make sense from a scientific or medical point of view. She could come up with explanations, but all of them involved new experimental chemicals or touchless surgical procedures that did not fit the low-quality medical facilities on the base.

One thing was certain: watching him settle into that blissful relief made her even more aware of the pain in her back and calves. She'd been on her feet, standing on the concrete floor for hours. Perhaps days. They'd allowed her to eat twice, but it barely touched the feeling that her stomach was trying to swallow itself. She realized her heart was racing, tachycardic.

Strange.

A wave of dizziness swept over her. *Psychosomatic?* She could fight through this. *Just need to . . .*

The two guards remained still as her legs buckled, and she bounced off the patient bed onto the floor. She never passed out. It was an energy plunge. Her liver—an amazing reservoir of glycogen that could keep her in action long past the point of starvation—had cut her off. Or maybe she'd hypoventilated and acidified her blood. It was hard to focus on all the possibilities. Regardless, a moment of rest would get her back on her feet. The concrete floor felt warm and soft against her back.

She wondered if she had hit her head.

Now the two were above her. Rough hands hooked under her arm pits, fingers digging into the sides of her breasts and down into her pectoral muscles. Then she was back on limp feet. The guards guided—dragged—her from the infirmary to the table where she'd eaten the previous two meals. She sat there dazed until they brought her a reddish plastic cup smudged with dirty fingerprints. Inside was a dark liquid, but the vessel was more interesting.

Where did they find a red solo cup? she wondered.

The question lingered, floating through her mind like a ship adrift. No purpose, no destination. Just interesting to watch.

"Drink," spoke a voice.

Her body shook involuntarily from the startle response, and a jolt of adrenaline helped her focus on the present. She was in what she considered their break room. Dozens of metal folding chairs surrounded six rectangular wooden tables that looked more residential than military. Her guards sat across from her, but the voice had come from behind. Someone new.

She turned, and her heart caught in her throat.

Him.

He was sitting there, casually, in the room's back corner, just beyond the reach of the fluorescent lights. His features were hard to make out, but she remembered enough to fill in the details. He wore the standard issue military uniform of the other officers, but those drab, olive-green shoulders and breast pockets were covered in a lot more flare. The individual symbols meant nothing to her but combined, they seemed to mark him with the respect—fear—he commanded from the rest of the military staff.

But what caught her attention as someone to avoid was those two wicked knives strapped next to his holstered pistol. One was long and thin. The other was wavy, almost decorative, but came to a point sharp enough to cut air. The faded crimson stains on his sleeves didn't help either.

"Drink," he repeated. "If you do not drink, you will lose your strength. If you cannot heal the others, you will hurt them."

She resisted the urge to shrink away from the aura of brutality radiating off the man in the shadows and took a swallow of the dark liquid. Grape juice. The thought that it was poisoned or drugged seemed academic at this point. They could have just left her on the floor if they'd wanted her incapacitated. If this was how they turned people into zombies, they probably wouldn't take no for an answer.

The metallic knife handles clinked together as the man rose and approached. Dr. Pat turned to set her solo cup down and saw that her guards were now watching with wide-eyed uncertainty. "Go," whispered the man, and the two hurried out of the room.

He sat at the table and looked her over as she might a new patient during an intake exam. Countless men, both wanted and unwanted, had studied her physique over the years, but nothing about this was sexual. He was seeing through her orange jumpsuit, beneath the skin to her organs. Looking for a place to make his first incision.

"Thank you for the juice," she managed. Compliance. Gratitude. *I matter.* Dr. Pat was human, not a cadaver.

"It is an American icon, this cup," he mused, finally making eye contact. "Does it give you hope for home?"

"It gives me hope that the ones I heal will go home." *Can't be selfish, and he seems to place some value on healing.*

"Because you think they will come?"

"Who?"

"The rescue heroes of your military."

She shook her head. "The only ending I hope for is one achieved through diplomacy." Years of practiced professionalism was the only thing keeping this monster from digging in. She'd vomit the triple-tight box knot out of her stomach later.

"There will only be bloodshed. But," he brought his face closer to hers, "I hope it begins with your rescue heroes." He looked around as if someone might overhear before adding, "I don't trust *them*. I want to see how they handle a *real* fighting force."

As he said it, the hooded figure in the black robe entered the room.

CHAPTER 5

UP ANCHOR

Hard rock pulsed through the ship as America's heroes readied themselves to answer the call once again. Over 400 United States Marines and equipment were now scattered throughout the expansive hangar deck. Pops and metallic clicks mixed with lively chatter as weapons and gear were checked, rechecked, and stowed.

Charlie Company—the C-monster—was assembled near the ramp to the flight deck. Its four platoons were stacked into tight rows, ready for a parade into hell. Pride of the battalion, they were the apex of modern romp and stomp warfare. Three rifle platoons grabbing angles and locking down positions backed by the show-stopping Heavy Weapons Platoon, which, once bolted in, could go toe to toe with just about any big metal the enemy could field.

The C-monster didn't probe. They weren't dainty. They didn't slip down quiet nylon ropes hoping to choke out an unsuspecting victim. They thundered in on flying death traps, suppressed, advanced, and gored the enemy right in the ass. They went big and then they went home.

"Thought that there full moon was a no-go, boss," LCpl Fischer said, remembering their conversation at breakfast. When Francisco didn't reply, he paned the high rows of desert-style beige, brown, and gray MCCUU battle dress uniforms around them with a smile. "This all must be for show, 'cause no way Nickels was right. Right?"

"Just because the winds are high, and the Earth's gravitational constant is out of adjustment doesn't mean they won't still ask you to take the shot," deadpanned Francisco. He hoisted his cumbersome SPC vest over his shoulders for effect. Those plates he had loaded in there were no joke. NIJ Level IV—the heavy shit that could stop a rifle round, maybe two. Seeing that stuff draped over the guys carrying machine guns and mortar tubes was one thing, but Francisco was the company's senior marksman.

Ain't gonna be no mobility and discretion in this fight, Fischer realized. It was going to be white-knuckled trigger action. Up close and personal.

"I hear ya," he said, pulling Francisco's shoulder straps snug. "Startin' to wonder if I shouldn't grab myself a carbine, too."

"Keep it light," said Francisco checking over Fischer's pack job. Unlike the base of fire-support units like Sgt Smith and Cpl Nickels, a Marine sniper was a delicate creature that made discrete adjustments to enemy numbers from a position of concealment. The twenty-five pounds of body armor notwithstanding, a rifle, some ammo, and a few granola bars to steady the blood sugar were all he needed.

In optimal conditions, anyway.

"You don't think I'm better off playin' the short game till you land?"

"Distance is safety is carelessness. They won't be in a hurry to get in your face.

"Yeah," agreed Fischer reaching down to give his M40A5 Marine Corps sniper rifle a pat. Even if everything went according to plan, there was plenty of cause for jitters. He was taking the classic long gun into battle. Not as a support spotter or on guard duty for the designated marksman, but as the trigger man. And while the higher-ups promised heavy support and a tacked-down, lit-up shooting gallery, those folks were known optimists.

Francisco tossed a banana peel back in his seabag, where Fischer caught sight of a conspicuous black Pelican case tucked in with his laundry. He gave it a good long look to make sure Francisco knew he knew before asking, "What was that about distance and whatnot?"

Francisco shrugged. "Always be prepared."

"You gonna risk bringin' the Bullpup 'cause the Boy Scouts told you to?"

"I haven't decided yet."

"Yeah, right. Y'all're a classic case of indecision," Fischer said with a laugh. Francisco was the kind of guy who planned his meals out weeks ahead. For him to even consider checking that excellent instrument of unfailing run and gun marksmanship cemented the fact that he planned to be knee-deep in the shit. Beyond balls deep. *Touching assholes,* as Cpl Nickels would say.

"This is uncharted territory for us. Our true roles will become evident when we're on the ground."

"Yeah. Still can't believe they're splittin' us up, though, boss," Fischer said, adjusting the straps that molded his own body armor to his torso. "I feel like I just got kicked outta the nest and gotta start workin' these big ol' wings." He hooked his thumbs together and flapped his fingers.

Francisco smirked and took aim at the pretend bird with a finger pistol. "Take it as a compliment. Saunders wants his best shooters staggered."

"Ye-huh. More like he don't want you getting all dead in that there death contraption." Command had pulled Fischer from his pairing with Francisco in Third Platoon just a few hours ago. It reassigned him to the Rapid Air to Ground vehicle—the RAG—as First Platoon's designated marksman.

Francisco paused at the mention of the RAG. "I think it'll work."

"Have you seen it?"

"No. But I heard it flies."

"Yeah, that ain't the part that worries me."

"You'll be fine. One hundred mile per hour tape always survives to contact."

Fischer chuckled at the image of a raggedy chopper held together by bubble gum and duct tape.

"And you'll get first pickings at a confused and disorganized enemy," added Francisco.

"But no carbine?"

"You're ready."

You're ready. Fischer ducked eye contact, hoping to avoid showing just how much that comment meant to him. It was probably the biggest *attaboy* he'd ever received in this military occupational specialty where Francisco was the gold standard of assessment.

"We'll sync up when I land," said Francisco. "By then, the lines will firm up, and the enemy will be bunkering. Some tough shots to be had. Saunders is going to want us paired at that point."

"Welp, y'all can take your time. Got me plenty of snacks." Fischer slung a small CamelBak over his shoulders.

"Hey." Francisco grabbed his arm. "Only water in there, right?" Most other hydration support devices in Charlie Company were filled with varying flavors and intensities of energy drinks. Ultra-caffeinated sugar pop that promised to replace adrenaline in moments of great need. It was fine for the hard chargers, but marksmen needed steady hands.

"Pure as the day the Earth was created."

"You get some shuteye?"

"Thought you said I was ready, hoss?"

"Check, check, and recheck. That's how we load our dice."

"Gotcha. Had me a good three-hour nap. Rocksteady." He held out his hands and extended his fingers.

Francisco nodded and hoisted his mission pack. "One more thing. Saunders is going to be on the ground with you. This isn't him flying a bunch of screens and appearing as a calm, collected voice over some headset. He's going to be knee-deep in the blood and guts. At least in the beginning. Keep an eye on him if you can. He's . . ."

"I heard the stories."

"Right. Just make sure he doesn't get into any tight spots."

"Wilco."

"All right, you know your places. Good luck and God bless. Dismissed," ordered Captain Saunders dispersing the collection of officers and staff NCOs from the officer's wardroom. Final confirmation had come through; they were still a go. He wasn't surprised, given his earlier meeting with Admiral Bowman. Still, they'd burned him so often this close to an operation that expecting a stand-down was second nature. Especially with something like Operation *Sea Monster*.

We're invading Pakistan.

It was surreal. Extraordinary. But since he was part of the machine, it also felt like just another day. Nothing miraculous got them here except that the enemy punched first. The rest was built in, innate. A steady flow chart of procedures and timing to make war.

Folks back home might tip their hats, but danger aside, this was nothing more than a magnified version of most small-scale operations. Pilots would take off from Kandahar, drop their loads and head back. Some would zip around pushing buttons and watching radar signatures vanish. Others in trailers back state-side would operate what the military called RPAs and ordinary people called drones to fill the battlespace voids men could not. And the Marines would fire their rifles, just as they always had.

"Sir," came a rasp.

Saunders looked up into the grizzled face of Gunny Brines. He hadn't put on his paint yet. "Mike?"

"I ah, seem to recall the plan being that First Platoon's chopper lands at the objective. Not crashes, sir."

"It's all about the delta T, Mike. Under fire, a chopper needs a small one."

"By . . . uhm, 'T' you mean exposure time. Right?"

Saunders considered turning back to the whiteboard and writing out the equation for Brines just to razz him. But they had a dwindling T of their own, and just because Brines didn't visualize math in his head didn't mean he couldn't understand. "Right."

"What happens if you die?" Good ol' Brines. Straight to the point.

"Third Platoon will learn from our mistake and attempt a regular landing." Off to the right, First Lieutenant Lyons—Charlie Company's executive officer—swallowed hard. Lyons was a good guy, great in a fight and destined to take Colonel Ridge's job one day, but a little high-strung. The one-way ticket aboard an experimental aircraft wasn't helping.

"Sir, why don't you let me take yer seat in this thing." Brines thumped a hand on Lyons' shoulder. "I'll look out fer the lieutenant."

"Negative, buddy. Privilege of command. They need me on the ground ASAP. It's all very complicated. You understand, right?"

Brines worked his lips into a rare smile at the sarcasm. It was refreshing to see this close to an operation, given his friend's demons. "I understand that in a situation carrying a high risk of death or dismemberment, you are depriving me of some pleasure."

"Corporal Nickels should provide plenty of in-flight entertainment."

The smile vanished, but a playfulness lingered in those sky-blue eyes. "Nickels is the in-flight meal."

———

Awash in the sterile, soft white of the hangar deck's halogen lighting, clusters of monochromatic Marines snapped salutes and cheered as the 25th

MEU's commanding officer, Colonel Jake Ridge, made his rounds. Combat prep was complete. This was a time for last-minute photos, handshakes, and each Marine to get that look from the battalion CO.

You're important.

Spirits soared; stomachs settled. Straps were snug, clips were locked, snags debrided, pictures pocketed, and rifles slung. *Sea Monster* was still green, still a go.

Charlie Company had fragmented into their fireteams and squads for final instructions from the staff sergeants. It was more pep than talk as slaps and antics ran rampant beneath the beat of the sound system. Then, unordered, they were back at attention.

All eyes locked onto the starboard hatch as the geared-up torso—resembling the hardened chassis of a top-heavy tank turret wrapped and strapped in 550 cord—of Gunnery Sergeant Brines glided through.

With his helmet between his left arm and hip, and the other hand gripping a heavy M4 Carbine with attached 40mm grenade launcher, Brines met their stares.

Don't look at me like that. I'm just as much a bullet sponge as the rest of you.

But all they saw was the active-duty Navy Cross awardee, the E7 so hard he was running a goddamned company. All they saw was a larger-than-life beacon to guide them through hell, and no one, not even their mommas, could tell them any different.

Glare at me, damn it. Spit in my face and yell at me fer making you earn yer hazard pay.

He couldn't say that, though. He'd been in their boots, trying to calm his green nerves by building up his heroes. The memory of his first company and First Sergeant Abe Ward—a tough son of a bitch who'd cut his teeth in Kuwait—surfaced. Abe was retired now with a bad back, four kids, and fifteen credit cards. Last time Brines met up with him for drinks, Abe pricked his fingers at least twice to get his sugars under control. But back when he'd stomp out before a mission in full gear, he was invincible. And that made Brines invincible.

And now, Brines made *them* invincible.

Captain Saunders followed on his heels and tossed a nod. The anticipation on deck was tangible, with Marines chomping at the bit. Brines wished he could somehow convey what combat was about to take from this group. Instead, he asked them in the native tongue of the Marine Corps, "OORAH?"

The Marines roared in response.

"You ready to do this shit?" Saunders asked, slapping him on the shoulder.

Brines began to kick back a motivational one-liner but stopped at the sight of his friend. Saunders' usually immaculate 'inside' boots were gone, replaced by his worn Marine desert issue in which his MCCUU trousers were tucked. His athletic trim was buried under the same chin-to-groin NIJ Level IV plate carrier that Sgt Smith's assault squad from Third Platoon wore. Standard loadout for a dig-in firefight. But then there was that nine-inch Ka-Bar USMC fighting knife hooked to the left side of his chest.

"Yes, sir," Brines rattled through his worn vocal cords. He respected the knife. Every bit of weight was ultimately a choice, and while that mass-produced shank was a toothpick compared to his own signature blade, it set the tone nicely. *We ain't givin' an inch without those hostages.*

The only question mark settled on the captain's primary weapon. Instead of the standard issue Colt M4 assault rifle, he was sporting an MP5 close-quarters combat gun. It was a short-barreled machine pistol designed for the sort of breach and clear tactics that were part of SEAL's mission, not the Marines. It was probably nothing, a minor issue. Not a control issue because Brines didn't have control issues. But a small snag that would pick at his brain. He hated those because they seemed to make sense at the worst times.

"All right, I'm gonna check in," said Saunders staring at Colonel Ridge like . . . like what? *Pissed because he's gotta earn that hazard pay?* Nah. Distracted was more like it. Ron's mind was in a whole other world of checklists, protocols, nine-lines, ratios, call signs, and probably his most recent fight with Sarah.

Yeah. I'm reading too much into it.

———

Captain Saunders found Colonel Ridge mid-compartment receiving a status update from Alpha Company's Captain Rogers.

"Alpha's good to go, no problems on my end."

"All right, Rogers, do the final checklist and assemble your men behind Charlie. Ah, Saunders, good of you to show up. Your boys good to go?"

Saunders locked eyes across the deck with 1stLt Lyons and got a thumbs-up. "Lean and mean, sir."

"Right. All elements are reporting green. You load up in fifteen. Any questions?"

"Any chance you want Alpha to take point?" asked Rogers with a laugh. The two companies were technically qualified to execute the mission. Rogers had spent just as much of his intellectual capital building out Operation *Sea Monster* as Saunders, but the fact was he'd come in second.

Col Ridge shrugged. "You'll get yours, Rogers. After we step in this Pakistani shit, I'm betting it'll be a while before we can clean it off our boots."

Saunders' stomach tightened. *So much for being home next week.*

"Yes, sir," said Rogers with just a touch too much strain in his neck muscles, as if he literally was having a hard time swallowing it. Saunders had trouble sympathizing. If anything, Alpha was in the best possible position. They weren't being cannibalized like Bravo or totally sidelined like Delta. Their mission was to secure the forward arming and refueling point *in country*. On the ground but out of harm's way. *Worst case scenario: Mina Bazar goes south, and they swoop in to save the day. Heroes!*

"Dismissed," finished Ridge with a deliberate look at Rogers. He took the hint and parted with a quick salute.

Saunders stayed and pulled a folded white envelope out of his pocket before Jake could voice whatever was on his mind. "Sir, I figure you'd be the one to . . . uh, *go*." He let that last word linger. He didn't want it to sound like a request, but the seed was planted. As battalion CO, Jake would be the one assigning the duty.

"And," he continued in a lighter tone, "since you'll be safe and secure in the LFOC for the duration of the mission, I can't think of a better place to stow it." A slight frown made Saunders regret that phrasing. Jake hated it when it was implied he was somehow *safe* back in the truck while they were kicking in doors. No one ever felt safe because everyone's ass was on the line.

The Landing Force Operations Center's Command Element would be just as white-knuckled as Brines ham-handing that damned knife.

"Anyway, I'm no great author. That was Dad and his dad. Just something handwritten. Something from me. You know?" He vaguely wondered if Jake would stuff the postcard from hell into a bouquet of flowers.

Colonel Ridge took the letter and nodded.

"Just make sure I'm really dead this time before you go," added Saunders with a chuckle.

"Report back alive, and there won't be any confusion." A smile lingered on Jake's lips, and then it was back to business. "Look . . . Ron." His eyes fell to the slung MP5 slung, and he lowered his voice. "Be careful out there. A fifty-fifty chance to grab an extra hostage or two isn't worth a careless discard of your life." From his grim expression, Colonel Ridge wasn't too happy with the change of plans either. But regardless of whether the two men could agree privately, they both had their orders.

"We're not leaving anyone behind, sir," Saunders replied. "I know the layout of their tactical operations center like the back of my hand."

Colonel Ridge, not Jake, moved in closer, his hot breath puffing and hissing into Saunders' right ear. "Let me be clear. Don't go anywhere near that fucking bunker unless you get explicit orders from me. It's a waste of Marine resources, and it's a waste of you. The VIP isn't worth shit to me. You read? I will destroy that goddamned C4I shitbox and everyone in it without a second thought if I think it's unattainable."

Saunders resisted the urge to take a step back. He wanted to protest, to agree, to look for someone higher up for guidance. Instead, he counted to three and blew out a breath.

"Copy that, sir."

Colonel Ridge leaned back, satisfied. "Good luck Marine." The men exchanged salutes and parted.

———

Three minutes till go.

Captain Saunders studied the ranks with satisfaction and a bit of detached awe. Charlie Company comprised the highest caliber products the Corps could produce. As infantry, they had chosen the most brutal medium of warfare and excelled. Now that excellence would mesh with all the tactical elements in the Joint Services' arsenal to make good on that age-old promise that kept America's enemies awake at night.

We don't negotiate with terrorists.

"At ease," came a rasp. Brines' voice was already hoarse, and they hadn't yet tasted the night air. The man had a strange set of pipes, though. Where Saunders' voice would wane after hours of shouting, Gunny Brines' intensified. The graininess added to the ambiance as if it operated at some primal frequency to which all Marines were attuned. *Like a baby's cry cutting through thunder.* Saunders clicked his head ever so slightly to the right and snapped off a dangerous line of thinking that would ultimately lead to Tommy and Sarah.

"Our objective is the PAF airfield Mina Bazar deep inside contested Pakistan," Brines continued, trekking across the deck with every helmet turning to keep pace. "We never done nothin' like this. We read about it, watched movies about it. But the world of big infantry died a long time ago. Now it's all drones, mech, tech, and fuckin' rocket-powered cracker jackers."

A murmur of laughter.

"Most'a you've kicked in doors with me." He paused. "This ain't gonna be like that. There ain't no support. There ain't no QRF." Saunders raised an eyebrow at the slight deviation from the script but remained silent. The mission had a ton of close-in air support from the Aviation Combat Element—callsign: Vulture. And Alpha Company was essentially the "quick reaction force." They just weren't super quick. It was all relative.

"We're droppin' over seven hundred fuckin' klicks behind lines in a country who don't know which way's up or down no more. I don't care how many jets and choppers they got flying around up top; we're gonna be the ones in the lead pissin' contest." He stopped and faced them.

"Two lines. Us and the enemy."

Every Marine a rifleman.

"And they gonna come at us with everything they got. Like bats outta hell lookin' to notch a belt with American blood. They're gonna be hungry as fuck for you." The Marines ranks shifted uncomfortably.

Brines breathed that hint of fear in and gave a rare smirk that folded his face along that vertical scar on his cheek. "You ain't gotta worry about that shit, though. What yer feelin' now is anxiety. Like when you walk up to a girl at a bar. You think she's outta your league, got a boyfriend, or flat out she's gonna say no and yer gonna feel like shit. Well, that's all in yer head. The moment you make contact, it's gone. Then it's drinks, flowers, steak dinner, and balls deep on the balcony of someone else's hotel room."

Chuckles and a couple hoots.

"'Cause you done it before. Different girl, same deal. Experience. That's what we're gonna do tonight. The nerves and fear are gone the moment we touch down. Then it's training; it's by the numbers. They'll come hard, but we'll be harder. We'll take the best they got straight to the chest and give it right back at 'em."

"Oorah!" belted the C-monster.

Semper Fi.

Satisfied, Brines turned and shared a thumbs up with Alpha's first sergeant. "Good to go, sir."

"Great speech," Saunders said. "When did *esprit de corps* become balls deep on a balcony?'"

"Day you met Sarah, sir."

Saunders shook his head. "Okay, it's go time."

Gunny spun and threw the switch.

The men hustled to their sticks where Combat Cargo was waiting to lead them to their assigned aircraft on the flight deck. Brines fell in with Third Platoon prompting cheers. Captain Strom came over the 1MC to wish the Ground Combat Element smooth sailing. The call to General Quarters sounded, and the ship thrust her bow into the wind.

Adrenaline was pumping hard through the infantry organism as Saunders got in line with First Platoon. Unlike Third Platoon, these Marines were tight-jaw forward, probably trying to reconcile fact from rumor about the RAG. And 1stLt Lyons was right there with them, quietly waiting in line for some bad news.

The moment you make contact, it's gone.

Saunders sifted through the ranks and found a radioman. An intense jamming package was being deployed for the operation, so personal communications gear had been nixed. Only the larger backpack units had enough power to cut through. Constant contact with the Aviation and Command Elements was essential, and there was no way he could juggle a radio with the rest of his gear. He put his hand on the nervous radio operator's shoulder and said, "PFC, you're on me out there. I need you close, copy?"

The private first class—an unusual rank in the special operations capable Marines—hesitated. More of that anxiety Brines was talking about.

Hell, this kid was still boot-camp lanky and probably sporting a few pimples under his war paint.

Saunders didn't need to push. The added responsibility was enough to jack up anyone's heart rate. Still, he trusted his instincts. This kid was assigned to the RAG for a reason. He had some fight.

He was a Marine.

Confirming this, PFC Licht—David was his first name if memory served—lifted his chin and squared his shoulders. "Yes, sir." It came out just a hair too loud, as if he were trying to impress a superior. Saunders could relate.

"Good. Loosen up that grip on your rifle; I need you cool and steady out there."

"Yes, sir."

"Oorah?"

PFC Licht swallowed. Those eyes were still wide, still unblinking. But they weren't saying *no*. Finally, a slight nod.

"Oorah, sir."

Saunders turned to the rest of his Marines and belted another *OORAH*. They hit it back louder.

The hangar deck's lighting went red, and the ramp alarm sounded.

The thumping rock&roll gave way to the patriotic Marine Corps Hymn, and Combat Cargo led America's elite up the flight deck tunnel to their transports. Outside was a storm of flashing lights, wind, and the thunderous whine of the massive gray Super Stallion transports on standby. Almost lost in the bombardment were the naval airmen waving from the decks of the island.

While the other platoons made for their usual choppers, Saunders and First Platoon drove forward into the wash of salt and humidity toward the RAG. It looked as bad as it sounded, with hastily welded hatches lining the perimeter and a patchwork of additional armored plating. Underneath it all was a Super Stallion, the same as the other transports. Still, it was a stark contrast to the beauty of the twin-rotored, vertical take-off/landing MV-22B Osprey on landing pad five, which a black-clothed SEAL team was now boarding.

Captain Saunders snapped a mental photograph as his men, strong and menacing in their combat gear, marched onboard. He, too, grappled with anxiety. The fear that some of those bright, young faces might fade to ghostly visages or that Sarah and the boy might be left alone in the world. The moment passed, and he gave the nod to Brines, promising to see him on the ground. Then he entered the beast.

The inside was thick with fresh paint, oil, and recent machining. But the welds and bolts were tight. Nowhere near as rickety as it looked.

The RAG was packed to the brim within minutes. Saunders lingered near the cockpit and exchanged a few words with the pilots before giving a thumbs up and taking his seat. "We're still a go!" he shouted over the roar of men and machines. "We're still a go! Departure in one minute."

The Marines bellowed their war cries, and precisely on schedule, the entire helicopter fleet lifted off the three ARG flight decks and disappeared into the night. In formation with their AH-1Z Viper attack helicopter escorts, the Ground Combat Element flew toward the Pakistani coast. They went *feet dry* at 0121 hours on the twenty-eighth of August in the year 2018.

Two days before the scheduled execution of 126 Americans.

CHAPTER 6

OPFOR

Despite the late hour, Mina Bazar's operations center thrummed. Rumors of a government offensive had ebbed and flowed over a wash of breathless days and sleepless nights, but the tide seemed near its peak. The command staff was fevered, bickering like children at times. Still, their hearts beat strong for war and for Kôz.

Kôz.

The true herald of this revolution. It was the prophetic teachings of a great reckoning that no man of faith could ignore once his ears and eyes were open. Guised by false names, it long slept in the hearts of many, waiting to be awakened in capable hands. For Guard Captain Ahmad and many thousands more, those hands belonged to Major General Khel.

Aki Hajul Khel was a man of no family and no background. A humble worker whose natural athleticism and lust for danger drove him to the Army. From there, the Inter-Services Intelligence. His quick feet and sharp mind paced him with the Mujahedeen in Afghanistan. First as an advisor and then as a brother. There he found his faith, and the first embers of Kôz began to glow.

When he reintegrated into the Army, the boy had become a man of vision. He played their games well, laughing and smiling with his enemies while uplifting his brethren. As a lieutenant general, he was placed in command of XI Corps and tasked with protecting the northern border.

When the West invaded Afghanistan, it was his greatest moment.

Blood and oil money in one hand, and the fierce lions of the just and holy in the other, he forged mud to metal. Thousands were saved, and the great cogs of imperialism left to rust. Kôz was homaged by all, no matter their name, country, or faith.

As with many before, pressure from the West and weakness in Islamabad eventually decided Major General Khel's fate.

But by then, Kôz was stronger.

The general survived the assassination attempt and fought back a thousandfold. Entire divisions knelt to Kôz's promise, and traitors were purged. What remained of the government was limp, inept, and begging the West for aid.

It was a dream only imagined.

But how much was truly faith and fury? Captain Ahmad wondered. There were many whispers in dark closets, but few knew the facts of Koz's victories. General Khel was instrumental, vital, and a herald in his own right, but there was more.

Allies.

Some called them the will of Kôz. Others believed them risen from fables or benevolent spirits. A few thought them the promised Beast from Middle Meccan who would purge the world of sinners when faith was strongest. Whatever the truth, the men in black robes arrived in a time of need, and the general accepted their aid.

Ahmad believed there was a fourth possibility. Such an impossible boon in a time of perceived need was perhaps a trick or what foreigners called a *scam*. Kôz thrived through the vision and tactical execution of a great man. *Not these . . . conjurers.*

Dashing these treacherous thoughts from his mind, Ahmad made his way toward the operation center's kitchen with an empty ceramic mug. There would be time to consider the past later.

This morning will decide much.

A leak, more reliable than others, confirmed that the forsaken remains of the fledgling government were poised to make a last, desperate strike with the coming dawn. *Fitting,* he thought, *that they who now stood beyond the light should so fear the darkness.* That fear had given Kôz time to prepare.

Brave warriors stood in defense of Mina Bazar as planes, logistics, and scaled defensive plans came together in these final hours. Together, here and on other fronts, his brothers in arms would be more than enough to drive the enemy back to Islamabad.

But what then?

Even Ahmad, a company-grade term officer with faith in Pakistan's journey, saw that the world was too well policed. Too tightly bound to the whims of a few powerful nations. The puppet government would whore itself out for allies. Kôz would find itself surrounded, suffering a lingering death at the pleasure of the rich countries as they milked their prey for political gains.

It pained Ahmad to admit it, but the answer was faith in something other than Allah or His people.

The Advantage.

It was a powerful gift borne by the robed ones, which General Khel had welcomed as a catalyst of revolution. Although Ahmad believed Kôz was strong enough on its own to grow into the beautiful flower of pure faith that it was, the results were hard to ignore. With the Advantage, they'd lashed out as a sprout. A leap of folly, but the victories soon came. Great victories.

Impossible victories.

What shall history write about the coming battle? Will it be Kôz or conjurers that save the world?

Ahmad shook his head. Weighing the value of this mysterious Advantage against traditional battle metrics across the grand campaign was an idle muse. His duties did not include counting the planes, tanks, fighters, and food stores on either side or making bold, predictive timelines of success. Minar Bazar, with and without the Advantage, was his charge.

The new colonel felt confident, because General Khel felt confident, that both the government and the American forces knew the hostages were here by now. Even if they guessed the true importance of this base, they had rules. If they came, they'd come slowly. With men. Living, breathing, and vulnerable men on the ground.

That was Ahmad's duty.

To win the pitched fight in the dirt as it should be. Such a victory would inspire and rally the blooded of Kôz throughout the nation, perhaps the world. And he would be rewarded.

Ahmad, Guard Captain, patriot, devoted of Allah, and father of three, tried once more to quiet his grandiose thoughts as he entered the command center's cramped kitchen. He filled his cup with a rich coffee derived from an Arabic bean whose lineage remained unique to the Middle East. The West could only dream of such purity. However, to his dismay, the staff added hot water to create the same dilution as the Americans drank. No cream, though. It was far from a steaming espresso with close company, but the loss of life's luxuries affected him little at this time. The drink was a necessity now, a tool to ensure his wakefulness through the night.

Thank Allah it is not yet Ramadan, he thought. The first few days without coffee always gave him a headache.

A hushed conversation among a trio of officers in the mess pricked his ears. They were discussing a report from a recent patrol. A speculative report. *Or so the colonel would have us believe.*

Whispers of American operatives lurking among the shadows in the surrounding countryside were nothing new. Still, recent talk of booted tracks and buzzing drones came from more experienced and reliable sources. Fact or fear, enemy spies were a surety. But should they become bold and step out of the shadows, Ahmad was ready.

He himself had designed Mina Bazar's interlocking gun emplacements that wove a tight web against intrusion. The fields of fire overlapped and were rapidly collapsible to adapt for different attack patterns. Artillery stations had also pre-registered all predicted ingress paths the enemy would take.

Thinking in the context of his professional military education was comforting. It was the confidence of tried-and-true battle terminology designed to instill a sense of infallibility.

Or is it a crutch? Perhaps fancy words spoken from safety belied the reality that Ahmad's defensive layout depended on a mix of conventional and irregular units who'd never been tested as a cohesive fighting force. All of them could kill, but there would be friction.

There would be losses.

The plan accounted for this, though. If a supported and determined enemy breached the detention center, the base garrison would move from a defensive space to full counteroffensive operations. The Americans—all believed it would be Americans—would then find themselves trapped, much like their kin they came to save. And then that cage would become a tomb buried deep in a white-hot hail.

He was confident the plan would succeed, but not because of superior battle tactics. It was the men. Man to man, the city-dwelling Americans—who spent much of their fortunes paying others to do their fighting—paled against true Mujahedeen warriors. Fueled by the furry of Kôz, passion alone would bring them victory.

A sour taste crept along the sides of Ahmad's mouth. *The Mina Bazar garrison will hold. We don't need the Advantage.*

The debt.

He exited the haphazard kitchen and found raised voices in the hall.

"Perhaps your years of loyal service can offer another explanation . . ." said the first man. He was a uniformed Pathan major who bore the insignia of the ISI—Pakistani Inter Services Intelligence agency—and a detached, almost amused look on his face. There was only darkness in this one's eyes.

And wit.

The second—older and prouder—wore a decorated Pakistani military dress uniform. Ahmad knew little of him beyond his rank of colonel and that he'd replaced Mina Bazar's former commanding officer at the onset of Kôz. Beyond that, he'd seen the reclusive man two or three times.

"The general would know of it by now. We have many allies."

The major raised an eyebrow. "Eyes, you mean. And all of them report to me." His words hit Ahmad's ears as clear Urdu, his birth tongue, but he knew the original speech was Pashto. *Another gift from the robed ones.*

"Then the burden of proof is on your head, Ra'num."

Ahmad blinked, but not at the challenge. *Ra'num.* He'd been working with this stranger from the ISI for six weeks and hadn't gotten more than rank out of him. Knowing he possessed a name almost diminished the mystique.

Major Ra'num's lips thinned, and his right hand drifted south to one of the blades hanging next to his pistol. "Silence says much. A broken network, perhaps. Consistent with the reported RADAR blackouts." His eyes bored the colonel's, daring him to refute the evidence. "It is a sign of attack."

"It is a sign of rusting equipment."

"Rust? On the eve of battle?"

The colonel sighed. "The RADAR net remains tight enough to catch the planes they send at dawn. Captain Ahmad here has prepared our defenses against ground attack. We hold their people as shields to their bombs. What remains of the government knows this. America knows this. At dawn, we shall be safe. This night, we are safe."

"Afghanistan was safe once, too."

"Afghanistan did not have Kôz. It did not have the Advantage. A million men could not take this base."

Major Ra'num stretched his fingers as if limbering up the muscles to grasp his blade's handle. "That is the sole source of your confidence." His mouth twisted. "Respectfully, you place this cursed Advantage too high above the jobs of your brothers."

The colonel glanced down at Ra'num's knives. "If you're looking for a challenge, it can be arranged. Would you like me to call them here? How fast is your draw?"

Them. Only one of the dark robes was assigned to Mina Bazar, but the others were never far away.

Major Ra'num shrugged and clasped his hands behind his back. "Perhaps after Kôz has overtaken its enemies."

The colonel leaned back, satisfied. "Our place here is secure. Under the cloak of night, our brothers take to the front lines to brace for the coming offensive. We cannot draw them back on speculation."

Major Ra'num nodded, no longer appearing interested.

"We must have proof," the colonel continued, "and the first step is in there." He pointed down the hallway toward the infirmary. "Our need to know what she knows has never been greater." He then drew his hand to his chest with an abrupt grimace. The moment passed, but it served to irritate him further. His yellowed eyes bounced between Ahmad and the major for a moment before a sudden intensity bade them a silent parting.

Major Ra'num watched the colonel disappear around the corner. He shook his head as he turned to Ahmad. "Men such as ourselves will hold sway over the fates of us all." He looked up and down the hallway as if aware his voice might be carrying. "*They* have their own purpose, I suspect. Keep your trust in Kôz. The Americans will come for their people."

"Yes, sir."

Hand firmly planted on the hilt of his shorter, nastier blade, Major Ra'num headed for the infirmary.

Ahmad sighed. He wasn't sure what they expected to learn from her, but he did pity her. He never understood why the enemy put their women in war zones.

It was like cooking in someone else's kitchen.

Well, a kitchen where the stove was a firepit and all the perishable meats were still inside the animals bleeding out in the barnyard. The garbage can was a hole in the dirt, and the dishwasher was an ecological triad between the human tongue, a few brave rats, and the scariest insects imaginable.

Don't forget to clean your plate!

Dr. Pat hadn't given up on the concept of sterility—everything was being boiled as fast as possible—but twenty-eight new patients were stressing a system on its last legs. They were all polytrauma victims airlifted from some distant battlefield. But what sealed the deal was trying to effectively assess and triage them with three "nurses" and thirty-year-old soviet medical instrumentation. Dr. Pat didn't have the time to learn how an oscilloscope with a hundred different buttons, switches, and knobs could be fine-tuned to produce a wave pattern.

Instead, she went into full paramedic mode. Gloveless. Feeling pulses, counting breath rates, releasing tourniquets, and pushing fluids. Some would live. Her only salvation was the massive stockpile of antibiotics in the pantry. She pumped them all so full of anti-microbials that nothing would grow here for weeks.

They wouldn't die from infection.

They would die from the array of gunshot wounds, blast concussions, and burns coupled with poor field care that was already compromising their peripheral blood flow. Then came necrosis: a sterile pathology where healthy tissues decayed into toxic generators, poisoning the rest of the body.

Sepsis.

Treatment options amounted to chemical or physical amputation of the affected areas. Fluids, pressors. Early transfusions might help, but blood was in short supply, and many were too far gone by the time they'd reached her. Even in the best trauma centers, some just didn't make it.

Micky was the exception. She should have died hours ago. Maybe she had. Just because the body looked alive didn't mean the critical organs weren't oxygen-starved and suffocating beneath her skin. Perhaps she was nothing more than a brain stem with a heart and lungs counting down the hours until they too were poisoned by rising blood toxins.

No, if that were true, there'd be distal limb rigidity, Dr. Pat told herself.

Micky was alive. And keeping Micky alive was the only thing keeping her sane and standing.

The door burst open, and both guards jumped to their feet. Dr. Pat recognized the newcomer from the clinking of knives hanging from his belt. It was the creeper who'd given her the grape juice earlier. She refused to look up as she applied a layer of sanitized cloth over a burnt arm destined for removal. The clinking stopped near Micky's bed, and the hairs on the back of Dr. Pat's neck stiffened. Still, she refused to turn.

"You've given this one great care," came that chilling, perfect English from the break room. "Were you friends? Or is it because everyone else here is your enemy?"

Dr. Pat didn't want to react, but it seemed the man knew how to push her buttons. She'd worked just as hard at saving everyone else. There were no favorites. Everything stayed detached and professional. *We are Doctors Without Borders, boundaries, or political . . .*

Yeah, Micky means more.

Annoying little Micky.

"Enemies are rarely earned," he continued in that disturbing, almost fake voice. "They are constructed by governments to serve the governments. Had you and I grown in the same place, we might have been friends. Not lovers, of course. I doubt you share my particular tastes. But friends."

Her heart was racing. *What the hell is about to happen?*

She spun and gave him a cold stare. "I grew up with plenty of people who aren't friends. Some hated my guts. I wouldn't turn any away from the clinic. Can you say the same? Would you show any of us compassion?"

His eyes narrowed and fell on Micky's pale form. "Release from the pain of this life is compassion, no?"

Dr. Pat's stomach knotted, and she regretted her challenge. One wrong word and he'd snuff the fragile life out of Micky without a second thought. She changed tactics. "I am thankful you have let me tend to their wounds."

"But have you tended enough? Could others live if she were dead?"

Tears.

Dammit, not tears. Not in front of this monster. She scoured her medical and interpersonal training for an answer. "She . . . she has a . . . a family." A lie. For all her touchy-feely stuff and talkativeness, Micky never mentioned much about herself. Not a word about where she was from, other friends, and especially nothing about a family.

The man in the standard Pakistani Army uniform—clearly no common soldier—shook with laughter, jingling the knives on his belt. "Of this, I am sure." His amusement vanished. "But I know that *you* have a family. One of particular importance." He slipped the straighter of the two knives from its sheath and ran the tip gently down Micky's cheek.

Dr. Pat swallowed hard, uncertain of what he thought he knew. Or worse, what he thought *she* knew.

"Soon, we will be attacked," he whispered, barely audible. She involuntarily leaned closer to hear. He smiled. "This news excites you? Of course, it does. It gives you hope. But what is the basis for that hope? Does the thought of government artillery pounding us for weeks thrill you? Or is it because your American rescue heroes are the victors in your fantasy?"

She blinked. The news of instability within Pakistan's government had been building for weeks preceding the attack on Hudud. Still, even retrospectively, it hadn't sounded like a big deal. His reference to a "government" attack put it all together.

There's no law and order.

These people were criminal animals who answered to no one. She took a breath. "If someone is to affect our release," she said evenly, "I would hope it is accomplished through diplomatic channels. Any act of violence threatens us all."

"Says Patricia *Bowman*." He let the last name hang in the air between them. "Daughter of an admiral whose armada is parked off our coast as we speak!"

Her cheeks burned. *Dad . . .*

Until now, she'd never considered that his command would be part of the military response. *Isn't the Army or even the FBI in charge of hostage rescue?* She honestly didn't know, but she did understand conflict of interest. If the USS *Harry Truman* was really out there, they must've relieved him. Because if he was in charge . . .

They'd be coming.

The wild-eyed creeper stroked his smooth chin studying her response. "Will he save you?" he asked finally. The knife stopped moving, and the tip pressed into the pale, clammy skin of Micky's neck.

"He's … he's just an administrator," she stammered. "He doesn't have that kind of authority. Even if he … and he … and he wouldn't. He wouldn't risk our lives attacking you."

That's what this is about. Possible hostage rescue plans.

"Because there is risk, you believe. Or he believes. Yes?"

Now she felt like a student being walked into a logical *gotcha* moment by an aging professor who got off on his superior knowledge and experience. "A risk to us, yes," she stated.

"A risk that he will fail."

"Because you will kill us." She willed stillness into her ever-shakier body. She could detach from the mortal terror facing her, but the rest of her physiology had no problems displaying its nervousness in full fury.

"No, because they will fail," he insisted. "Tell me of what you remember from the victory."

The Victory™.

Must mean Hudud.

The blue beam of light that obliterated Camp Dud flashed in her mind, and she must've worn that recognition on her face like a bright neon sign. He smiled in the way a cat might at a mouse. "Tell me the exact moment in the battle when your Army was defeated."

"Marines," she corrected.

"Marines!" he hissed. The knife pushed deeper, drawing a small pool of deep crimson from Micky's skin.

Dr. Pat couldn't help studying the blood's color. It was too watery, too dark, meaning Micky was hemodiluted and hypoxic. This strange line of questioning needed to end so she could return to work. "I remember a light from the sky. I'd never seen anything like it in real life. It destroyed the Marine outpost. Vaporized it or something."

"And what was that light? The origin?"

"I don't know."

"You do!"

"A laser, maybe."

He cocked his head to the side. "Laser …" he tried to repeat, his voice suddenly thick with accent and uncertainty.

"Yes, a … a laser. A big one. From a plane, maybe?"

"It sounds very technical," he said, his perfect English returned to him.

"I don't know what it was. No one does! Only place with anything like that is in a movie."

He withdrew his blade from the base of Micky's neck. "This . . . ah, weapon would be a great threat to your military, yes?"

"It already is. Isn't it?"

He nodded to himself. "And if they were aware of its presence, they would not want to risk their armada so close to Pakistan's shores. Yes?"

"I . . . I guess."

He leaned back as if that's what he needed to hear and slipped the blade back into its sheath. "You occupy a strange place in this world, Patricia Bowman. Your concern for," he gestured to Micky, "her is genuine. Perhaps such a narrow focus is good." He turned for the door, ignoring the two guards who'd held themselves at strained attention for the entire conversation. Before leaving, he turned back and said, "You may continue to care for your friend. For now."

Guard Captain Ahmad took a draught of coffee as he exited through the operations center's steel blast door. The flatness of the diluted brew was more apparent now that it had cooled. What little power the aroma had to bolster the scant taste was gone.

Privileged concerns.

Pining for luxuries was unbecoming, especially in front of the stout-hearted soldiers manning the two heavy machine-gun nests outside the entrance. They remained sharp-eyed and eager and tossed him respectful but subtle nods as he passed, which were returned in kind. No overt gestures that might flag rank or importance were permitted.

He was among good men.

Ahmad wondered how the government staging points looked at this late hour. If their wire was manned by eagles and lions, or sheep bought with riches stolen from the people. He imagined scores of paper soldiers haunted by their own inexperience, fearing the dawn.

Are we so different?

His own question was startling, perhaps treacherous to the wrong sort. He glanced over his shoulder back at the command center, where flood-lights burned bright against the shadows. No place for robed ones to hide and watch or . . . *hear.*

Major Ra'num now believed the nature and capabilities of the Advantage were unknown to the enemy. It fit his belief the Americans would strike ahead of the dawn offensive. Still, despite Ra'num's reservations, the major still weighted the Advantage heavily in the coming battles. For all his unique talents, he could not see through the smoke to the substance.

We are what matters.

Kôz had attracted the best of Pakistan. The brothers defending Mina Bazar were far from common fodder; General Khel had seen to that. Many even had fought the Americans in Afghanistan before Kôz in Jihad. That experience brought strengthened convictions that spread among and inspired the garrison. The base was ready.

The Americans, though.

They were the great unknown. They alone could brighten spirits within the government camps with false promises that a barrage of bombs and contraptions would do the hard fighting. Perhaps the government's forces were perfectly comfortable this eve, nursed by the thought that they would never face a united front of hardened Mujahedeen. Never face the greatest of reckonings.

Now beyond the operations center's gravel parking lot, Ahmad began his walk down the bright path toward the detention compound. The night air was electric with anticipation. Watch towers loomed in the distance casting their lights in all directions. Heavy patrols of men with guns were always close, offering cheerful gestures in the place of salutes. Even those at their posts looked alive, talking and sharing in late meals.

Speculation about the despairing government forces was more idle fantasy, Ahmad realized. Facts were the only actionable elements, and everything he needed to know was within sight. Within the strength of Mina Bazar.

Reflected in the eyes of the men.

Or is it? his dammable self-doubts asked. Was it the fruits of military planning and discipline his brethren were seeing or were they like Ra'num?

Intoxicated by the Advantage.

Ahmad's pace quickened as the buzz of the base's command area fell into the distance, and the emptiness of the pervading night began to pick at the back of his mind. The true nature of the Advantage was known to few or perhaps none. Those who'd taken Hudud had witnessed something incredible and were forbidden to speak of it. Still, whispers floated through the ranks.

True power.

More than changing Pashto to Urdu in the ears of men or invisible tricks claiming credit for victories. It had scooped the American fighters from the Earth and smashed them against the heavens. Difficult to believe, but there were few doubters. And, if such stories had spread among the men to drive inspiration, then surely something had leaked to the Americans.

A bit of paranoia rose as Ahmad considered the difficulty of defending against spies. Nearby shadows beneath humming streetlights grew darker and shiftier. The instinctive animal within twitched and began to chip away at calm reason. Before long, his rifle took the place of the coffee cup in his hands.

He wished he had taken a car as he reached the main road south, but fuel was precious. If the men had to walk, so would he.

The sense of being watched flowed from primal instinct to pure reason. If the Americans wanted the hostages, they'd need to slip in and protect them with small, elite teams. Snipers with quiet weapons would then pick off lone individuals—such as himself—to soften the base before the big invasion. In fact, they might focus their search on him, considering his area of oversight.

Executions.

Ahmad held single-order kill authority over the hostages, as distasteful and woefully illegal as it was. And while there was some deeper purpose for their captives that he let Ra'num handle, the world knew this was no bluff. The general had made it clear in his broadcast that Pakistan now abided a greater power than the legal bindings of men.

If war came to this place, he would be a priority. The no-salute zone did little to hide his rank, position, or importance. They would know who he is because no mission launched without a target. Their spies were capable and wealthy. The garrison mixed with the civilians of uncertain loyalties from the nearby cities and countryside. Men could be bought. Perhaps even the Advantage—if it was as powerful as they said—could do little to protect him.

He forced the rising bile in his throat to the pit of his stomach. It was easy to fear the improbable when it carried the risk of death. *The airfield is secure.* The defenses were tuned against small unit incursions. Floodlighting projected in every direction covering the kill strip between the berms and c-wire. And the Americans always started off with their bombs. Word of action would come over the radio long before they had to take cover from sniper fire.

Still, he couldn't shake the feeling of loneliness among the garrison. He passed the entrance to a low-profile bunker designed to be mistaken for a refuge instead of a hardened garage for their compliment of armored vehicles. Inside were several friendly faces from the motor pool reseating a heavy 12.7×99 mm Browning M2HB machine gun on a flatbed truck. His business at the detention compound was not urgent, so he turned toward them. A quick laugh would raise his—

BANG!

He hit the ground.

Spitting and gagging on dry dirt, Ahmad was all elbows pulling his Kalashnikov rifle out from under him. By the time the weapon was free, and he could breathe, the unexpected arrived at his ears.

Laughter.

No cries for Allah's aid, officers shouting orders, or weapon reports. Just laughter from the motor pool.

The truck had backfired.

Lifting himself up, he silenced the amused men with a glare and brushed the dust off his battle uniform. He resumed his journey on shaky legs and cursed himself for such a display. Fears only deserved acknowledgment so they might be crushed by reason. Not given occupancy.

Perhaps I am getting old.

A deep breath of the early morning air was rejuvenating, and his worries came under control. Reaching the Mujahedeen bivouac, he rested to gaze at the darkened heavens. The star-spangled sky held a crystalline sharpness, cloudless and humbling. Ahmad's knowledge of astronomy was lacking, but that did not stop him from admiring the dusty star formations and dazzling designs. Allah truly was an artist. This night's black canvas was a work of great labor, a clear sign that God considered this an important day for both men and Kôz.

One crafting that decorated the heavens—constellation was the technical term—resembled a butterfly if he imagined the stars to be points on a wire frame. His eyes traveled to the surrounding stars looking for another shape, and he realized the butterfly was connected to something larger. As Ahmad tried to imagine an image over the new frame, something happened.

A change.

The brightest star, seated near the middle of the new shape, was suddenly swallowed by the black.

Allah has erased it!

Not an instant later, it reappeared.

Has He changed His mind?

Ahmad never heard the air disruption of the stealth B-2 bomber, nor did he detect the whistling of over a dozen CBU-58B anti-infantry cluster bombs as they fell earthward. But, as one set of bomblets deployed from their SUU-30H/B containers a tad premature, the northeastern quadrant of the airfield was the first to erupt.

That he heard.

Time slowed for Ahmad as the initial burst tore across his horizon. His training overrode the urge to gawk at the scintillating pattern seconds away from enveloping him in fiery death, and he dove beneath a vehicle.

A moment of stunned silence washed over Mina Bazar as the remaining weapons blanketed the area with anti-infantry bomblets.

They've come.

At once, the air became fire. Molten shrapnel swept through meat, flesh, and bone alike with little regard for the body armor only a few wore.

The open-aired Mujahedeen bivouac took enormous casualties since their tents offered no protection from the firestorm of five-gram titanium pellets. The men of the motor pool were likely safe in the bunker since these weapons had minimal penetration against hardened positions. For sure, they were no longer laughing.

Ahmad remained unscathed beneath the light protection of a pickup truck. Outside, his brethren were dying, and he longed to aid them as in the old days. But cold logic told him they were a distraction; he existed now to fulfill a singular purpose.

The concussive roar gave way to the moaning of wounded. Grasping his hand radio as he crawled out from beneath the truck, he prepared to give the execution orders. But before it even reached his ear, he knew communications were compromised. He tossed the device with its incoherent noises aside and cocked his rifle.

A frantic look at the airfield caught a series of bright lights accelerating and burrowing into both runways. The resulting explosions heaved gigantic sections of thick pavement into the air crushing any hope of their planes mustering.

They will know pain, he thought, suddenly reversing his opinion of the Advantage.

It was a gift. A godsend.

Ahmad tore his eyes away from the carnage and gritted his teeth against the rising rage within.

You have condemned your people!

A single directive echoed in his mind. His sole reason for living now, ordained by God who had spared him, was to make sure that none of the prisoners lived to see the rise of dawn. Only his direct orders could trigger the executions. Radios were useless, and he couldn't trust that the hanging landline between the operations bunker and the detention compound remained intact. He needed to get to the prison cells. That was his only mission.

His destiny.

Tightening his grip on the wooden stock of his rifle, Ahmad set his sights on the last leg of his journey—the fenced compound in the distance. There was no time to dash between cover or wave down a vehicle.

So he sprinted through *jaheem.*

Blasts of heat baked him, and suffocating air tried to steal his legs. The ground shook, his face and lungs burned. Vision fading and head swimming, he came close to failing the test.

Then he was back in the cool night with the main gate just ahead.

As he redoubled his effort, more explosions thudded in the distance. *They are bombing the whole countryside.*

Wounded and dead lay everywhere, but hundreds more poured out of the shelters to man their fighting positions and aid the fallen. The brief reprieve ended as American missiles began hitting the radar and air control towers. Suddenly, Mina Bazar was a firestorm once more.

One sound, barely audible above the bombardment but a single source of comfort, was the thumping of flak cannons. The air defenses.

The American war machines will feel the sting of Kôz if they draw too close.

He reached the fence's edge and ran along the barbed wire toward the gate. Above him loomed one of the four concrete guard towers planted on the corners of the rectangular perimeter. The guards within were shouting, but the words were lost to Ahmad's thunder-shocked ears.

He ignored them; the prison entrance was his only concern.

The three gate guards were dead, caught in the open by the anti-personnel strike. As Ahmad passed into the yard, an earth-shaking wave of explosions rolled through the base. He looked southward as towers and buildings burst into plumes of white fire, fed by still visible missile smoke trails. Hordes of attack helicopters began a thundering flyover, crushing his hopes that the air defenses might hold.

Why does no force usher forth to smash them against the heavens?
Where is this Advantage?

He rallied, knowing he alone could drive a last spike into the American heart.

The prisoners must die.

Suddenly the air cracked behind him, and he was flying. He felt the flames before the kiss of dirt. Crying out in pain, he thrashed against the ground until the heat was gone. The agony was withering, but worse was the cold sweat that began to seep out of his pores.

The injury was mortal.

Perhaps there was a chance if he returned to the infirmary and . . .

No. The prisoners must die.

He rose, knees braced against one another, and staggered forward. The journey across the courtyard, only moments ago an effortless task, seemed like kilometers through the desert. Agony gave way to a weakness his lungs could not tend. Halfway to the door, when he thought he could go no farther, a new sound confronted him.

A steady thudding so pronounced that it threatened to interrupt the rhythmic beating of his own struggling heart.

He forced his chin to rise and searched for its source. Through the billowing smoke came one of their war machines. There was something odd about the configuration, but no doubt it was an American transport helicopter.

They're landing troops!

Through pain and a darkening fate, Ahmad smiled.

The air defenses no longer mattered; they'd fallen for his trap.

Soon the detention center would be a grave. A mass grave filled with American folly. And then the morning would find all the world stunned as Kôz crushed the government offensive and swept through the nation.

Perhaps the world.

Black smoke billowed from the chopper's engines as it vectored wildly, taking a barrage of flak straight to the belly. Wounded as it appeared, it looked like it would stay aloft long enough to come down right on top of the detention center.

Ahmad could hardly stand, let alone reach his goal before the helicopter hit. So, he aimed his rifle and pulled the trigger. The heavy gun bucked in his hands in a satisfying spray of fully automatic fire. To his surprise, the bird suddenly lost all thrust and smashed into the ground between him and the door, sparing the structure. It didn't explode. Once it came to a final rest, it was clear that the chopper's fuselage was crumpled, the rotors were gone, and the tail section was utterly detached and smoldering.

Ahmad looked at his rifle. A win for Kôz.

With what voice he could muster, he allowed himself a cheer. American blood could spill well enough, and their machines were still bound by God's laws. Dust kicked up by the crash was thick, but he could still see the chopper's markings.

USMC

He moved to reload his rifle when, suddenly, the wreckage sprang to life.

CHAPTER 7

STIFF PARROT

The RAG.

The official designation was Heavy Lift Rapid Air to Ground Insertion Vehicle or H.L.R.A.G.I.V. But once the Marines got involved, it became the RAG.

At its core, it was an up-armored, turbocharged CH- 53E Super Stallion convert. Similar to the three monster birds hauling Charlie Company's other three platoons. In practice, it was Ronwill LLC's—a subsidiary of Sikorsky—answer to the age-old problem of a helicopter's vulnerability during landing.

Eliminate the landing; eliminate the vulnerability.

The RAG was (potentially) a one-way ride that touched down like it was pushed off the side of a building. Seats were stiff-bottomed and supported with independent suspensions to prevent whiplash and other immobilizing injuries. Multiple hatches were also cut into the fuselage that could be released by explosive force after airborne functionality was no longer required. Estimates put a platoon at 90% capacity after a hard landing.

The sell, of course, both up and down the chain of command, was that the crash capability—*hard landing*—would be employed as a last resort. It was a comfortable reserve, really.

An option.

At this point, the expectation for Mina Bazar was light resistance and to go in soft while using the rapid deployment capabilities afforded by the multi-hatched design.

The truth was everyone bought the bullshit because they needed a working plan. But deep down, the Marines of First Platoon knew they were rolling the dice to be part of the 90% who could still feel their legs after smacking into the dirt.

And survival estimates always ran a tad high.

"Licht, you a good shot?" came a shout from the captain.

PFC Licht jumped out of his contemplative trance. The muffled roar of the RAG's three heavy lift engines made him forget his active ear plugs were pass-through for voice. Swallowing, he patted his Colt M4A1 assault rifle and said, "Yes, sir. 132 out of 150; second highest in my class."

"Great. I'm going to need you trigger-happy with that bitch between radio breaks. Copy?"

"Solid copy, sir," he replied, hoping the captain couldn't see the bundle of nerves in his throat. And that was just for the landing. Then it was war, real war.

"Two minutes, motherfuckers!!" boomed the pilot's voice over the intercom.

Now Licht's intestines were pretzelling. His legs started twitching, and a wave of nausea rolled in. Two minutes was a microwave setting, not an expiration date. He sucked at the warm, oily air that had already passed through numerous sets of lungs, finding no relief.

A spike of terror lanced him at the sudden realization that no force of command would get him on that battlefield. Nothing. He couldn't move now; he wouldn't move then. No way could he will himself toward his own death. Legs bouncing like they were self-actuating to run away, he couldn't even sit here and wait for it.

I can't die in this messed-up chopper. I need to get out.
Right now!

"Dude," came a voice to his left. He recognized it through his paralytic terror as the semi-ok guy from the other company. Greg. Lance Corporal Greg Gladstone.

"Remember that corporal from breakfast? Nickels?" Gladstone shouted over the rising storm of concussive thunder outside the fuselage.

"Y . . . yeah."

"He told me a combat drop is like getting blown by a dude."

"Huh?"

"Yeah. Don't look down."

Suddenly Captain Saunders was standing above him, hanging onto the webbing for support. *Why are you out of your seat?* The captain's wild eyes answered the question. Then came the laugh and, "Don't look down!"

"Don't look down!" cheered the men within earshot.

It took a second for Licht to process the twisted meaning but seeing his fellow Marines strapped in awaiting the same fate was worth a lifetime of therapy. He wasn't alone.

"Don't look down!" he shouted.

———

Saunders nodded at the PFC, who was now breathing easier. Odds of a freeze-up were 50/50, but he'd just have to cross that bridge when it dropped. Until then, there was only forward.

The cabin shuddered again, not the healthiest of feelings from an aircraft, and Saunders took stock of the men. Some were deer in headlights, while others were shouting random one-liners from movies. The rest were eyes on their CO.

Keep these men safe and victorious. Semper Fi, Amen, he mouthed in silent prayer. He'd be lying if he wasn't scared shitless too.

Standing to his full height in the cramped transport, he announced, "All right Marines, get those IR beacons online so Vulture knows who not to fuck. Make sure you and your seatmate's active hearing plugs are in and working. Secure your shit and bite down on something. LZ's hot, and the *hard landing* is a go."

The aisle came alive as everyone fumbled with their friend/foe identifiers and ran buddy checks. Saunders reached for the radio on PFC Licht's back.

The kid shifted in his restraints as if trying to evade him. "Sir?" He looked up with a furrowed brow caked in striped war paint. "I thought we were radio silent until touch down."

Saunders ignored him and spoke into the calibrated handset. "This is Limulus Actual; deploy Parrot Package." Limulus had been Sarah's idea after one particularly playful night at the beach cottage. Someone signing the guest book had referred to the metal horseshoe crab sculpture (dust collector) on the coffee table as a "Limulus." It sounded sexy as fuck, and the name stuck. Later she'd dared him to seed it in as a callsign. So it was.

Saunders imagined the specially equipped Aviation Combat Element pilots sporting amused smiles as each flipped a small switch on their consoles. The result was a small but significant alteration to the broad-spectrum jamming signal disrupting communications.

From tonal pulses to *pulsing.*

PFC Licht's brow furrows deepened as he puzzled out what "Parrot Package" might be. It was probably a better occupancy of his brainpower than projecting how the next 30 seconds of his life would play out.

Just as the kid opened his mouth to ask, electric guitar riffed from the chopper's communication system. A cheer rose in the cabin, and the torrent of anxiety and apprehension dissolved into amusement as vocals joined the rhythm.

Stiff Parrot, Stiff Parrot,
That girl, she can have it.
That girl, she just has it,
that girl, she can have it.

I'm a pirate, I'm a pirate,
I'm the captain of my pirate ship.
I'm the captain of my little skiff,
the captain of my parrot stiff.

PFC Licht smirked as he connected the dots. *They're using jams to jam enemy coms.*

From his training, radio jamming was a subtler act involving the disruption and dampening of enemy receivers by a type of silent noise so as not to arouse their immediate suspicions. But the garage band hit "Stiff Parrot" blasting over the full spectrum of communications frequencies was anything but subtle.

It also explained the obsession over his qualifications on the new SINCGARS upgrade, which was completely due to him being the new guy trained on the new shit. Marine man-portable transmitters relied on burst, and the new one could pop off tighter data packets with more power. The plan to shut down coms must have raised questions about whether the older SINCGARS would still cut through. A testament to the high-powered emitters they were using.

The use of culturally offensive music was another layer. Radically different from what he had learned in class, where everything was amplitude ratios and wave theory.

This wasn't a hearts and minds operation.

A deep vibration, unlike any turbulence anyone should ever feel in an aircraft, rolled through the cabin. Captain Saunders ordered everyone to ball up into crash positions, and the chopper began to bank left and right.

This was really happening.

Explosions, probably flak, cut through the roar of music and thrust. *Guess the bombardment didn't get everyone.* The thunder soon gave way to a pelting score of pops and pings as the enemy fire zeroed in on them. Then, one of the intercom speakers exploded in a shower of sparks, and the cabin depressurized. Licht's ears popped, and someone yelled, "OORAH!"

Another volley sent more metal flying through the hull. The cabin filled with the acrid vapor of ruptured batteries and smoldering electrical conduits. Licht gritted his teeth and tried not to inhale as he fought against the sharp seesawing of the death wagon. Finally, the flak let up, and a singular, peaceful moment endured long enough for him to enjoy the guitar-soaked lyrics:

> *I get a stiff parrot when that girl walks by,*
> *stiff on the lip and hard on the tip.*

before he was jerked forward into pain.

CHAPTER 8

CONTACT

Deep within the hull of the USS *Storm* sat the Landing Force Operations Center (LFOC). A state-of-the-art C4I electronic laboratory designed to connect the Command Element (call sign: Hawk) with the action.

As Operation *Sea Monster's* nerve center, it was humming with energy. Every aspect of the mission was integrated into a multitude of inputs and outputs from various assets such as orbiting satellites, RPA (drone) pilots from the Air Force's 25th Attack Group stationed at Whiteman AFB, across-services Special Operations Command coordinators, air traffic controllers in Kandahar, NASA, the NSA, other foreign and domestic intelligence agencies, and the internet. It was all prioritized and routed to the LFOC for further distillation by an assembly of Marine and Naval operators that resembled a small version of NASA's mission control.

"Still quiet along the Indo-Pakistani border," came a voice relaying the summation of high-altitude surveillance intel from Central Command (CENTCOM) out of Qatar.

Colonel Ridge, stationed at the round table with the Command Element, nodded but not out of responsibility. He'd been briefed, the same as everyone else, that the push to ensure a complete and total stand-down of Indian armed forces was why Operation *Sea Monster* was even feasible. Behind closed doors, diplomats had hammered out an international agreement allowing the United States to directly—and, as it turned out, unilaterally—support the legitimate government of Pakistan with military intervention. He was not, however, privy to the enormous list of concessions it took to get that done.

India and Pakistan were nuclear powers with long histories. Keeping the Indians from using this distraction to grab ground in the hotly contested Kashmir region was critical. The Pakistanis retained complete control of their nuclear forces—a net positive—but might be trigger-happy if their conventional forces were over-committed.

Which they are.

One nuke meant more nukes, maybe all the nukes, from both countries in a bid to out-retaliate each other. So, it was nice to hear India was playing along.

More reports floated through the speakers.

"Pakistani government forces report 37% mobilization."

"Visibility over objective still nominal."

"Target mitigation success over Peshawar not assessed."

"Alpha Company check-in confirmed."

"Kandahar and Whiteman confirm reports singular B2 ordnance malfunction on the last run. Premature detonation."

"Vulture Group not meeting target mitigation timeline. Interference from anti-air," said LtCol Danielle 'Rousey' Baud, Commander of the HMLA-167 Light Attack Helicopter Squadron. Vulture Group.

That last one piqued Ridge's interest. The Aviation Combat Element was primarily composed of Bell AH-1Z "Viper" attack helicopters. There were only a few AH-1W Supercobras in the mix but talk to anyone on deck, and they were all *Cobras*. Only the pilots cared about all the updated, high-tech acquisition and delivery systems on the Viper variant.

Vulture was the close-in support designed to hunt short-transients—mobile threats on a fluid battlefield that could not be pre-targeted and destroyed. The swarm had escorted the CH-53E troop transports most of the way in, only to zoom ahead at the last moment and rake the base for anything the initial bombardment missed.

Apparently, they were hitting some snags.

"That's what the drones are for," said Admiral Bowman. He adjusted his headset and spoke to an operator over the mic. "Coordinate through CENTCOM to ensure the RPAs prioritize those twenty mike-mike guns."

Redundancy was good for execution. The remotely piloted aircraft carried the same Hellfire II missiles as the Cobras but were unmanned, smaller, and more maneuverable. They could get in close and take the risks the manned vehicles couldn't.

So far, so good, thought Ridge. Then he noticed Admiral Bowman staring off into the distance as if preoccupied with something. As if the heart-pounding war-feed wasn't attention-grabbing enough. He was also fidgeting with the gold ring on his left hand.

Wrong time to focus on personal issues.

It was the same behavior Ridge had noticed during that shit-show briefing earlier. The admiral had been distracted—at best—while attempting to deliver the bomb that Ridge needed to send his Marines on what amounted to a suicide mission for some . . . "asset." Before it could consume any more of his attention, a report came through that the RAG had landed.

Landed. That could mean anything.

"Status?" Ridge asked.

"They haven't checked in. SEAL is five minutes out."

Col Ridge leaned back in his chair and rested his hands on the table.

This was going to be a long five.

———

The crushing pressure of abrupt deceleration and screech of crunching metal finally subsided. The Marines of First Platoon stared at each other through the darkened cabin in silence.

Touch down.

Saunders wanted to give them their moment to bask in the afterglow of almost dying, but outside their little aluminum can, the fires of hell were stoked. "Easy part's over; get ready!" he yelled, tearing free of his restraints. The MP5 snapped to his shoulder as the smoky compartment became a flurry of limbs and gear.

Staff Sergeant Riccardi cracked the whip up front while First Lieutenant Lyons went rearward for a head count.

Between the fumes, bodies, and gear, the compartment was getting claustrophobic. Fast. Saunders eyed the hatches. They were rigged to blow on a what had seemed like a short delay during the design phase. *Definitely way too long during the* sitting ducks *phase.*

Thumbs up forward and rear, along with two beautiful gloved hands curled into clear **0**s, indicated they had beat the fuck out of the odds. No casualties. *Thank God.*

The hatches blew.

"Go! Go! Go!" shouted everyone with lungs.

Marine fireteams snaked into the night and immediately started taking shit. Some dropped prone, as they were trained to do, and set themselves up to respond. Others pressed the advance, hoping to secure cover positions around the main detention center.

Saunders let his instincts guide him forward as bullets rang off the fuselage. The base's power was out, but there was enough moonlight and backlighting from unseen fires to forgo the night vision goggles. A crop of shadows delineated various structures, hard points, and hidden dangers.

Flickers marked enemy positions.

Smoke and dust billowed seductively, creating a ghostly shroud that seemed to select whom it wanted to conceal. Right now, it favored the Marines, and Saunders took advantage as he sprinted through the firefight. His goal, barely visible, was what he remembered from the base schematic as the detention center's eastern gate.

Zigzagging through the dirt and sweeping streams of small-arms fire, Saunders was surprised to see a lone soldier emerge from the haze directly in his path. Oblivious to or unconcerned with the battle, the figure held his ground, bringing his AK-47 to bear in a smooth but slow motion.

The bolt of the MP5 shuddered, and the man pitched backward, his rifle bucking harmlessly into the air. No great contest ever took place between the two. No clash of wills, convictions, or strengths; the Marine captain just fired first.

Suddenly, as if reacting to the report of his machine pistol, the shroud of smoke and dust pulled back, leaving Saunders exposed in a zone of heavy fire. The air came alive with supersonic pops and zips as twin streams from low-profile nests closed in like a pair of scissors.

He scoured for nearby cover. Nothing.

With speed as his only friend, he was out of options. A panicked voice in the back of his head begged him to drop prone. He was microseconds from complying when a Cobra attack helicopter strafed a chasm into the real estate occupied by the gun emplacements.

The bullets stopped.

The rotor wash from two more Cobras shoved the veil of smoke back in place as they circled the embattled First Platoon providing highly accurate and lethal cover fire.

Oorah.

Saunders used the respite to drive for the blasted-out gatehouse. He dove into the twisted metal and registered a searing pain in his shoulder as it grazed a piece of red-hot iron. Dirt and sparks spit into his face as another position opened-up on him.

Panting, he was surprised to feel the heavy bump of a body rolling into him from behind.

PFC Licht!

No time to talk; just do.

Waves of incoming pelted the broken structure. Saunders waited for the breaks to pop his head out and get eyes on the enemy positions. His movements were quick, each amounting to a snapshot of flickering muzzle reports scattered over the darkened battlefield for *post hoc* analysis while under cover. Any longer, and he'd feel the tug of several high-velocity bullets pulling his brains out through the back of his skull.

After a few looks, he had a firm bead on the enemy positions and turned his attention back to the detention center. The haze had lifted again. It exposed everyone but also offered a clean view of First Platoon's progress.

They had secured the entrance and were expanding the defensive perimeter around the building. The landing zone was not secure, but the enemy was in no position to move on it. For the moment, the Marines were hitting back so hard that Saunders' position looked to be the only one taking fire. And even those gun nests turtled as Vulture's Cobras made another strafe across their front lawns.

A hush—a breather—fell over the detention center. Then, at once, the MV-22B Osprey appeared out of the darkness, slipping down through the shroud of swirling dust and smoke to deliver the SEAL team with near impossible precision.

The plane-like helicopter landed on a pinhead beside the RAG's corpse. Not missing a beat, the black-clothed hostage-rescue team charged down the rear ramp in a tight column and slithered through the building's entrance with their guns at the ready. The Osprey gunned its rotors and vanished back into the night.

Holy shit, by the hair of my ass!

Whatever happened topside, the hostages now had a chance. American servicemen—brutal fucking warriors—would stop at nothing to ensure their safety.

Saunders vowed to testify to whoever would listen about what those pilots just did, wished SEAL luck, and turned his attention back to holding the line.

———

"SEAL delivered. Ground Element reporting fierce resistance," relayed one of the operators.

Col Ridge blew out a breath he'd been holding. There'd been a brief debate on whether to delay SEAL. Ultimately, it'd been the Osprey pilot's call, and he'd performed beautifully.

Read: lucky.

The entire mission was predicated on SEAL operating inside that detention center. Sailors trained in hostage rescue and close-quarters combat who could whip through the dark corridors neutralizing *tangos* and forming an ever-strengthening shield between friendlies and the enemy. The topside action was just sheer violence. A matter of who wanted it more. And there was no question that the Marine Corps had more fight to give.

"What's the status of their air defenses?" asked Admiral Bowman, seemingly unmoved by the news of successful SEAL insertion.

"Vulture Group reports better close-in operations. RPA strikes successful near detention center. Visibility is now a larger point of failure," replied a naval operator from combat flight. "They're throwing up some sort of smoke screen."

"What about infrared?" Admiral Bowman asked.

Ridge smirked at the old-school reference to the modern Electro-Optical Targeting System (EOTS) that used long-wavelength infrared to cut through everything from a cloud to a sandstorm. However advanced they made it sound with their fancy terminology, Ridge was pretty sure it was the same infrared they used fifty years ago in 'nam. Better software and resolution, but nothing space-age.

"Pilots report intermittent high-density pockets breaking target locks."

"And I'm just now hearing about this?" asked LtCol Baud.

"Sorry, ma'am," replied the operator.

"What the fuck is fucking with our EOTS?" Baud demanded.

"Unknown."

"Might just be some nasty shit burning down there," Ridge offered.

"Grab a spectral analysis of this . . . smoke. Feed the intel to Central and see if they can find a hole," said Admiral Bowman tapping a finger as if this was some sort of pivotal finding. "Meanwhile, clearing that anti-air around the LZ remains top priority."

———

Someone shot off a flare.

The sky lit up, illuminating a nightmarish tapestry of smoky tentacles and columns spiraling toward the heavens. It reminded Captain Saunders of pictures from the Gulf War when the enemy would torch oil fields to cut air-to-ground visibility. Whatever was burning or spewing into the atmosphere now completely blocked out the pale glow of the full moon and explained why Vulture was dialing back their assault.

Nothing new, he thought, turning back to PFC Licht.

"Okay, we've got two nests hitting us. One's forward left, the other's forward right. Eleven o'clock and two o'clock. The right's got some cover, and we can't hit 'em."

PFC Licht nodded and reached for his radio handset to call in a fire order.

Saunders grabbed that hand and pointed skyward. PFC Licht's eyes followed and fell in disappointment. Nothing up there but the occasional stream of anti-aircraft tracers disappearing into the thickening shroud.

No incoming missile trails.

Both men glanced back at the detention center. Still secure, but First Platoon was pinned down and doing their best to hold their fledgling perimeter. No help there.

Every Marine a rifleman.

"Give me your carbine," Saunders ordered, thrusting his own MP5 into the PFC's arms, "and cover me."

The M4 Carbine, a short-barreled variant of the standard-issue M16, was designed with close-quarters combat in mind. Reduced barrel length translated to some compromise in effective range. Still, it was a hell of a lot better than the MP5—basically a long-barreled pistol with an automatic bolt. If he'd known the mission would be so dependent on small arms, he would've loaded everyone out with M16s.

And automatic grenade launches.

Fuck it, some damned tanks into this shit-pissing contest.

"Right," shouted PFC Licht, the rifle visibly shaking as he handed it over.

Saunders wedged his left leg between two pieces of metal and shouldered the PFC's M4. It was a nice setup with a red-dot sight embedded in non-magnifying glass and easy-adjust windage and elevation turrets. There was no time to re-zero, though, so he'd have to correct on the fly.

He focused on the left nest's bursting pattern. Regardless of training, humans tended to become predictable when repetition was perpetuated, and this gunner was no different. He was engaging multiple targets with the goal of suppression until his buddies could mount a counterattack. Saunders calculated the gunner was allocating three bursts per target with a five-second pause between each.

On the third burst, Saunders took a half breath. He leaned out using his rock-hard abdominal muscles to stabilize his position and sent his first 5.56 mm round sailing right through the gunner's skull.

Holy shit, one in a million!

But before the lifeless body could even finish slumping forward, more of the nest crew was re-manning the gun. Saunders capped off several more rounds, wounding another, before pulling himself back just in time to avoid a storm of angry return fire. Attrition would take forever at this range even with more lucky shots like the first.

"Shit. Gotta advance," Saunders growled, sliding around to the other side of the wrecked guard post to keep the enemy guessing his precise location. This time he only managed to squeeze the trigger once before the metal hail drove him back.

If they bring up anything heavier, we're fucked.

He pulled the PFC's head close to his so he could be heard over the metallic bangs and twangs, which were cutting through the active earplugs. "Find out long until the rest of the mission lands. And tell Lyons to get us some help over here ASAP."

Nodding, PFC Licht fumbled with the gun and radio handset. Suddenly, he bolted to his feet and rattled off two bursts with the MP5. Despite all his apprehensions, the kid handled the weapon like a pro.

A quick peek into no man's land revealed two crumpled forms close enough to piss on. The remains of a fucking kamikaze charge.

The PFC's inexperience unmasked itself as he stood a moment too long, letting his mind process the fact that he had just taken a pair of lives.

Saunders moved fast, sweeping the kid's legs with a kick and pulling him behind cover. "Cover, shoot, cover!" he said as bullets popped through the air the PFC had just occupied.

"Yes, sir," he gasped between frantic breaths.

"Roll over."

"Okay."

Reaching for the radio mic, Saunders couldn't let the moment go unnoticed. "That was good work, Marine."

Damned good. *And damned close.* This was why officers weren't frontline material. Too many operational distractions to stay focused on the fact that two assholes might be charging in with their machetes. *Or I slipped up.* Maybe a combination of both.

For his part, PFC Licht sat breathless, no doubt trying to process what had just happened within the context of a major battle. He'd deal with those new demons later. More encouraging was the look of pride in his eyes, like a kicked dog that finally found a way to hunt.

"Limulus Actual to Hawk," Saunders yelled into the receiver

A few seconds passed, the twisted metal structure rang loudly from another volley of gunfire, and finally, the headset came to life. "Hawk, go ahead."

"Need support. Two nests about 350 meters east of the detention center are suppressing advance and putting a lot of heat on the LZ."

"... gonna ... sit tight." The air coordinator's response barely emerged from a wash of static. "Vulture Group taking heavy ground-fire."

From what? Saunders wondered. He could see intermittent tracers from maybe two different 20 mm cannons. Nothing too serious. "Negative on sitting tight, enemy's advancing and reinforcing. Status on remaining Ground Element?"

"Trying to find a hole ..."—more static—"... heavy delays."

Saunders mouthed a silent *fuck.* "Copy. Get 'em down here. Over, out." The enemy was presenting a stiffer, more organized resistance than expected. Which was to be expected, of course.

The zips and pops of incoming fire faded as the shifting shroud of what looked like, but did not smell like, black smoke shielded them from view. The respite was unsettling, however, because—as PFC Licht took a second to point out—the enemy could now advance.

Hesitant in his position, Captain Saunders felt his body physically weigh the options: charge into the breach or retreat to First Platoon. He was the Ground Combat Element's operational commanding officer. Military tradition, etiquette, and a sense of self-preservation told him to fall back. The Marines fighting for their lives to hold the perimeter were counting on his leadership. It was his duty; it was where he could most effectively ensure the mission's success.

But then again, a good defense was a stronger offense, and time was short. That and he inherited a great deal of his grandmother's Italian stubbornness.

Fuck it, let's—

"Comin' up!"

Saunders turned to see two of his emerge from the swirling shroud and slide behind cover. One carried a standard M4 carbine with a slung M40A5 bolt-action sniper rifle, the other a standard M4 with an M1014 Joint Service Combat Shotgun strapped across his modular pack. It was challenging in the spastic light and thick layers of accumulating grime, but he recognized them as Lance Corporals Fischer and Gladstone.

"Status?" Saunders asked. LCpl Fischer was turning into an excellent marksman under Francisco's tutelage. *That long gun could be a game changer right now.* The combat engineer was an attached element to the Company and expanded their skill set considerably.

"Poppin' heads, sir," drawled LCpl Fischer.

"With a carbine?"

"Visibility's too low for the big boy, sir. Lyons said y'all were out this way and thought we might give ya a hand."

Lyons is a good man.

Saunders nodded; it was decided. He had a fireteam and an objective. There wasn't much high-level executive stuff he could do until the LZ was clear anyway. "Excellent, we've got two nests to kill. Oorah?"

LCpl Fischer smiled that wicked smile he'd seen on countless gung-ho Marines, but LCpl Gladstone was a little wider in the eyes. Still, they both shot back the same reply.

"Oorah."

Trading the PFC's M4 back for his MP5, Saunders poked his head out and beheld the dark shroud of obscurity.

Whatever was causing it, the effect was essentially that of a smoke screen. It swirled and shifted against the flickering light of the Marine flares and numerous explosions that continued to rock the area. Eerie. Disorienting.

Cover.

Barely able to see his next position, Saunders listened for the burst patterns of the gunners buried within the fog. The pattern had dissolved, and the gun's incoming tracer rounds showed his accuracy drifting to his left—the enemy was blind.

"On me, let's move!" Saunders hefted his two-hundred-pound frame along with full combat gear into a sprint. The three Marines followed unquestioningly, and the fireteam zigzagged forth into an atmosphere alive with lethal fragmentation, flying debris, and a dark secret.

———

Guard Captain Ahmad lay motionless, the sensation of air passing between his lips now lost to him. He felt nothing, heard nothing. The world was quiet and empty, as his body would soon be.

He'd taken several hits when the enemy sprung from their crash. The first burned a hole in his stomach, and the second left him without feeling and unable to function. He was thankful to meet the ground on his back, his face toward the heavens. Another soldier had shot him again in passing but spared Ahmad's head.

He now measured the passage of time in distance from the sensations and concerns of the world. His mind had receded from the incessant noise of the base material, no longer concerned with a dying body that could not nourish it. The battle was now meaningless—a concern for those who would continue living. With more time, he might've marveled at how fast the mind disconnected from a lifetime of information. Accumulated names, faces, motivations, and all things necessary to function in society were suddenly hollow when the remaining breaths could be counted on one hand.

Finally free, Ahmad's mind was a totality of clarity and perception. He could see everything that was not of the eyes and focus with absolute concentration. He was surprised to find it was not a reflection of his life or longing for his beloved that occupied his last few moments.

It was the Advantage.

Staring into the swirling abyss above, he finally understood. As a flesh and pumping blood man ensnared by the material world and its constant prodding, he could not perceive it. But here, divorced from a constructed reality, anything was possible. The Advantage was beautiful, the hopes and dreams of all men.

And.

His vision dimmed, and his world shrank to a final word.

Evil.

CHAPTER 9

MICROMANAGEMENT

"Negative on that delay, Hawk. We're pants down holdin' our dicks up here. Land us!" bellowed a pissed-off Gunnery Sergeant Brines.

It was loud enough to jump right over the CH-53E's thudding rotors and "Stiff Parrot" blaring out of the loudspeakers. Sergeant Smith jerked upright to full attention. He couldn't hear the reply, but Gunny's fist slamming into the bulkhead that separated the cockpit from the main cabin conveyed it just fine.

Someone somewhere had lost their nerve.

Details were light, but 2ndLt Weber passed word earlier that enemy air defenses were still online. Excuses.

Lost their fuckin' nerve.

The chopper banked port again. Circling. Some high-up, smart-ass officer would call it an "orbital holding pattern beyond weapons range." Truth was Smith's brother Marines were getting ground to hamburger while he sat safely on his ass. Not just that, but the longer they waited, the more pressure was on First Platoon to hold that LZ.

He checked his watch.

Fifteen minutes off-mission. A smoke break.

A combat Marine's life expectancy.

Gunny Brines smacked the radio handset out of the 2ndLt Weber's hands and started rearward in a rage. But then, something stopped him. With a grimace, he cleared his face, looked back at the officer, and mouthed something Smith couldn't hear. 2ndLt Weber put up his hands and shook his head with a smile. Water under the bridge.

Old Gunny, with his "control issues," woulda put on more of a show, Smith thought. Old Gunny would've hung back and screamed the word *fuck* so many times that the dictionary would have to rename itself The Fucktionary.

Smith straightened up a bit as that boxy frame came down the aisle. Didn't hurt to look the part of the pump he was feeling in front of the senior company grunt. But then he caught sight of a mischievous grin forming on Cpl Nickels' face.

Of all damned times to start fucking with Gunny . . .

It was double-edged, though. Smith's plan to shine in his new role as squad leader might be headed for the dumpster, but at least Jersey was showing a spark of life. He'd been quiet the whole trip. Hard to tell if he was giving out the cold shoulder—the guy could be an emotional pogo stick when he was in a mood—or if something new was eating at him.

Smith shook his head at Nickels trying to get him to lock that shit down, but it was too late. The scar that no war paint could hide beneath two blue eyes bleached out from watching the world burn was in his face. Still, it was better than the view of Gunny's ass that Jersey was getting. The feud was clearly two-sided.

"Smith," Gunny began in a controlled voice, "I want both'ya on me when we touch down." The inflection of "both" included Jersey, but the only direct communication Gunny would have with Nickels was through his ass. "Captain's unaccounted for."

Shit. "You got it, Gunny."

Brines didn't smile, but his grimace loosened, and he said, "Good man." And then added loud enough for Jersey to hear, "That's why yer a sergeant."

Thanks for bringing that up, again, Smith thought, holding a neutral expression. Nickels claimed he was playing around about the stripe envy during breakfast, but Smith knew there was some truth that he felt passed over.

Gunny spun about and glared at Nickels. The two didn't exchange words, but Smith saw Nickels' head bob in acknowledgment. Maybe hearing the bit about the captain put the motherfuckery on hold.

Or it was pure gratification knowing that Gunny came crawling over with a problem.

Jersey had authority, personality, and social issues, but he was also a damned badass with the squad automatic weapon (SAW; M249). It was like getting shot at stabilized his mood and brought some sort of weird focus. At least twice in Afghanistan, Nickels stayed calm and cool, cutting lines when plenty of other Marines were froze up.

Satisfied—if that was even possible for the guy—the larger-than-life gunny headed for the rear loading ramp to be first in line if they ever landed.

Smith felt a thrill rush through his body. It sounded like a bigger shit storm was raging down there than just losing track of the captain. Licking his lips, he decided to test the waters with Jersey. "Think he's all right?"

"Fuckin' Gunny ain't all right; you've seen that shit angry."

"I hear ya," Smith said, nodding. "Seriously though, the Cap'n?"

"Always pulls through."

"Yeah, but we usually there to back 'im up. Gunny ain't the only one who gonna pop if we keep fuckin' around up here."

"Relax, man," slurred Nickels. "Command's plan is infallible. Just gotta wait for it to unfold like the beautiful flower it is."

Smith snorted. "That the same command that said the head only need one-ply toilet paper?"

"True that, bro." Nickels cocked his head rearward to grab a look at Gunny. The legend was standing before the closed landing ramp, hanging onto some nylon mesh with a free hand. Probably asking himself if he was hard enough to survive a jump out.

Nickels turned back with a sudden fire in his eyes. "Who knows what's goin' on down there, but I bet you it's harder than a bull-dyke's strap on if he wants both of us to tag along." He patted his SAW with a genuine smile. "We'll get it done, Bone."

"That's what I'm wantin' to hear." Smith was also packing the M249 SAW, a devastating firearm capable of a cyclic fire rate around 800 rounds per minute. Typically comprising the base of fire for a four-man fireteam, the gas-operated, air-cooled, belt-fed light machine gun had more balls than the M4 carbines. So it took a special breed to carry into battle. Chambered for the standard 5.56 mm ammunition, it had the punch and endurance to suppress just about any hostile in a small arms firefight. Everything a guy could hope for.

Sergeant Smith turned to the Marines in his squad and shouted over the ambient roar, "We're on the Gunny out there. Means we're goin' straight into the heat instead of fillin' up the port flank as planned. Oorah?"

The resulting refrain, "oorah sergeant," thudded with confidence, a testament to adaptability.

Corporal Nickels, in turn, called over to his own squad leader to explain his new orders and the change in plan. While irritated at the sudden loss of Nickels' fireteam, Sergeant Kim took one look in Gunny's direction and let the issue drop. They weren't designated as an offensive unit, so pulling them off the line wouldn't big a big deal.

Nickels slapped his knee like he just got permission to stay out after dark and hadn't been dishing out the silent treatment the whole trip. "Fuckin' A. I've been pent up on that ship, Bone. Feelin' like I'm gonna empty some motherfucking boxes out there. Heavy trigger action."

"Yeah, just hope you don't drop the ball like the last time I needed some cover fire." It was forced, but if Smith could keep the conversation on the good times, he might get a shot at what was bugging his friend.

Nickels' eyes went wide, and he jumped into his version of the epic rifle malfunction that almost planted both of them in the middle of a cold mountain desert. It stayed friendly, two buddies remembering the time they pulled each other out of a mess.

"The good ol' days, man," Nickels said finally. Instead of capping the conversation, it came out like a sigh.

"Hells yeah, dawg, getting' back to the shit!" Smith gave it all the enthusiasm he could muster, but with Jersey going dark again, it was fake as fuck. The guy probably looked fine to anyone else, just another Marine before the ramp drop, but Smith knew his friend. Jersey was running unstable, and it felt like more than just the promotion. Like maybe Smith had made a pass at his girl or something.

As far as he knew, that hadn't happened.

Maybe she broke it off with him? Fuck, it could be anything. And Jersey was doing an obscene job of bottling it up. Honestly, it shouldn't've pinged Smith's radar in the middle of all this tension, stress, and the fact that Nickels was a legendary dick on a good day. But it did. Haters could hate, but Smith liked his friends.

A weird silence floated between them. Gunny was still ten turns too tight, and 2ndLt Weber still shouting into the radio. Now was as good a time as any to clear the air. "Look, man, while we got some time, I was wonder—"

"Man, I don't need you trying to be my sergeant right now," Nickels snapped.

Smith wanted to hit him.

The fuck is up? Hot, cold, hot fucking cold. "Bro, I ain't your sergeant, and I ain't your problem. Why you takin' this promotion so hard?"

Nickels cocked his head to the side. "That's not what I . . . No. Yes. Yeah, you know what? Fuck you for getting a promotion, *dawg*. Beat me to it. Guess I'll just have to punch my E4-eight, full-severance pay card while the rest of you suck dick for stripes. Guess I shoulda worked harder on my fake jive to get ahead. Least I woulda gotten some head."

"Sayin' shit like that ain't gonna get you promoted."

Nickels threw his arms up. "Look, man, you don't get it. I don't give a fuck about promotions right now."

"Then what the fuck is up with you?"

He pushed his palms forward to stop the bull from charging. "Let's . . . not now. Okay? Let's just fuckin' do this, man. You and me. We can talk about shit after. Okay?"

"Nothin' I want more. But this ain't done."

"Yeah, it ain't."

An announcement cut through their moment, and "Stiff Parrot." Second Lieutenant confirmed what the whole compartment knew: still in a holding pattern awaiting greenlight.

The wave of groans mirrored Smith's own frustrations perfectly.

Ready to be done with this shit, he thought, drawing a deep breath and flexing his bulk against the restraints as the aircraft banked port yet again.

Longest goddamned flight of my life.

————

Ten thousand feet of pure fog from gray, pregnant clouds wanting nothing more than to piss in your face, and then the peak. Clear as day.

The similarities to mountain climbing ended there as Captain Saunders, chest heaving, stumbled out of the murk in full view of the enemy.

Instead of taking in the scene or grabbing breath, he slammed the accelerator and put everything into finding a desperate place to hide. The cornered animal was in control now, feral and looking for that inch of cover.

It dove for a depression on the right. Something he wouldn't chance in a snowball fight against a toddler, let alone trying to cram into with three other Marines and gear.

Face down, pressing into the dirt and gravel, he waited for the burn of bullets ripping across his back.

Nothing.

They didn't see us.

It was a miracle on top of miracles. Visibility was shit just about everywhere except in this neat little bubble encompassing both offending machine-gun nests.

The Marines behind him squirmed to shrink themselves down, eager to start firing. But even at this range, pissing off that closer MG3 machine gun was a terrible idea. The nest was fully stocked and taking shit from no one.

For now, anyway.

"Want I should go to work on 'em, sir?" asked LCpl Fischer, flat on his stomach, sighting his carbine. The long barrel of the M40 slung over his back pointed askew as if this fight were not worthy of attention. True enough, they could probably do some damage with their service pistols at this range.

"Negative. Cover fire."

He felt PFC Licht, scrunched up against his left thigh, suck a quick breath as if the extra pressure from his lungs would keep his heart from skipping a beat. LCpl Gladstone lived up to his nick name "Stone" and didn't flinch. But neither did he shift his weight in anticipation of a quick rise to action.

No one was looking forward to this.

They were in a shit position here. Element of surprise, but no margin for error. The moment the enemy got a bead on them, they'd be taking fire from multiple protected positions. Risk of a freeze-up was not zero.

Fuck it, they followed me this far.

Saunders produced an M67 fragmentation grenade and pulled the pin. "Boom and bang." *Not a shot till this motherfucker goes off.*

Three thumbs up confirmed his faith in Marines.

PFC Licht and LCpl Gladstone rose to a low crouch, ready to follow. Adrenaline surged through Saunders' veins bringing mind and body into combat focus. Breathing slowed, and the hellish roar of the battle drowned beneath the sound of his heart hammering against his rib cage. Rational fear died against an irrational need to go beat the fuck out of someone. To win.

"On me!" shouted Saunders releasing the spoon and hurling the grenade at the target.

He broke ground fast, with the two Marines following behind in a loose wedge formation. The grenade found its mark, inciting a frenzy from the darkened shapes within the sandbag perimeter. A dull thud and a puff of smoke hid the radial spray of white-hot fragmentation ripping through the nest.

Stillness.

Saunders held a breath as his legs pounded earth. Then, two figures rose and opened fire.

Damn. Professionals.

A significant step up from some rag-tag rebel army.

Fighting the insatiable urge to scatter and find cover in the face of two well-protected shooters, the Marines spread out and zigzagged their approach. They took turns running and gunning, and a steady stream of cover from LCpl Fischer kept the enemy from owning the exchange. It was a mess of frantic shuttering from Saunders' MP5, heavy breathing, and perfuse sweating.

Then three became two as Gladstone slammed into an invisible wall. His legs flew out, and gravity made him its bitch by driving him down flat on his back.

Fuck! Man down. Drive on.

Charging into a well-defined enemy kill zone slowed time, but the exchange only lasted a second or two before the MG3 gunners managed to bring the heavy, fixed-position machine gun back online. Saunders' lizard brain wrestled for control of his muscles, nearly throwing him to the ground as it clawed for a place to hide. But he kept moving, kept firing as the monster gun opened up just meters away.

The line of red-tracered heat came in, another ending for Saunders and PFC Licht—impressively still in formation.

But then it flew wide as a well-placed 5.56 mm NATO round hammered the gunner's skull. The MG3's barrel arched and bucked as they tried to bring it under control. LCpl Fischer fired again, blowing the second gunner's shoulder apart. The gun pitched downward and went silent.

No time to celebrate.

Scoring a headshot on one of the flanking riflemen with the last few rounds in his magazine, Saunders let the MP5 fall to his side and drew his service pistol. Handguns were his specialty—the first round he ever fired as a child was through a Berretta 9mm—and he let the enemy know it. He drove two soldiers behind cover and scored several center mass hits on the last MG3 gunner. Then he was sailing over the sandbags into the three-foot deep hole that comprised the interior of the enemy position.

His bulk came down on one of the reloading shooters, and then he was face to face with more men than he thought could occupy a bunker this size. All were moving slow, wounded, but still had plenty of fight.

Saunders fired wildly into the tangled mass of limbs and metal with his right while beating the man entangled beneath him with his left fist.

Finally, his pistol thudded empty, and there was nowhere to run.

———

The sandbags fed PFC David Licht dirt as he dove to avoid the crackling gunfire sweeping in his direction.

Gladstone's down.

Captain Saunders was inside the nest, swimming in enemy soldiers.

What if I shoot him?

The thought never reached his forebrain as his legs found traction and that M4 scaled the sandbag wall.

It was dark. No time to drop his night vision goggles.

Something indistinct was moving on the floor of the pit. Something alive.

He couldn't just fire blindly. Shouldn't. Right? But then he was.

PFC Licht drove tacks into anything that looked like shit. Because Marines weren't shit. It kind of made sense.

A gloved hand suddenly grabbed the barrel of his rifle. He resisted, but it was no use. He couldn't leverage his weight in his precarious position. He let it go and kicked backward, scrambling for his sidearm.

"Licht!"

He stopped cold. His mission in the Marine Corps was radio operations for a reason. He'd always had excellent hearing. Even in the noisiest places, he could pick out individual voices. And here in this hell of bombs, bullets, and those ear plugs, the firm voice of Captain Saunders was loud and clear.

Please don't be hurt.
"PFC. Get the fuck in here!"

———

Saunders waited for PFC Licht to climb into the nest before handing him back his M4. "Brownie points for saving my ass. Get on the mic and make sure Vulture is reading our beacons so we don't get fragged." He'd tossed a portable IR beacon in addition to the ones they had on their persons to mark this as a Marine position. Overkill on any other day, but with visibility this poor, he wasn't taking any chances.

"Yessir."

The kid was shaking hard, but his eyes were electric. Pure adrenaline. Saunders missed that rush. It tended to diminish the more close-calls one survived. And this was definitely too close. *The fuck was I thinking?*

This PFC is gonna get a Christmas ham and then some. That's twice in a row. Stone's down . . .

Fuck. No time for it. Gotta get some guns on the wall.

Two more forms rolled over into the nest, careful to keep their weapons aimed high and non-threatening. It didn't stop Saunders from grabbing at the empty space on his vest where his knife used to be, though. *When did I lose that?*

"Shit, y'all are nuts," breathed LCpl Fischer crawling to the far corner to set up against a possible counterattack. He pointed back to the second Marine. "Found that back there."

LCpl Gladstone.

"Status?" asked Saunders, careful not to get his hopes up. He'd seen plenty of dead men walking through a war.

"Good to go, sir," gasped Gladstone through labored breaths. "Vest stopped it. Just got the wind knocked outta me."

"Y'all can thank me later for pickin' your lazy ass up," Fischer said, pulling his M40 sniper rifle off his back and sighting the scope. The air was clearing, and the long game was about to heat up.

"Good man, Stone," said Saunders, silently thanking God. A hit from a 7.62 mm round was like taking a sledgehammer to the chest. "Any chance you can get that gun operational and light up the twelve o'clock nest?"

"I'll see what I can do," grunted Gladstone pushing the dead soldiers away from the MG3. Fischer set himself up on the sandbags at two o'clock. The rifle cracked once, then twice.

Saunders took a breath and felt his gloved hand connect with the hilt of his knife. At some point, he'd planted it squarely into an enemy combatant's chest but didn't quite remember doing it. It was a purely instinctive kill; Brines would be proud. He pulled the knife free as streams of enemy fire chewed into the sandbags above his head.

"Nest on our twelve is talkin', sir," growled Gladstone furiously, trying to figure out how to clear a jammed round from the enemy machine gun.

"Incoming foot on our four," shouted Fischer before sending more bullets downrange with his bolt-action.

"Fuck. Keep watch on four," said Saunders ejecting the spent magazine from his MP5.

Fischer rolled over and said, "Sir, they movin' fast. Gonna flank us."

"Don't let 'em dig in. Licht?"

PFC Licht crawled over the fresh corpses, looking like he might puke, and handed over the radio handset. There was only so much sliding around in the various wet and slippery gobs of tissue, blood, and sinew that a grown man could take.

Everyone heaved eventually.

"Hawk wants you to report in," said PFC Licht bringing his gloved hand to his nose to mask the foul metallic odor of sulfur and blood.

Saunders started speaking into the handset just as Gladstone's MG3 went loud. A solid five-second torrent sent the enemy a memo that zero fucks would be tolerated. *Impressive.* The E3 Marine probably hadn't taken a formal course on foreign weapons but seemed to be making do.

The response came as a pelting of 7.62 and the bone-popping thuds of explosive ordnance falling nearby. Saunders radioed that the Landing Zone was no longer under fire from the two nests, but time was short. He begged for relief from Vulture.

"Negative," came the reply. The Aviation Combat Element was occupied by the sudden emergence of enemy armor deploying from a bay the missile bombardment had missed.

First Platoon was still pinned down, and Hawk refused to give a clear answer on the ETA of his other three fucking platoons. Forty beat-up riflemen could not hold, especially if enemy armor was now in play.

Saunders said his piece, reported his situation and then rejoined his team in the fight. Every attempt to return fire was suppressed as the counterattack became more coordinated. With no additional support, and that damned black shroud hiding enemy movements, their position was soon surrounded.

CHAPTER 10

SECOND WAVE

Captain Case 'Padilla' Rath burned the rotors and yanked his AH-1Z Viper into a jarring forty-five-degree starboard bank. Everything below was still murky, but at least he could make out the embattled Marine positions now. They resembled headlights in a thick fog.

Flickering headlights, lots of them.

Fireworks, really.

Fireworks in the fog. He'd tried using his rotor wash to clear some air, but it just sucked the shit into the intakes, nearly stalling the engine.

"Talk to me, Gurka," he called to his gunner through the aircraft's intercom.

"FLIR still ain't cuttin' through this shit. Who the fuck got a read on armor down there?"

"Came from Hawk."

A pause.

"Guns hot," Gurka announced. Rath held the cyclic steady as the twenty-millimeter cannon came to life.

"You find the armor?" Rath asked. "Need another pass?"

"Negative, just some boots."

"Better than nothing. I'm going to pull us around and try coming at them from two-seven-five again. Hawk says zero surface-to-air threat on that approach."

"It was shit hunting last time. I just wanna rock out with my cock out."

"It's a mess down there; no hip shots," Rath said, pulling back and veering off from their original plan of attack. The thick murk seemed to encircle them, blinding them at every turn. He'd flown through plenty of fog, smog, and smoke in his five years since flight school, and there was always a layer of clear air. Sometimes it was up, sometimes it was down. Usually, he could gauge it by wind speed. Higher up, higher winds, faster clearing. But this shit was stagnant.

"Let's take it higher, Padilla. Lift this bitch till we can see the moon. Like Batman," spoke Gurkha's voice through his headset. Captain Rath had to reach back into his mental archives before getting a vision of the chopper punching through the cloud layer. It rose high enough to bask in an oversized moon before stalling out. Gurka probably watched *Batman* a few hours ago, along with every other '80s movie.

"Roger that, buddy." He yanked the lever and felt himself grow heavier in his flight seat. Within a few seconds, they were basking in the pale moon light.

"Batman, baby."

"Yeah, but are you seeing this shit?" Rath asked, turning the ultra-responsive craft around and skimming an ocean of black tendrils reaching up at them.

"Looks carcinogenic."

"Fuckin' Mordor."

"Huh?"

"Never mind." Gurkha's pop culture references never left the '80s for some reason.

"We've seen a lot of blown-up, burning battles, and they never looked like this," said Gurkha. "Lowest bidder combustibles?"

"It's moving against the wind . . .," Rath muttered, staring down at the instrumentation. It wasn't just a gentle breeze either; the wind up here was howling at thirty knots. Strange, the weather report had called for calm conditions.

"Got vehicles!"

"I see 'em," said Rath.

"About time, baby. Got a lock, eat shit motherfucker!"

The craft rumbled as a Hellfire II air-to-ground missile rocketed into the murk. Gurka was already lining up another shot while Rath continued the run. They were taking no flak and operating at a solid range. Unless the Ground Element needed some seriously close-in shit, he planned to spend the rest of the mission in this sweet spot.

"Score! Next one locked," came Gurkha's somewhat echoey voice through the headset. There'd been some frustrations, but now it was grind time. Anti-armor was the apex role of the Marine Corps' Viper fleet. Those tanks were about to wish they'd stayed parked and covered.

And then something went wrong.

All at once, Rath felt his stomach drop out from under him. It was an air pocket, he told himself. A transient loss of lift. The thought evaporated as the altimeter began to spin.

Free fall.

The controls were non-responsive. The rotors were still turning; no sign of malfunction. There was just nothing to grab.

"The fuck, man? Yank it up!"

"Lost lift; dropping hard," replied Captain Rath slamming the throttle and redlining the engine.

Nothing.

Black murk swallowed Rath's view of the night sky. He looked up. The rotors were still there, spinning hard, max pitch, everything perfectly aligned. *We're just . . . fucking falling.* The aircraft was operating in a vacuum. It was impossible.

Fucking impossible.

"Options?" asked Gurka, jerking his controls around and coming to the same conclusion. Everything was working fine, the boards were green, and the Earth was rushing up at them.

Rath considered shutting the engine off and doing a restart but felt strangely resigned to his fate. They were about to crash, plain and simple. "This is Vulture two-four. Mayday. Mayday. Mayday. We're in uncontrolled descent. Cause unknown. Coordinates inbound."

Sixteen hundred feet.

"Fuck it, man. Got a lock! I'm taking it!"

Rath turned his head to watch as the Hellfire popped off and zoomed toward its unseen target as if nothing was wrong in the world. It didn't make sense. He yanked at the controls dredging up memories of old war stories from hundreds of pilots pulling out of worse shit.

But nothing worked.

They were accelerating past expected terminal velocity as if the atmosphere were utterly gone. Yet, he was still breathing and could hear the rush of air outside the cockpit. Something was pulling them down. But what?

He caught sight of the ground rushing up silently at him a half second before it connected.

Shit.

———

"Lieutenant Lyons confirms LZ no longer under fire from eastern nests. That's our window," said Vulture Group commander Baud, her thin trigger finger flexing as if she'd just heard the target lock tone go off in her mind.

You can take the pilot out of the cockpit . . ., Colonel Ridge thought absently.

"Land 'em," said Admiral Bowman slapping his palm against the steel table.

"Ground Element insertion is a go, I repeat . . ." said LtCol Baud into the mouthpiece of her headset. Ridge's shoulders tightened at the thought of those huge Super Stallion transports dropping their loads into a hot-as-fuck landing zone. But he was more relaxed now that Saunders had checked in.

Saunders.

That ballsy motherfucker hadn't wasted a moment charging dick first into the fray instead of trying, for once, to operate in a leadership role. This mission was already as danger-close as possible, and he *still* managed to move the goal posts.

The real kicker was that if—and it was a big *if*—Saunders made it back alive, him taking that nest was going to be a brand-new Marine Corps legend. It'd get so blown out of proportion that no one would believe it, but everyone would tell it.

Everyone would love it.

"F-15 down over Peshawar. Activating TRAP," came an operator's voice spoiling the mood. Most of the faces around the table held like stone. It was the inevitable bad news they'd been waiting for. It was the reason Tactical Recovery of Aircraft and Personnel (TRAP) teams were strategically prepositioned in the areas of operations.

"Pilot status? Shot down or, ah . . . malfunction?" asked Admiral Bowman, wringing his hands.

Malfunction?

"Ejected and clear. Looking like a lawn dart. Uh, malfunction, Admiral," replied the operator.

"A-10 Thunderbolt supporting sub-operation *Pakistan Dawn* now reported down too. No word on pilot. Uncontrolled dive, no explanation," said another operator.

"Two F-16 escorts for a KC-135 Stratotanker just dropped from the scope."

"Mayday from the KC-135, now."

Suddenly, overlapping reports of these insane aircraft malfunctions and maydays from pilots all over Pakistan inundated the LFOC. Questions arose, but the Command Element could do little more than react in silence to something most of them couldn't understand. And it wasn't clear whether Admiral Bowman knew something or just got stupid lucky. Regardless, it was an Air Force problem. Baud still had a firm grip on Vulture, and Ridge tried to stay focused on the feed from his Marines.

The transports were on target, coming in smooth.

But soon, coms chatter from Air Combat Command was white hot and couldn't be ignored. Over a few minutes, they'd lost more aircraft than they had in the past two decades combined.

Everyone was in disbelief.

Was it atmospheric phenomena? A systemic computer virus? Directed energy weapons? Nothing made sense. There was no warning, no information, just pilots losing the ability to fly and pulling their *Oh shit!* levers to eject.

"Vulture two-four reports mayday."

The LFOC went silent save for the blood rushing in Ridge's ears. *Vulture*. If the Marine aviators were affected, his men were in serious trouble.

"Vulture two-four is down."

Admiral Bowman pounded his fist on the table so hard that Ridge's laptop got a good half-inch of airtime. More than that, Bowman's reaction wasn't one of frustration but that of a gambler who just rolled snake eyes.

"Can we abort?" Ridge asked, breaking the silence.

Admiral Bowman shot over a crazed look. Like one of those cats with different colored eyes that always seemed to have two conflicting thoughts about something. "No," he said finally.

"Vulture one-five reporting malfunction."

"Baud, pull Vulture out of contact," ordered Admiral Bowman.

The aviation combat element commander opened her mouth to protest, but another Zulu Cobra reported mayday. "Get 'em back to the FARP!" she shouted into her headset. The Forward Arming and Refueling point was their best chance to regroup, but it fucked Saunders.

It was Ridge's turn to pound the table. "That leaves my Marines completely exposed!" No one was listening.

"Vulture two-two down."

"Vulture one-five down."

"Vulture pulling back to regroup."

"Vulture one-three reporting mayday."

"They're not going to make it; we need to ground those aircraft ASAP. Find them a harbor," ordered Baud to the combat flight operators.

"Christ, it's a slaughter," muttered Admiral Bowman.

"What about the Marine transports?" asked Ridge.

"They're committed," answered Baud getting up from the table. "And, until we figure this shit out," she took a seat by a flight operator pointing at a map on his display, "stranded."

It was all happening too fast, too widespread. In a world of information overload, an intel blind spot this big was unbelievable. Still, the enemy had pulled a fast one, and an entire company of Marines, Navy SEALs, and a mess of civilians were all caught in what appeared to be a well-orchestrated trap. A vision of them encircled, drained of their ammunition, lined up, gagged, and blindfolded for some kind of medieval savagery flashed in Ridge's mind. Their last thoughts longing for home.

No, we just need time. The analysts would discover the source of this new weapon or systemic malfunction, and the operational window would reopen.

Saunders can hold. Especially if . . .

The secure line—what would've been the "red phone" in the olden days—chimed.

Everyone stopped talking.

Admiral Bowman took the call, and his face drained of color within seconds. There was no back and forth, no arguing, just him listening. Hanging up, he took a moment to collect himself before addressing the entire LFOC.

"CENTCOM is suspending all in-country air operations and completely grounding the 455th and 22nd Expeditionary Wings."

No one breathed. No one moved.

They'd have sooner expected that an ICMB exchange just wiped out 80% of the planet before hearing that order issued during an operation.

There was absolutely no contingency for a complete suspension of air operations.

"We have men in harm's way . . ." breathed LtCol Baud.

But it didn't matter, and everyone knew it. The priority order came directly from USCENTCOM, and there was no questioning it. No protesting it. No one short of the president could countermand it.

And just like that, the unthinkable was a reality. The United States had lost air superiority.

———

". . . I gotta get my parrot going drip, drip, drip!" sang the Marines of Third Platoon over the clanging pots and pans of a flak-riddled fuselage. Their chorus was their armor; the lyrics, a mystical spell to keep those S-60 HE-T flak rounds from popping a hair closer.

Sergeant Smith added his big baritone to the song but kept an ear on the hail of fragmentation hitting the hull. If this was considered safe for landing, he didn't want to think about how bad it was on the ground. Still, he'd take feet firm over this death trap any day.

Getting in line behind Gunny for that ramp was looking better by the minute as the chopper lumbered from side to side. This was more than just dodging those anti-air cannons; they were fighting to stay on course against the air turbulence and heat coming off the base.

Like a fly trying to land in a fire.

Stable ground, that's where Smith needed to be. Plenty of guys got their rush from scampering up mountains, jumping out of planes, surfing one hundred-foot waves, and other psychotic shit like that. *Not me.*

He was the mountain. *And mountains don't fly.*

The pilot made some announcement over the intercom, and the pops and pings of incoming fire suddenly ceased.

This is it.

Grabbing his restraint harness to pull everything extra tight, Smith braced himself for touchdown. Seconds later, a bone-chattering shock ripped through his body, and his teeth slammed together. A distressed vibration then rolled through the cabin along with a sickening groan of metal in protest. Finally, for the first time in a month, the constant swaying of ships, boats, and aircraft was gone. He was back on stiff, stable, rock-solid earth.

For a dazed moment, Smith wondered if maybe he was in the RAG all along. Gunny's voice then thundered through the haze ordering everyone to the ready. Shaking it off, Smith blew out a sigh of relief and spot-checked his squad.

Thumbs up all around.

Grunting *oorahs,* the Marines tore themselves out of their safety harnesses, grabbed their gear, and stacked up. The ramp dropped, and Sergeant Smith and his men charged after Gunny into the fight.

———

Gunny Brines led the forty Marines of Third Platoon into the Landing Zone and had them take cover by squad. The detention compound was dark and hazy from what looked like thick, black smoke. It felt wrong, but that shit had covered their approach and was keeping them out of the crosshairs.

First Platoon's positions were hard to see, but their thin, ragged line encircling the compound was easy to pinpoint.

Because it was lit up by exploding ordnance.

So much so that it seemed like the fight was a lost cause. But between detonations resided the wonderful, coordinated sound of Marine weapons platforms spitting back.

They're holding.

Brines had two squads hold fast to maintain LZ security for the remaining two inbound transports, and the rest went straight to the perimeter.

The effect was immediate. Word of reinforcements spread among First Platoon and spurred a renewed vigor to the engagement. Suddenly less concerned that each shot was a countdown until Marine rifles ran dry, the formerly fledgling defense smacked back.

Hard.

The enemy blinked, the skies parted, and the unceasing rain of ordnance ended. Not a single mortar or stray round found an American target as the second and third CH-53Es landed and offloaded their lethal Marine cargo.

Gunny Brines held himself together until satisfied that the C-monster had fully disembarked and waved the three birds clear. However, instead of lifting off and disappearing into the swirling black blanket of shit that hung over the area, they powered down their engines.

This ain't no parkin' lot . . .

Brines tapped LCpl Buontempo—the radio operator attached to Cpl Nickels' fireteam—and ordered him to report that the Ground Element was clear. That the transports were vulnerable on the ground and needed to get the fuck out.

The response, direct from Hawk, was chilling.

"All aircraft grounded until further notice."

Brines didn't have time to complain or otherwise speculate. *No air support. Got it.*

Drive on.

Brines and his hand-picked team advanced beneath the cover of billowing dust kicked up by the rotor wash. It felt better than trusting that evil dumpster fire shit that was moving against the wind. They followed the gear-laden Heavy Weapons Platoon to the detention center's service entrance on the western side.

The site was dug into the ground with concrete ramps and paving, marking the structure as a former warehouse. The doors at the ends of those ramps were reinforced with sheet steel, and iron supports to prevent access . . . or escape. Right now, the loading pit was a rally point for Marines moving between the command post and the northern front where fighting was fiercest.

Brines sent two squads from Second Platoon ahead while Heavy Weapons got set. Once the Ground Combat Element hit full strength, the report of 5.56 mm NATO began to drown out the whizzing pops of 7.62s flying overhead. Finally, incoming fire dropped off all together.

With some sense that they finally had the foothold the battle plan called for, it was time clear the pit of their wounded. It was out of direct fire but didn't have any top cover. The command post inside the concrete main entrance, however, did.

Hauling and supporting Marines—most of who still had enough wind to crack a joke or two—Gunny Brines and his men arrived at the CP to find a very much relieved 1stLt Lyons. The lieutenant was covered in soot, and several rifle magazines were missing from his vest, but on the ball and directing traffic. Morale was strong.

Brines smiled. This was the element. Not war, per se, but men struggling against adversity to get shit done. The Corps issued every Marine a mess of hats, but only one rifle. Lyons was owning it.

He sent Sgt Smith and his men back for another group of wounded while he sidled up to 1stLt Lyons.

"Status?"

"We're at 90%, Gunny."

"Where's Saunders?"

The lieutenant reached into his pants pocket and yanked out a small map of the base. On it, he'd hand-drawn enemy positions. Brines couldn't help but smile at the fact that many were also crossed out.

"He headed east with a fireteam and took a nest, here. Currently taking shit from this nest, here. He's the reason you're on the ground, Gunny."

"I'll pay that shit forward. Why'd they ground Vulture?"

"Don't know specifics. A few Cobras went down, and they pulled air support. We're on our own for now."

"That's a raw fuckin' deal. Timeline? Whadda they need from us?"

"No timeline. No needs." 1stLt Lyons wasn't shaking his boots, but Brines could see that slippery slope of uncertainty forming behind his eyes. *Where do we go from here?*

He placed a hand on the lieutenant's shoulder. "We're good till they can figure it out. Copy?"

"Solid copy, Gunny," he said, squaring his jaw.

"Right. I want to grab the captain first. Any contact with those downed pilots?"

"None."

"Fuck. We gotta keep 'em in mind."

"Orders are to sit tight."

"Negative, we gotta get movin' behind their lines. Take it to 'em before they learn our air's offline. Agreed?"

"Captain's call."

Brines glared, but he had what he needed. "Fair enough." The lieutenant had more backbone than people gave him credit for. Few men in the violence of battle would resist Brines' advice. Ron would, of course, but from experience, he had brass in more places than just on his uniform.

"Go get him, Gunny. He's pinned down, and we haven't had the resources until now."

"Yes, sir." That was everything.

Lyons was here to run the mission as designed. And fortunately, he recognized the fact that he didn't have the experience to deal with the unexpected. Other men might've given Brines lip, been afraid to send their senior NCO into the fray. And they woulda found themselves with a big fuckin' problem on their hands. But Lyons was a good man. They could decide on the new ground plan later.

Ron Saunders first.

———

Faces, not tactical data, now occupied the large LCD screens looming over the LFOC's war table. Hell of a time for a meeting, but these were unprecedented times.

Colonel Ridge first recognized the one belonging to the Honorable Wayne Ford—the recently appointed Secretary of Defense for the United States of America. He had attended the pre-operations confirmation briefing earlier via video teleconferencing.

It seemed like a lifetime ago. But at that meeting, those little blue veins weren't popping out of Secretary Ford's temples, and his face wasn't so beat-red it posed a fire danger to the trimmed, white hair above.

"I'm hearing reports of thirty-nine aircraft down. Zero explanation," Ford said.

"I'm hearing requests from the Pakistani President for immediate aid because his forces are getting hammered by a peer-adversary. Not peer to them, peer to *us*. A peer-fucking-adversary fielding numbers no one predicted or can account for," Ford said.

"I'm hearing that India is on full alert. In fact, everyone is on full alert. POTUS is being moved as we speak," Ford said.

"I'm hearing shit from our allies about the status of our goddamned operation before I hear it from you!" Ford shouted.

No one spoke. Answers were for actual questions.

Secretary Ford drew a long breath. That pause was filled with the overlapping voices of operators coordinating with every military and contracted expert they could find. Men were dying, and armies mobilizing. Seconds mattered.

"Tell me what you need," he said finally.

"Air power, sir," said LtCol Baud.

"Denied. We just lost a billion dollars in aircraft."

It always came down to money, but Ridge was surprised how quickly they'd run the numbers. His Marines also had a dollar value attached to them. Likely, a small one.

Admiral Bowman cleared his throat. "Secretary Ford, the value of *Sea Monster* cannot be calculated. It is a fact that we need a win here."

The two men appeared to make eye contact through the VTC screen—if that was even possible given the positioning of the cameras—and held that gaze for more than a few seconds. A report came through Ridge's ear indicating Charlie Company's lines had stabilized, and they were hunting for Captain Saunders. No question his men could handle their ground game. But not indefinitely and not if the enemy could now reinforce.

"Agreed. But we need alternatives until we can get a read on this new weapon."

Admiral Bowman pointed to Colonel Ridge.

Ridge straightened himself. There hadn't been time to brief his superior officer, General Harrell. Everything was happening too fast. He was the one under the lamp now. "Mr. Secretary, the 25th MEU is now on full alert and gearing up. We're fast-tracking a plan for an amphibious landing. We have the manpower, the ordnance, and the will to onshore and prosecute operations for thirty days. Problem is that our best scenario puts the timeline for securing the objective at three days. More like one week, given enemy resistance. Without air support and supply drops, the Ground Element won't last."

"It's not ideal, but move it forward."

"If I may," interrupted a new voice. It was the Combatant Commander of CENTCOM, Major General Larry 'Castle' McNeal. "We've got a preliminary analysis of the affected aircraft."

Everyone leaned a little closer to the screen, desperate for any scrap of information that might shed light on this unexpected enemy advantage.

"By all means," Secretary Ford practically begged. Ridge wondered what it must be like to oversee so much and yet be so far away from the actual blood and guts. And then Captain Saunders' words echoed through his mind.

You'll be safe and secure in the LFOC . . .

Everyone had their place, and the grass was always greener.

"There are three geographic regions over which our aircraft were affected: Peshawar, Mina Bazar—our current objective—and Rawalpindi," said General McNeal. Rawalpindi hung in the air like a bad note.

"Rawalpindi is . . ." began Admiral Bowman.

"The staging area for the Pakistani X Corps and their Strategic Command," finished General McNeal.

The importance of Strategic Command was lost on no one.

"They're making a run for the nukes," muttered Secretary Ford.

"And there's not a damned thing we can do about it while we're grounded," added LtCol Baud. Everyone was past formalities by this point.

"The important finding here," said General McNeal trying to keep the conversation on track, "is that since Rawalpindi has remained firmly under government control, it looks whatever is disabling our aircraft operates on a mobile platform. We've got the folks at the NSA pouring over every inch of satellite and regional imagery taken over the past two weeks. Train cars, trailers, new encampments. Anything. They've promised a quick turnaround."

Ridge's shoulders slumped. "Any idea what 'quick' means to them?"

"Strategic effort, Colonel."

"Got it."

"But we've got news for our short game too. Neither drones nor stealth aircraft have been affected."

That was pivotal.

"I'm on it," said Secretary Ford, motioning to someone off camera. "Will have a decision on the stealths in minutes."

"We need every fucking RPA within range launched immediately," said Admiral Bowman to the combat flight people. Between the USS *Truman*, the ARG, and Kandahar AFB, they had deep reserves.

"Yes, sir."

"How many do we have operating in the AO?" asked Ridge.

"Fifteen, but we're short on missiles," said LtCol Baud. "Get me a count on weapons."

Moving stealth aircraft into place would take time. Maybe an hour. Maybe longer. The remotely piloted aerial systems (RPAs) would help, but they were a garden hose against a four-alarm fire. The truth was that they needed a plan to get Vulture back in the air, but a complement of stealth F22s would have to suffice. They could at least curtail enemy mobility and provide cover for evacuating ground personnel. It all came down to whether Secretary Ford could convince the president that McNeal's analysis was valid.

Then it was up to Saunders to survive.

———

The silhouette of Gunny Brines strobed against the background firefight. Everyone else was behind cover, hugging the dirt. But not him. He was a pissed-off wolf looking for his cubs.

"Captain's pinned down east of here. Everybody on me!" came that grainy voice above the din.

Sergent Smith gave Nickels a nod and chopped his hand forward. They set themselves on the flanks while the rest of the squad wedged up behind Gunny, rifles shouldered and eyes sharp.

Rounds were snapping over their heads within seconds of leaving the smoky compound. Probably from some gunner set up pretty nice in a hardened position. The saving grace was that this nasty black stuff in the air meant he was shooting blind.

Smith signaled the squad to open their wedge a bit and to stay low. The enemy probably knew something was coming but didn't know it was a moving wall of death waiting to crash down on them.

The air crackled and twanged as they sprinted the last ten meters to some wrecked metallic structure—likely a guard station for a vehicle checkpoint. They took cover with a First Platoon fireteam.

"Glad to see ya!" shouted a fellow sergeant whom Smith knew only by his last name. Gilbert.

"SITREP," demanded Brines as he strolled up to the structure, not bothering to duck down behind it.

"Hey, Gunny," said Sgt Gilbert. "We'd just about shut that eleven o'clock nest down but lost eyes. Now that it's clearing up, it looks like they're back online. Orders are to hold."

"We ain't holdin'."

"Roger."

"Smith, Nickels, give 'em a taste."

Nickels flashed Smith a wicked smile as the pair popped up with SAWs cocked. Gilbert was right: the air had cleared considerably in the span of a half minute or whatever. Smith had no trouble spotting the gun and the whole fucking rat nest. Eleven o'clock was a big motherfucker, too, laid out in the shape of a three-leaf clover. Fortunately, *intimidating* was a Marine word, not the enemy's.

Both SAWs went live, and high-velocity 5.56 mm NATO rounds ripped at the sandbags protecting the MG3 gunner. The torrent drove him to use the large gun as more a shield than an instrument of offense. The second they let up, that stream of hot steel returned and forced Smith, Nickels, and even Gunny back under cover.

This wasn't going to be a quick kill.

"Fuckin' Christ, we ain't got time for this shit," shouted Gunny firing back at the well-protected position in anger.

Smith reached over and patted the attached Colt M203 40 mm grenade launcher hanging off the bottom of Gunny's M4 Carbine. "Think we can hit 'em with one of these, Gunny?"

"Gotta get closer," he growled.

"Heavy Weapons?"

"No time."

"Got a nice crater 'bouta hundred meters out, Gunny. Should be enough," offered Sgt Gilbert.

Shit. Smith's stomach tightened as he turned to his men. He had to pick someone. Probably two to cross the distance over open, exposed ground covered by a heavy machine gun. It was a death sentence. This was the part he hated. He might as well be pulling the trigger himself.

"Smith, Nickels, get ready to lay down some fire," said Brines rising to a crouch before Smith could issue his orders. "Gilbert, get a smoker on that nest."

"Gunny let one of us . . ." began Smith and Gilbert simultaneously.

"Shut it and cover me."

Smith watched as the legend himself spat in the face of the odds and sucked a deep breath. Gunny was all man, authentic. But it only took one bullet. Pop, *thank you for your service.* Or the guy survived but could never get off the couch or take a piss without help.

It was a razor-thin line between badass and on-your-ass.

But before Gunny got to his feet, someone shouted a *head's up* from behind, and a beige Marine rolled behind cover between Smith and Nickels. By the numbers, he propped himself up on one knee, took aim with an impressively heavy-looking, thick-barreled rifle, and pounded one at the nest. The MG3 fell silent.

"Somebody order a round?" the new arrival asked.

Without turning to see who it was, Cpl Nickels yelled, "Right in my ear! Fuck you, Francisco."

Slamming back the bolt of his signature Barrett XM500 'Bullpup' rifle and ejecting one of those expensive-as-fuck .50 caliber rounds, Smith's buddy and the C-monster's senior scout sniper replied, "Don't hate."

Smith smiled. He hadn't seen Francisco sport his prized possession in a long time. The Bullpup was an ultra-powerful, shortened sniper rifle that never touched an assembly line. Instead, Francisco somehow got ahold of a concept model and had the gunsmiths at Quantico make it lethal.

Beautiful deliverance, Smith thought as the rifle exploded again, nearly folding another soldier attempting to re-man the knock-off Rheinmetall machine gun.

A momentary reprieve from incoming fire and the fact that Francisco just saved the lives of at least two of his brother Marines were more than Smith felt he deserved. To pay it back, he tapped Nickels on the arm, and their SAWs purred together as dual streams of white-hot metal tore at the enemy.

Just like old times . . .

———

Brines considered his rifle grenade as Smith and Nickels' SAWs kept heads down. It was a solution for the nest, but now they had new problems. Francisco shutting down that MG3 had been like turning on the lights in an infested basement. Brines shouldered the M4 and started snapping away at multiple small infantry groups moving for their flanks.

We ain't helpin' no one from here.

Firing his last shot through the torso of a rifleman darting from cover to cover, Brines dropped down to reload. A new mag in his M4, he crawled over to Sgt Gilbert and tapped him on the shoulder. "Lyons said the captain's hol' up near the IR beacon. Confirm?"

Sgt Gilbert pressed his head close to his and yelled over the SAWs,

"Roger, that's them at two o'clock. They were rockin' and rollin' on the nest's gun a while ago. But those flankers are keepin' their heads down."

Brines didn't respond. From what he could see through his rifle's minimal optics, Gilbert was correct. Ron's position was still active but taking much more shit than it was giving. Despite Smith and Nickels' efforts, the nest at eleven o'clock was already starting to collect itself.

More soldiers were moving to replace the dead and reinforce a solid skirmish line advancing on Saunders' position at two o'clock. Every moment he delayed brought a more brutal fight to the captain in the next.

Of all fuckin' days to lose air support.

Suddenly a blast whacked him in the back and tossed him on top of Gilbert. A fucking mortar. The guns around him fell silent as Marines checked their persons and pants. Ignoring a new pain in his right calf, Brines roared, "Goddamn it! We need support."

Sgt Gilbert tapped LCpl Buontempo to see what they could raise on the radio. Brines gave in to reckless rage and fired at anything moving. It wasn't a control issue, though. Not at all. He just needed to see someone die for fucking up his leg.

Firing made him a target, and the air began popping and zinging around him with increasing fury. Frustration and feeling trapped behind this piss-poor excuse for cover drove him back to the verge of doing something macho and rash.

Grenade's the only play I got.

He scoured the bled-out kill zone for a route of attack. That crater was nothing more than a shallow grave, but it was better than—

Suddenly, the eleven o'clock nest popped with a bright fireball and deafening report.

Even before Brines recovered from the flash blindness, a powerful surge of adrenaline began to build. His Marines erupted in cheers as Sgt Gilbert reported that command managed to prioritize an RPA and the enemy had just gotten a big *fuck you* from a Hellfire II missile.

Brines locked eyes with Sgts Smith and Gilbert while hurtling over the concrete barrier and boomed, "Advance!"

———

Dr. Patricia Bowman tried to focus on the young man squirming on the table.

Not what put him there.

Not the battle thudding through the concrete walls.

She wasn't a soldier, nor were the men being brought to her. Not anymore, at least. They were currency now. A way to stall, to extend her life. Extend the lives of all the hostages.

Thunder shook the room, and a metal instrument tray clattered to the concrete floor.

That was close.

When it all started, she was paralyzed by the prospect of bombs crashing through the ceiling at any second. That every thought might be her last, and she'd never know it. Or, worse, the structure would collapse, and she'd spend the rest of her short life knowing the pain of Crush Syndrome.

But the explosions had trailed off, and, in time, even the whine of helicopters racing overhead disappeared. It wasn't over, but the danger felt less immediate. And then they brought in the first wave of wounded. She never had a chance to fantasize about rescue, never dared think that she might be left behind. She was just trying to stay alive, and for now, the more people she treated, the better her odds.

She worked feverishly, not even noticing that her two guards had left until she ran through the stock of half-assed hemostatic dressing. She considered switching to gauze and packing the hell out of the puncture wounds, but the dressing was more efficient, even though it sucked.

Dr. Pat finally stole a look up from her work. Everyone was stable for the time being, and no one was watching her.

I need dressings.

The door was unlocked, probably because it wasn't a priority to the last pair of soldiers dragging in their bloody comrades. She crept into the hallway, suddenly aware that she was a mix of days-old, caked-on sweat and the radiant heme of blood. Downright wafting.

Who am I trying to impress?

She made for the break room, thinking it would be a waste of an escape attempt if she didn't steal some food. Raised voices from within stopped her cold.

Occupied.

The heated discussion was in that too perfect English. Every other hallway led to more guards or closed doors she dared not open. So, she listened.

"With the bat of an eye, the wave of a hand, their air force is dismissed! Why now do we allow their transports to land and fighters to fortify?" came the voice she knew best. The sicko in the officer's uniform with those disgusting knives.

Ra'num.

"Question not their ways!" spat a second.

"I would question any who allows his allies to die when it is within his power to save them."

Pat felt the cold, logical part of her mind engage. In an analytical, objective sense, she agreed. Her captors obviously had some weapon capable of winning the battle. She'd seen it herself. The laser. Why not use it?

Please don't be American troops out there.

"It is a matter of study," came a third, monotone voice that she recognized as belonging to the psych-case who always wore those black robes.

"Study?" demanded Ra'num. "Study them after they're dead."

"Death is a finished tapestry that only hints at the process and passions of the painter. If we are to learn, we must watch the artist work."

"Colonel," began Ra'num with a more level, restrained tone, "you condone this experimentation on your men? As if they are monkeys in some Eastern Bloc laboratory?"

"Ra'num. Without the Advantage, this very place would be rubble. More lives are saved than sacrificed."

"And this will bring our brothers comfort?"

"The strength of Kôz is their comfort."

"Bah, it is your folly, then."

"The end will come," came the monotone, detached voice again. "My brethren and I have removed their air wagons, and your enemy fights upon the land itself. As men should. This is where I will learn much."

"But if you are dead from a sniper's bullet, how can we hope to learn much from you?" quipped Ra'num.

"Nothing can harm me."

"Ra'num!" scolded the colonel. "You will provide him with an escort to ensure he gathers what he needs. Then we finished this and turn toward *Kôz Dawn.*"

Before Ra'num could respond, the low voice of the black-robed fellow said, "A listener . . ."

Ra'num's voice then asked a question, but it was in another language and unintelligible to Dr. Pat. More conversing in foreign tongues made her wonder why they would bother speaking English at all. Suddenly, she was in the grips of rough hands. Her two guards dragged her back to the infirmary silently, ignoring her protests and pleas for supplies.

Packed gauze it is.

———

"Ackgh," cried LCpl Fischer gagging on a mouthful of exploded sandbag. It was better than taking a full pelting from the grenade itself, though. He spat a gritty wad off to the side before recovering with a clean shot through the grenadier's chest.

Captain Saunders was still seeing stars from whatever thunked against his helmet with that last blast, but he kept his stream of fire steady.

The enemy was going to pay for every inch.

LCpl Gladstone was done screwing around with the MG3 after it jammed for the seventh and final time. He hoped that the captain didn't think it was operator error. True, he'd never fired this weapon, but it worked the same as everything else.

Except when a freaking casing tries to feed sideways.

Pliers and ten gallons of lube were not an option right now.

The broken gun was bittersweet, considering the incessant malfunctions probably saved their lives during their initial assault. Gladstone switched to his tried-and-true pitching arm—*thanks, Mom, for driving me to little league all those years*—and began lobbing their compliment of M67 frags into the many bombed-out craters the enemy was using for cover.

They were *that* close.

And they just kept coming, like one of those survive-the-swarm video games. No matter how often he hit a position, it was immediately repopulated.

PFC Licht noticed the others were ducking more than they were firing, and the hot air above his head was increasingly alive with cracks and pops of suppressive fire. He swallowed down yet another building wave of anxiety.

Or fear.

Panic? It was a sludge of the worst, most despairing, mind-fucking sensations offering eternal bliss if he would just curl up and cover his ears.

Instead, he chose to keep his rifle up, if not always his head, and sling lead down range. He was good at it, after all. And because of that, the captain kept looking back at him like he mattered. The soldiers he was putting down were a job well done.

Points.

Maybe even atonement for having to report that Hawk pulled air support. Of course, it wasn't Licht's fault, but he always felt that people liked blaming him for things. Nothing worse than telling the boss that the heavy ordinance he was counting on was reduced to just one heavy weapons platoon that couldn't be reinforced. Oh, and everyone was now trapped here, too.

Bile seeped back into Licht's throat.

After a time measured only by the rate at which the enemy tightened the noose, Licht cried out in terror. An armored, wheeled vehicle that he should've probably been able to identify by name rolled out of the thick haze. The nasty-looking gun on top began cutting through the sandbags with high-caliber rounds. That was endgame.

Suddenly, it exploded.

Licht blinked, thinking it was a trick. Then he spotted the air-to-surface missile trail still visible in the pulsing light of a recent flare. *Air support!*

The celebration was short-lived. For one, it appeared to be an isolated incident. Two, the enemy seemed accustomed to fighting under bombardment from American aircraft. Losing that vehicle only pissed them off more, and they came hard like Gunny promised: *bats out of hell and hungry as fuck.*

"Shit, I'm out," said Captain Saunders feeling the hollow click of his machine pistol's bolt lock in the open position. He ducked behind the sandbag barrier as low as possible and called over to PFC Licht, "How's our six?"

The kid hesitated, his grip on that rifle so tight Saunders could see it shaking from the effort. After a moment, and clearly against his instinct for self-preservation, the PFC lifted his head over the sandbags to check it out.

Licht couldn't understand how Captain Saunders and the others could take a quick peek from behind cover and instantly know the position of every enemy soldier. Movement in the open was rare and usually accompanied by a ton of suppressive fire. When it was safe to look, everyone was back in low-profile positions blending in with the shadows and dirt. By the time Licht focused his eyes on something that didn't look like a natural part of the environment, he was running the risk of seeing muzzle flashes. Which meant bullets were already flying through his skull.

He wasn't nearly fast enough.

Presently, the haze and dying flare light only gave him two burnt-out vehicles, a few bodies, and the crater-ridden road leading off into the darkness. All that was backdropped by the impressive light display around the detention center where Charlie Company was hunkered down and battling for their lives. It was only a glimpse, but still too close for comfort. The enemy wasted no time in focusing their efforts on the space his head just occupied.

Breathless from stress and cumulative exertion, Licht said, "I . . . I think they've gotten around behind us, sir. But I can't see where."

"I know. Keep an eye out for when they go all in," Saunders said, rummaging through bodies and equipment for a replacement rifle. The reprieve from that second nest blowing up was over.

If PFC Licht was right about spotting the landing of at least one additional Marine platoon, the enemy knew they were running out of time. Pretty soon, no sacrifice would be too great. It was times like these when the American military doctrine was weakest.

It was hard to defend against someone with nothing to lose.

"They've thrown up smoke on our six, sir!" cried PFC Licht, but the warning came too late. The world heaved, and sandbags flew in every direction. Saunders found himself on his backside, breathless and ears ringing.

That wasn't a grenade or mortar. It was something fired from a cannon.

Gasping for air, Saunders drew his service 9mm and held his wavering aim at the plume thrown up by the blast. He thought he heard Fischer shout a warning and could see Gladstone's prone form to the left shimmying for cover.

A gentle wind—just a draft that had remained unnoticed until this point—began to clear Saunders' easterly visual field. Within seconds he realized that the sandbags now sported a gaping hole.

We're completely exposed.

In what seemed like slow motion, the flicker of muzzle flashes proliferated among the enemy positions, and rounds began ripping into the space occupied by the four embattled Marines. Squads of rebel soldiers then swept out and advanced, confident that their prey had nowhere to hide.

CHAPTER 11

CHUGAGIN'

"The RPAs are ineffective. They don't have a fraction of Vulture's firepower and, of that, their hit rate is below 50%," said Colonel Ridge. He was repeating information that had already been passed around the compartment a dozen times. But now, he wasn't trying to be informative or spark a theoretical debate; it was an accusation aimed directly across the table at Admiral Bowman.

"Any update on why that might be?" asked the admiral absently.

"No explanation, *sir.*"

"Well," he shrugged, "it's better than nothing. They're mostly a deterrent t—"

"Bullshit," Ridge shouted. "Any Marine worth his salt will tell you that a bunch of flies buzzing around won't deter shit. And the moment the enemy armor moves, we lose this fight." The outburst was totally inappropriate, insubordinate, and disrespectful, but he wasn't going to stop now. Calm voices and reason prevailed when making plans, but action required balls. He didn't give a fuck about the politics or behind-the-scenes promises against which the admiral was measuring each word.

I want results, not a goddamned star on my collar.

When no one moved to shut him up, Ridge let it fly. "I want that C4I bunker back on the fucking target list!"

"Negative," said the admiral, eyes a millimeter wider from the outburst.

"Why not?" asked LtCol Baud, who had been nodding in agreement. "If you can't kill the body, cut off the head."

"Because ..." Ridge began. He was pumped up and getting damned close to dropping hints about Operation *Sea Monster's* classified component.

"Because we're not having this discussion," snapped Admiral Bowman.

The glare that followed told Ridge to choose a different tactic. He wasn't an idiot. Outbursts between men in a war room were one thing but breaking a promise to the Department of Defense was suicide.

Ridge sucked a breath and pulled himself back from that ledge, but he wasn't backing down. "My Marines are about to get creamed."

"A fact we are well—"

"And then?" he continued, "SEAL. And then? The goddamned hostages. What part of this is confusing? Destroy their operations center, and we'll have a chance at salvaging something from this mission."

"It might shut down this . . . this weapon or whatever's killing our pilots," added Baud.

"No." The admiral licked his lips. "No, we can't go wasting a bunch of perfectly good tank-killing missiles on a hardened bunker."

Ridge sat back. All the reports he'd read suggested that C4I tactical operations center—TOC as the men would say—had less top-down reinforcement than most high schools back home. One well-placed Hellfire II from above should rip it a new one. Yes, that probably meant icing the VIP and a few other hostages, but someone had to make the hard decisions. "We just need one."

Admiral Bowman fidgeted with the gold band on his left ring finger. Whatever was going on behind those shifty brown eyes was impossible to read, but he clearly recognized the logic. The problem, Ridge decided, was that people tended to cling to the irrational, to the extremes of probable outcomes. Grabbing that VIP might've sounded great back when the fucking Air Superiority Doctrine was still an ironclad given, but the situation had changed. The whole thing was fucked-up beyond all recognition.

"Maybe the Heavy Weapons Platoon could—"

"Missiles, not men, sir." Ridge insisted. He sucked a breath and slid his following few words in calm and collected, a veiled ultimatum that only an idiot could reject. "If we lose this engagement, we lose initiative. We lose our ability to conduct follow-on operations. We lose those hostages."

He waited a five-count and added, "*All* of the hostages, sir."

Silence.

The seconds ticked by like one of those damned anti-smoking commercials. *Every minute someone dies from lung cancer.*

"One attempt. On the western wing. That's it," the admiral said finally.

A few orders later, the big screen showed the RPA feed. The drone was operating high above the "shroud cover," as the operators were calling it. It looked like an angry sea filled with black stalagmites reaching up to snare anything that might fly by.

Could that be the weapon? Ridge wondered. *Something screwing with the aircraft engine intakes?* Numerous analysts had ruled it out, although they couldn't explain precisely what the shroud was either.

The screen switched to the missile's infrared camera, and *fox one* came over the com. It punched through the whispy stalagmites without issue and streaked toward the grainy image of the airfield. The inbound angle made it hard for Ridge to orient himself with his mental map of Mina Bazar, but the intermittent flashes mixing in with periodic frame freezes to the left of the screen gave him a sense of the vector. Seconds later, a familiar structure took shape in the center of the screen, and he held his breath.

Five seconds to impact.

Suddenly, the feed went dead. An operator later reported that the missile had exploded midair, leaving the enemy C4I bunker completely untouched.

No one spoke.

Fucking lung cancer.

———

It was crunch time. That moment when the cornered animal became a creature of pure excellence. When the only option was all-in because everything was on the line. Anything less than the best was an evolutionary failure, and Captain Saunders' wasn't the product of a billion years of iterative failures.

He was the apex.

But as that boilerplate backstop of pure survival spooled up to roar back against impossible odds, something interfered.

Amid the scramble for cover, men shooting and shouting, an image flashed. It was vivid, the beginning of a thick memory being laid over his current reality.

Saunders shook his head, trying to clear his vision and roll back behind cover. The sandbags were breached, and he saw a quad of soldiers advancing steadily from cover to cover. Their movements were so quick that he only had splits of a second to snap off rounds from his sidearm in their general direction. From another angle, bullets were kicking up dirt beside him. He called out to his men.

He called for someone to cover the gap.

Then the rear two soldiers cut left, and Saunders trained his sights just ahead. They were close enough now that he could do more with that pistol than make noise. But then the problem with his vision settled into his limbs. His arms became leaden, and his aim slipped. The snapping battle blurred, and he found himself spacing, reality slipping through his fingers.

He never took the shot.

The world dulled and darkened as if consumed by that strange shroud blocking the sky. His mind tore at its disembodied cage, desperate to understand what was happening and to get back in the fight. But his efforts proved futile, and he was soon engulfed.

. . .

It was quiet.

The transition between a 160+ decibel firefight and a near-total sensory void was disorienting at best, never mind trying to explain what just happened. The only thing that mattered was rapidly unfucking this situation.

Saunders ran a system check.

He could wiggle the toes in his boots and his fingers but couldn't raise his arms to check for injuries. After a few seconds, sound returned: the rush of air through his nostrils and the soft rubbing of cloth on rope as he flexed his tired muscles against unseen restraints.

His heart raced; questions bubbled up from murky depths. *Am I a prisoner? A casualty? Did I frag someone?* He could hear but not see. It was either pitch black or hurt too much to open his eyes.

Suddenly, there was a voice.

At last, one worthy of our attention. We have traveled far to find you.

The voice was new to him, resonant and powerful, yet had a degree of familiarity. It should've startled him, but he was dull to it as if he'd heard it a thousand times. In fact, the voice that he'd never-before-heard-in-his-life was so ingrained he'd long since forgotten whether he was actually hearing it or if it was all inside his head.

With the voice followed a desire to respond and a detached sense of the conditioning and trauma one might receive after years of imprisonment and torture. But while he had more than enough memories of torture and confinement, they were nothing like this.

Saunders tried to lock down his mounting confusion. Lock down the horror that, for whatever reason, his mind and body had become foreign, responding in ways he couldn't understand. The part of him that felt most like himself was just an observer.

I accept your yield.

The voice was reassuring now, and he was elated. Operation *Sea Monster,* the firefight, and even the Marine Corps faded into a distant memory. It was long ago, fuzzy even. Time had washed away urgency, and he was merging with his new reality.

Stubborn resistance against something so powerful was useless, he realized. The pain was already unbearable, and they had an infinite capacity to inflict more. He was too frail, too old, a breath away from collapse. They offered the hope that part of him would be left intact or at least put to rest in comfort.

Surrender.

Hard stop.

Fantasy, delusion, waking dream, or not, Saunders recognized a command when he heard one. And it hadn't come from his team, his people. It was an alien word, the ultimate violation of freedom and everything he held dear. It was the doorway to a fate worse than death and the wrong damned thing to say to a Marine.

It was a trigger.

And that trigger said to fight.

To kill. Kill. Kill! *Kill till there's no one left!*

So, he fought.

His shrunken mental form exploded out of confinement and wrestled hold of his eyes, ears, and mouth. He screamed as muscles jerked and spasmed back under his control. The body was his, and he threw himself at the restraints.

Suddenly, the volume shot up to one hundred as the firefight pounded back into his skull. He could see. He was still in the nest. His men were nearby, fighting for their lives.

He never left.

Disoriented, he tried to take stock of what had just happened. His body was cold and awkward as if it had just been jolted out of sleep.

Am I hit?

Did I blackout?

No. He was just in a bad place, and some remnant of his childhood brain was driving him toward a nice fetal position and a long thumb-sucking. It made sense too. Maybe if he stopped resisting, the advancing soldiers would let him live long enough to see what it's like to be drowned in gasoline and set on fire.

Fuck that.

The scene he just witnessed or imagined where some broken version of himself was purring like a newborn kitten at the idea of pleasing his tormenters was sickening as fuck. Saunders had fought the odds his whole life thanks to a debilitating stubborn streak. The better schools were always above his grade point average, GT scores were never enough for the good jobs, the team was always looking for better players, Kyle taunting that the mountain was too technical, *Sarah was out of my league,* and death was supposed to be permanent.

But he'd put a face to those average marks, gotten every promotion first look, trained day and night to forge himself into a competitive athlete, climbed the mountain anyway, sold himself to Sarah, and survived bigger dungeons than this shithole nest.

He sucked sulfur from the burning air and wrenched his right arm free from the torso of a still-limber corpse. Along with it came his pistol. His gaze tracked to the breach in the nest's former defensive wall. Beyond it, soldiers were charging, raising their rifles at point-blank range to light him up.

No. Fucking. Bueno.

He kicked against the corpses, ammo boxes, and other shit littering the ground, propelling himself backward. The enemy was close enough, and he was a damned good shot. Might get one before they zeroed him, maybe two. But that was it. Facing down multiple squads carrying automatic weapons while on your ass was something Hollywood didn't even try to pass as possible.

He got a flash of his son, Tommy—that boyish smile overtaking his face whenever he saw his Daddy—as he opened fire.

The 9mm popped twice in his hands before clicking hollow.

Empty. Jammed. Fucked.

He reached for another clip.

A thud buffeted him from behind. Something heavy had crashed into the sandbag perimeter he'd backed into. Next, someone was climbing over the wall above him faster than his body could respond. He watched as his free hand stopped groping at empty ammo pouches and began a slow, agonizing journey toward his chest, where his Ka-Bar sat in its sheath.

Tommy's red cheeks and wet eyes whenever he had to say goodbye to his Daddy.

A pair of strong arms grabbed and hauled him up out of the nest.

Surrender.

Saunders denied the voice.

He clawed for his knife and fought with every ounce of his strength. If his arms or legs or teeth were free, he could maim or kill. He would live or die here, but there was no way in hell he would suffer capture again.

Despite his energy and determination, the struggle was short-lived. His captor pinned him in a full body hold, arms and legs flopping uselessly in the air. It was rare for Saunders to meet his match, but it seemed like the enemy had discovered steroids.

Before that cornered animal could take another crack at surviving the impossible, something pressed into the side of his face. Something his assailant wore. It was smooth and grooved.

A handle made of bone . . .

Then came the rasp clear through the ear plug in his left ear, "Friendly, sir."

Saunders blew out a breath as Marine rifles dropped onto the sandbags above him and hit back at the enemy. Then he was staring into the face of Mike Brines, sporting the faintest of smiles through his mask of stone.

"With all due respect, sir," Brines said with a smack to Saunders' helmet, "thought you needed a fuckin' reminder that no one kicks yer ass but me."

Saunders could've laughed, but the situation was still hyper-hot, and seconds mattered. More Marines emerged from the smoke screen they'd thrown up and established fighting positions around the besieged nest. Saunders rolled away from Brines and began coordinating the influx of men while pointing out enemy vectors.

Gladstone. Licht. Fischer.

It was too early to tell, but no one came near that nest without a complete understanding they had friendlies inside.

Brines' reinforcements expanded the line behind the remains of the sandbags, and their rifles started blasting away like firefighters battling a raging backdraft.

Saunders got eyes over the bags. The enemy columns were pushing hard as if driven by a greater fear of retreat. It was almost enough to overrun the nest, but Marine 5.56 mm NATO took its toll. The ranks thinned. Formations scattered.

The enemy advance collapsed.

The Marine wall of death pressed the advantage, refusing to let the enemy regroup for a counterattack. A continuous stream of highly accurate fire raked through the prone and desperate repeatedly. It was lethal suppression, and Saunders could imagine it sent a clear signal to the enemy commanders that their window of opportunity was closed. And the Marine window had just blown wide-open.

It was time to stop thinking about dying and start thinking about winning.

As he sealed off the mental compartment of this entire clusterfuck and moved into the next phase of the operation, a distance voice—indistinguishable from his own thoughts—called after him.

There are others . . .

———

"Giddown, dawg!" Sgt Smith bellowed as he skidded into the thigh-high sandbags. There was no telling which Marine was hanging out on the wrong side of cover, but the kid was strapped with a shotgun and froze the fuck up. The guy Gunny was hauling out of the nest looked like the captain. Smith hoped he was alive.

After a quick scramble to get his legs back under him, Smith popped up to see what they were up against.

A shit-ton of infantry.

They were all out in the open and closing fast. *Someone cracked the whip.*

Flexing the huge muscles in his back, Smith wondered if that someone had counted on a Marine fireline stomping out of the smoke. The smarter ones were already breaking formation and second-guessing what they were running toward.

The time to capitalize on stupid was now.

Smith threw his shoulder into his rifle's stock and squeezed the trigger. The powerful M249 SAW jackhammered into the advance, pissing casings onto the ducking Marine just a foot and a half below. The enemy kept coming, field crackling with rifle flashes. Then they were weaving, trying to run and gun and dance around the bullets cutting through their space.

Bodies dropped.

Some stayed on their feet, but the ones with half a brain—literally—learned their respect for the SAW and went prone.

And then Nickels was next to him, his SAW pounding more heat into the kill box. And the poor Marine on the other side of the sandbags redoubled his efforts to cover his ears and bat away the rain of hot brass.

You'll thank me in a minute, dawg.

Incoming fire died down as the enemy went defensive. The rest of Smith's squad spread out along the flanks, some found sandbag cover, and the rest set up on elbows out in the open. Training, experience, position, Marine marksmanship, and a hail of 5.56 mm combined to devastate the remnants of a futile waste of human life.

"Shit's gonna turn into whack-a-mole pretty soon, Bone," shouted Nickels between bursts.

"Shit's the truth." Smith didn't dare try to count-up the bodies littering the kill zone, but just as many had managed to fall back. On a positive note, they weren't taking fire anymore.

"Hold up!" Smith shouted with a raised hand.

The barrage ceased, but no one lowered their rifles.

Holy mother of fucks that just happened.

They literally just destroyed a platoon. Stormed out of the smoke, dropped anchor, and blew up on those motherfuckers with a full broadside. To Smith's left, Captain Saunders was up and shouting orders. Alive and well.

Beat the clock.

"Oorah!" Smith boomed, his attention shifting to his squad. Everyone was fine, and he was sporting a wicked adrenaline pump. He tried to stay focused, but that was bad-fucking-ass. They'd just put up a wall and run the enemy right into it. No bullshit. Hot, heavy, and fast. Satisfying.

"Yup, bunkering," said Nickels. "Blew my load already; cover me, Bone."

Smith groaned at the thought of getting embroiled in a rolling bunker battle. It was a waste of Marine resources and bought the enemy time to reinforce. But that foreknowledge didn't mean he couldn't live in the moment a bit. "Shit! Weapon jam," he shouted.

Nickels shot back a panicked, incredulous look before he saw the obvious smirk. It took him a second to compose himself before he could get his mouth working. "Thought we weren't playin' out here. But it's on now, motherfucker. Twelve inches of all-you-can-eat soup can, bitch. Williamson! Reloading."

LCpl Williamson, the assistant automatic rifleman in Nickels' fireteam, crawled over. He carried the reserve ammo to keep that SAW spraying all night, but Smith wondered if it wasn't another cold shoulder moment.

Nickels still had at least two full boxes.

Before Smith could over-analyze the situation, a voice came out from under his bulky, box-fed rifle.

"Corporal Nickels?"

Shit forgot about the guy in the nest!

Smith peered over the sandbags to find a semi-familiar face staring up at him beneath a layer of dirt and spent shell casings. It was the Bravo Company dude Jersey was harassing at breakfast. LCpl Gladstone.

"You feelin' good down there, bro?" asked Nickels, also spotting a look to see who it was.

"Oorah."

"Chugagin', am I right?"

LCpl Gladstone, lying among a mess of blood and guts, shook with laughter. It got going so hard it turned a few heads from others still focused on the kill zone.

"Chugaging!"

"Much obliged, Gunny," LCpl Fischer said, patting himself down for injuries. He missed the bus that hit him, but somehow it didn't leave anything bleeding. Gunny was standing over him in the space that just a minute ago was whipping and popping so fierce it put out heat like a bon fire.

If that ain't him sayin' get the fuck up, *then nothin' is.*

Fischer sat up, dirt and bits of metal raining off his chest. He knocked crud off his formerly immaculate rifle like it was some range-mule, all-weather, replace-every-5,000-rounds disposable. *Maybe the boss has some lens wipes.* A splash of water and his sleeve on those premium optics wouldn't cut it. He started to pan the Marine reinforcements for Francisco but was distracted as his eyes settled on a motionless form.

"Shit."

Staying low, he crawled to a lifeless PFC Licht and searched for dark splotches on an otherwise bright beige uniform. From behind, Gunny boomed, "Fuck, need a corpsman!"

Rolling the PFC over, Fischer inspected critical areas for signs of blood or injury. Finding none, he raised a hand.

"Uhh, hang on Gunny." After a few vigorous shakes, Licht stirred. "You okay, man?" Fischer asked, checking his pupils with a penlight.

"Ugh."

"Where ya hurt?"

"Uhh, I don't. I . . . uhh. Nowhere."

"You sure? You hit your head? You seein' all right? How many toes I got in my boot?"

"I'm fine," the PFC said at last.

Fischer could've sworn that Licht's face started burning bright red through the face paint but didn't call attention to it. Instead, he offered a friendly smile and tossed a thumbs up back to Gunny. "He's good to go."

Looked like Gladstone made it, too, even after taking that hit to the chest. Everyone said that body armor stopping a straight-line rifle round was like getting hit by a sledgehammer. The way Stone had flown back, it looked a lot worse.

But they were alive. All of them. It was the amazing, against-all-odds win with what felt like incredible rewards.

However, seeing Gunny and the Captain plotting and pointing into the darkness made it clear that the only thing behind that jeweled grand prize door was the chance to play again.

Damn, this job kinda sucks.

———

Watching Fish help the PFC collect his shit and haul his sorry ass out of what was left of the nest made Cpl Nickels laugh. It felt good to laugh. Freeing.

That's all I needed. Just a fucking win.

But even as he thought it, his chest began to tighten. Or maybe it was always tight but temporarily forgotten. With it came the reality of that phone call.

It was wrong to laugh.

Wrong to know any joy at all . . .

Nickels got hit by a sudden head rush—his brain trying to do a back-flip inside his skull—and crouched behind cover. He wasn't dizzy but felt like he could pitch forward any second.

Not now.

He clenched every muscle in his body as if he could crush the sensation of rising panic through sheer might. He needed air. He couldn't fight like this.

He had to get out of there.

Everyone is going to fucking die!

"Jersey, you gonna share or what?"

Nickels practically jumped out of his trousers. *Christ, leave it alone, man!*

He used what little control he could muster to compose himself and meet Smith's questioning eyes. And then felt foolish as he realized Bone was looking at the canteen clutched in his hand. Most everyone else had CamelBaks, but he and Smith stuck with canteens. No tubing to get nasty when it was filled with something other than water. Right now, he had some flat energy soda. Every sip was a half cup of coffee and a porno mag. Cherry flavored. Smith probably had orange.

"If you worried about mouth AIDS, dawg . . ."

Nickels handed him the canteen with a relieved chuckle, grateful for the distraction. The weight on his chest lightened, and the dark thoughts receded. Standing, he slapped Smith on his bicycle-pumped arm and said, "Looks like the captain popped their combat cherries real good."

The rest of Bone's hard-earned muscle mass shook with laughter in the growing shadows as he handed the canteen back. "Yeah, but Fish and them took it better than you di—"

A lighting flare popped over the kill box.

Smith's head snapped left.

Nickels didn't think.

It was the same as when chilling with the bros at a bar and one of them broke eye contact to check something out. Instinct correctly relayed the information that he was eye-fucking some ass that trumped and required everyone's immediate attention. It was unspoken because to bring it up was to lay a claim. Worst thing that could happen was not looking too. Because— in love, married, ten babies, and a thousand promises or not—it was how dudes operated.

Hunters.

Nickels jumped up with his freshly reloaded weapon and drew down a line at the dim target. He was faster on the draw than Bone but never got the chance to fire. A sharp, distinctive crack from the rear iced it first. A rush of irritation followed as he was battered by the smugness radiating off the motherfucker casually walking up from behind.

"You guys slowing down already?" asked Francisco. *Francis,* as Nickels liked to call him.

"'Bout time you got up here, Pete," said Smith.

"Yeah, we showed them bitches what balls in the face feels like," said Nickels thrusting his weapon out toward the field of bodies. "Where were you?"

Yeah, where the fuck were you, bro?

He was never going to understand what Bone saw in this Italian-looking half-breed. Francis wouldn't survive ten minutes as a short-line cook. But he'd probably do okay in a sausage shop.

The hot-shit sniper squatted down, cast his eyes out over the field, and shook his head. "Ah, never mind, I don't think you guys can see them from here."

"Sure. Sure. S'all right, dawg. Jersey and I'll take your word for it."

"I'm not taking no one's word," Nickels spat.

"You guys are gonna miss me if I ever get transferred outta this outfit," Francis said, lowering his helmet-mounted night vision goggles. Nickels watched him pan their handiwork and then turn back to where the choppers were parked.

Nickels lowered his NVGs and also looked, but only from pure muscle memory. Not because Francis was sending any sort of correct hunting signal.

The air was clearer than he remembered. In fact, that shitty smokescreen was now like a foul stench that lingered exclusively over those rebel assholes. The choppers were safe, for now, outside of direct fire behind the detention center. But it only took one genius with a mortar to change that. The bulk of the Marine position was another story.

The battle was raging. The enemy was coming in hard from the north and landing a ton of munitions on their boys. It looked like a nightmare. A nightmare he and Bone needed to get in on. Right now, with the chest tightness coming back, Nickels just needed violence.

Pain.

A distraction.

Something to numb-out everything else.

Let these snipers take care of this eastern wasteland.

———

Captain Saunders plumbed the magazines that Brines had considerately brought along into his war vest and snapped the bolt closed on his reloaded MP5. Then he paused. Never in his wildest dreams was he burning through over 200 rounds with a close-quarters combat weapon on this trip. Most people didn't even piss that much ammo on the practice range.

I'm alive.

The realization hit him with a muted thud since it guaranteed nothing going forward. However, he still enjoyed the mild sense that he'd won the lottery.

So, what am I going to spend it on?

The SITREP from PFC Licht was grim. Hawk was short on ideas and shorter on assets. Their silence on critical operational elements was the really scary shit, though. At least the initial fears about certain Marine radios not working were unfounded.

Around him, the men were amped up. They had the initiative, but the window for action was closing, and there were already a few heads stealing eager glances back at the detention center. He empathized but sending them back to reinforce their besieged brethren would be little more than a drop in the bucket. Out here, they were deadly. They could harass, open new fronts, and act as true force multipliers against a numerically superior enemy.

In Saunders' role as the ground commander, the opposite applied. Right now, he was just another gun. But back at the detention center, he was at the helm of the C-monster.

An image of a great tentacle composed of Marines all strung together formed in Saunders' mind. And then it slapped down on hundreds of pathetic enemy soldiers running for their lives.

"Francisco," he called over. "Assessment?"

The veteran sniper scanned the eastern part of the base through his night vision goggles before crawling over to him. "They've taken up position in and around the rubble at two o'clock. Map reads it as what's left of their barracks."

"Ain't no place like home," muttered Brines.

"That was a high-priority target. There shouldn't be much left," Saunders said.

"There isn't," said Francisco.

"Any armor?"

"Just smoking hulls. Threat from east flank is minimal."

"How many boots we talkin' here?" asked Brines. "Hundreds?"

"Negative, a few dozen at most."

"Sir," urged Brines, the old Brines. The Brines before he "gave up" drinking. The Brines before he even started drinking. "We can take 'em."

Saunders had no doubt the men Brines brought were sufficient to clear the barracks, but he wasn't sure of the value. It was an extra angle of attack and possibly a shot at that C4I bunker down the road. But more likely, it'd be a liability because if they got into trouble, they'd be on their own.

Divide and conquer rang negatively in his mind.

"What do you hope to gain?" Saunders asked. "Vulture's out. Intel is spotty because of this black crud they're spewing into the air. We can't be certain of their numbers, and I don't need a last-minute mission to find a pinned-down squad. We need to yank it fast when it's time to go."

Brines shook his head. "Already got men pinned, sir. Pilots."

"Shit."

"Besides, we ain't takin' off 'nless we do some serious damage to that northern front. We gotta get an angle on it. Clearin' those barracks will let us swing around and remind 'em they got asses."

Saunders stroked the greasy stubble on his chin. No one ever talked about a five o'clock *AM* shadow. Tactically, the barracks was a wasteland occupied by a broken, demoralized unit looking to survive until the fighting ended. Francisco could probably cover that mess alone while the rest of them moved to the northern front. That would be the logical choice for playing defense tonight. Saunders glanced down at the bodies and equipment that, not so long ago, comprised a hardened fighting position.

I'm not playing defense.

The northern front was a challenge. Air support was gone, as fucking nuts as that sounded. It was the one damned thing he'd absolutely counted on. And that was his mistake. No matter. If winning was the new plan, they needed to stop raiding a base and start fighting a war. That meant dynamic fronts, mobility, charges, and feints. That meant sending his men out to increase his zones of control. To shove the enemy into a box, for a change, and kill them before reinforcements arrived.

Plus, and Saunders was not happy about this particular positive, positioning them for a run at that C4I bunker—the TOC—kept all options on the table. Presently, it was unreachable without a reckless and psychotic expenditure of resources. Still, just because he couldn't visualize the objective didn't mean he couldn't continue maneuvering his pieces to take advantage of new opportunities. The decision came down to playing it safe to assure some success or staying all in.

Sea Monster *was always high risk. Why stop now?*

"How many men do you need?" he asked finally.

"Just what I brought, minus Macko and Westermann."

"Can they walk?" Saunders asked. Brines wouldn't have said it so casually if it was serious.

"Yeah, put 'em in with First. They can still shoot."

"Okay. Do it. But do it slow. And maintain a clear line to us. We're a bubble, Mike, don't get pinched off. Copy?"

"Understood."

Saunders nodded to himself. With a lane open, he could still pull them back if the northern front got out of hand.

A shaky voice interrupted his thoughts. "Uhh, sir?"

The PFC.

"Licht, you operational?"

"I'm fine," he said with a forced depth to his voice, "but a Major Matt from SEAL just reported in."

Saunders' mouth went dry. This was that pass or fail moment.

The hinge of so many lives. "And?"

"They got to the hostages!"

Saunders punched his fist into his glove, a mountain of pressure off his shoulders. Of course, all it did was slam down the other mountain sitting on top of it. He'd take what he could get at this point, though.

"Fuckin A, details?"

"He said it's by the numbers just like they planned. Only issue is that they're light on the headcount. Most of the rest of the message was the word *fuck*. They're sitting tight for now."

"How light?" Saunders yelled, startling the kid.

"Uhh, he didn't . . . I uhh." He took a breath. "I'll ask, sir."

"Tell me what Matt said." Always felt weird calling them by their first names. But it was some sort of special forces, OpSec coding.

"Something about an alternate location."

"Fan-fucking-tastic," swore Brines.

"I'll ask them again," the PFC offered.

Saunders shook his head. There was no longer any question in his mind that the VIP had been moved. Some of the hostages being dead was a possibility, but SEAL was professional. They wouldn't speculate something this huge over the air.

That C4I bunker loomed at him from an impossible distance, another mile ascent to the top when he was already breathing hard and seeing double. But there was no turning back.

"Why don't you look surprised, sir?" asked Brines, the word *sir* hanging in the air as if a great distance had formed between them.

Time to improvise. Brines knew the drill, even if he would drop his two cents at every opportunity. That whole thing about no control issues was total bullshit.

"Intel floated the idea of an alternate location. High risk."

"Where?"

"TOC."

Brines pulled out his map and a small red light. "Fuck." Then after a pause. "Guessing it's still standing?"

"Yeah."

"You coulda just told me you wanted it bagged, sir."

"We need it bagged, Mike."

"Anything else you don't want me to know about in there?"

"No."

Brines stared through those dead blues long enough to convey his displeasure at being kept out of the loop. But then a wicked grin spread across his lips. "Another shot to shit plan beggin' fer a band-aid. And the best part is there ain't no one comin' to rip it off when the job's done."

"We just can't win today, man."

"We can win, sir. We gonna sweep around and end up in that shithouse TOC instead of hitting their lines from behind. We'll do it justice. You just gotta make sure we have an out."

Saunders nodded and drew a deep breath. *Mike's volunteering for this,* he reminded himself. He just hadn't expected the TOC to move up on the priority list so soon. It couldn't be helped. The plan was set; time to hold up his end of the bargain.

He turned back to PFC Licht. "It's all us now. Radio Lieutenant Lyons and tell him I'm coming back." There was no option but optimism. He had a company of the best armed and trained Marines on the planet, and nothing was off the table. If they needed to leave this place a burning sore on God's Earth and ruck it back to the coast on foot, they would.

Brines met his eyes with glowing excitement. "Let's not fuck this up," Saunders said. "I want you back on us in a hot minute when we get extraction figured out."

"Yes, sir."

Rising, the captain twirled a finger in the air and shouted, "Gladstone, Fischer, Licht, Macko, and Westermann, on me. Let's move."

LCpl Fischer looked back at Francisco and shrugged.

"Captain's going to need a deadeye with him," said Francisco to change in plans. "Go get some, Fish."

Saunders took another look at the darkened battlefield capped by a thick layer of . . . of murk or whatever instead of thundering support choppers and falling bombs. It was some new weapon that would totally rewrite modern infantry doctrine. He wasn't just sending Brines against a strong enemy unsupported.

He was sending him against the unknown.

And that's when PFC Licht tagged him on the shoulder. "Sir, I can't raise Lyons."

———

"Major Ra'num! Major Ra'num! We must push hard, now," shouted a tall, bearded Mujahid catching up from behind. Rank and name came accented in a Syrian dialect of Arabic. The rest of the words were in perfect Pashto due to the Advantage. Breathing hard, he dropped a weighted satchel to the ground.

Ra'num stopped, eyes falling to the bag. The details were lost in the dim light, but the dark splotches seeping through the canvas were suggestive of its dire contents.

"The men cannot break them unsupported."

The bloodied bag held no special meaning to Ra'num nor, he suspected, to his dark companion. Perhaps it was just a prop, an opening to conversation. *Effective.* Still, he offered no reaction and kept his attention focused beyond the warrior to the not-so-distant flashes and muffled thunder coming from the prison.

"The tanks must roll!"

Ra'num considered ignoring the pleas, but then he was distracted by a twinge of pity. Or perhaps it was just a memory of the emotion from his childhood; from before men were just things to be broken. His hand drifted to the hilt of the sleek, pointed blade on his belt. His favorite dirk.

Like the robed creature—the Black Robe, as he had come to call it—that stood silent at his side, Ra'num's mission here was greater than the sake of the common troops. If all war was a game of chess, he was the nuts and bolts of the table that held it aloft. A minor tweak here and a loose screw there could topple kings faster than any single play or grand strategy. Spending time on this Mujahid was spending time on the pawns, or worse, perhaps one of the checkered squares upon which the pawns walked.

Still, too often did the prize blind men to grander opportunities.

As evident from their experiments in the prison, pawns were what these Black Robes most desired in their search for these ... *Corsan Carre*— the strange term that failed to translate. So let them have a taste of more than frightened hostages and ordinary soldiers.

Let them see the battle-hardened Mujahedeen of Kôz.

Only the strength and determination of the Mujahedeen forces kept the Americans from sweeping the base like wolves through a herd of sheep. "They will roll, brother," Ra'num assured him with practiced sincerity.

"These words come from the colonel?"

"Yes."

Hesitation. "I must hear them myself."

"He is busy."

"We are dying! The orders to attack are given in thoughtless haste. No support, no care for the fallen. Where is Captain Ahmad? His plans die cradled in incompetent hands!"

Ra'num shrugged. The colonel had made it clear that he supported this "study" of battle the Black Robe desired. And that meant running perfectly good men in suicidal charges against the American lines. "Their helicopters are gone," he offered.

"And with them, the danger to the vehicles. What more is needed?"

Ra'num opened his arms with palms faced upward as if asking a higher power for forgiveness. It also had the effect of displaying the infamous knives strapped to his waist. "The greater plan demands patience and sacrifice. I beg we have the strength to endure." He kept one eye on the Black Robe, hoping for a reaction. There was none.

The Mujahid spat at the display but then remembered his place. "I seek only to know when the tanks will come."

A better idea came to Ra'num, and his voice chilled. "The vehicles are held for the offensive at dawn."

"What?"

"The colonel has decreed it. They must be kept safe from the American weapons."

"You said the vehicles will roll!" said the Mujahid, quivering with rage and sadness.

"A lie."

"What? What evil takes your mind?" Narrowing eyes shifted to the Black Robe for the first time since their discussion began. "Is it you?" He kicked the bag to the being's feet. "Answer."

Ra'num remained silent, still holding the pseudo-religious pose as if it were out of his hands. Because it was. The armored column would roll when he and the Black Robe arrived at a good vantage point. But first, he wanted to see this harbinger of the Advantage react to the suffering of soldiers. To the reality of denying them a quick victory.

The Black Robe took a step forward. "This day's blood will nourish your future," he said in that deep, flat voice that was so calm it drove Ra'num wild with desire to make it scream.

"Demon talk. Have we not given enough?" asked the Mujahid, struggling to stand firm against a power he could never comprehend.

"It is not the blood that should concern you," the Black Robe replied, taking another step forward. The warrior held his ground and grabbed his rifle. Ra'num raised an eyebrow but made no attempt to interfere.

A tension filled the air, and Ra'num perceived a deep hum at the lower edge of his hearing.

The Mujahid raised his weapon with great effort as if it weighed a hundred kilograms. He grimaced, mouth working, but no sound emerged.

Then the warrior's composure faltered, and his arms went limp. The rifle dropped to the pavement.

The mouth kept moving, and Ra'num's ears perked up in anticipation of a renewed dialogue between the two. Any words of wisdom were lost as the jaw fell slack as if disconnected from the mind.

The fierceness drained from the warrior's eyes, and they locked forward. He stopped blinking and seemed less aware of his surroundings. Ra'num thought to test this theory by waving his hand in front of the man's face, but that might've produced unexpected consequences.

Then the battle-hardened Mujahid's expression changed. His features softened, and he stumbled forward. At first, Ra'num thought he was making a final effort to strike out against the Black Robe. But the look on the man's face told him otherwise. It was not defiance or rage. Quite the opposite.

It was longing. Perhaps love.

"I am yours," whispered the human shell to the Black Robe.

———

"Jesus Christ," shouted 1stLt Lyons as Captain Saunders entered the make-shift command post in the detention center's concrete vestibule.

Jesus Christ yourself, Saunders thought, relieved to see his executive officer alive.

Long-range communications problems had been anticipated with all the electronic warfare crap they were throwing down. Still, when Lyons stopped answering his radio, it screamed *Marines dead.* So it was nice finding him and the platoon officers inside and out of direct fire for a moment. Still, the tension in Lyon's face said it all: any sense of security was an illusion.

"Report."

Composing himself, the lieutenant dismissed two runners back to the lines with fresh loads of ammo and ushered Saunders deeper inside.

"We're holding."

Holding.

That one word spoke volumes. It was what people did in the face of sheer uncertainty when the last letter in the word *hope* was a question mark. They held on, hunkered down. Just enough to remain, but with no foresight of the future and no plan for self-actualization. It was time to change that.

"What's our strength?"

"Latest report put Second at full capacity. First is on crutches and half of Third took off looking for you."

"Gunny's got a team working on the eastern flank. Should lighten the load. Any more from SEAL?"

Lyons shrugged. "A couple of them came up a little while ago, took a look around, and headed back without saying much."

"Probably waiting on us."

"Yeah."

Time to talk about the elephant in the room.

"Our radio just went on the fritz. Tried to give you a heads up and got back a wash of static. But we're using that upgraded model we thought would handle the jamming signal better. Maybe it's shit?" said Saunders with a hint of hopefulness.

Lyons kicked his boot against the dusty cinder block wall. "Yeah, we're out too."

"Fuck."

"Resorted to runners."

"It'll do for now. Last report from Hawk mentioned something about armor."

"Yeah," said Lyons. "After they pulled Vulture, the RPAs spotted more vehicles coming out of a bunker just north of here. I'd show you, but I think you know what I'm talking about."

"Affirmative," replied Saunders conjuring the image in his mind of the sizeable reinforced-concrete structure rated as a priority target. "That was supposed to be blasted to shit by now."

"Before Vulture went offline, Hawk was reporting widespread ordnance malfunctions. Several key targets were missed. Last we heard, they were working on clearance to get stealths back in the air, but all we're seeing here is the occasional RPA."

"I'm aware. Gunny and I owe one of those remote pilots a round of beers. How are we handling their armor?"

An explosion thudded near the entrance, and a plume of black dust sprayed inward. A pair of Marines emerged from the cloud, coughing. Saunders caught LCpl Gladstone's eye and received a thumbs up.

Nodding, he turned back to Lyons, who kept talking without missing a beat. "Heavy Weapons is locked and loaded, but the armor hasn't made a run at us yet. And frankly, we don't have eyes on any of it. A few personnel carriers were lurking around when we landed, but First Platoon handled them."

Saunders frowned. "So, no contact, but no idea where those tanks are either?"

"Sir, this smog-shroud stuff limits visibility to effective rifle range. They could be 500 meters out, and we'd never know it." Lyons scrubbed his hands together, searching the darkened concrete walls for answers. "Hawk reported it's a mix of wheeled vehicles and T-70-whatevers."

"Yeah, main battle tanks. No big deal," Saunders replied sarcastically.

Lyons relaxed a little and mopped his brow on his sleeve. "They probably think we've got some serious hardware, and that's why they're holding back. Maybe waiting till the air clears and they can scout us better. The second they see we've only got Javelins, they'll come hard and fast."

"Yeah, close that gap before we can pop too many tops."

"But on a good note, we've thinned their infantry significantly."

"Main threat is the armor, got it," said Saunders.

And time.

All the elegant electronic warfare, jamming equipment, and "Stiff Parrot" delayed, not prevented outside interference. Even if the proximate enemy units in the surrounding countryside were under a total blackout, it didn't take a lot of brain power to determine which areas might be under attack. And that assumed they didn't already have an automatic deployment/return-to-base plan in case of severe coms failure. Which, being a professional military, would be hard to believe.

The trifecta was that mysterious anti-air weapon that took a chunk out of their Cobra fleet and effectively changed United States air superiority doctrine forever. Saunders was more convinced than ever that the enemy C4I tactical operations center held critical intel, if not the weapon's control center. The fact that the VIP was also conveniently located there plucked at the back of his mind, yearning to make some connection. But he didn't have time to deal with it. All roads seemed to lead that way, and he needed it under Marine control. Still, he fought the urge to reinforce Gunny's team.

Baby steps.

Right now, he needed to stay grounded and on mission. This was still a rescue operation, after all.

Saunders snorted and ground his teeth on the dust and grit caking the inside of his mouth. "Those fucking tanks. They're just waiting for us to start loading the choppers. We've got no choice . . . gotta clear the way for the evac." He turned back toward the entrance. "Licht, keep trying to raise Hawk. Transmit that we're getting ready to move and need assets. Anything they can give us."

"On it, sir."

He turned back to Lyons and made no effort to hide the wild look in his eyes as he said, "No more holding. Rally the sergeants."

CHAPTER 12

ALONE TOGETHER

Gunny Brines and the four Marines who'd followed him were like rats in an undersized burrow squirming for position. Limbs and gear clunked together as everyone tried to hug the precious earth of the shallow impact crater. It was their oasis, their lifeboat. It was the only thing keeping them alive as enemy fire snapped over their heads.

Panting, Sergeant Gilbert called out, "That was a little fuckin' farther than 200 meters, Gunny!"

"Quit bitchin' and get those smokers off so Smith's squad can move up!"

Fuckers are makin' us work fer it.

The enemy was a few more than Francisco's "dozen or so" and dug in tighter than an over-torqued barrel nut. And that oily, thick haze they'd counted on to cover their movements had blown itself out of the base's eastern portion. Good for the snipers and the drones, but bad news for the men on the ground hauling the duty.

That was about to change, though.

Staying low, Sgt Gilbert slipped the M32 MGL 40mm grenade launcher off his back and fired three M680 canopy smokers fifty meters forward. Seconds later, the enemy muzzle flashes faded into the white plume.

"Stay down!" bellowed Brines as a storm of pissed-off lead poured in around them.

Yeah, I'd be mad, too, if I couldn't see me coming.

Explosions slapped the atmosphere against Brines' ears, and molten flashes against the billowing backdrop hinted at the true visage of hell. But for all their ferocity, the enemy's fixation was on the cloud itself, which was forward of the Marine position.

Ultimately, a waste of ammo.

In time, the laws of thermodynamics caught up with the enemy as their weaponry required cycling and reloading. The second incoming fire began to wither, Brines gave permission to fire the flare—the signal for Smith's squad to advance.

We got 'em. We got 'em . . .

Skirting the northern edge of the smoke screen, Sergeant Smith was practically tiptoeing as he led his exposed squad forward. The objective was close, a waist-high perimeter wall marking the barracks' beginnings. Random bursts of blind-fire spit pavement and debris up at his legs as they pumped against overburdened fatigue, but he was confident the element of surprise remained.

Even if it didn't, Gunny counted on them grabbing the other angle. Francisco said there was enough shit out here to turn it into a bunker battle if they went straight in, but not enough to protect both flanks. A crossfire would kill the enemy position quick, and then they could put the hurtin' on that TOC.

Breathing hard and feeling like he was running his boys across a tight-rope, Smith resisted the urge to drop prone as the air came alive with a fresh line of gunfire. It was just a few more meters to cover. He could taste the sulfur of his fully automatic retaliation.

Movement.

It was scant, just out the corner of his eye. Something dark on a small knoll in the distance. Nothing around it. Might've been his imagination.

Or a sniper.

The thought of being in someone's crosshairs spiked more adrenaline into Smith's blood. He put that extra power into zig-zagging the final distance to cover.

Need to flag that knoll for Francisco ASAP.

Suddenly, a flash cut across his vision, followed by several disturbing and disconnected sensations.

Ringing.

Stinging pain on his left side.

The taste of fruit.

The smell of blood.

The stiff bones in his legs turning to rubber.

Smith became a passenger in his body, just along for the ride. Momentum carried him into a forward summersault with the SAW jamming itself between his diaphragm and the blacktop. His lungs seized with an awful grunt, and he crumpled face down on the pavement.

His mind raced, pulling at the controls of his uncoordinated muscles. He was exposed. Wasting time. Gunny needed him on that wall. *So damned close!* He pushed his palms into the ground, struggling to rise. The weight of the world forced him back down.

Panic rose, the fear of being trapped within himself. *Why can't I get up?* Years of physical training, heaving hundreds of pounds off his chest, and now he couldn't do one stinking sissy pushup?

He called out for Nickels, who was right behind him but didn't get a response. With a great effort, he turned his head and saw the body of another Marine. Face down, no telling who it was.

Smith tried again to push himself up, but his arms were jelly. Struggling to catch his breath, the pain in his side began spreading across his belly. He tried to concentrate on what it meant, but wild thoughts and daydreams began to slide across his mind blurring the lines between reality and fantasy. One thing he could be sure of was that through the rising chaos around him, he could clearly hear the screams of a human being caught in the depths of terror. And he recognized who it was.

Nickels. Nickels was screaming.

———

"Smith should be in position, Gunny," called Sgt Gilbert, checking his watch.

Brines nodded, and the five crouched Marines readied themselves. While he didn't have eyes on Smith's squad on the other side of the smoke, that's where the bullets were flying now. One way or another, the enemy was distracted.

Time to hit 'em in the ass.

"Go!" ordered Brines, thrusting the fireteam into the smoke screen. Hugging the cloud's periphery where visibility was better, they worked their way across a bombed-out parade ground. The dying light from the last round of flares was barely enough to keep them from tripping over debris and each other.

They tightened up into a single-column formation with Brines bringing up the rear. Under normal circumstances, a run through the oily, sulfuric plume that emanated from those smoker rounds would bring up a hacking spasm with each breath, but something about combat negated that effect. The air could have been that of the sweetest spring morning for all Brines cared. All he knew was the training guiding his movements; all he knew was where they needed to be to complete the kill.

Suddenly, the air thickened, causing Sgt Gilbert's point man to stumble over a stack of wooden pallets. Then the smoke swirled skyward as if caught in some updraft. A second later, it slammed back down on them. As if finally deciding what to do with itself, it settled in and shot high-density pockets of smoke into their faces.

Disoriented, Brines called out, "Break right. Let's get outta this shit!"

They covered less than two spans before hitting a pocket of clear, crisp air. And on the other side of that impossibly clean bubble, about twenty meters away, stood a firing squad.

As time slowed, those angry, bearded faces—wearing uniforms that Brines recognized from his time in Afghanistan as belonging to the Mujahedeen—melted into the darkness of the dying flare. Then erupted as a line of flickering muzzle flashes.

———

The LFOC was in full crisis mode.

Mission-critical operators were handling traffic on an unprecedented level as the hysteria over Pakistan's new anti-air capability exploded. The entire United States defense network was on high alert, and the Pentagon had ordered all commands to DEFCON 2. The President, Vice President, and Joint Chiefs were relocating to nuclear-hardened command bunkers.

The world was taking notice.

Allies and enemies were enacting reaction protocols to the US DEFCON 2 upgrade. A storm of political chatter was lighting up the circuit boards, and media reports were beginning to surface about problems with a military operation titled *Sea Monster* that was ongoing in Pakistan.

CENTCOM was handling a lot of it, but only the Marine Command Element seated around the war table in the USS *Storm's* LFOC could answer certain questions. As such, Central was directing a high volume of queries and data their way.

It seemed like every DARPA-funded engineer with a modicum of clearance had been contacted, filled in, and already developed a working theory. The problem with theories was that they rarely offered answers without a shit load of testing. Every crack-pot idea required mission-critical assets like satellite time, in-theater scans of the electromagnetic spectrum, and some nonsense involving sonar from one of the subs escorting the fleet.

Colonel Ridge found it distracting and downright disrespectful. He still had men on the ground, and he was damned if he'd allow the egg-heads to sacrifice Marines for the sake of probing a scientific curiosity. Eleventh-hour, day-saving shit didn't happen in the real world. There was only one man whose quick thinking and quicker action might matter.

Ron Saunders.

"Getting back in contact with my Marines is our only priority, General," Ridge said. He'd long since passed insubordination. Yelling over admirals and secretaries of defense was just par for the course. One look from these men and his career was gone. But he wasn't bound by the golden handcuffs or a string of greedy dependents. He didn't have a family like Saunders, just a trail of broken hearts. Truthfully, most of those broken hearts were his— always picking the wrong kind of girl . . .

Major General McNeal snapped him back into focus with a sigh, barely audible over the forward video screen, and said, "I grew up in the Regiment, Colonel. Dad was a Ranger. I don't need a lecture on *no man left behind*. But facts are facts. A communications solution can only progress so fast. We need to be working on multiple fronts simultaneously."

"Right. And all those fronts need to immediately benefit my Marines."

"Categorically false," said Secretary of Defense Wayne Ford from the flanking monitor. "India's nuclear forces are on high alert, and they've cut coms with us National Command Authorities. They're terrified that the nuclear equation has become unstable. This is just one situation out of dozens that require immediate, if not exclusive, attention."

"Iran's another bucket of shit waiting to dump itself on our heads," added General McNeal.

"Less of an issue," dismissed Mr. Ford without elaborating.

"Right," said General McNeal flatly. "Anyway, Ridge. General Harrell has put his faith and confidence in you because you're closer to the action than he is. That's why you're still talking. I said I was sympathetic. Tell me what you need."

General Harrell was a good man. The first time Ridge met him was at a party when Harrell was still a full bird colonel. The man was all Marine. Gruff, direct, always had an eye out for the gung-ho, *oorah* types. He was the kind of guy who'd find his kids playing with explosives and yell at them first for not submitting a five-paragraph order and second for not using enough gunpowder. Yet, he was famous for his rock-solid command of reality. He knew the right people to do the right job and when to take charge himself. No one questioned him when he put a man on task.

Taking a breath and knowing they'd gone down this path several times already, Ridge said, "I need Vulture back online with the sole mission of destroying the armored threat. And I want Alpha Company in the air, on mission to reinforce Charlie."

Admiral Bowman closed his eyes and shook his head but remained silent. In fact, everyone was quiet, as if Ridge had just said something stupid. As if he hadn't been keeping up on current events, following along. As if he didn't know and hadn't been repeatedly told that the Marine Aviation Combat Element was totally grounded and off the table as a viable option. But none of them had Saunders' goodbye letter burning a hole in their breast pockets.

No way can I deliver that to Sarah.

"Denied," said General McNeal.

Okay, Plan B. Ridge opened his mouth to demand authorization for the immediate amphibious deployment of remaining Marine combat personnel to invade the fucking country and extract their people. A glare from the admiral closed it.

"However," said General McNeal raising a finger. "We will maintain Vulture on the highest alert while aggressively pursuing options to deal with or work around the threat to our air components. Any indication that there's a hole, and we'll fast-track 'em. It's the best we can do without casually discarding capabilities and lives."

It was an improvement, Ridge admitted to himself. He'd gotten them to budge from engines-cold grounded to full readiness. What was left of Vulture had retreated to the forward arming and refueling point where the four combat-ready platoons of Captain Rogers' Alpha Company were stationed. That put them fifteen minutes out from greenlight to reinforcing Mina Bazar. But it wasn't a bad lead time. And now, there was only one hurdle between his men and support.

"What satisfies the burden of proof for this 'hole?'" he asked.

Both high-ranking men on their respective screens frowned, clearly searching for the right way to say, *to be determined.* But, before they could speak, an operator came through the speaker with a priority message.

"Admiral, we're reading the build-up of an anomalous electromagnetic signature."

Bowman's posture straightened like a cattle prod just poked him in the back. "Go ahead," he managed, trying to keep his composure.

The fuck is the admiral not telling us? Ridge wondered, convinced the man was withholding more than a few mission-critical details.

"It resembles a nuclear thermal pulse, sir. But protracted over minutes instead of microseconds."

The compartment went dead silent.

"You reading this, General?" the admiral asked McNeal.

"We're getting it too. Running a comparison. Standby."

As they waited with bated breath and racing minds, Ridge's thoughts wandered back to Sarah Saunders. Giving her that terrible news was becoming more of a reality by the second. Of course, he'd do it in person. He was man enough, but the thought of delivering that killing blow turned his stomach.

How had the seventeen intelligence agencies employed by the United States missed such a major game changer? Of course, he already knew the answer. *They lost that VIP.* That's why this whole mission got fast-tracked in the first place. *Talk about putting all your eggs in one basket.* In this era of ultra-rapid and secure communications, it seemed inconceivable that one person could hold all the cards.

"It's confirmed," came the sober voice of General McNeal. "Same signature we recorded at Hudud."

Wait, what?

"Your people ID a source, McNeal?" asked Admiral Bowman, tapping the table.

"Negative. Signal's diffuse. Wait, standby . . ."

"What happened at Hudud?" Ridge asked to a deaf audience. The official story was that the 24th MEU garrison got overrun by a helicopter-borne attack. Hostages taken. Village torched. No mention of nukes.

"Got localization," said General McNeal with a frown. "But it doesn't make sense. It reads as a column six miles tall and a mile wide. Fifty miles above the airfield."

"Some sort of aircraft or satellite?" asked Bowman with total sincerity.

Ridge raised an eyebrow. A moment ago, these men were giving him the stink eye for suggesting the use of aircraft, and now they were entertaining the possibility of gigantic airplanes. He fought the urge to call up General Harrell and start screaming until he was either thrown in the brig or operational command was transferred back to the Marines.

"Negative, the Landsat spectral bands are reading clear."

"What happened at Hudud?" Ridge repeated.

"Still tracking the same way as Hudud's?" asked Bowman.

"Yes."

"How long until it peaks?"

"Twenty minutes. That is two-zero minutes."

"Options?" asked SecDef Ford.

"Hit it with an SLBM," suggested General McNeal. "We've got a sleeper sub within intermediate range; the timing could work."

I'm in a meeting where the nuclear option is being seriously considered . . .

"Hudud was non-nuclear. The President has made it clear that we do not nuke first."

"And we have no idea if anything is even up there," said Admiral Bowman. "Might just be a trick. Ghost signal or something."

"Talk to the President," General McNeal told SecDef Ford. "Give him the facts. A W76-2 is low yield, less than ten kilotons. That far up, it shouldn't affect our men on the ground. But it has a good chance of disabling this weapon by direct contact or electromagnetic pulse. More importantly, it'll remind the world not to fuck with us."

"Policy is policy. We do not pre-empt," repeated Ford. "But we need to take measures to protect ourselves. Admiral, are you still in contact with the forward arming and refueling point?"

"Yes, sir."

"Tell them to pack it up and evac."

"On it," said Admiral Bowman snapping his fingers at LtCol Baud to relay the message.

"No!" protested Ridge, but his voice was lost in a flurry of activity. The SecDef made a hurried exit to brief the President, and General McNeal shot him one last sympathetic look. The LFOC darkened as those two monitors cut off. Ridge could hear the blood rushing through his ears as his heart tried to pound its way out of his chest.

The Marine Corps Commandant regrets to inform you that your husband . . .

No! He locked eyes with Admiral Bowman in a desperate attempt to salvage something, anything from the situation. "What happened at Hudud?"

"Combat outpost Dud was vaporized by an unidentified energy weapon."

Ridge's jaw dropped. But instead of pointing fingers, he swallowed that twenty-inch sausage, nodded, and said, "We need to contact Saunders. Give him a heads up."

"We can't."

"There's still time for the civilians, at least, to get on those choppers and make a run for it." How had this gone from helping Saunders destroy an armored column to sheer desperation for five seconds of mic time?

"Colonel," said Admiral Bowman, seeming to come to grips with something himself, "we need to start thinking about the lives we *can* save. Alpha Company, the men on this ship. Hell, the entire fleet may be in danger."

"But . . ."

"Captain Saunders has his responsibilities, and we have ours. He's on his own."

———

"So, we're bait?" shouted one of the squad leaders over the nearby exchange of gunfire.

First Lieutenant Lyons peered into the dark, dirty, demanding faces of Second Platoon's sergeants and resisted the urge to shrug in admission. Instead, he wondered what Gunny Brines would say at a time like this. Definitely not a limp-wristed *captain's orders*. No, it was time to own it.

"Bait with balls, Sergeant," he shouted back, projecting as much gung-ho confidence as he could. Normally he'd descend into a long-winded explanation calculating their assets, liabilities, and overall odds, but he was starting to see why Marines spoke short and acted fast. There was just no damned time. Plus, there wasn't a good way to sugar-coat the order to charge. No. It was step one, then step two. Right now, they needed a breakout.

The sergeants eyed their temporary platoon leader, 2ndLt Weber. Second Lieutenant Franklin got caught by mortar fire earlier while rucking a wounded Marine to the temporary field hospital in the detention center. Hero shit. Now he was sitting this one out, waiting on a MEDEVAC that might never come.

Any uncertainty about Weber vanished as they took in his gaunt face, which seemed chiseled out of grim determination in the dim lighting. So, the men looked among each other, shrugged, and, much to Lyons' relief, came back with wild-eyed *oorahs*.

The huddle broke, and the sergeants moved out to update their squads. Lyons gave Weber a slap on the back—a departure from his usual three feet of personal space at all times. Weber returned a firm handshake and solid eye contact.

Then he was gone.

Lyons was left with a pang of regret that he wouldn't be leading those men. He had planted First Platoon after that psychotic crash landing, held the lines, and now gotten Second Platoon juiced for the meat grinder essentially on his own. The looks he was getting meant, for the first time, they saw more than just a checklist officer. And that was tough in a company with Marine Corps giants like Captain Saunders and Gunny Brines casting long shadows. He hoped this wasn't goodbye.

"Incoming!"

LCpl Gladstone had a fraction of a second to turtle-up before the thick atmosphere hammered down with a deafening bang.

What the hell was that? he wondered, waiting for the waves of disorientation to pass and fresh oxygen to reach his starved lungs. Between the pounding they were taking and the fact that his chest ached with every breath from that round he took earlier, he was having trouble staying motivated.

A body flopped down beside him and nuzzled into the sandbags as another score of explosions ripped through their position.

"Great day in the morning," shouted a familiar southern drawl as Gladstone's hearing began to return. "That was a goddamned time on target!"

"A what?" said Gladstone, probably ten times louder than he needed to. He looked at the Marine and was relieved to see LCpl Fischer's perpetual smile aiming back.

"That's when them artillery rounds all blow up at the same time. Big fuckin' boom."

"We're being hit with artillery?" *Not good.*

"Mortars. Whatever," said Fischer resting his M4 Carbine on top of the sandbags as if getting ready to return fire. Gladstone eyed the weapon and couldn't help but notice the scoped sniper rifle slung over his back.

"Thought you were getting set up with a spotter?"

"Can't see shit out here tonight. Captain said to hang onto the tack-driver and get ready for the fuckfest."

"Shit."

"Yeah, it's all balls in the face. Thought I'd pair up with you 'cause you got that pretty-as-fuck shotty. Plus, we had all that fun in the nest back there." As if on cue, a fresh burst of molten fragmentation peppered the area, and a torrent of steel-core tore at the sandbags just inches from their heads. Fischer kept his rifle up but made no attempt to respond.

"I can't see a damned thing, and they're just lighting us up," said Gladstone knocking the smoldering bits off his uniform before they burned through to his skin.

Fischer shook his head. "They can't see shit neither. They just know the lay of the land better. Besides, we got body armor." He jabbed Gladstone lightly in the chest as he said it, and Gladstone nearly doubled over wheezing, his shattered chest plate crunching with each spasm. Taking that round was probably the worst pain he'd felt in his life, and some of that crunching was probably his rib cage. As he waited for the agony to die down, his frazzled mind oddly wondered how it compared to childbirth. Probably worse. *God, that'd be terrible if it wasn't.*

"Sorry, man, I forgot. Hey, you okay?"

"Yeah." Gladstone could breathe again, at least.

"Look, I got somethin' that'll make you feel better."

"What?"

"Word is the captain's goin' in with us."

"That's crazy. Why?"

"I tell ya, it don't make sense to me neither. But Captain Saunders has a streak about him if you ain't noticed."

"Yeah," said Gladstone wishing he could get his hand beneath the layers of Kevlar and cracked ceramic plates to massage his sternum.

"But if I wager a guess, I'd say it's because we're in a pretty big bind, and he needs every man he has."

"How is that supposed to make me feel better?"

"'Cause, do or die, we all goin' to the same place. And misery loves company."

———

Ra'num was surprised, perhaps pleased, to find himself marveling as the Black Robe lowered its frail hands and clasped them together. The American squad advancing this far beyond their battle lines had been unexpected; Captain Ahmad's concerns about their elites appeared well-founded. Instead of a firefight, though, the Advantage showed itself at last by casually casting the threat aside.

Its will unto the world through no device of man . . .

The twisting of the Mujahid warrior's mind was impressive but dismissible as with any trick. Perhaps the two conspired together. But watching the Americans succumb to a bolt of pure light shot from the Black Robe's fingertips . . . It was the power men had sought since the dawn of time.

Wizardry.

A practice old as time, if the right fables spoke to truth, but long-buried by the modern world of reason and logic. To suggest such now was to enter the realm of wild fantasy or mental illness.

Ra'num now knew different.

He was beginning to understand how the Black Robes could watch so many die in the name of study. The brilliance of their power blinded them to the tiny lights of common men. Even he, Ra'num, was small. A master of so much, yet little more than an ant beside the Advantage.

The creature of magic—perhaps a man in appearance alone—set its gaze to the battle near the prison. As he prepared to dismiss it as a mere annoyance, Ra'num wondered why they needed Kôz at all.

"So many with potential," said the Black Robe seeing something that Ra'num could not.

"A conclusion from your study?"

"It is a separate matter but valuable. For now, their hearts beat to a rhythm we know well. They take to the attack."

"Then do not delay." It had been a long time since Ra'num felt the thrill of combat and his senses so alive. When the Americans charged out of the smoke, there was even fear, a fleeting desire to seek refuge instead of holding the knoll.

The Black Robe hesitated.

Interesting.

There was enough battle to study; what use was seeing more of Kôz fall to the coming attack? Ra'num cared little for *a* life but much for the lives of many. Letting his brethren die purposelessly was disrespectful, disgusting, and insulting. His hand slid to his dirk, remembering the colonel's question as to the speed of his draw. Perhaps it was time to find out.

Valuable.

The word rang loud, and he retracted his hand. *The Black Robe has a need,* he realized. Something Ra'num could provide. The possibilities exploded in his mind, a rush of insane desires from his darkest fantasies now made possible by the Advantage.

"Perhaps a few may live?" asked the Black Robe.

Ra'num smiled. Clearly, the Black Robe wanted human capital with which to do as it pleased. Regardless of how small Ra'num might seem to them, the Black Robe remained bound to whatever agreement had been made with General Khel. And Ra'num was the executor.

But what do I want?

Power.

He kept his expression neutral, stifling the rising storm of excitement and terror. This was a delicate negotiation, and he needed to speak from a position of abundance and confidence. "You may have ten," he said. "But I seek knowledge of the Advantage."

"Knowledge?"

"To wield," Ra'num hissed.

Silence—the agonizing quiet of decision.

Will my jaw go slack and eyes vacant for asking? Is this the end of Ra'num?

"It is possible . . ."

"Then share it with me," he said quickly, "and neither General Khel nor my brethren shall ever know of your prisoners."

The Black Robe was still, blending into the darkness of the surrounding night. Ra'num once again considered the speed of his draw, his fingers aching to wrap the Kris' ornate handle instead of the dirk. The wavy blade was shorter and cumbersome, but a single strike would ensure the kill. He understood little of this being or its motivations other than that it was powerful, and the element of surprise was his only friend. He stayed his hand, though, trusting in his intuition about the intentions and needs of others.

"Very well," came that lifeless voice through the darkness.

"Will it take long?" Ra'num asked.

"No. I have made my selections; the fight ends."

Ra'num meant the process of becoming a god, but no matter. He turned his attention to the battle around the prison, which was intensifying into a blinding exchange. The Americans were expending an unsustainable amount of ordnance in preparation for their attack. Ra'num's heart raced anew as he readied himself to witness all that energy snuffed out in a great breath.

The Black Robe raised its arms and wove them through a series of unfamiliar gestures. The movements seemed important, so Ra'num committed every detail to memory. Then a light flashed in the heavens—the same from the stories of Hudud—and Ra'num sucked a breath.

For Kôz, Allah, and spite of men that brings them to war!

Suddenly, the night air began to snap and pop around him.

Gunfire.

Ice poured through Ra'num's veins as he hit the dirt with his rifle. The thrill of combat brightened the battlefield, and he spotted a lone soldier charging toward them, rifle blaring away.

Another team?

"My prize comes to me," breathed the Black Robe, unmoved by the bullets zipping past. "We shall claim this one first."

CHAPTER 13

A RECIPE FOR PTSD

"Take cover!" bellowed Gunny Brines bolting away from the enemy fire line.

It was a split-second decision, infinitely too slow. In the open, dead to rights in the enemy's iron sights, Sgt Gilbert's team had zero chance of effectively engaging. The Mujahedeen were calm and collected, putting a dot on the side of a barnyard door while buttoned up with the profile of a mouse. There wasn't a chance in hell of hitting them with anything less than a howitzer. And even then, the Marines would only get one shot.

Brines' full-powered course change happened fast. He couldn't keep eyes on his men and had to trust that they heard his order, reached the same conclusion, or were just following his lead for once.

Unfortunately, the report of Marine rifle fire filled the air.

Shit.

He managed to steal a glance back, just in time to see Sgt Gilbert waving two Marines behind him as his rifle popped wildly in his other hand.

And then Gilbert jerked and twisted at odd angles as a massive burst of 7.62 mm Pakistani shit unloaded on him. The ceramic plates in his vest absorbed enough early hits that the pathways between his brain and legs remained open. He kicked himself into an awful-looking stagger, a man trying to run on stilts, which ended abruptly as the meat around his knees and femur splashed off in huge chunks. What was left of him pitched forward and slapped face-first into the dirt without making any effort to brace for the fall.

Brines resisted the overwhelming urge to turn back.

Suicide.

The other two Marines were just as fucked if they didn't kick it into high gear. The third was nowhere to be seen. Brines just had to hope they'd find cover as he pounded sand without regard for anything other than hauling his mass into the nearest defensible position.

The air was electric as the pops and sparks of tracer-loaded steel core zipped between his legs. He zigged and zagged like a football player dodging invisible yet highly tangible bad guys.

It's on you, Mike.

You led them into that shit.

A blast—likely a grenade—threw up dust and debris on his two o'clock. He dove for the plume as if it were a bunker forged by God Himself. Rolling behind the screen, he dropped prone and tried to meld his body with the ground as machine-gun fire snapped inches above his head.

Goddamned ambush. Where the fuck is Smith?

Brines knew the answer. He'd bit off a fuckload more than he could chew thinkin' with his balls, not his head. Now he'd fucked half a platoon out of their lives.

It's on you, Mike.

Yeah. He took stock of his situation: no new hurts, still mobile, and still armed.

Angry.

Goddamned Gilbert trying to protect his team would keep him up at night for a long time.

Fuck. This. Shit.

Suddenly, he was back in that cage all those years ago. He could hear his friends screaming and gasping. Hopeless. Their organs set out on display, a death blow that would last for hours. Good strong men reduced to wide-eyed feral animals by the time the work was done. No last words or thoughts. Just meat and mess.

And then it was his turn on the table . . .

Never again.

Another loud bang brought him back to the fight. He needed to move; it wouldn't be long before some asshole bombed his sanctuary with a grenade. He scanned the scarred landscape against the flicker of the fight and spotted a new objective—a small knoll with some sandbags at its base.

Thirty meters. He could make it. Make a stand.

The enemy found something else to engage, which drew most of the fire off him.

It was time.

Brines popped up and raced toward the knoll. The ground was shit but manageable now that the murky top cover had thinned out and some moonlight was getting through. He was halfway there when he caught the silhouettes of two men. They were standing on Brines' fucking knoll as if casually observing the blood bath in the distance.

A thrill rushed through him, renewing his hopes for a meaningful death. It might just be a couple of snipers setting up, but there was always the chance it was a company commander trying to get eyes on the fight. Either way, it would be fitting revenge.

Surprise, motherfuckers!

Pure muscle memory from years of training jerked his weapon into alignment with his shoulder, and he fired without hesitation. The rifle's report was lost in the roar of battle—that or his hearing had long since jumped ship—but he could feel the shuttering recoil. He was putting rounds on target.

One dropped immediately, but the other figure remained standing like he didn't give a shit he was being shot at. All too soon, Brines felt the hollow thud of an empty magazine.

Before he could even think about slamming in a fresh one, gravity went apeshit. The ground spun up to smack his helmet, then flipped back down to receive him on his ass. There was no pain, but that didn't stop blackness from swallowing him.

———

Shaking.

It was the first sensation Sergeant Smith had perceived since entering the place of velvet-wrapped nothingness. Annoying, like an alarm clock blowing up on a Sunday morning when he was sleeping so good and didn't need to get up for anything. He tried waiting it out, waiting for that numb bliss to return, but it only got worse.

Curiosity.

He didn't usually shake. Unless he was cold.

Awareness began to expand beyond the confines of his skull to the rest of his body.

Not cold. No, he was a furnace, sweating in places that only got wet running through a carwash naked. Tired, too, as if he'd been exerting himself all day.

Or all night . . .

Was it an earthquake? Big earthquakes didn't happen where he lived in Kansas City, Missouri. It was nice, flat, and stable, just like he liked. Fuck the mountains and fuck earthquakes.

Wait, I ain't in Kansas City no more . . .

The sudden urge to jump into a bathtub or something for cover gripped him. Or was it hide under a tree? Where was his rifle? Through his jumbled thoughts, he became aware of overlapping voices.

"Come on, Jay. Wake up, goddamn it. I can't lose you too. Not you, man," the loudest voice pleaded.

Smith thought it sounded familiar but wrong. Too serious. Then again, it was hard to make out over the popping noises.

That ain't popcorn, fool; that's gunfire. Get the fuck up.

A cold adrenaline spike kicked his eyes open, bringing his huge muscles back under control. Sergeant Smith lurched into a sitting position, nearly throwing Cpl Nickels backward.

The shaking stopped.

"Oh, shit!" cried Nickels scrambling forward and grabbing Smith's face with his fingers. "Tell me you're okay, dude."

Smith batted Jersey away and did the three-slap check—both legs and dick were still attached.

"Jay, you hit? Where are you hit? Tell me where you're hit," Nickels demanded.

Smith worked his mouth to clear out the lingering cobwebs in his head and tried to muster a reply. But as he locked eyes with his buddy, he saw something that woke him the fuck up.

"Bro . . ." Smith began.

"Yeah, Jay?"

"Are you fuckin' crying?"

"What? No. Fuck no. Fuck you, Bone; it's hot as balls out. You know? Working overtime trying to wake your ass up. Sweat and shit running up under the lids. You're fuckin' seein' shit."

The memory download hit, and Smith just stared back. Nickels wasn't injured but had been screaming in some god-awful, mortal agony before things went dark.

He froze, Smith realized. *Lost his shit.*

It didn't make sense. He and Jersey had seen Marines killed in action and been in some damned tight spots. Neither of them ever froze; they always had each other's backs. Always. And even now, he wouldn't have believed it if not for staring right into those wet, frantic eyes. Pure panic.

Calm him down.

"Man, I feel like shit," Smith said, changing the subject. "What's our status?"

Nickels wiped his face and looked over his shoulder to that short wall they'd been running for when it all went to shit. "Not good. Two dead, three more down like you."

"Who dead? What you mean like me?"

"I was hangin' back, babysitting Francis over there when whatever it was hit you guys."

Smith peered through the darkness at the Marine sniper propped up against the side of a concrete divider snapping off rounds with an M4. Pete's rate of fire was rhythmic, almost soothing, and unrepresentative of the danger they faced in their precarious position. It was also a curious sight to see his Bullpup slung.

Enemy must be close.

"Sanchez and Nguyen got smoked, never saw it comin'," continued Nickels.

"Shit."

"I got up here fast. Man, I . . . I fuckin' thought you were done. I let 'em have it, y'know? But I was shooting like an asshole—just making noise to keep their heads down. I was sure they were gonna come hard. I . . . I woulda . . . I . . . and there was no way I was gonna let them gank our corpses for a load of ammo. I woulda taken care of it. You know?"

Bullshit, Smith thought. But now wasn't the time to call him out on a lie. Instead, he laid a heavy hand on Jersey's shoulder and said, "Yeah, man. You did good." He also wasn't going to waste his breath telling his friend to calm down. That'd be gasoline on a fire.

"Yeah, I uh, kinda lost my shit a little, too. Hell of a time we're having this morning, lemme tell you."

That admission was huge; Ryan Nickels rarely got real with anything less than a pint of whiskey in him.

It wasn't the best time to discuss anything other than staying alive, but Nickels was no good if his head wasn't on straight. Plus, no one was getting up until Francisco dealt with whatever was pinning them down. "Surprised you held 'em off for me," Smith said, stretching to reach his SAW a few feet away. "Figured you'd be gunnin' for my job the way you been actin' today."

"What? Man, no. I told you: fuck your job. You got that 'cause you ain't a fuckup. I'm just razzing you about the sergeant shit. You know that, right?"

"Then why you been acting all squirrely?"

Nickels dumped eye contact. "Just forget about it. I told you: we'll talk. Later."

So, somethin' else is *goin' on.*

Smith flashed back to the episode on the ship when he found Nickels in his bunk muttering to himself. Shit must've gone down before they even launched. *And I was too pumped up to think it was anything but jealousy. Fuck.*

Nickels took a breath and offered a rare, genuine smile. Smith acknowledged it (as buddies do), hoping their little chat was a big enough band-aid to get them through the next couple of hours. Or minutes. Maybe seconds if they kept wasting time.

With a quick glance at Francisco, Nickels registered the urgency and continued. "Well anyway, this bitch finally decided to show up and iced some of their heavies. Then me and Light managed to drag you, Williamson, Buontempo, and Garcia outta the line of fire. Hodgies haven't had the balls to move on us yet."

LCpl Light waved from beside LCpls Williamson, Buontempo, and Garcia in various stages of sitting up. It was like someone had hit them all with the *stun* setting. Apparently, Sanchez and Nguyen weren't so lucky.

Another loud pop and Francisco shouldered his rifle. Raising his night vision goggles, he shouted something inaudible.

"Say again?" yelled Smith.

Francisco shimmied over and said, "Pressure's off. Glad to see you up, Jay. Still intact?"

"I still got everythin' worth lookin' for."

Nickels laughed, a refreshing sign that he was getting his head back in the game, and said, "Bone, don't go teasing him about hardware he never had."

"Never had in my mouth," quipped Francisco.

"You motherfu—"

"Hang on a minute," said Smith sliding between the two men. "What happened to Gunny?"

———

Brines figured he'd taken a round the way his chest hurt. Still, his lungs were grabbing oxygen, pulse thudding steadily through the massive carotids in his neck, and nothing was sopping wet.

Vest must've stopped it.

He didn't remember hitting the ground.

Did I black out? Fer how long? He groped for his rifle but came up empty. He then went for his sidearm and tried to get his bearings. A mess of dark and blurry shapes danced among sandbags. *Must'a made it to that nest.* He shook his head, trying to clear his vision.

One of the shadows leaped at him.

Brines knew men on a primal level. When they wanted to kill you, they went for it. And when they thought they could gore you with a knife, they tried.

The pistol was caught under him, and there wasn't time to waste freeing it. Instead, his hand found the bone grip on his blade, and he slashed at the glinting steel of his attacker in one smooth movement. The figure's weapon disappeared into the darkness, and he hopped back, clearly caught off-guard by the straight blade-on-blade parry.

Brines launched a side kick, catching the man in the thigh and further propelling his rearward momentum.

That bought time. Vision clearing, Brines struggled to his feet, caring less that some sniper would pop his dome from afar and more that his death might be literally *at hand*. Facing the man on wobbly legs, chest pumping atmosphere, his free hand started again for his sidearm.

But then something else, something older within, forced his attention to the whites of those eyes glaring back at him. And the two men bore into each other for one of the brief eternities that dot the intervals between gunfire on the battlefield.

"You and me," came the enemy's challenge in a low growl.

Brines wasn't surprised the guy knew a few canned English phrases but being able to communicate seemed to kill the mood. It was short-lived, though, as a new sensation arose. The knife in Brines' hand felt impossibly right. The thought of discarding it now, when it was so close to tasting flesh, blood, and bone, was sickening.

He needed this kill.

It was his redemption, his revenge, his right. This fight had been preordained; no need for words.

Then, Brines felt a wash of icy blood flow through his veins as the man whose face seemed to cast its own shadows drew a glistening, wavy blade from his belt. It was not the sort of weapon carried by any front-line grunt in any army during any period of warfare in human history.

It was, however, the instrument of an assassin.

Suddenly there was no battle, war, Marine Corps, or anything else save the man in the nest. For the first time in a long time, Mike Brines realized he was being confronted by someone who not only wanted to feel him die but was probably quite capable of doing it too.

CHAPTER 14

BLOOD ON THE SIDES

The calm before the storm.

That moment of drawn breath preceding a great blow. It was a time of peace and reflection as previously pressing worries were crushed by the sheer magnitude of the impending threat.

Watching the blinding exchange of crackling gunfire and blast munitions between the Marines and remaining rebels, Saunders' thoughts strayed to his earlier phone call with Sarah.

Tell li'l T I love him.

Sarah was strong; she'd struggle through and probably have forty guys lined up to take Saunders' place in a hot minute. Eventually, she'd move on. But . . . Tommy. He would be the one to suffer if Daddy didn't come home. The kid was old enough now to start understanding the world and permeance. It wouldn't just be him growing up without a father, as it might've been a year or two ago.

He'd have memories of Daddy.

He'd have memories of Daddy's casket. And, for the rest of his life, Daddy wouldn't be there for him.

Saunders swallowed hard. Nothing was going to hurt Tommy on his watch, not even him. He had to survive.

Still, a strange sense of longing soaked through his steadfast determination. It was as if that call had happened years ago, and he wouldn't be able to share his joys and heartaches with Sarah for many more. It was a sense of impending distance, like saying goodbye.

Operational stress is a motherfucker, he decided, gripping his weapon tighter and forcing the thoughts down below.

He needed to be 100%.

The fireworks from First, Third, and Heavy Platoons suddenly intensified, while Second remained almost ghostly quiet around him. It was now or never.

"Lieutenant Lyons is thumbs up. Ten seconds!" shouted PFC Licht fumbling with his M4 combat rifle.

Saunders gave him a reassuring nod and gazed back over the Marines. LCpl's Gladstone and Fischer were crouched on his six with their weapons shouldered, eyes wide from either excitement or fear—or both—and ready for action. They were all a commander could ask for: men who put aside their most basic and powerful hesitations for trust in their leader's decisions despite a battle plan that had scraped by and teetered on the verge of collapse all morning.

The rest of his column was staggered throughout the wreckage, parts of concrete walls, haphazard piles of sandbags, and whatever else had been providing them with protection. Young eyes, some hard with experience and others still fresh and soft, met his with the same message, *oorah*.

It was inspiring because they all had someone back home too. A few—2ndLt Weber for sure—even had a young kid or two. *Babies having babies.*

Saunders' reservations drained away, and he turned cold and hard toward his enemies.

I'm going to survive this shit.

———

"They're fucked."

Admiral Bowman's final assessment resonated throughout the compartment. The nation of Pakistan was in flames as a new kind of war raged through its streets. The enemy, thought contained and ready for a final blow, was flying bombers over government-controlled cities and military targets with near-total impunity. Fleets of ground attack choppers harried staging areas. Signatureless munitions rained on safe houses and weapons depots with impossible precision. Enemy forces were repositioning with inexplicable mobility.

The only element that wasn't a question mark was what would happen next.

The inevitable clash with ground forces.

Pakistan was a sinking ship, and with it, the hope for regional stability. It would be a loss of an important ally, an opportunity for Iran to extend its influence, and in all probability, the tipping point for a nuclear exchange with India. The *what-if* scenarios were endless and exhausting to entertain. But at that moment, no one in the LFOC gave a damn about politics. Their eyes were glued to the big screen, showing an intensity-enhanced infrared contrast of the Ground Combat Element at Mina Bazar. The quality was terrible and clouded by the mysterious shroud cover, but the Charlie Company's intent was clear. They were massing for a futile attack on the enemy's complement of armored vehicles.

"There's got to be something," urged Colonel Ridge. "What's the status on the stealths?"

"Back in play," said LtCol Baud with a sigh.

"And?"

"And?" she said, throwing her hands up. "Are you looking for something else to get angry at? Everyone is screaming for air support, and every three out of four bombs dropped misses its target or fails to detonate. Causes unknown."

Standard operating procedure at this point; no love for the Marines. Next, thought Ridge.

"Well, why don't we try another Tomahawk? Or fifty fucking Tomahawks?"

Admiral Bowman massaged his temples. "You saw what happened to the last bunch. Whatever they've got is nullifying our over-the-horizon capabilities."

Ridge hadn't forgotten what happened to those ten cruise missiles. They flew perfectly from the point of launch only to explode a half-mile from the target. No missile defense system in the world was that accurate. They all blew up precisely at the same spot, give or take some drift in their approach vectors. It was almost like they'd hit a wall. An invisible wall.

Like . . . a shield.

He rolled his eyes at the thought. *Great, now I'm grasping at science fiction for answers.*

Still, it wasn't like anyone else was saying shit.

"I find it impossible that we can't talk to them," continued Ridge doing everything he could to fill the vacuum of brainpower. "What about the crash kits on the choppers? Do they operate on a frequency that isn't being blocked?"

"We tried everything, sir," responded a coms operator. "Full spectrum broadcasts, burst transmissions, the works."

"What about shooting a laser in there, tapping out the evacuation order in Morse code?"

"Colonel," began Admiral Bowman.

"Shoot the laser at a cloud, anything. Just get something flashing."

"Colonel!"

"What? We need to be thinking and spitting out ideas right now, *Admiral*."

"Nothing we or they do will matter because, in a few minutes, that energy build-up discharges. And it'll be like Hudud."

The compartment went silent.

"What we need to be doing," the admiral was now addressing everyone, "is paying close attention to what's about to happen. Because in the next battle, the stakes will be higher."

———

LCpl Gladstone lowered his night vision goggles and scanned no-man's land. What was once a grassy field cut by a road was now littered with trash and pocketed by craters. The rest faded into the creepy shroud save for sporadic flashes of Marine mortars detonating on the enemy lines.

"You boys ready?" shouted 2ndLt Weber, crouching low with a nearby fireteam.

"Hells yeah!" replied LCpl Fischer. He jabbed Gladstone in the arm. "It's gonna be thick as cow shit in there. Mind if I hang behind that big ol' shotty you got there?"

"I like to keep it handy for close encounters," Gladstone shouted back, quoting one of his favorite movies.

"I heard that," replied Fischer with the proper response.

Gladstone laughed. It probably wasn't the right time to be thinking about new friends, but something about serving in a combat zone made him feel like he'd known these guys forever. It was almost enough to counter the sense of dread building since that hell-fight in that nest they stupidly took. A sense that they were all about to die. Almost.

There was no need for a specific go-signal to get Second Platoon on its feet; the ordinance from the first, third, and heavy platoons was about as show-stopping an event as any. This was their final effort, and they held nothing back. The Marine Ground Element's biggest and best anti-personnel munitions became an angry, molten ocean crashing down on a lonely beach. An enemy beach.

"On me!" bellowed Captain Saunders leaping his fireteam over the concrete rubble and sprinting toward the fiery wash.

Gladstone pushed his emotions down into the pit of his stomach and bolted forward, shotgun ready. As he did, he felt the entire platoon moving in sync as if they were all connected by a giant array. Suddenly, this wasn't just him on a suicidal charge. He was part of an organism. A big one.

The C-monster.

Gladstone moved fast through the barricades into the foreboding openness of the grassy field. The dozens of boots crunching on spent brass around him were comforting but also highlighted the eerie quiet that had settled over the battlefield.

No one was shooting, not even the enemy.

He pushed himself hard, struggling to keep up with the captain's four-man stack as they drove into the murky haze. Over the road and back onto the worn grass, they advanced uncontested.

Maybe they can't see us coming? Gladstone thought, huffing and puffing in a struggle to see through the greenish fog displayed by his night vision goggles. It was getting thicker with every step. Soon, he found himself having trouble tracking the captain's team. He sped up but nearly banged his knees into the waist-high wreckage of some vehicle. He went around it, but then the captain's team was gone.

He crouched low and kept to his original course. The rest of the platoon was still moving all around but slower. His finger drifted reflexively to the shotgun's trigger. Visibility was ten feet, barely enough time to react if some dude came at him with a knife.

He was walking now, the silence of the fog giving him pause with each step. He felt like he was in the woods, fearful of stepping on a stick or crunchy leaves. Afraid that any sound would give away his position.

'Thicker than cow shit' is right, he thought as the fog enveloped him. Now he couldn't see anyone. He could hear them; it felt like everyone was still on plan, but being unable to see was disorienting. He checked his six, and a figure moved through the mists. Probably Fischer. He didn't dare call out.

Gunfire ripped through the night. Someone had made contact.

Gladstone lurched toward the noise. A bombed-out structure came into view. Finally, something to use as cover.

More reports filled the air as the exchange heated up. A spread of bullets ripped across the ground. Gladstone jumped as something tore at his boot, and he hit the deck.

A flash, strangely absent of noise, blinded him, and he reflexively knocked the night vision goggles off his face.

These pieces of shit are supposed to buffer lights!

He struggled to get his bearings. It was like standing in the shower, eyes stinging with soap, as the killer pulled back the curtain. Everyone was shooting but him, it seemed.

Where am I? Lost? Turned around?

The black spots floating across his vision started to shrink. He rose, shotgun at the ready, to get his back against that wall . . .

And came face to face with a human being.

It was blurry, but he could clearly see the sickly yellow of the enemy's uniform and shitty Kalashnikov rifle being aimed at his chest.

Gladstone fired first.

———

The big blast of Gladstone's twelve gauge was a relief to LCpl Fischer. Searching awkwardly through the haze for something to do other than bump into other Marines who were just as lost wasn't working. The firefight sounded close, but he couldn't seem to get there.

Chasing down the shotgun's punctuating report with his M4 cocked and shouldered, he soon caught sight of a building that was blown all to hell. It stirred a memory, something about staying away from blast zones because enemy artillery—

Whistling.

It was the unmistakable sound of incoming.

Fischer dropped and rolled until there was ground between him and the building.

Shouts for cover all around.

The shockwave roared overhead. Heat, pain. Deafening. The active earplugs couldn't stop sound from traveling up through bone. There was nothing to shoot back at, so he tucked and covered until it stopped.

When it was over, he saw a figure crouched against a portion of the building's wall that was still standing. At first, he figured it must be Gladstone. Still, as he stared at it, he could clearly make out the yellowish uniform of a Pakistani soldier.

He aimed his rifle but held off on the trigger. The other Marines around him were eyes forward but weren't reacting.

Could it be Gladstone?

Fischer shook his head and took another look. Clearly a Marine with an M4 strapped across his back.

Christ, must be getting sloppy. Almost fragged my new buddy.

"Movin' up!" he announced so Gladstone wouldn't make the same mistake.

As he got closer, Gladstone tossed the shotgun to the ground, pulled the M4 off his back, and unloaded at something around the bend. Fischer double-timed it and skidded next to him, ready to assist.

But something was wrong.

Between shots, Gladstone was screaming a nonsensical stream of curses mixed with guttural sobs at whatever was out there. The second his weapon clicked empty, he was down on one knee trying to slam in a fresh mag with shaking hands.

Fischer grabbed his arm. "Bud, calm down! Let me take a whack at 'em."

"I . . . I . . . it's . . . fuckers . . . it's," stammered Gladstone, wild eyes snapping back and forth in their sockets.

"You hit?"

"N . . . n . . . not me. Fuckers!" Gladstone's extra mag found its home in the base of his rifle, and he started to rise.

"Hold back. Let me get a look."

"NO!" Gladstone surged, his lanky frame pushing back with surprising strength.

Fischer, a corn-fed doughboy if there ever was one, had a bigger fight on his hands than expected. But weight won out, and he kept the smaller man pinned until he stopped resisting. Satisfied, Fischer turned to find out what was out there, what it was that set Gladstone off.

The fog was thinner up ahead. Through the night vision goggles, he could see plenty of hiding places among the rubble and jagged pieces of concrete poking out of the greenish mists in the background, but no human shapes or flickers of light. Then he panned down to the ground.

It was a Marine.

"Corpsman. Need a corpsman! Man down!" he shouted back into the deaf-and-blind haze. Maybe someone would hear him, but from the looks of the body, it was too late. The Marine's helmet was gone, along with the entire top of his head. Only a soft flap of barely recognizable face lay draped over the remains of his skull.

"Cover me," he shouted to Gladstone, crouching low and approaching the body.

Loadout said it all, but Fischer had to be sure. He pulled the left glove off and saw the glinting steel of the wedding band on his ring finger. Confirmed. *Damn.*

It was Second Lieutenant Weber.

Dropping back behind cover, Fischer understood Gladstone's rage. He must've seen it happen and lost his shit. Fischer shouldered his rifle. First thing he saw was getting drilled and planted. *First fucking thing.*

The enemy struck first.

Fischer's visual cortex registered movement; the next thing he knew, he was on his back, and his ears were ringing. The exposed areas of his skin stung like a boiled bullwhip had gone to work on them. Gladstone was looking down at him from farther up the wall shaking his head, mouth wide.

It took a moment, but eventually, the words navigated the chaos between Fischer's brain and mouth. "I . . . I ain't dead, man," he reassured his buddy.

Another explosion clapped, and the air came to life with a score of snaps and zips as whoever was out there poured on the heat.

"We gotta get out of here!" shouted Gladstone, finally making sense.

"Gotta pull the body back," said Fischer shaking it off and climbing to his feet. "We can't let 'em have it."

"No time; it's too hot," insisted Gladstone.

"I don't give a fuck."

"He's gone, man. He's fucked. He's bait."

Bait.

Gladstone was right. Fresh bodies were a predator's dream, and they had that shit zeroed with more than just artillery. Fischer was damned lucky he fell back when he did. They probably let him go, hoping more Marines would come forward. Corpsmen.

Fuck these assholes.

"All right," Fischer said finally. "But them fuckers just became my project. Let's break right, see if we can't get an angle on 'em."

Instead of agreeing and booking, Gladstone just stared back all cock-eyed. Like he was trying to figure something out. More likely, he was on the verge of shutting down.

"Come on, bud. Gotta do our job."

Gladstone studied him for an uncertain moment. But then, his eyes focused, and he nodded. "Let's get it done."

———

Life sucks, thought Saunders.

Whomever they were trading shots with had scurried back into their hidey-holes within the rubble, a classic feint to lure the Marines deeper into the murk.

The enemy wasn't stupid, but Saunders had prayed they weren't configured for a well-organized defense. Morale was everything right now and while running his men at breakneck speed toward an earth-shaking storm of explosions was daunting, it gave the Marines the initiative and momentum. A hope that their plan would work.

With stillness pouring in, every step forward into the thickening oily smoke and nauseating fumes felt like they were lambs to the slaughter. Lambs with horns, but still to the slaughter. All their built-up steam was cooling off. Fast.

Saunders slowed his pace to a crawl keeping his MP5 bolted to his shoulder and sweeping for the slightest wisp of movement. With his combat senses heightened, he could feel every step and stumble of his fireteams traversing the large chunks of asphalt, twisted metal, and other wreckage littering the pocketed terrain.

Suddenly, he spotted a contrast bright spot and sucked in a short breath.

Contact!

Wait. Scratch that. It was just a severed hand.

Someone laughed. A low chuckle but deafening to his ears. This wasn't the time to get into a shushing battle. The men knew their places, and he'd take a giggle over a scream any day.

Still, that hand was fresh enough that the blood still glistened on what remained of the wrist.

They had reached the enemy defensive line.

He signaled the men within eye-sight fan out and take cover. His experience was that even the most impressive bombardments—from land, sea, or air—had 50% attrition of enemy forces as an upper ceiling. Large, mechanized targets pushed that percentage higher. Still, despite all the propaganda about how efficient, smart, and powerful the Marine Corps' weapons were, it was never wise to underestimate a man's ability to burrow and survive. Hell, he'd seen it today with a veritable army still standing after the initial strike that was supposed to destroy infantry combat capacity.

Stillness.

He ordered his Marines forward. They were urban assault, now, moving in tandem from cover to cover through the ruins of a once vibrant and lively administrative park. It used to house the airfield's civilian coordinators, perhaps even American advisors before the coup. But now, it was shadows of half-formed, broken structures fading into a greenish haze to their vision-enhanced eyes, cut off from the rest of the world.

It was the enemy's battlespace.

The base's garrison had lived, breathed, and fought here all morning. Judging from the coils of new barbed wire and developed fighting positions with interconnecting trenches, they'd planned to lose the detention center. *Smart.* And aside from the hand and a few bodies, they'd clearly been successful in falling back.

But to where?

The infuriating quiet continued save for crunching boots, labored breaths, and the sporadic rattle of gunfire to the east, which Saunders hoped was Brines kicking ass. Or at least methodically opening another front against these fuckers and making progress toward the TOC. He already regretted not giving Brines more men. Hell, maybe even the bulk of the company so First Platoon and SEAL could run the evac while the enemy's guns were turned east.

The *what-if* scenarios on what he could have done differently would probably drive him wild for the rest of his life—which would be a long while because he was going to fucking survive this. So, now wasn't the time.

The Marines kept moving, crawling over smashed gun emplacements, bodies, shredded chain-link fencing, and lines of barbed wire. The tension was tangible; it was that instant before the scales tipped, the dam cracked, the legs buckled, the bough broke, the heart stopped, the phone rang . . .

Every inch forward was another past the point of no return.

Until all hell broke loose.

———

As PFC Licht dove for cover behind a mound of dirt and rebar-spiked concrete that couldn't hide a five-year-old, he couldn't help but admire the other two Marines in the captain's fireteam. Baker and Carvalho didn't flinch, bitch, or waiver. They planted their feet and ripped into the soldiers pouring out of the haze.

Fearless.

They were the kinds of men Licht had always looked up to, always envied. The ones who'd get the medals, the girls, and the knowing smiles from those who mattered. Guys like that went home every night more sung than blamed.

The ground between Licht's knees popped and sparked.

He tried to compress himself against the mess of rubble when something like a maul pounded him on the back. He went flat, weapon and arms pinned beneath him.

"Cover! Cover!" yelled the captain over the exchange.

Licht hurt but figured the pain would be much worse if he had a hole in him. Until it felt like death, he was still in the fight.

He moved slowly, the air crackling in all directions, super self-conscious about accidentally sticking out an elbow or a foot. A body fell beside him with a sickening thud—compliments of the active earplugs. It was one of the Marines who held his ground.

"Cover fire!" shouted the captain again.

No excuses; Licht just needed to move fast and start shooting back. *Fire enough rounds and the rifle becomes the cover.*

Go.

Licht readied himself for a pushup and quick left roll into a new fighting position when his earpiece went live.

A voice.

At first, he thought it was filtering through the ambient noise, but then a burst of static said it was coming from coms. The words were garbled, confusing.

Compelling.

He strained to listen. It came again, but fainter this time. He was sure he could grab it if he stayed put and muffed his ears. *The firefight can wait,* he found himself thinking. Listening to the radio message was more important.

Then he caught a glimpse of the face on the body beside him.

Baker.

Licht shook his head. Marines were dying; fight and win first.

He forgot about the two-sizes too-small defilade and rose to one knee. Rifle free, he dove into the fight. An enemy helmet popped out of the dirt like a gator coming up for a breath. Licht lined up the shot. Before he could pull the trigger, the radio whispers whipped into a screeching howl. It was almost enough to make him yank out the earpiece.

Almost.

Instead, he found his focus by driving high-velocity bullets into that gator head and at two more soldiers running between defilades. The pair dropped and rolled out of view. But Licht was pretty sure he'd scored some hits. They'd be hurting.

Keeping his rifle bouncing from one possible hiding spot to the next, he grabbed a few mental snapshots of his fellow Marines. They'd made quick work of that squad, and more beige forms were leaping from cover to cover ahead of them. The captain directed another fireteam toward a long concrete wall blocking their view north.

Licht's eyes settled on Baker. Crimson dribble bubbled up from his lips and trickled down his face. He was still, eyes fixed skyward. Unfocused. It still looked human, but it was meat. The same meat for sale at a grocery store. Just dead mass. It didn't sicken Licht, but he felt terrible that there weren't any last words.

Felt bad that the guy wouldn't be getting laid.

He gritted his teeth as his overactive mind began questioning and replaying the decision to dive for cover. Captain had said cover, so he took cover. It's not like he ran away in terror. It was an order. Everyone should have ducked behind something before fighting back too. Right? Baker paid for standing his ground, not because Licht ran for cover first. Right?

Covering fire . . .

Dread filled Licht as it became hard to remember exactly what the captain ordered. Covering fire was a lot different than the order to cover. But something was wrong. It was like a new memory was implanting itself over the old one. It felt odd, unnatural. If it wasn't so fresh, it might've fooled him. But it didn't. The captain clearly said *cover,* and Licht followed orders. Nothing was his fault here. Nothing at all.

It is your fault.

That stopped him cold. As clear as day, he just heard a fucking voice. It might've been the radio, but it had none of the usual digitized audio. And it definitely did not pass through his ears.

No, he'd just heard a voice in his head. Battle fatigue, shell shock, concussions, and all that stuff were real and probably explanatory. But it was also a lie, messing with his mind. He needed to lock it down.

Not your fault, not your problem. Sack-up and follow the captain, he told himself.

He lined up another shot, a blur moving past a gap in a ruined building, and iced it no problem. Then two Marines moved up and hooked the arm pits of the body next to him. There were no shouts for corpsmen or any attempt to check a pulse or something. They just dragged Baker out of the way.

Another flicker of movement commanded three shots from Licht's rifle.

A low growl radiated from his earpiece. Probably not a priority contact from Hawk. It sounded like frustration, but Licht refused to spend any more time thinking about it. He'd seen what happened when men listened to the voices in their heads and interacted with them. It made them look crazy.

David Licht wasn't crazy.

The captain slid out of cover and waved his fireteam toward that concrete wall. Other teams shored up his flanks. Licht followed, eyes running over every crevice, searching for stray or not-completely-dead enemies. Focused, in the zone, not crazy.

Others, rippled the voice one last time.

———

The shroud hung heavy in the air despite the steady breeze blowing across the ravaged landscape. Beyond the reinforced wall Second Platoon was using for cover, nothing was recognizable as human construction. It was blackened rubble, a mess of shit where small pockets of enemy fighters lay like mines hoping to slow the Marine advance as their larger groups retreated.

LCpl Gladstone should have felt relief, but the murk was thick and felt like it had settled deep into his chest. A new weight threatened to crush his soul with every breath. That fateful shotgun blast replayed in his mind, and he nearly doubled over from a wave of nausea.

A loud crack and a *whoop.*

Gladstone turned to his right and saw LCpl Fischer's face light up as he studied something through the scope on his M40 sniper rifle. Gladstone held his stare until Fischer took up the offer of eye contact.

"Ain't no one gonna have trouble grabbin' Lieutenant Weber now," Fischer said solemnly.

Gladstone nodded, but inside, his heart was hammering boulders. When this was all still contested territory, there was a chance that Weber's body would get left behind in the chaos. But now, the fight was cooling, and the enemy appeared to be in retreat. More than one Marine had already been pulled back. Weber was just a matter of time.

"Your rifle workin' there, hoss?" Fischer asked with that smile still splayed across his face.

There was no way Fischer could know. But suspect? *He might suspect.* At the very least, command would figure it out soon enough. There'd be enough evidence to raise questions. They'd interview everyone and figure out Fischer was the closest witness. After that, it'd get pieced together.

Court martial.

Prison.

No question about it, considering I'm the only fucking one out here with a damned shotgun!

"Bro, you alright?"

Deny. Lie. Deny. Lie.

"Yeah. Just wondering why they're falling back."

The concern was as genuine as it was a convenient subject change. The rebel effort to retake the detention center had been well-organized and determined despite the Marine Corps' shit-ton of high-tech disruption equipment. Even after getting repelled, they still fielded a sizable force. It didn't make sense for them to run now when they held such a solid defensive advantage.

"Maybe they're just stringin' up some new fightin' positions to tear us all to bits if we advance again," mused Fischer dropping his eye behind his scope. Gladstone wasn't sure if those precision optics were even helpful when they could barely see beyond pistol range. Still, seconds later, the long gun cracked the disquieting night, and Fischer seemed satisfied.

Hide. Survive. Hide. Survive.

The words rippled across Gladstone's mind like a ship's wake through a stormy surf. They were his thoughts but felt forced or artificial. He couldn't be sure if it was something he'd heard or imagined. But then the small, primitive animal within him caught up, and he suddenly needed to hide.

Hide and survive.

Gladstone ducked down, frantically searching for better cover. A hole or cave in which to burrow until the storm passed.

"You see something?" asked Fischer, joining him.

Gladstone opened his mouth to explain but couldn't find the words. In that space between breaths, Fischer's ears perked up, and he swapped out his sniper rifle for the M4.

"You hear that?" he asked, head snapping back and forth. "There's somethin' out there, man."

In the world where their ears had become their eyes, Gladstone couldn't hear whatever Fischer was talking about. But, somehow, he knew what was coming.

Hide. Survive. Hide. Survive.

Struggling to follow Captain Saunders, watch his footing, and stay aware of the shadows and innumerable hiding places, PFC Licht found himself numb to the fact that every breath might be his last. The terror that had initially seized him when the captain slapped him on the shoulder and said, "You're on me," remained. But it was muted, oddly enough, by his sense of self-preservation.

Forget the fear; fight the thing that's tryin' t' kill ya.

Gunny Brines' words. Somewhere between that fateful day when Licht decided to make something of his life and now, the Marine Corps replaced the basic human tendency to flee danger with a compulsion to engage. Far from the invincibility he'd felt with friends while getting in trouble back home, it was a sort of logic plated over his original programming.

A demand for rationality over primitive animal emotion.

Licht crouched to cover an advancing fireteam. The team made good time despite frequent checks for tripwires and anything that might mean the place was boobytrapped. When they reached the big wall blocking the way north, Licht started to fantasize about how safe it would be behind something so solid and sturdy that it had survived all the fighting pretty much untouched. Of course, the captain would probably set them up on its more crumbled end, but at least they would have that angle covered.

Captain Saunders chopped his hand forward, and Licht rose to follow. The fireteam at the wall turned around and started waving. *Signaling all clear,* was Licht's first thought.

There was no second thought.

The world vanished. His skin stung from an invisible slap that passed through and hammered against the back of his skull. He dropped flat on his ass, incapable of thought. It was the most shocking, painful sensation he'd ever known, something he would have nightmares about for the rest of his life.

Disoriented, he lay paralyzed as Marines scrambled in all directions. Then Captain Saunders was under his arms, shouting and dragging. Licht tried kicking his legs to help support his weight, but nothing was answering the helm.

Breathing hard, the captain dumped him behind some cinderblock rubble.

More cinderblocks.

Everything was made of cinderblocks here. *Was there a special on cinderblocks at Lowes when they built the place?* As other funny thoughts percolated through his detached fugue, he rolled his head to see where that forward fireteam was. *Probably running like hell.*

BANG!

That strong, concrete wall became a rush of debris shooting overhead as though blasted from a gigantic shotgun.

Whoa.

"Fall back!" the captain screamed as another section of the wall exploded, swallowing two Marines in a gust of smoke. The muffled flash and directional spray from each hit triggered a distinct memory in Licht's mind from Marine Combat Training. Specifically, the day they were invited over to the Advanced Infantry Training Battalion to watch some tank target practice. It was a lot of fun.

The sludge of thoughts oozing through the folds of his brain made it hard to focus on the importance of that one memory. It was somehow related to what the captain was saying and why no one was returning fire.

Another blast knocked the sense back into Licht, and all those ungraspable dots suddenly connected.

The tanks!

Captain Saunders kept calling for a retreat. The rumbling and creaking of treads were audible now, just beyond the wall. The captain stole a frantic look back the way they came and sorta froze. Like he wasn't sure what to do or something.

Getting himself back under control, Licht turned his head, hoping to spot their next objective so he wasn't just following blindly. Instead, he saw what Captain Saunders' desperate eyes saw.

Nothing.

There should have been at least an aerial flare indicating the direction of the Marine perimeter, a signal punching through the swirling blackness. But they'd come too far. Or maybe the murky shroud had thickened again. Whatever the case, Second Platoon had succeeded in luring the tanks out but were too scattered and disorganized to rally rearward before those tanks could roll right over them.

A flood of thoughts: *the Heavy Weapons Platoon can't see us, can't help us. Gunny Brines and his men haven't opened any second front of attack. The skies are closed, and we're not—*

Another round landed, muting Licht's world.

The captain pulled him up, and they ran, hunting for cover. When Licht's hearing returned, Captain Saunders was calling for everyone to find cover.

Only, it sounded more like screaming than an order.

CHAPTER 15

INFANTRY DOCTRINE

You feelin' good, sir?" Sgt Smith asked. He scanned the wheezing Marine's olive-green flight suit for dark splotches as the rest of his men secured the crash site. Gunny had said there might be friendlies out here. Only a priority by proximity, though.

"When I'm not breathing," croaked the pilot with a faint smile.

"Think you can walk?"

"Yeah."

Smith tossed a thumbs up back to the rest of his patchwork team and panned the scattered wreckage of the downed Viper attack helicopter. There was almost nothing left bigger than a mailbox, and most of that was unrecognizable.

"They shot it up pretty bad after we hit," the pilot said. "Seat cracked loose and took me with it. Landed right over there. I got lucky they didn't search around a bit more."

"You the only one?"

"Yeah," he replied with a frown. "Captain Case Rath."

"Sergeant Smith."

"A damned pleasure, Smith." He looked around at the wreckage and winced at some memory. "We hit on the nose. Gurka . . . ah . . . my gunner didn't make it."

Smith shook his head. "Day's been fucked up, sir. Coms is down. You lucky we stumbled 'cross you."

"Find anyone else? Before the crash radio cut out, they made it sound like there were some other *maydays*."

Smith steeled himself. It wasn't his call. It really wasn't anyone's call.

It was just a fact. "Ain't a priority right now."

Captain Rath dropped his eyes and sighed. "Figures."

"Yeah, well . . . though it hurts, you still breathin'. Dig?"

"What's the plan?"

"We gunnin' for the TOC."

"The ops center?" he asked with eyes widening as they panned over the remains of Smith's squad.

"Yeah, we got chopped up pretty bad. Lost a lot of good people gettin' this far; ain't gonna bug out now."

"Looks like you need every man you can get. Mind if I tag along?"

"Respectfully, sir; you sure you can hack it?"

Capt Rath took one more look back at the wreckage and climbed to his feet. Then with a small, wheezing laugh, he croaked, "I can hack it!" It was a decent impression of Private Cowboy from *Full Metal Jacket*. The smile faded. "Damn, Gurka loved that movie. Ready."

Smith had LCpl Williamson bring up an extra rifle and set Capt Rath toward the rear of their formation, where he'd least likely be the first one to die. Keeping his M249 SAW up and sweeping, Smith joined Nickels on point. The way forward appeared clear, and a thumbs up from Francisco confirmed it. Low and quiet, the squad resumed its trek through the darkness.

Aside from scattered rifle cracks and booms in the distance, the battlefield was calm. Especially compared to that barrage they'd heard not too long ago. It was so quiet and under control that Smith's thoughts wandered back to the look on Capt Rath's face when he realized there wouldn't be any body recovery. It hurt. Smith would've made the same face, maybe worse. But until this shit show let up, that's how it was.

"You ok, man?" asked Nickels. He'd gone from losing his shit to motherly, and Smith wasn't sure which one was worse. "You're like . . . quiet."

"We movin', dawg. Hush it."

"Slide back a bit; I got point covered. You might have a concussion."

Smith shook his head, which was a painless affair reinforcing the fact that he did *not* have a concussion. "Chill the nanny crap. We got a war to win." He tried thinking back to when Nickels first started acting weird. He was fine at breakfast, formation, all day, really. It wasn't until Smith found him sitting on his bunk talking to himself.

What was he saying?

Jersey had been whispering, but Smith caught at least part of it. Unfortunately, the exact words were lost in the lifetime of brain damage that had occurred since then.

"Yut," whispered Francisco, skipping past him and Nickels with his Bullpup shouldered. The big gun may have been a shortened variant of the regular .50 caliber sniper rifle, but that didn't mean it was wieldy like the lightweight carbines. It was a heavy-barreled son of a bitch meant to be fired prone, not standing. *Only a bad man rocks one of those like an assault rifle.*

Smith held up a fist and his squad scattered into the shadows. "Talk to me, Pete."

Ignoring him, Francisco crawled up the grassy hill they'd been using to conceal their approach to the TOC. At the top, he dropped his night vision goggles to his eyes and panned. A moment later, he shimmied down.

"Got a view on the objective. They're stocked and staged."

"Be pretty dumb if they weren't," said Nickels crouching nearby.

"Only one shooter with glass, though. The rest are big guns and mean dudes. And a fucking submarine door buttoning up the entrance."

"We got somethin' for that," said Smith smiling.

"Oorah," added Nickels.

"I can probably clear out the shooter and two or three of the gunners before they concave the fuck out of this hill," said Francisco.

"We'll circle around, push hard and light 'em up, Pete. They won't get near you."

"Appreciate it, but I'm going to get mobile after the third round."

"It's you, baby. Aight, we got a plan." Sergeant Smith waved the rest of the squad forward. They'd trained for this. Assaulting a fixed position was a rifleman's bread and butter.

Cut open a hole in the enemy's overlapping positions, push in, and gut them.

The problem was what happened after that. They'd done plenty of breach and clear building-to-building operations, but those were with cordons and some intel on the interior situation. There was no telling the layout of that bunker beyond the door. He needed a minute to think.

"Let's grab a quick sip of water," Smith said when everyone was within earshot. No one disagreed. He twisted the top off his canteen full of cherry-flavored taurine, but Jersey was in his face before he could get it to his lips.

"Bone, let's get you back to the LZ."

"You hurt, Jay?" asked Francisco.

"Nah, bro. Jersey's just bein' tender."

"Fuck both of you. Everyone feels fine, and then they die. That's how it works."

"You want to fill me in here?" asked Francisco.

"Concussion," said Nickels.

Francisco reached over and managed to unbuckle the chinstrap and pull Smith's helmet off in one swift motion. He then ran a gloved hand over the freshly shaved scalp and slapped him on the side of the head. Smith playfully batted the hand away.

"I think you need a head injury to have a concussion," Francisco said, returning to his rifle.

"Nuh-uh," insisted Nickels. "The brain can rattle or . . ."

Smith wasn't listening anymore, although he kept one eye on his two buds to ensure no one else was trying to broadside him again. The other eye settled on the remaining four Marines and Marine Pilot.

At best, we got two teams.

Keeping Nickels as a fireteam leader was the real issue. He had the rank. But his head was screwy, and this concussion shit was just nails in the coffin. On the other hand, slapping Jersey in the face by replacing him with a subordinate might check him out permanently. At minimum, their friendship would be on life support. Smith could argue both sides but ultimately had to go with his instincts.

"Aight, listen up, break's over. If we wanna go home, we gotta clear this bunker. We goin' in bayonets fixed. No bullshit. Two teams—"

This is it: pull him or don't? Ah fuck. You chicken!

"—Corporal Nickels leads Alpha; I'll lead Bravo. Alpha takes the right flank, and Bravo's goin' left. We get into position and assess. Do our thing the second Francisco drops their heavies. Then it's the door, the sweep, and the fuckin' jewels. Got friendlies in there and maybe a super weapon. Fucked up?"

"Fucked up!" cheered the squad.

It got a chuckle out of Capt Rath.

————

Something was different.

The steady stream of soldiers bringing wounded had stopped. Her two guards were gone. *Again.* And Dr. Pat's "helpers" had clammed up, spending an increasing amount of time eying the room's only exit. Probably a consequence of the once distant thumps and rips of gunfire that were getting louder by the minute.

The door flew open, and the uniformed man everyone addressed as *colonel*—likely the base commander—stuck his head in with wild eyes. They settled on Dr. Pat. He barked something, which she either didn't catch, or maybe he was speaking in his native Urdu. It didn't matter; she was done trying to figure out their mind games.

"What?" she yelled back, astonished at how taxing the effort was. *I'm running on fumes.*

His dark, bushy eyebrows popped up as if surprised by her voice. Then, scowling, he spat something unintelligible, turned, and fled down the hallway without bothering to close the door.

Her heart fluttered as she processed the fact that, once again, her cage was left open. It was so compelling that she forgot about the whimpers coinciding with the slight rise and fall of Micky's chest and stepped toward the dim opening to peer into the hallway.

The sight of men dragging some gigantic machine gun immediately cemented her feet back in reality. Those dirty, bloodied soldiers didn't look happy, but they weren't beaten either. They were gearing up for a fight to the end, which meant she had no chance of slipping past.

What am I doing?

She turned back to the makeshift infirmary. To the occupied cots, the dirty blanket beds on the cold concrete floor, and the moaning wounded lining the walls. One look at all those drooping heads as they waited on the chance to be seen was all she needed. *I have no business leaving.* Even if the entire building was surrounded and all she had to do was slip out the back door. They needed her.

Micky needed her.

So, she closed the door and turned to her helpers. She gave them a cold, practiced stare. The no-bullshit, trauma-ward invocation of authority above bodily and worldly concerns. And any glimmer of hope in their faces melted into cowed submission.

"No one is leaving."

———

Brines fumed.

He prided himself on his ability to eat shit the last mile of an uphill marathon and smile as they told him to turn around and do it again. But as he got older and the fights got harder, he was butting up against the point of failure more often than he cared to admit.

It was his own damned fault too. *Legendary* Gunny Brines was a fucking recruiting pamphlet, not an infantry tactic. Instead of respecting that, respecting the new man he was trying to be, he let that ego operate his mouth. Let that legend make promises he and, worse, his men couldn't keep.

A fucking gunnery sergeant shouldn't be running fireteams full of lance corporals like he's some spring chicken.

Abe.

Sergeant Major Ward was the real deal. A towering figure because he inspired from his position, not positioned himself to inspire. Not positioned himself on the frontline so he could get shot in some insecure attempt to be legendary.

The worst part of this colossal failure was that Brines had let Ron down. This wasn't some no-name operation in the desert. It was happening right in fucking front of the whole world. Goddamned Colonel Ridge probably saw Sgt Gilbert and his men die from a hundred miles up. Every media drone in the world was probably feeding it onto YouTube. Millions laughing at the geriatric gunny who couldn't handle his shit. Led his team right into an obvious fucking ambush.

The world doesn't matter, he told himself, *just the men.* But as far as he was concerned, they were everyone. So, it might as well have been the world. How the fuck was he gonna have the balls to ask them to follow him into battle going forward?

Fact was, he did have the balls. But that didn't mean he liked it.

He panted his feet and dodged a thrust using only his waist. Brines was at the wrong angle to get in a counter stab—too damned slow—but landed a nice elbow shot to the assassin's chest. It slid up and connected with the fucker's chin, driving him back. Huffing, Brines felt a sharp pain in his side.

A cut!

He will kill you.

Brines backpedaled, suddenly uncertain of what disturbed him more: his opponent landing a strike with such a novice move or that he was starting to hear voices.

———

Fireteams Alpha and Bravo swept forward mechanically, keeping their angles and each other covered. Sergeant Smith would've marveled at how well shit was working without any bitching and moaning, but then he would've needed some wood to knock on.

Shots rang out in the distance, and the exchange between the bulk of the Ground Element and dug-in rebels reignited. Although it sounded closer than before, Smith tried to concentrate on their goal. He was behind schedule, and every second risked exposure. The enemy would be on them like fire ants if they got caught out here.

To his relief, the area was still calm and dark when he got his binoculars on the unscathed enemy TOC.

The reinforced concrete structure was exactly as Francisco had described: a classically engineered refuge. Its low profile and sloped roof were made to deflect incoming ordnance, while the only visible entrance was protected by two heavily sandbagged machine-gun nests positioned to repel infantry. More sandbags also lined the foundation walls.

"Wait for Francisco," he whispered to Bravo. He took a moment to shift the tight straps of his modular pack. Felt like a bucket of cool water poured over his shoulders. Carrying all that gear also left him soaked in sweat. So much so that he was probably redlining dehydration and running on pure adrenaline. And taurine.

Hope that's enough.

As the seconds ticked by, it felt like this was too easy. No way the TOC guards were oblivious to the chance that they were sitting in somebody's crosshairs. They must've known that the Marines were operating outside the detention area after their ambush team went offline.

Maybe they think they're untouchable 'cause the TOC ain't takin' fire yet.

Also, the guards were low profile, decked to the tits in body armor, and probably thought they had a chance behind those big guns. But shit, it couldn't have been that reassuring.

On the other hand, maybe they were wondering who would be crazy enough to attack a hardened facility.

Suddenly, Smith's thoughts were interrupted by something . . . unusual. Familiar.

It rose over the battlefield from back the way they came.

A howl, wild and primal.

Now we gotta deal with animals out here too?

Bomb sniffers or even junkyard attack dogs would fit the bill. The Marines around him tilted their heads, listening for it again. *That ain't no damned dog,* Smith decided. It was something etched in his brain. Recognizable. Like . . . like someone's voice.

His veins turned to ice. *It's human. The hell is happening out here?*

Francisco's Bullpup thundered, and Smith put the howl out of his mind. It was go time.

———

Molded bone—still white after countless years.

A battered and worn Marine Corps emblem sat fused into the ivory pommel. The adiabatic shear banding that they all said made the blade weak rippled outward like a determined ocean rushing toward the world's edge. Two-sided with a four-inch serration climbing the stout spine into a wicked concave curve that could whip through flesh and crack rock, the knife was anything but weak.

They said Brines got lucky with the M390 steel—new age shit that would forgive his mistakes. But anyone who'd ever touched a forge knew better.

Knew something different when they saw it.

Maybe it was the carbon, some unique contaminant in the alloy. Maybe it was the cryo-quenching. Maybe it was the hate he put into every hammer swing. But his blade could slice corneas and parry a crowbar.

It was a last resort weapon in a wireless world. And once again, despite all the technology and advanced weaponry of the modern battlefield, it was unsheathed.

The enemy studied him, having withdrawn a few steps in response to the primitive roar that consumed the thunderous battle around them.

Brines didn't mean it to come off as macho as it did. It was an automatic reaction one might give to scare off a dog or meth addict in the heat of the moment. But the deed was done. Both men now appreciated the challenge they faced. Clearly, they shared the fact that neither of them expected to find an enemy here with more substance than a smoking barrel.

The moment was brief but memorable. "Ra'num," the man said.

"Brines."

Ra'num's wavy dagger slipped in to take a piece of Brines' forehead.

Brines dodged and tried to counter, but the blade swooped around and drove down toward his right side, trying to capitalize on a perceived defensive weakness.

This time he managed to twist out of the way, but it almost cost him his balance.

The assassin moved to exploit the stumble, but Brines learned long ago how to turn every bit of momentum, even a misstep, to his advantage. Using the raw strength in his upper arms and shoulders, he snapped a respectful thrust and swipe.

Ra'num's eyes widened, but he jumped back even faster.

Goddamned ninja shit.

Shifting stances and the orientations of his hands as though he were reeling in a fish, Ra'num lunged three more times with dynamic styles of attack. It would've cut down most other men, but Brines was starting to warm up. Parry, dodge, feint. All countered with an increasingly efficient defense.

Definitely getting' into the zone, Brines thought as warmth spread through his arms into his core.

Now he stood a little taller, and Ra'num grew timider in his approach. Something stirred within Brines through the swirling mix of rage, fatigue, guilt, and desire to right his wrongs. The skills he honed so long ago were awakening and reintegrating into muscle memory.

He struck.

He blocked.

He anticipated.

The old Brines—the animal long locked away in the darkness—rattled his cage.

The assassin thrust, and Brines parried.

Another stab and Brines smacked the offending arm down.

Enraged, Ra'num launched himself into a flurry of attacks. Brines worked his forms hard, weaving his hands and the blade through a narrow ribbon of operating space to deflect, counterattack, and deflect again. But it was too much. The assassin finally forced him on his heels.

Fuck he's good.

Defeat was inevitable at this pace. Brines was out of gas and probably dealing with a concussion from whatever knocked him out before.

In that moment of weakness, two things happened: Brines lowered his eyes in resignation and . . .

The cage broke.

The old Brines seized the reins and reveled in the privilege of dying a free man.

Ra'num sensed it immediately, the change within his adversary. Suddenly, he wasn't fighting a man with hopes of a future; he was trapped in a pit with a wild animal.

With his blade tucked close, Gunny stared deep into Ra'num and saw what he craved.

Fear.

Ra'num struck with a swipe that would have unseated most men. Gunny knocked it aside without breaking eye contact, a master toying with his student. Ra'num raised an eyebrow and muttered something in his native tongue that sounded nasty enough.

Suddenly, the battlefield lit up as new flares managed to break through the thick haze. Gunny took in the sight of his prey in the fresh light. He was wiry, which spoke to his attack speed and body-weighted style. A crescent moon ISI emblem was clearly visible on his outstretched right arm. Brines wondered how much of the intel for *Sea Monster* had been provided by corrupt ISI agents.

A nod.

A glare returned.

Gunny then drew a breath and relaxed his muscles. Sometimes, control was letting go. And everything was about control.

Ra'num struck fast at the neck—as expected—not realizing his mistake until his arm was fully extended. Gunny's left hand whipped around to grab the man's wrist and then pulled forward. The wavy blade slid harmlessly past its target, exposing Ra'num's guts.

Gunny's killing blow was smooth and merciful.

———

"Jersey, that door gonna be a problem?"

Corporal Nickels lifted his head out of the shadows and studied the reinforced steel entrance to the TOC. After a few seconds, he started rummaging through the outer pockets of his pack and waved LCpl Garcia over. The two of them soon came to a consensus, and Nickels shook his head *no*.

"Good," Smith said. His lower back was already tingling from the start of another adrenalin pump. How much more did he have to give? *Unlimited*. They'd secured the TOC's perimeter like the swinging dicks they were, and now it was time to hollow it out. "Wire it, bro. Everyone else stack up and stay frosty."

Dropping one-liners from movies was a sure sign of how tired he was. Still, no one was complaining.

The distant thudding escalated again into what sounded like a serious ass-pounding and, with it, a new sense of urgency. Francisco had said it looked like the other Marine platoons were trying to advance. Smith hoped they weren't because whatever made those big booms was nothing short of a vehicularly-mounted motherfucker.

Otherwise known as a tank.

"Double-time, guys," Smith urged.

"Heads up," hissed the darkness seconds before Francisco sprang up from behind one of the sandbag barriers.

"You just got this Viper pilot's heart going, buddy," breathed Captain Rath.

"We're on the clock, Smith," said Francisco.

"I know. Get yourself on overwatch. Cap'n Rath, you cool to back him up?"

"Roger."

"Think the six of us are enough to take this place apart?" asked Nickels, molding their compliment of clay-like explosive into the door's frame. That ten-inch-thick bitch wasn't budging for anything short of a 120 mm sabot round, but the supports were just concrete and steel contact points.

"We gonna make 'em feel our pain, bro."

Nickels stopped. It was hard to make out in the mix of shadows and sweat-smeared face paint, but he was pretty sure Jersey was wincing at something, maybe a memory.

"Yeah, man," was all he said.

———

Brines checked the corpse for signs of life before reaching down to pluck the wavy blade out of death's grip. There wasn't much to see in this light, but it was going in the collection. He unhooked the sheath from the corpse's belt, taking note of the second empty sheath—home to the other blade that had gone missing—and then moved to recover his weaponry.

After a second thought, he paused out of respect for the fallen. This Ra'num might've been his enemy and a traitor to his own people, but the fight had been clean.

But why?

This wasn't a cage match or a sanctioned title shot. This was a knock-down, drag-out, tooth-and-nail, throw-your-shit-in-his-face fight. There weren't any rules. Was this guy some fanatic hell-bent on an honor code? Brines could respect that, but he didn't buy it.

You relied on your blade as well.

Brines would've jumped ten fucking feet if his legs weren't filled with lead from the adrenaline dump.

That fucking voice!

No way would he give it the satisfaction of hearing him scream for it to get out of his head. No way, but damn, it was tempting. *This me snapping?* He'd seen bigger vets than him lose their shit, just sit down in the middle of a firefight and open an MRE like it was chow time.

Everyone had their limit. One mission, ten missions, it was inevitable. Problem was he thought he snapped a long time ago, and this was the glorious aftermath.

You have potential.

Brines spot-checked himself for injuries. Aside from the cut on his side, which stung just a bit and had already stopped bleeding, he was fully functional. *Maybe I knocked my skull harder than I thought when I blacked out?* Whatever this voice was, it was a distraction. Sergeant Smith's team needed him. Taking that TOC was their only chance of going home.

It is their tomb.

Brines drew a breath that felt like a full drag on a motor-oil-black, thick-gauge stogie, but he didn't cough. Instead, he focused the pain deep into his chest, hoping it was enough to reboot his fried brain and purge the voice. He was tired of the mindfucks and only had time to deal in raw information. He had an objective and a war to win. He just needed his rifle.

Then the shadows shifted.

———

Sgt Smith gave the nod.

The blast pounded the stillness out of the besieged TOC and engulfed the heavy door in a burst of billowing debris and smoke. It was hard to believe from the ringing in Smith's ears, but most of the concussive force traveled inward, causing the entire structure to heave and then exhale dust from a thousand little cracks.

Before the asbestos-laden rubble finished raining down, the Marines were on their feet.

Smith posted LCpl Buontempo and LCpl Garcia on the entrance to cover their six, and then he and Nickels fired a spread with both SAWs through the doorway. They gave anything still living a three-count to respond before the two teams of two charged in side by side.

Smith's SAW was leveled and hungry as he entered the structure. Visibility was poor but sufficient. He was greeted by a long, wide hallway that reminded him of an elementary school with its painted cinderblock walls and few flickering fluorescent lights overhead. At least there weren't any crayon drawings of little stick-figure kids holding onto their taller stick-figure mommies and daddies.

Children were a no-go. A game-ender. A pack up and go home I-ain't-getting-into-a-firefight-in-or-around-any-kids deal breaker.

Three bodies (adult sized!) lay behind scattered sandbags set up as an anti-intrusion defensive barricade. Otherwise, there was no sign of life. The corridor was wide. Broad-shouldered Smith and Nickels easily had enough room to stand side by side as they swept forward as a united front.

Suddenly, the overhead lights shut off, plunging them into darkness. Emergency lighting from individual battery backup units came on, but they were shit with all the dust in the air.

Smith lowered his night vision goggles and ensured Light, Williamson, and Nickels did the same.

It was quiet. Aside from a smattering of papers and trash on the slab floor, they encountered nothing remarkable until finding an intersection. Smith motioned for the others to hold and flattened himself against the wall. Nickels passed forward a mirror, and Smith held it out to face down the left hallway. Two pairs of closed doors lined the walls, and more trash littered the floor. The only threat came from the anemic emergency lighting as it flickered like someone trying to scare away a dog with a flashlight.

Clear.

He tossed the mirror back to Nickels, who rushed past and aimed his SAW down the shorter hallway. After a quick check, Nickels signaled that it was empty and contained a single doorway.

"Go."

Nickels covered the right. Smith went left. He rushed up the hall and knocked the closer door off its hinges with his boot. LCpl Williamson was right on his six as he got clear and tossed in an M67 fragmentation grenade. Then they hugged the walls flanking the door.

A spread of gunfire ate the space between them.

Shouting.

Scrambling.

The crack of the grenade and the silence that followed.

Smith and Williamson swept into the room like a rush of fresh air and pounded several controlled bursts into the disoriented survivors.

The space was larger than expected. Given the upturned tables and quality of the dishware, it appeared to be the officer's mess. Smith checked over the bodies—no civvies—and realized that he just got lucky as fuck with that grenade. He needed to remember they were clearing for friendlies and needed to take it slow. A doorway on the far end led to a small kitchen, which appeared empty. After confirming that, Smith called back to Nickels, "Clear!"

That's when it hit the fan.

A shout for cover and the deafening report of gunfire out in the hallway ended with an explosion. Still in the kitchen, Williamson made a beeline for the fight and nearly went ass over tea kettle—literally—stumbling through a mess of pots and pans that had fallen on the floor. Smith caught him with one arm and ordered him to hold fast. The rattle of enemy weaponry filled the blast's void, followed by more cries to fall back.

The exchange sounded one-sided during that frenzied bubble of acute time dilation in which firefights reside. Smith's arm ached from the act of holding Williamson back but keeping someone from helping their buddies hurt his pride more. He knew the correct way to proceed, but that didn't mean he was bred that way. The Marines broke people down and trained them up to do the opposite of what their instincts sometimes screamed. In some cases, that meant running toward the fire. In others, it was squashing that raging hardon to *get some* and letting the situation evolve.

The agony of listening to his brothers eat shit soon fell to worry. *Did Jersey freeze up again?* LCpl Light was a good Marine, but his zero social skills were the absolute wrong stuff to mix with a panic attack.

It went on too long, and Smith felt his body engage, now fuckless for protocol. But then, the sweet sound of Marine hardware finally joined the battle. The purr of Nickels' SAW was empowering, like that moment when old-school Superman regained all his powers and crushed every bone in that one motherfucker's hand.

A concussive boom slowed the exchange, but both sides kept at it. Smith listened a moment longer and then grabbed Williamson's attention and cocked his head back toward the kitchen. The Marine nodded, and the two of them moved as one.

Angles. Everything in war was angles.

Smith kept his step light and away from the cabinets under the stainless-steel countertops. For whatever reason, he had a persistent fear that some motherfucker's hand would come out and shank his ankle or something. It wasn't just in enemy TOCs, either. At home, he always kept one eye down while cooking.

Finally, they found a door that exited back into the hallway. Smith told Williamson to hold fast and got into position to breach. The Marine gave him a pleading look, but he shook his head and whispered, "Cover my six."

Then, Smith let the testosterone take over.

———

"Frag out!"

Nickels hoped Smith was hunkered the fuck down as LCpl Light pitched another grenade down the hall. He gave it a two-count before turtling. In the narrow space, there was nowhere to run except back outside. But they already tried that. It brought LCpl Garcia into the fight but left them feeling like their backs were totally exposed to the whole fucking war.

No thanks.

Francis and that pilot weren't nearly enough of an overwatch.

The smoky hallway blew big with a pelting mix of hot fragmentation and debris. His helmet took a few hits, but nothing touched the hair.

"Sound off!" he shouted, his voice muffled inside his skull.

"Yo!"

"Yut!"

"Clear back here," called LCpl Buontempo from the entrance.

Nickels stood and aimed his SAW down the hallway. It would take a full evacuation of his brain cavity to stop him from putting fifty rounds through the next thing that moved.

A bullet to the head.

The thought floated by like a distracting pair of bikini-waxed thighs. Forbidden fruit. That irresponsible release.

Total bliss.

"Corporal?"

Fuck it. Kill or be killed but kill first. Marine Corps.

"On me," Nickels growled, shaking off the delusion.

The image-enhanced, green-tinted haze he was getting through his night vision goggles didn't provide much information on the enemy's whereabouts. Still, he advanced fearlessly. Anger and rage were his focus, and he was Mosses stomping into the Red Sea.

Part for me, bitch.

But this wasn't faith; it was balls. Brass fucking balls.

Nickels counted himself lucky when that first burst of panic fire sailed down the hall and missed those balls. He sucked a half breath and sent the message to squeeze the trigger and show them what the fuck was up.

Blind.

The green haze went white hot, searing his eyes. He had no shot.

Disoriented and perceiving similar cries of surprise from the men behind him, he ducked toward the left wall. Head pounding, he slapped the night vision goggles off his face, plunging the corridor into near-total darkness. No light at all.

What the fuck kind of malfunction was that?

His eyes refused to focus as he struggled to get a bead on the shooter. Panic rose; it was taking too long.

He was too late.

An enemy version of Moses strolled around the corner and leveled a machine gun at Nickels' fireteam. In the elapsing milliseconds where the brain works faster than the body can respond, Nickels realized that nothing short of a head shot would stop that guy from shredding all of them.

———

Sergeant Smith fired first.

Dumb luck collided his bullish charge back into the hallway with the enemy's decision to advance on Nickels' team. Maybe in another universe, he would've given a verbal offer after catching some backsides in his sights.

But all Smith saw was a big gun pointed at his boys.

The solid line of explosive-pumped projectiles smashed into the enemy machine gunner like a medieval javelin, folding him in half and shoving the body back into his comrades. Then it was their turn. Within seconds, what remained of the threat wasn't just down but pulverized.

"Clear!" boomed Smith, still marching forward.

Nickels called out some sort of reply, but Smith barely heard it over the blood rushing in his ears.

At no point during the operational briefing did 2ndLt Weber say anything about them wandering through some enemy bunker kicking in doors and shit. Hell, Smith's whole squad was supposed to be stationed back at the detention center behind a mountain of ballistic protection. Not smeared across another military miscalculation.

Anger at the loss of Marines on their first combat mission together bubbled up and dissolved what remained of his restraint.

It's on now.

Smith snapped the next door with a side kick and stomped in with a wild burst from his SAW. He didn't even look at the meat it tore up as he stepped aside and let LCpl Williamson peg the leftovers. Instead, he moved to the next door and hammered the rest of his box through the shitty plywood. By now, Nickels had caught up and caught on to the fact that the United States Marine Corps now officially owned the hallways and weren't taking shit from nobody.

Distantly, the word *friendlies* floated through Smith's head. But it was lost in the rush of pent-up rage.

Nothin's friendly here.

He reloaded, crashed another room, and jackhammered the place to fuck.

"Hold up!" shouted Nickels by the last door at the end of the hallway.

"Lemme at it," Smith snarled, ready to end this fucking war. That super weapon, or whatever, was in there, and he was going to punch it in the face.

"Bone, no. It's reinforced."

Smith pushed past Nickels and slammed his shoulder into solid steel. "Fuck!"

"Bro, we'll cover it. Clear the rest. Oorah?"

"Fuck no. Whatever they gots in there, we gotta take it out. That's the whole damned reason we came here. Whole damned reason we lost Gunny, lost Sanchez, Gilbert, Nguyen, and the others. Fuck everything else," Smith shouted with a spray of spit.

"We don't know what's in there."

"Somethin' that needs to die."

"Yeah? And we'll need some serious hardware to get at it."

"Anymore C4?"

"No."

"Fuck!"

"Fuck is right!" said Nickels. "While we're standing around talking about it, we've got half of this place unsecured. Who knows how many fuckers are left just waiting till we're busy to bust out and pop us in the ass."

Smith punched the door again. It made the sick sound of a steak slapping down onto a cold, cast-iron pan. Solid through and through. Jersey had a point.

"Look," continued Nickels, now the voice of reason as tempers cooled, "we'll put a man on it and clear the rest of this shit out. Okay? Maybe get lucky and find their armory. Something big enough to crack this bitch open."

Smith brightened up. "Yeah, man, the armory. Grab us a cannon."

"Fuckin' A, Bone."

"Williamson, you on the door. Somethin' come outta there, you fuck it up."

"Oorah, Sergeant."

"Aight, Jersey. Fuck this place," said Smith, turning his attention back the way they came. LCpl Garcia, one of the two Marines he'd set at the entrance, was in the intersection securing the opposing hallway. It looked like he entered—probably to back up Nickels—and engaged the right wing. Two new bodies were piled up at the end of the hall like they tripped on their way in.

Garcia crept forward with his M4 aimed into the far doorway's gaping darkness and kneeled against the wall. "Two down," he reported.

"Good man," replied Smith, motioning for the four Marines to gather in the intersection. Once they were there with rifles covering every angle, he said, "Listen up. We got three rooms to clear. After that, they're hol' up behind that metal door. Think it's their ops center. Gotta clear the rest of this shit hole out first. Lookin' for something to blow that door. Oorah?"

"Oorah."

But before Smith's men could get on it, a frantic voice from outside the TOC stopped them cold.

They were out of time.

———

It was quiet for the first time in days, weeks, maybe months.

The work was mechanical now: cut, clip, suture, and clean. Clean and bandage. There were no orderlies, so she'd be the one doing the dishes after those who could be saved were stabilized.

Dr. Pat's mind wandered.

Grassy fields and a warm breeze. Trout were biting, so the boys were happy. No way was she going to let them clean the fish, though. She wasn't in the mood to stitch up a three-inch laceration. *Assholes with knives.*

She drew a suture extra tight, eliciting a gasp from the patient and a strange word that was meaningless beyond its profane nature.

Everyone had stopped speaking English except for a few broken phrases here and there. *Stress response?* She'd once dated an Indian boy who reverted to his native tongue after about six beers. Then there was a Russian colleague who'd completely lose the use of articles in a sentence whenever he was ill.

Everyone was crazy. The other "nurses" poked about—arms bent and drawn to the chest like chickens—not doing anything beneficial. The wounded moaned incoherently.

Some were dead.

With no free hands to disconnect their IV drips, saline pooled in their bloating, clogged veins uselessly. The infirmary was never close to meeting modern medical standards, but now it was goddamned horror show.

Dr. Pat huffed as a gob of fluid splattered onto the patient below her. Another fell.

Then another.

Is it raining? her sluggish mind wondered.

A hole in the tent's canopy made sense. She just needed to fetch a pot.

The guys would be back soon if it was raining. The rain brought the fish, but they were all a bunch of pussies when it came to getting wet. And it was getting cold, wasn't it? That's why she was shaking.

Shiver response: a nervous attempt to generate heat by muscle action.

Dr. Pat looked at the nearest nurse and tried to say something, but it came out as a sea of slurred spit, and the effort exhausted her. At least she knew now where the leak was coming from.

She was caught somewhere between running on autopilot and drooling in her sleep.

———

Brines dove behind a half-sized Hesco barrier—the last bit of evidence that marked this crater as a former fighting position—and wicked the knife into his left hand.

Impressive duel, rumbled that low voice again.

Brines leaned out and scanned the darkness. There was shit to see except a beautiful M4 carbine with an under-barrel grenade launcher about ten feet away. The rifle was out of reach for the moment but still served a purpose. It was a reminder that he had a fucking pistol strapped to his side. He sheepishly yanked it out of the holster.

I have borne witness to better, of course. But in this dead place, I had thought all blades decorative. Useless in clumsy hands. Relics.

Brines strained his ears, but they did not help him locate the speaker.

There was no directional component. It reminded him of listening to head-phones, something he rarely cared for.

I am glad it is you who made it this far. The others I found are too entangled in the chaos of your fight. I hoped to remove them before too much mixing, but there were many surprises. A shame since it began so clean and orderly. Two sides facing off. Simple lines, never touching.

Brines gritted his teeth and forced thoughts of violence and murder into his head. Anything to drown out the fucking guy's musings and stay focused. Forgetting about the rifle, he and his pistol scooted around the other side of the barrier to get a bead on where he'd seen movement.

What he saw sobered up every memory he had of being drunk.

An asshole in black robes standing out in the open.

Some kinda religious nut job?

But the impatience of men still drives them to grapple, no matter the circumstances.

Brines grabbed another look. No visible weapon, but that didn't mean the guy wasn't backed by a couple sniper teams. He vaguely wondered what happened to Sgt Smith's squad. *Be nice to have them on an angle right now.* He remembered hearing a SAW during the knife fight, but he never trusted his adrenaline-fueled memories.

Gotta take 'em quick.

This study was too early, too dirty to be fruitful. But it is enough to prepare us for the future. I had thought myself resigned to claim your adversary as my prize. My . . . specimen, to use your words. But now I have you, the victor. The Obantum shall be pleased.

Prize? No fucking way.

Brines raised his pistol but hesitated as he felt a sudden urge to rush the rat fuck and gore him in the heart with the knife. His left arm shook violently, yearning to stab, slash, and cut. It was a good thing new Brines was back in control and did NOT have control issues, or he'd have a real problem with the sudden, uncontrollable urge to gut a bitch.

Reason won, and Brines launched out of cover with a sideways roll. He figured it would buy him a couple seconds as any potential snipers readjusted their scopes.

He landed upright on a knee and lined up a clean shot well within pistol range.

No hesitation.

The semi-automatic cannon bucked in his hand until the clip went dry. Nothing.

The figure in the robe never budged. It was as if the gun was firing blanks.

Brines reached for an extra clip but stopped as he smelled something burning. His leather glove was smoking. Confused, he looked at the pistol. Glowing, fucking molten. Shocked, he tossed the gun and tore off his glove.

His options were dwindling; he was out of grenades and short on time. The rifle was about halfway between him and the target. Bitch was empty, and slapping in a fresh mag would be an eternity he didn't have, but the launcher had a round in it.

What the fuck just happened to my gun?

In all his years, he'd never had one heat up like that.

Do you feel your significance waning? Stripped bare of your weapons, you are naked in a dangerous place. Will it not be easier to seek a new shepherd who can protect you in the coming chaos? Someone who can heal your wounds and still the storm that rages within.

Brines spat and launched himself at the rifle. He crossed the distance fast and dove the last five feet to clamp down on the *T,* as Ron called it a lifetime ago.

With his fingers just inches away, the weapon scooted into the darkness as if yanked by an invisible cord. Brines landed flat on his face and somehow lost all the momentum he needed to roll out of the dive. Frantic, he tried to push himself up, but something wasn't working. It felt like a weight was pressing into his back, keeping him down.

Soon you and I will be all that is left in this quiet place. I shall not bother humbling you by crushing the small nut of your mind with my might as with the others. I shall soak it in pain until all that remains is the rotten meat at its core. Then, together, we will dine.

Brines felt himself grow cold. He couldn't figure out what the fuck sort of setup he'd stumbled into or what on earth was pinning him to the ground. It was a comedy of psychotic missteps with some cosplay motherfucker holding the microphone. But he did realize one thing as his body armor's ceramic plates crunched into his chest. Mike T. Brines had control issues.

And there never was any *new* Brines.

His heart fluttered as his true self, repressed by years of practiced denial, changed the beat. Harder, not smarter.

Harder!

Brines felt something lunge from his core and slam into that invisible weight, desperate to lash out against the nut in the robe. That energy then ricocheted between his spine and the ground, bucking his torso uselessly against enraging immobility.

It sought escape, vengeance. It gnashed his teeth and kicked his legs until finding its way into his arms.

There it found freedom.

There it found a way to leave the confines of his body.

The knife launched from his free hand as if it were the last shout of anger from an obsolete, sinking battleship.

The figure in black made no attempt to dodge. Instead, he accepted the throw, cackling as the white handle disappeared into his flowing robes.

The cackling stopped.

The weight on Brines' back vanished.

"How?" asked the man stumbling backward, his words now clearly coming from his mouth.

Brines moved fast and got his legs under him. He closed the distance between them in seconds.

"A bone of the Vissl . . . here?"

The robed man's back cracked as Brines tackled him to the ground. Then it was a scramble to wrap up the legs and get mount. The frail fuck put up almost no fight, and soon Brines' fingers were wrapped around his knife's—strangely—hot handle. No way was he letting go this time.

"We are not the first . . ."

A yank freed the blade, and he hoisted it high to finish the job.

Right in the goddamned beating heart!

The man whispered something, and a flash sent Brines flying backward. He landed in a heap, right where he'd been pinned to the ground by *god knows what*. He clambered back to his feet, ready to charge.

But he was alone.

———

Colonel Ridge bolted upright. "Say again?!"

"EM signature just vanished, sir," reported one of the operators.

"Discharged?" asked Admiral Bowman.

"Negative, sir. Rectangular drop-off, zero decay constant."

"The fuck does that mean?"

"Try bringing up the satellite image again," said Ridge, white-knuckled and heart racing. They lost the feed a few minutes after Saunders launched what looked to be a platoon into a clear enemy trap.

"Yes, put it up on the main screen," added Admiral Bowman.

Ridge kicked his chair back from the table and stood. Then he began pacing, near wild with impatience as the process of switching inputs took forever. Finally, the huge liquid crystal display lit up, and he released a stale breath.

They're alive!

Visual was back for the airbase, right down to individual heat signatures. The Marines still held the prison complex, and multiple squads had advanced north. His celebration was short-lived as the analytical part of his mind studied the board and calculated the next moves.

They were in big trouble.

"So, did it happen? Was it like Hudud?" asked LtCol Baud.

"No," replied the admiral fucking around with his gold ring again.

"They need support," managed Ridge trying to comprehend the strategy of sending those men north. *What was Saunders thinking? Bayonets fixed, no bayonets . . .*

"I wonder what happened to the interference?" mused Admiral Bowman as if blind to the fact that the Marines were being overrun.

"Admiral," shouted Ridge, "Vulture and Alpha Company need to get airborne and on mission to reinforce Charlie. Now!"

"Agreed," said LtCol Baud slapping her hand down on the table.

"What? Why?"

The admiral was either clueless or feigning ignorance because he was a balllless fuck scared to make a wrong move. Either way, Ridge's career as a Marine infantry officer had started in the ground, grown in the ground, and the only reason he was on this fucking boat was because the *gators* could get him to new ground. There was no way he would be out-manned by this fly-boy ranker.

"Alpha Company!"

"Totally denied. Their mission is the FARP and making sure we get our people out of country," replied the admiral, finally focused on the discussion.

"Then get Saunders his air support," Ridge growled, locking eyes. Alpha was a farfetched request, even he knew it. Pakistan was imploding and fast becoming a denied area. Throwing Captain Rogers into the fray was that desperate gamble at the night's end when you were unbuttoning your shirt to fund one more toss.

"It's bigger than any of us in this room, Colonel. We need an explanation."

"Fine. I have good reason to believe the atmospheric phenomena, the EM signature, and the new anti-air weapon are all connected. And I believe someone just took it out."

"Believe?"

"See for yourself: we've got Marine localization at that 4CI, and suddenly the feed's back. Look, the shroud cover's gone. Admiral, that more than satisfies the burden of proof for Central Command."

"There's no way to know—"

"I'm not asking you to know," Ridge said. "I'm asking you to untie our hands so we can pull my goddamned men out of there." He held his gaze, boring into whatever soul the man had.

Admiral Bowman's eyes shifted between the table and the screen where the Ground Element was fighting for their lives against a major advance. After a moment, he said, "You're asking a lot."

"I . . ."

"Let me finish." The admiral rested his hands on the table. "If we do this, I need something in return. Understood?"

Ridge swallowed hard and looked up at the real-time satellite image again. Saunders had sent at least a squad after that C4I bunker. Two friendly IR beacons near the entrance indicated that they'd left a couple of men on overwatch outside. Intermittent signals indicated that more were inside, but it wasn't clear if they were moving.

A start, but miles from the finish line. The admiral's hard-on for that C4I was so painful that the prison battle was almost a distraction. Ridge surmised this "need" was simple: execute the order as written. That meant Saunders himself had to make positive identification on the VIP before he could even think about evacuating, considerably reducing his odds of returning safely.

But his odds were zero if Vulture didn't get back in the air.

General McNeal could override the admiral, but getting approval and bringing him up to speed would take time. Time Saunders didn't have.

An image of Sarah looking down at the letter in Ridge's pocket flashed in his mind as he answered.

CHAPTER 16

TOP-DOWN ECONOMICS

Captain Saunders lamented.

He'd cast one too many gutsy rolls in his life, and lady luck had finally hit menopause. The entire linchpin of the plan involved luring those tanks out so the Heavy Weapons Platoon could engage on their timetable, not the enemy's.

But that shit the bed.

Second Platoon was configured for counter-infantry operations with no capacity to effectively handle armor—a fact being explicated by every Marine within earshot. All they could do was hunker down among the crumbling foundations of the former administrator park and hope the enemy commanders popped their heads out for a look as they drove past. But really, without anti-tank munitions, his Marines were little more than squishy speed bumps.

"Sir . . ." came a wavering voice to his left. PFC Licht.

Saunders waved him off and kept popping up to search for an escape route. His men were still mobile, but the mass of anti-personnel and main battle tanks, spanning decades and continents in terms of technology, was moving fast. Three groups of four were bearing down on them, keeping tight to support each other in the absence of a significant infantry escort. For all he knew, this was just the first wave.

He kept watch for any break, any obstacle that might divide their formation and offer him a hole for either egress or a chance to slow them down. He racked his brain for historical and tactical data that might help him escape this situation, but nothing practical emerged. He scolded himself for making the age-old mistake of miscalculating visibility.

If he had just stayed on the Marine defensive perimeter, Second Platoon would at least have a chance to buy time for Heavy Weapons to fight back. Instead, Lyons was about to find himself knee-deep in fucking tanks. They might be able to take care of the wheeled vehicles, but it would be ugly taking on that eleven-inch-thick armor in close quarters. The FGM-148 Javelins needed range to gain altitude before slamming down on the weakest point—the turret.

And those turrets would waste no time in destroying the transports.

The moment we lose those choppers, this is our graveyard.

Saunders considered sending some runners to give Lyons a heads-up. Order him to pack it up and burn it out of here, anti-air weapon be damned. But looking back at the wide-open field they'd have to cross, he realized his men wouldn't get far. It was a shooting gallery.

Wait.

He could see the field.

And the silhouette of the detention center in the distance.

He lifted his night vision goggles and looked skyward.

Stars.

"Sir!" shouted PFC Licht, probably trying to communicate something important, but the rising cacophony of screeching metal was more demanding. The lead vehicles were through the destroyed concrete wall. Saunders pulled a grenade. *Maybe the treads . . .*

An old Soviet-made T-72 Ural—complete with its vintage cast-steel armor casing and trailblazing 7.62 mm PKT coax machine gun—spearheaded the drive into the center of Second Platoon's fledgling line. The Marines scattered, making a hole with the hope of flanking the beast. Some clutched grenades with the same idea as their captain. It was hopeless, but it was something.

Suddenly, the tank's turret exploded.

Saunders raised an eyebrow.

The unmistakable hiss of another FGM-148 Javelin cut through the air and smashed right into the turret of the second vehicle. Wide-eyed in surprise as the clanking tank burst into a shower of molten metal and flames, Saunders slowly connected the dots.

Heavy Weapons could see them. Heavy Weapons could help them.

And Heavy Weapons made it rain.

Explosions engulfed the enemy armor from the shoulder-fired anti-tank weapons, and cheers erupted from Second Platoon. Saunders stuck his head up and gawked in wonder at the smoldering wreck. However wrong it might've gone, the plan was somehow unfucking itself.

"Sir!" insisted PFC Licht.

"What?"

"Coms are back up. I've got Hawk online."

Son of a bitch. "Give me the mic. It's time to finish this fight and pull the fuck out."

"Yessir," came the reply of a young man in disbelief.

Brines crouched low, blending with the shadows and silhouettes of a cooling battlefield. He couldn't find his rifle, so he grabbed a 7.62 mm AK-something-or-other as a replacement. It stayed slung, though, in case any of his men were still out there. It'd be his lucky day that they'd ID the weapon before his uniform or friendly disposition, and he'd never live long enough to get drunk and tell the whole bar about the crazy shit he just saw.

Did any of that really happen?

He played it over in his head, wishing he was calmer and better able to recollect the details. But right now, the adrenaline-buzzed memory was all he had.

He remembered knifing two *whiskey tangos*. Confirmed by the blood caked over the glinting surface of Gramps' blade.

Was that second guy really trash-talkin' the entire time? In English, no less. *Shit, was there even a second guy?*

He had one corpse, for sure, but the second guy had disappeared right after that flashbang or whatever went off.

Brines checked himself for wounds and burns again. Not a grenade. Not at that range. Still, he might've lost consciousness and never known it. Guy might've had time to run off. *The guy in the fuckin' death cult costume.* Hallucination was sounding better by the minute.

A score of explosions ripped in the distance. The fight wasn't over.

Brines remained still, though, alone in the shadows enjoying feeling like his old self for once. Someone would be along soon enough; this was a choke point for anyone traveling between the TOC and the prison.

And then they'd meet the old Gunny, lying in wait.

Until then, he kept himself entertained by dreaming up ways to explain what just happened. To leadership, to Ron. At the very least, he would get some laughs with that story. At the bar.

At the goddamned bar.

———

With the atmosphere purged of whatever mess of pollutants the enemy had thrown up, the C-monster was free to conduct warfare as God intended.

The Heavy Weapons Platoon let loose on the enemy armor as it slowed to navigate the dragon's teeth of ruined structures and abandoned trench networks. Second Platoon stayed low, catching their breaths as they waited for the enemy infantry to bail out their trump card.

Instead of pulling back, the tanks doubled down. Learning from the mistakes of the lead vehicles, the two rear groups took to the flanks. The heavy-tracked T-80 battle tanks charged for open ground, barreling through reinforced concrete and smoldering vehicle husks with impunity, and began trading shots with the Marine defensive perimeter.

Behind them followed the smaller, more maneuverable T-55s, T-72s, and a few wheeled vehicles that reminded the Marines of the tribal fighting in Afghanistan.

Second Platoon—dismayed at seeing one of the T-80s shrug off two Javelin hits—let them pass, keen on the infantry clusters lurking in their wake.

LCpl Fischer traded his M4 for the M40 sniper rifle and handed his buddy LCpl Gladstone a spotting scope. The pair went to work on the stubborn heads springing up across the shattered landscape.

PFC Licht, breathless with a deep fatigue soaking into his bones, forced himself to keep up with the captain.

It was a struggle and a juggle.

Along with two other fireteams, they swung around the left flank to set up an angle against the enemy's follow-on support. Hawk was back online and in his ear, demanding a SitRep. First Lieutenant Lyons was also screaming for some sort of answer about the nearly indestructible T-80s coming his way.

Run. Stop. Radio. Rifle. Run.

It was an insane ballet, but it worked. Licht even added another notch on the company belt during some downtime.

"Tell Lyons to ignore the T-80s," shouted Captain Saunders as the fire line let loose on an enemy squad caught in the open.

Licht shook his head. "He's insistent, sir."

"Don't have time for this; tell him it'll take care of itself."

That made exactly zero sense. Licht opened his mouth to ask the obvious question that would be part of the cuss-laden first lieutenant's reply, but something held him back. It might've been the military training crushing his desire to question a commanding officer, but, on second thought, it was trust. *Real trust.*

The realization gave David Licht pause.

He looked over to Captain Saunders. Gone was just another ego to feed, boss to disappoint, guy who would leave him high and dry. Saunders was a brother Marine and a genuine person. Lieutenant Lyons wouldn't question the order, just as no one had questioned Second Platoon's headlong charge at several enemy tank platoons. No one could predict the future, but Saunders made everyone confident that he knew which roads would get them there. After twenty years of mistrust, Licht found himself accepting someone at his word. And that was a beautiful thing.

Sure enough, it wasn't surprising when 1stLt Lyons came over the mic cheering a few minutes later. Licht looked back in time to see a pair of bright flashes engulf two of the heavy tanks, followed by the thunderous roar of attack helicopters.

Vulture was back.

———

Mina Bazar was in the tip zone.

The enemy still fielded a substantial ground force and remained a significant threat to Marine ground and non-combatant evacuation operations. But their advantage was spent.

And with it, their morale.

Long after the Americans had expected, command and control finally disintegrated. The PAF regulars broke first despite retaining sufficient combat power to deny the Marine advance. Next came the facility garrison—men fighting for their home soil. Lastly, the Mujahedeen were left to decide if Kôz was bigger than a single battle.

Second Platoon pounced on the rout with all the speed that months of urban assault training afforded them. Return fire was sporadic and in-effective as even the battered rebel rearguard broke cover and ran like hell toward the northeastern airfield. Out in the exposed expanse without that mysterious shroud to protect them, Vulture Group descended.

Captain Saunders signaled for Second Platoon to hold fast as a barrage of 20 mm cannon fire took the stage. Seeing men powerless against such a force was tough, but it had to be done. Some of the severely unlucky fleers even managed to step on and trigger some of the unexploded bomblets from the initial cluster munitions dispersal. A final kick in the ass for going up against the title.

"Last of them o'er yonder are outta range, sir," said LCpl Fischer pan-ning the wrecked runways through the black scope on his M40. "Want us to slink on up there?"

"Negative," Saunders said, bringing up his binocs. The ominous C4I tactical operations center, reportedly under Marine control, leered at him in the distance. More critically, the enemy hadn't bothered to retreat there. They'd concentrated their remaining manpower securing the northeastern access gate. That could only mean one thing.

"PFC, the mic."

"Sir, was just about to tell you that Hawk wants a word."

A word?

Saunders raised an eyebrow at the kid. His face was unreadable as he focused on completing the task of handing over the mic. A more senior operator would've added some flavor, any flavor to prepare him for what the fuck command wanted to talk about. "A word" didn't sound like an ap-proved evacuation plan. It sounded like . . .

Saunders turned back toward the C4I tactical operations center—the final toss after a wild streak of luck—and a wave of exhaustion washed over him.

No.

Mina Bazar was a death trap, and the only thing keeping its jaws from snapping shut was sheer Marine muscle power. They were alone out here, barrels smoking and lungs heaving from carving out the tiniest escape win-dow. Scouring that bunker was an entire operation itself, another trap, or at least a quagmire that threatened the whole mission.

For what?

He knew the answer, but that didn't mean it was equitable. After everything they just went through and the high probability of incoming enemy reinforcements, there was no way in hell he had enough time.

CHAPTER 17

THE REMAINS

The quiet crunching of boots and swishing of fabric blew in with the smell of cordite. Brines considered popping that crappy, wooden-stock rifle into his hands. *Might be a good idea to pre-fuck any more psycho chit-chat.* But he recognized the pattern of movement.

"Yut," he barked.

The shuffling feet melted into silence, and a few tense seconds passed. Finally, a familiar voice replied, "Yut! Sound off."

"Brines."

Captain Saunders stepped out of the shadows with his MP5 raised but promptly lowered it. "Jesus, Mike. You operational?"

"Yessir."

"The fuck are you doing out here?"

"Got 'em caught in an ambush, sir."

Ron didn't flinch. *Looks like I ain't the only one having a bad day.* "Yeah," he said. "Smith reported you guys got hit. Thought you'd gone offline."

"Smith? He made it?"

"Affirmative. We're light on details, but they're dug in at the TOC.

Brines sucked a breath. He'd thought for sure they were all dead. Before he could get a full update, the other three Marines in the captain's team slipped along the edges of the blown-out nest. One, LCpl Fischer, crouched by Ra'num's corpse and put a light on the multiple chest lacerations.

"Hey . . . uhh, Gunny. Do you, by any reckon, need some . . . ah, ammo?" he asked.

Everyone stopped and followed Fischer's index finger to the knife still clutched in Brines' left hand.

"Hardcore," whispered one of the jokers. Ron just stared.

"Forget it. Job's done here," Brines growled, acknowledging the urgent look on the captain's face. "Let's get back in action. What's the objective?"

"Extract the TOC. Got that Osprey on station," said Saunders.

"Long fuse?"

"Microscopic."

"Shit," muttered Brines waving everyone forward. Going to the damned TOC to pick up the assault team didn't make sense unless they were offline or couldn't complete their objectives. But the fight was over as far as he could tell. To highlight this point, the last CH-53E Super Stallion transport lifted off from the detention center in the distance.

They were alone now.

———

"'Sit tight,' that's what they said, Sergeant," said LCpl Buontempo setting his radio pack against the cinderblock wall. He rolled his shoulders a few times and cracked his neck.

"Ain't make no sense," Smith muttered. He studied the men in the security post they'd established at the intersecting hallways. Guns were trained on every location the Marines did not control or had not cleared. The bunker remained an active threat; two wings were still in enemy hands.

We ain't done shit here.

"Anyone remember icing a super weapon?" he asked.

A few chuckles, but now that the choppers were back and the enemy was running for the hills, their focus was on leaving. Leaving before some asshole decided to ground the entire Air Force again.

"Yut," came a call from the entrance. It was Capt Rath.

"Yut," Smith answered.

"Heat's off for now. Your man Francisco says some trucks are hauling ass up the north road, but it doesn't look like they'll get far. Everyone else is pooling at the northeastern gate."

Smith nodded. Twenty minutes ago, Capt Rath was standing in that blown-up doorway, telling them they were facing down a whole platoon with a fuckload of heavy weaponry. Smith, who'd gone more than apeshit with his ammo, was looking at the impossible defense of a crossfire position at the end of a disastrous mission. No backup. No hope of rescue. Nothing but a bullet to the head or ten years in a dark cell with daily waterboardings as thanks.

Then, poof, it was all different: the Marines were winning.

It couldn't be that easy.

"So, they ain't all leaving, sir?" Smith asked.

"No," said Capt Rath, "but what's left of my squadron is up there giving them plenty of hell."

"Yeah, but maybe they expectin' some backup. More reason to get the fuck outta here."

"Speakin' my language, Bone," said Nickels. "That big door ain't happenin', but let's finish what Garcia started with the other one. Bang and boom. Then book. Oorah?"

"Can't, orders."

"Orders were to search for friendlies and destroy a super weapon. Super weapon sounds like it went down. Hostages waitin', bro. Wanna dick around till they all get their heads shot off?" Nickels flexed his trigger hand. "Let's just rock this shit out."

"We holdin'."

"Fucker. That's the concussion talking."

"Ain't no concussion. But I got just as big a hardon for goin' home as you. Buontempo, call in and find out how long we gonna be on our asses here."

"Shouldn't be long," said Capt Rath joining the security post. "Francisco spotted your relief team inbound. He wanted me to tell you that it looks like your gunnery sergeant needs a new rifle."

"They found Gunny?" It hit like the first warm sunrise after a bullshit winter. In all this insane death and ruin, Gunny was the tower. Nothing about today made sense without him.

"Figures," muttered Nickels.

———

Dr. Pat braced her knees against the cold metal table and held onto the fluid drip stand for support until the room stopped spinning. Soldiers were talking out in the hallway. Most of it was muffled, but a few choice words—*bang and boom* and *hostages*—came through loud and clear. In English. So, maybe that was a thing again. Not for her nurses, but nothing made much sense. Well, except that Ra'num had probably sent the soldiers. He did say she'd be useless if she couldn't tend to the wounded.

Do you care for her more because she is your friend? Or because she isn't your enemy?

His words echoed in her mind. She refused to consider the possibility of Micky dying here. Dr. Pat tested her grip on the straight scissors in her free hand. Another wave of dizziness hit.

It was getting late, and the boys still hadn't brought her any fish to clean. *What are they up to?*

She could hear them talking and carrying on, but they were still far away. Didn't they realize it was dinner time? The first few wisps of smoke curled off the hot oil. *Where are they?*

Shouts at the door.

The soldiers were angry. Dr. Pat wondered if she should hide, but then she might fall asleep. No, she needed to be awake to stab that motherfucker Ra'num. The one who hadn't so much as touched her yet left her feeling violated. And if she stabbed him, maybe he'd need a doctor to patch him up.

The fire was down to the coals, and the wind was blowing. They missed dinner, and now there was a storm coming. She wondered if she should search for them, but she couldn't leave. No matter what, she had to stay here. With the fire. No, the pan. Wait. *I need to stay with Micky, she's—*

A bright flash and a clap against her ears brought Dr. Pat back to the infirmary with an instant headache. She was disoriented, black splotches floating across a sea of blurred movement and muffled shouts. The soldiers were coming in.

She coiled. Maybe she wouldn't get a stab at *him*, but certainly the first fucker who put his hands on her. They needed to be taught a lesson for staying out so late, worrying her half to death.

More shouting, maybe they'd caught a fish. She tried to focus on what they were saying; it was the same thing repeatedly.

"Down! Down! Everybody down! We are Americans! Get down! United States Marines!"

Definitely speaking English again. That was nice. Now she could ask them what the hell took them so long, right before she stabbed the first fucker to put his hands on her.

Two soldiers appeared on the other side of the table, speaking fast.

Not soldiers, Marines.

They seemed to be in such a hurry. Her face felt tingly. Maybe her blood was acidifying.

Dr. Pat blinked away the last of the flash blindness and felt a mild frustration as her mind struggled to process all the new information. These guards were bigger than the others she'd seen around the infirmary. Who needed that much gear for fly fishing anyway?

"Ma'am, can you understand me?"

What a stupid question. "Yes," she tried to answer in her best doctor's voice of confidence and control. It came out as a slurry drawl like she'd been dipping into the guys' cooler. She scolded herself and snapped to attention.

"What do you want?" she demanded, tightening her grip on the scissors.

The one with green eyes and a soft face slung his rifle over his shoulder and raised his hands. "We're friendly. Gonna take you outta here."

"I'm not going anywhere."

Green eyes looked at another one who was carrying a much bigger and nastier-looking gun. And this one didn't bother relaxing his grip.

Big Gun shrugged and said, "Chick's totally checked out. Probably a concussion."

"She doesn't look hurt."

"They never do, dude. Bone's still on his feet."

"He's not hurt."

"You ain't a doctor."

"Neither are you."

"I am," said Dr. Pat, somewhat annoyed. "Your friend will have to wait until I'm finished here." No way was she going to let another front-line grunt with a flesh wound step in front of Micky.

A third, taller man approached, and the other two stepped aside. There was something familiar about the way he carried himself. An air of authority, perhaps. Tall Authority. *The park ranger? Shit, where's my fishing license?*

"Ma'am," he coaxed, trying to slip past her walls. "We're leaving. Is there anyone else besides yourself and her?" He pointed down at Micky.

Dr. Pat saw red.

"You leave her alone!" she screamed, lurching over the table to plant the scissors in the side of Tall Authority's face.

An invisible force folded her at the waist and plucked the scissors from her grip. Then she was staring at the dank ceiling with its half-lit fluorescent lighting.

"None of that now, ma'am," rasped a voice from below.

She squirmed against the ironclad hold of her captor until her body went limp from exhaustion.

"Micky . . ." she whimpered.

"Sir, we are ten past done. Need to go," rasped the one holding her.

"Ma'am, we'll take good care of *Micky*. But I need your name," said Tall Authority.

The struggle cleared her head a bit. She was beginning to understand that these Marines were part of a rescue team. "Pat. Pat Bowman," she managed.

"No fuckin' way that's a coincidence," said another.

"Quiet, Corporal. Ma'am, are you two the last ones?"

"Yeah," she sighed, deciding to turn in for the night. Dinner had been a disaster. But plenty of people went to bed hungry and lived to tell about it. The infirmary dimmed—even darker than when the power went out earlier—and she floated away from the dream world of muffled voices, firecrackers, thunderstorms, and screams.

———

"This one ain't gonna make it, sir," said Brines.

Saunders wasn't an expert but had to agree the bloodied and bandaged brunette on the table looked terrible. If it wasn't for the subtle rise and fall of that yellowed bedsheet covering her chest, he would've guessed her long dead.

"Fuckers," spat Cpl Nickels shoving his boot into one of the pale soldiers propped up against the far wall.

"Enough of that," Saunders said, still trying to puzzle out who else they needed to extract from this blood-soaked shithole.

Nickels shook his head, but not to say *no*. It was too vigorous, almost involuntary. Enough to grab Saunders' full, undivided attention. The corporal's fists clenched, and he kicked another one. "Fuckers!" Then he was pointing at the woman on the surgical table—Micky, according to Dr. Bowman—as if seeing her for the first time.

No one moved; even Brines, with the doc draped over his shoulder, wasn't sure whether to jump in and shut shit down or give it space.

Nickels' jaw quivered like some tears might be on tap. Understandable after all they'd been through. Instead of breaking down, the guy with a squad automatic rifle strapped across his chest went left at the fork.

And exploded.

"Animals!" he screamed, snapping that SAW to his shoulder. Marine rifles went up, but not fast enough to deter him from stomping across the room toward the three Pakistani nurses cowering in the corner.

"Stand down, Corporal," Saunders managed, cutting eyes between him and Brines. Mike was just as shocked. Neither of them ever figured Nickels was the type who cared about anything outside of himself or his next joke.

Nickels got right in the nurses' faces and gave them a crash course on the malicious use of the word *fuck*. The veins in his temples and neck were visibly bulging, as if he was seriously considering executing a bunch of unarmed civilians.

"PFC, get Smith in here, goddamn it," said Brines swinging the doc around to give his free arm with the pistol a clear shot.

"Rein it in," Saunders ordered again, considering his options if the corporal didn't comply. The tension in the room was as thick as the clotted blood caked on its floor.

Sgt Smith marched through the doorway, missing his trademark smile. The sight of his buddy losing his shit did not seem to surprise him. "Jersey!"

"Look at this shit, Jay. Look at these fucks!"

"Look in the mirror, bro. You ain't thinkin' straight." Smith moved closer and held up his hand to Brines. "He dealin' with some shit, Gunny. But we cool."

"Five seconds," growled Brines, too low for Nickels to hear.

"Bro, look at me, not them," said Smith. Nickels didn't flinch as the sergeant laid a hand on his shoulder. "Look at me."

Nickels turned.

"You and me, aight? Ain't nothin' here worth nothin'. Job's done; we out."

"But they . . ."

Smith firmed his grip. "They a bunch of scared girls."

Nickels blinked like somehow that resonated more than quivering human beings on their knees. "Fuck. Fuck! Fuck, Bone, I fucked up," he stammered, lowering the rifle.

"No, you didn't. Just a little time lost. Ain't that right, sir?"

Brines shook his head, but Saunders said, "Fall in, Corporal."

"Aye, sir," Nickels said, stepping back. "I . . . I'm sorry, sir."

Disciplining this shit was as far from Saunders' mind as possible. *Evac without further incident.* "Stone, you and Nickels head to the front door and tell them we're ready to move."

"Yessir," Nickels said again, finally relaxing. Gladstone hesitated, but a nod from Smith got things moving, and they were gone.

Blowing out a breath, Saunders turned back to Brines.

"Been sayin' it fer months."

"Understood. Now, let's see about a stretcher or something for this one." Saunders pointed at Micky.

"You sure?"

"Yeah, she's coming. Dead or alive."

"Captain," said PFC Licht. "Hawk says the Osprey is inbound. One minute. All other ground personnel confirmed airborne and under escort."

"Copy."

"What about their ops center, sir?" asked Brines.

Before Saunders could delete it from the list of action items with an expletive, Sgt Smith cleared his throat. "We heard a few shots and somethin' like a grenade go off in there a few minutes ago, sir. Thinkin' they wasn't eager to get captured. So, we clear."

"It'll have to do." Saunders had long argued the point in the back of his mind. Would he suffer capture again? Or would he use that last bullet on himself? Without Sarah and Tommy factored in, the question was a no-brainer. Literally.

Thirty seconds . . .

"Smith, grab the lady on the table. No time for a stretcher. Brines, Licht: take lead."

A cluster of *yessirs* followed, and the Marines went to work.

Saunders held his breath as Sgt Smith slid his huge arms beneath Micky's slight form, causing her to whimper. To the big guy's credit, though, he was gentle, cradling the bandaged head like a newborn's as he headed for the exit.

Saunders was the last to leave the infirmary, keeping his MP5 trained on the "nurses" until he was back in the hallway. Nickels was wrong to go after them the way he did, but without a full body search, there was no way to tell what they might be hiding under those puffy scrubs.

Lance Corporal Gladstone stopped them in the main corridor with a raised hand. The characteristic crack of an M40 Marine sniper rifle from outside answered the unasked question—the enemy had returned.

"Dammit," said Saunders. "Chopper's inbound. We need to move. Smith, give me the wounded and take Nickels up there. Think you can cover our exfil?" It wasn't a question of capability, and Smith's slow nod said he was on the same page.

"Yes, sir," he answered without hesitation or even looking at Nickels.

"Right, once we're clear, you haul ass. The rest of you, on me. Oorah?" Saunders said, slinging his weapon and carefully accepting the limp form into his arms.

"Oorah, sir!"

A refocused Cpl Nickels and Smith disappeared into the night and added their SAWs to the rattling automatic gunfire of the battle. After what seemed like an eternity, the firefight was swallowed by the thumping, twin-rotary engines of the Marine MV-22B Osprey.

Sgt Smith stuck his head back inside and shouted, "You're clear! Move!"

"Ahuh!" bellowed Saunders hefting himself and the girl forward.

The others formed into a tight line and followed him into the stiff winds and choking dust of the chopper's rotor wash. It was quiet at first, giving hope that the hard parts were over. But halfway to the gray beast's welcoming maw, incoming small arms fire began to whip and crack around them.

There was no turning back or ducking for cover at that point. Only forward.

And prayers.

Seconds later, as if answering those prayers, a pair of Viper attack helicopters strafed the area of origin to the northeast giving the Marines a final break.

Saunders' legs burned from exertion and little bits of shrapnel that were just now making themselves known. Still, he pushed it hard and nearly hurled the lifeless girl up the loading ramp and into the waiting arms of one of the flight crew. Then he ran back down, gasping for breath, and helped Brines with the unconscious doctor as the others boarded.

Once clear, he waved over Sgt Smith's rear guard.

As the four remaining Marines raced to cover the distance, more small-arms fire began to ping off the chopper's hull. Saunders did his best to find a target to shoot through the swirling dust, but it was too dense. The enemy couldn't see him either, but all they needed to do was shoot at the big helicopter-sounding noise. One hit from an RPG, and they were done.

The seconds ticked by like time was being lowered into a vat of molten steel. Finally, Sgt Smith, LCpl Fischer, Cpl Nickels, and Francisco stormed on board and dropped like sacks of potatoes into their flight seats.

Amid the pops and pings of ricocheting bullets, Saunders slammed the retractor on the loading ramp. Then he stomped on the deck plate and pumped a thumbs up toward the cockpit. "Clear! Clear! Get us vertical! Go, go, go!" he yelled over the roar of machinery and mayhem.

The pilot responded by burning the rotors and touching the Osprey off the ground. The hell of war against the hull faded as the VTOL helicopter banked starboard and lowered its nacelles for horizontal flight.

Saunders staggered through the cabin and collapsed into the web seating. Exchanging his Kevlar tactical helmet for an intercom headset, he turned to stare out the single Plexiglas window.

Down below, red tracer streams snaked up at them in a last, desperate attempt of retaliation as a vehicle column poured through the northeastern gate.

Too fucking close.

Hundreds of little fires also dotted the darkened landscape giving the smoldering airfield semblance to the turbulent inside of an active volcano. It reminded him of his last phone conversation with Sarah. Suddenly the thought of a volcano as a vacation destination revolted him. No wonder she thought he was nuts for suggesting it.

I'm coming home, babe.

He leaned back and took in the shell-shocked silence permeated by the humming engines. The men were cooked, and his body ached in so many places that he couldn't tell the hurts from the numbs. Later would come the emotional toll, the loss of their brothers.

The letters home.

The grief.

Some defense mechanism in his brain staved off the tearful download, stopped him from running through the list of Charlie Company personnel he'd seen go down. Stopped him from wondering how many Marines they'd left on the ground in their haste to depart.

Left men behind.

He'd vomit that thought up later. Instead, he settled his eyes on Mike Brines, turning his signature fighting knife over in his hands, contemplative. The cabin was dim, but Saunders was pretty sure that wasn't mud caked all over it. And where did that other show-piece knife tucked into his war belt come from?

Brines wasn't the only one sporting the thousand-yard stare, either. Most of the men were unsettled, almost disturbed. They all seemed to be processing something awful. Maybe Nickels losing his shit was the canary in the coal mine. Maybe.

On a strategic and tactical level, everything that just happened was mind-numbing, terrifying. The balance of power in the entire world might've just fucking shifted. Saunders figured they had every right to be withdrawn. Still, he sensed there was more to it.

Something was nagging him, too, albeit on a personal level. That . . . hallucination, or whatever, where he was restrained and on the verge of cracking. It was like a bad dream that sat in the brain, real as any memory, with the eerie promise that it hadn't happened yet. As much as he tried to rationalize it away as dehydration, stress, or straight-up trauma, it stuck with him. Worse, whenever he tried to think about it or analyze it, his stomach felt queasy, and his heart raced as if he could feel himself being pulled in again.

What the hell happened down there?

———

Beneath the deep purple of the coming dawn, the place called *Mina Bazar* smoldered. The cries of wounded men echoed across the dying battlefield, but none would come to their aid. The able were fast fleeing, repurposed to other fronts. There was nothing left of their *Kôz* here.

. . .

Gallor Creetdel, Third of The Three, was alone.

He considered reaching out to the others with the Long Voice, but it was a fleeting desire. Neither the Second nor the First's knowledge of healing surpassed his own. And would that they possessed the talent to reverse the touch of the Vissl, their purposes far surpassed his bodily needs. Even a warning would be a useless distraction.

His long journey through life flashed before him.

Hated child.

Lost youth.

A student found.

A master in His cult. A lord in His legions. A brother of the Obantum Carre.

High in position though Creetdel was, he remained no one of great import and would be missed by few. A lovely face crossed his fading vision. Her name and house were lost to the toll of his injuries, but her affectation had warmed many a frigid evening.

The ground beneath him felt cold.

Strange how it had been too warm for his tastes before, but now that his life was draining away, it gave no comfort.

He shivered; an exhausting experience. His mind would soon follow his body. It already wandered aimless in the precious time he had left.

He willed himself to focus.

A whisper of command and his eyes stretched into the heavens toward the buzzing noise fading into the distance. The last of the Corsan Carre's flying wagons.

Rage flared in his body, providing the illusion of warmth. He'd allowed his study to go too far. Approached too near. It was an insufferable, haughty mistake. But while he held breath, their lives were his.

He shuddered as he relived the Vissl searing through his flesh and mind. The teeth-chattering blankness of pure discordancy. An impossible weapon in an unlikely place.

He tried to spit away the wetness collecting in his mouth, for it seemed he could no longer swallow, but instead, it came out as a sticky trickle sliding down his cheek.

Soon.

He let his rage grow, vowing to destroy the harbingers of his demise and spare his brothers the bite of that horrid weapon. In his weakness, though, he alone could not assure the destruction of the last flying wagon. Perhaps if he knew how the machine worked, he could make a small but damaging adjustment. A fleeting image of a Twelve-horsed Battle Carriage's hind axles snapping appeared in his mind. No, he would have to rely upon his agent already aboard.

Indeed, the agent's mind contained the necessary information. It would be a loss. Still, Second and First would find others.

But . . .

A thought came to him: It was unusual to find such potential in so small a group. Yes, they had resisted Enthralling and remained free. Even his agent was incomplete and still deaf to his whispers.

But perhaps they could still be sent. Here with their tools and countrymen, they were strong. But *there* they would be . . .

Prey.

A message to be consumed as a whole, then retched out and picked apart for its secrets.

The distresses of his brothers, the ministers, and the council had always dwelt on the men and the soil of this world. Different, separate. The Vissl rattled his thoughts again. Never did they imagine that something from their world was already here.

The council needed to be warned, and the losses of the Enthralled prisoners meant naught. *These Corsan Carre are the threat.*

His vision blurred as he summoned the last of his strength.

It was the only way to prepare the others. The Corsan Carre screaming at the hands of the Obantum Carre would be greater than any revenge he could conjure. That they had no inkling of their doom brought him one last taste of satisfaction.

Pleasure.

Gallor Creetdel released and was grateful to last long enough to witness the flying wagon vanish, swallowed whole into the place between places.

ACKNOWLEDGMENTS

I'm going to try and keep it professional this time. Straight to the point. Nothing weird, no national command authority first-strike jokes or alcohol references. I'm so experienced with communication now that brevity is all you get.

Half the second edition comes from my own evolving experience. Editing and storytelling. Also, the Realms' Anchor universe has expanded, allowing me to plant more seeds for the keen-eyed. The other half is you: readers—of course—but also the people who've written me with their *yeas* and *nays*. That's how writing improves. So even if you thought you were hard, it was welcomed and utilized. All the praise just went to my head and helped drive the sequels. Which was great; thanks there too.

Production of the First Edition took a team who asked for nothing in return. Ronald Volpicella was there at Realms' Anchor's inception and helped guide both the plot and characters. *Stiff Parrot* is also his creation. The manuscript received a mighty boon from Nick Pullen with a mix of developmental and copy-editing. Tom Kuhar provided invaluable content editing and advice through the publishing process. Sean Murphy also added his terrific insight into the structural details of novelization. My wife, kids, and dad were (and remain) the critical moral support that makes projects like this possible.

In the real world, when I'm chasing USD, I often come across people in the startup space. Amazing individuals who pour themselves into a dream that often fails. There are few guarantees and often limited promises of equity or payout.

But they drive it hard because they *believe*.

That's what the above folks did and do for Realms' Anchor. It's the same spirit keeping the vast majority of creatives in the game. I know it's unrealistic to expect you'll ever get to shake their hands but think about the people in your life who help press your dreams into the tangible. Thank them for me.

With beer.

Damn, so much for not mentioning a toxic product of yeast metabolism.

ABOUT THE AUTHOR

William H. Nugent is a biomedical researcher and author of the Realms' Anchor fantasy series. As a research physiologist, he works in the fields of reproductive physiology, combat trauma, sickle cell anemia, blood substitutes, and sepsis. Fictional literary influences are best represented by (but not limited to) Tom Clancy, Stephen Ambrose, J.R.R. Tolkein, Brandon Sanderson, John Scalzi, G.R.R. Martin, R.A. Salvator, and many more in the genres of military fiction and fantasy.

When Will is not writing, editing, reading, or begging for readers, he is lifting, running, and maybe gaming. He lives in rural Virginia with his wife and three children. Uh . . . Two cats. He has two cats, too. They eat food. Rock on.

Twitter handle: @Vagus001. That's two 0s, like James Bond's employee identifier.